MAGE
CATALYST

Christopher George

Mage Catalyst 1st Edition

This novel is entirely a work of fiction. Any resemblance to actual persons living or dead, is entirely coincidental.

Copyright © 2015 Christopher George

Cover design by Christopher George
Cover photography by Ian Harding Photography
Cover artwork by Megan Owenson
Typesetting by Odyssey Books

ISBN: 978-0-6485784-1-3
ISBN-13: 978-1981840571

DEDICATION

This book is dedicated to the waiting lounge at Adelaide Airport. Without you and your five-hour flight delay this novel might never have been started.

To my family and friends, thank you for your years of love and support as I struggled to turn myself into a half decent writer. It is still my fervent wish to one day achieve this goal.

ACKNOWLEDGMENTS

I would like to acknowledge Ian Harding for his beautiful photography work for the cover and Vanessa Verzaci for taking on the role of editor for my undisciplined scribbles. I would also like to acknowledge the beautiful hand of Sasha Hartdobler for her modelling and Megan Owensen for the digital artwork used on the cover.

I am also indebted to my brother, Daniel, for his ongoing critique and comments. Without him the storyline wouldn't be anywhere near as detailed and immersive as it is now. His attention to detail and ability to niggle every little point is greatly appreciated. (Well, it is now anyway.)

And lastly, Ms Penelope Alexander, without whom I never would have finished my first draft. Penelope was instrumental in keeping me motivated and on track during a very stressful and difficult time in my life.

Without you guys this book wouldn't have happened. Thank you.

Catalyst

'kat(ə)lɪst/

- A substance that increases the rate of chemical reaction without itself undergoing any permanent chemical change.

- A person or thing that precipitates an event.

PROLOGUE

I'm not sure when I became the villain of my story. But I'm now quite certain that this is exactly what I've become. It is no more clear to me as I stand atop a destroyed car park looking over my home. The smoke from still smouldering buildings billow off into the distance, almost writing my name into the skyline, but I do not care. It is no more than a grim signature of the suffering that I've caused to those around me. My name is Devon Wills and I am a mage.

I'm well aware of the stigma now attached to that title. However, to understand exactly what this title means, I will tell you my story. Perhaps you have seen us on the news; maybe you've even seen us in person if you've been unlucky enough. You know what we're capable of. We're not tired old men who smoke strange tobacco and brew up potions in kitchen pots. We're not haggard women who ride around on broomsticks and cackle into the night. We're able to send lightning arcing from our fingertips and burn holes through solid metal with just the mere flick of our wrists. In short, we're dangerous – but you already knew that.

You know the word "mage" – it means wizard,

sorcerer, magician or a variety of other terms for mystic, but do you know what it actually means to be a mage?

I didn't think so.

Let me educate you. When I use the term "mage", I mean someone capable of feats of power so great that they don't know what's real anymore. There are no limits, no restrictions – no laws. There is nothing to stop us should we go bad, and as you already know we *do* go bad.

When I use the term "mage", I mean someone so whacked out on sorcery that they hardly know what they're doing anymore. They don't care about anyone or anything other than the magic. They will do anything in pursuit of their powers. When I say mage I mean someone who is barely human anymore.

Where shall I begin my tale? I was, of course, born to two parents in the usual way and I grew up and went to school like any other normal child. I was not the product of a brutal tragedy, nor was I betrayed by my parents and cast into the river. I did not draw forth a sword from a stone. In fact my life was decidedly normal. My upbringing was not the stuff of legends and so, perhaps, it should not surprise me now to discover that I am the villain and not the hero of my story.

Despite my mundane upbringing I always knew that I was different from other children. I've always known it, though I never knew how or why. Somehow I was different, not in years, but in manner. It wasn't until several days after my eighteenth birthday that I found out exactly why – I was a mage, and my life would never be the same.

Understand that I don't say these things to defend my actions, nor to extol what virtues I do possess. I did what I did simply because I had no choice and I will not try to justify my actions to you. It is not for you to judge me – that is for my peers to do and I no longer have peers amongst the likes of you and your kind.

CHAPTER ONE

My story began on a cold autumn morning in Melbourne, Australia. It was raining as I recall, which wasn't surprising as rain and cold winds were not unusual in any season except summer. Our summers could be uncharitably and aggressively hot. It was almost as if Melbourne was trying to drown you for nine months of the year and then spend the next three months drying you out.

This day wasn't unusual from the one before. It didn't start any differently from the rest of my life. It wasn't until much later that I realised how just different this day actually was – for it was the last day that I could say without a doubt that I was a simple man, just like everyone else.

I was at school sitting through another boring English class, gazing longingly out the window. A gym class made its way across the oval. I envied them. It's not that I particularly wanted to join them – physical education didn't appeal to me – but anything was better than this class room.

"Devon, will you please pay attention?" snapped a sharp voice from across the room.

"The horror, the horror," I murmured, as my gaze returned to the slides on *A Heart of Darkness* projected on to the whiteboard. This was the seventh class we had endured on this novel so far.

"Very funny," our teacher, Mr Saunders, said gruffly. "Now, can you tell me what Kurtz means when he says that?"

"No, sir," I mumbled, annoyed at not having something more antagonistic to say. That wasn't like me – my form was definitely off today.

Mr Saunders ran his classes like a form of ritual detention and some of my class, myself included, played a game to see how far we could push him before he'd send us into the hall as punishment. It was immature, but seeing the shades of purple and red rise in his cheeks made it all the more worthwhile. It was a game I usually excelled at; however, today my wit had served me poorly.

Mr Saunders was your typical middle-aged school English teacher – balding, overweight, and short-tempered. He wore horn-rimmed glasses perched on the end of his nose and if he was particularly agitated he would remove them and clean them viciously with an old handkerchief in front of the class. He also wore business suits to class each day and spent as much time lecturing students on their bad habits as he did teaching. He wasn't my favourite teacher and I was far from his star student. He seemed to take delight in calling on me in class when he was sure that I didn't know the answer or if it was obvious that I wasn't paying attention. He took himself so seriously that we'd taken to calling him "sir" as a subtle insult, but I don't think he ever picked up on the jibe.

"What young Devon missed here is fundamentally important," Mr Saunders droned on. "*A Heart of Darkness* is a prime example of framed narrative."

Mr Saunders began to pace up and down the length of the whiteboard, a sure indication that he was gearing up for a long rant.

"A framed narrative is – of course – a story-telling device in which the tale is related by the narrator. Can anyone tell me another such example?"

Before anyone could answer, he turned back to me. "Can anyone tell me why this makes *A Heart of Darkness* such a psychological masterpiece? Mr Wills, perhaps?"

"No, sir."

I wasn't even trying anymore. Mr Saunders smirked and continued his rant. He'd won today's round and he knew it.

The darkness within, the thin veneer over the man, blah blah blah. Mr Saunders had drilled on and on about it when we first started reading the novel. Now, I understand the book, of course, but back then I knew nothing. I hadn't seen how people react when they are removed from the shackles of authority. At school my entire world was dominated by teachers and parents in authority, people I had to look up to, or at least listen to. We are taught in our childhood to respect and obey our governments, our police, our politicians – those in positions of power. It's all a sham though. What happens when we learn the horrible truth that they are just as dark and misguided as everyone else – that they're just hiding behind an enforced and ingrained system of societal control?

"…Man, what a drag."

"What? Huh?" I mumbled, looking up. I realised that the class bell had sounded and my friend Garry was staring at me expectantly.

Garry and I had been friends since the start of the year, when we had been seated together in English class. I got along well with Garry, although he could be annoying at times. He could provoke an argument with pretty much anyone about any subject. He was one of the smaller kids in the class and I guess he felt he needed to make up for that by being overly confrontational. I tried to avoid topics with him that I knew would lead to an argument. This worked most of the time, but it wasn't easy.

"Saunders, he just goes on and on," Garry moaned.

Our next class was on the far side of the school so I had plenty of time to hear Garry complain about Saunders. Normally I'd be participating in the Saunders-bashing but today, for some weird reason, I just couldn't find the enthusiasm.

"Are you going to your dad's this weekend?" Garry asked. He knew I always spent my weekends with my father and he also knew that I hated it. I gritted my teeth and nodded. I wasn't sure if he was just curious or if he was trying to annoy me. Either way I didn't want to be talking about this any further.

"What's the matter with you? You sure are out of it today," Garry snapped.

"Didn't sleep well," I said. "Just drop it."

The rest of the morning turned out to be no better than English class. I just couldn't focus. My mind kept drifting off. Two classes rolled by and I can't say what those classes were, let alone what was taught. It wasn't until lunch time that I was able to make any kind of effort to be sociable.

"Hey, Devon, are you okay?"

A soft voice beside me brought me back to the present. I was seated at a long bench in the lunch hall, but I had no idea how I had gotten there. I glanced up to see Sarah Bennett placing her tray down next to mine. She was my best friend's girlfriend and we hung out a lot.

"I know the food's bad but you haven't even touched it," she added.

"I'm okay." I nodded. "I was just thinking."

I'd always liked Sarah. In truth I'd had a little bit of a crush on her but I had no intention of making a move on my best friend's girl.

"Deep thinker?" she jibed. "Who'da thought…"

She trailed off quickly and looked away. I thought I heard a slight gasp from her, but when I looked up she was quietly unwrapping her sausage roll. She seemed fine, but something was definitely wrong here – Sarah was never like this.

"What?"

"No... nothing... It's nothing," she mumbled, no longer looking directly at me.

"You and Tony okay?" I asked. Maybe she was fighting with her boyfriend.

"Yeah, we're fine," she replied, her eyes looking deeply into mine, her look questioning, probing as if she was examining me. I didn't like it.

"Okay, out with it!"

"You looked a little funny before..." Sarah began tentatively. "Your eyes looked, I don't know, dilated." She peered into my eyes again. "It's nothing. They're fine now. I must have imagined it."

"You imagine me often?" I said in a hope to lighten the mood. I enjoyed teasing Sarah, although it wasn't often that I had the opportunity because Tony was always around.

"Oh, always – you're the last thing I think of before I go to sleep, and the first thing I wake up to." She rolled her eyes.

"Well, you're only human," I countered.

"Ouch!" I recoiled as her elbow caught me in the ribs.

You could only push Sarah so far before she retaliated. The elbow never really hurt me, it was usually just an indication that I'd gone too far.

"Hey guys!" Tony's voice boomed. I smiled as Tony sat down across from us, kissing Sarah on the cheek. I'd known Tony since the first year of high school when our teacher had paired us together in a hope that we would encourage each other to do our homework. It hadn't worked.

"How's tricks?" he chirped, as he began unwrapping his food. He was unusually peppy for this early in the morning.

"The rabbit died," I replied promptly.

"Rabbit?" his eyebrow raised slightly, looking at me as if I was crazy.

"The one in the top hat…" I trailed off, realising that I had sounded a little macabre. My jokes had a bad habit of doing that. I really needed to think more about how my jokes sounded outside the confines of my own head.

"Oh… You're quite the magician then," Tony said. "Dead rabbits in hats and you've probably got a whole deck of cards lodged in your underwear right now."

I didn't really have a suitable response. Tony always seemed to get in the last word.

"Hey, I wanted to talk to you," Tony began. "You're going to be at your dad's this weekend, right?"

I gritted my teeth. Again with the stupid questions.

I nodded as Tony continued, "This wicked new band are playing in the city this weekend. We can crash at your dad's – if that's cool?"

Tony had a knack for finding really good yet mostly unheard of bands. He hadn't steered me wrong yet. Going out sounded good, but I just couldn't feel enthusiastic about it. That wasn't going to stop Tony though. If I didn't say yes, he'd just keep hassling me about it until I did.

"Probably be okay," I said grudgingly. Tony wasn't going to just let this go.

"Ooh, I'm coming too!" Sarah smiled. "It's awesome that you're old enough now to come out with us."

I'd had my eighteenth birthday party last Saturday. I was the last of my friends to turn eighteen and Tony had brought a bottle of whisky to celebrate. It's customary for the birthday boy to get a little toasted; however, I'd pulled up fine. Gloriously drunk then no hangover, no headaches, nothing. I was untouchable!

I smiled back, remembering. "Yep, I can drink with the best of them. What about you, Tony?" I grinned evilly. Tony had had a little too much to drink and from what I'd heard, he was still violently puking the next morning.

Tony just shuddered. "Aah well. All is good now."

Sarah frowned. She was obviously still unimpressed with Tony's performance.

"There was nothing good about your Sunday morning," Sarah huffed.

I was feeling quite proud of my drinking accomplishments, especially given that Tony hadn't pulled up quite so well. It's strange the way we can only appreciate our own strengths through the opposite weakness in others.

"This band you mentioned? What are they like?" I asked as I began to eat my lunch.

I wasn't really listening to his response as I was more focused on the pie in front of me. It was awful, but I'd expected that – it was school food. What this pie needed was tomato sauce and lots of it. A problem as I didn't feel like getting up and waiting back in the queue for a measly few sachets of sauce. There was an unused packet of sauce on the other side of Sarah's tray, just out of reach.

Tony was still talking excitedly – this must have been some band. I hadn't seen him talk so animatedly about anything for quite some time.

"Uhuh… Sarah, have you finished with that tomato sauce?"

"Yeah, sure." Sarah nodded as her hands went to her tray and stopped. The sachet was gone.

"Uh, I must have dropped it," she mumbled, looking down on the ground.

I followed her gaze to the floor for the missing condiment.

"Oh, you already grabbed it. Sure you can have it." Sarah smiled and turned back to Tony's spiel, which was fortunate because it meant that she didn't see the look of confusion on my face.

The sauce sachet was just inches away from my fingers. How did it get there? I didn't reach for it; reaching for it would have meant standing up, and I didn't do that.

Yet, there it was, mere inches from my fingers. Weird.

"Anyways, mate," Tony drawled, bringing me back to the present. "I'd better go. I'll see you later." Both Tony and Sarah got up. I poured the sauce onto the remains of my pie and took a cautious bite. It was still a very bad pie.

"Don't feel too cocky about the lack of hangover!" Sarah called as they left. "I've heard that they can sneak up on you!"

I hadn't even felt dehydrated the next morning. I was pretty sure I was in the clear. But Sarah must have had prophetic vision or I had somehow offended the gods of poetic justice. During the next period I developed a headache – it was a real head-splitter. It came on suddenly and without any warning. My temples felt like they were on fire and a pounding reverberated throughout my skull with stunning force. Sarah had joked that hangovers could sneak up on you, but three days later? This was crazy.

Thud. Thud. Thud.

Pound. Pound. Pound.

Thud. Thud. Thud.

Light became unbearable, the sound of chalk on the blackboard became even more painful, and the dull monotone of Mr Cromby's voice made me sick to my stomach as shivers shook my entire frame. Why was he even using the blackboard? There was a perfectly good whiteboard next to it but our Maths teacher's response to progress and modernity was obviously to quietly ignore them.

I'd had Mr Cromby for Maths for several years and I'd always managed to retain a cordial relationship with him despite my grades and complete ineptitude at maths. I urgently raised my hand. I needed to get out of there – quickly.

"Mr Cromby, I think I need to go get some water or something," I mumbled as I swayed to my feet, taking the liberty of getting up before I had permission.

"Yes, Devon, that's fine," I heard him call as I made my way to the door. I contemplated going to the school nurse, but thought that some water would be a good first start. Maybe it was nothing more than just dehydration or something like that. Then the walkway I was following blurred and I had to lurch to catch the handrail. I quickly readdressed my decision to visit the school nurse but again chose not to – the bathroom was closer and there was the distinct possibility that I might now throw up.

I found that by closing my eyes, the pain subsided a little and so I clumsily made my way from the walkway into the toilet block at the end of the quadrangle without opening my eyes – an impressive effort that only resulted in my walking into things twice. Once inside the washroom, I staggered across to the wash basin and threw some water over my face. I gripped the edge of the basin as I let the water trickle slowly down my face. I breathed out as I prepared to open my eyes again – this was going to be unpleasant.

When I did open my eyes again I was immediately sucked into a world of hurt. My vision swam and I saw reflected sparkles dancing across vision. The effect might have been incredibly beautiful if not for the pounding in my head. I gasped as I looked down at my hands. A small particle of blue light was sliding up my arm. More appeared as I watched. They didn't appear to be following any sort of pattern. I pulled my shirt sleeve up to follow them as they moved further up towards my shoulder. I quickly undid the top three buttons on my shirt and pulled it open to see the particles lazily forming a rough circular pattern on my chest. I took several steps back to see the effect properly in the mirror.

There was nothing. The figure standing in the mirror looked completely normal. No sparkling lights. Amazed, I brought my hand up before my face – the particles were definitely there. They were rotating around my wrist and forearm, slowly making their way back up to my chest. When I returned my gaze to the mirror there was nothing. No, wait – that wasn't quite right either. I moved forward to gaze at my reflection. Something was definitely wrong.

My eyes, my God, my eyes!

The pupil of each eye was a tiny dot almost lost in the sea of blue that was my iris. In fact, I could see small tendrils of light sweep outwards from my iris expanding over the whites of my eyes. It wasn't affecting my vision at all, but the effect gave me an otherworldly look. I could see the irises of my eyes pulsing slightly, flexing as I gazed at my reflected face. A face that should be familiar appeared alien and threatening now. My changed eyes altered the entire balance of my face, giving me a malevolent look. I shuddered as my irises finished their transition, completely consuming the white. Then suddenly, as if someone had simply flicked off a switch, all the pain in my head stopped.

I quickly threw some more water across my face, closing my eyes and hoping when I opened them again that they would have returned to normal and that this was some kind of visual disturbance brought on by a migraine. No such luck, when I opened my eyes and gazed into the mirror – the strange eyes were staring back at me.

What the hell was happening? This kind of thing just doesn't happen in the real world. There was no rational explanation for it. This had to be some kind of hallucination or a weird reaction from cafeteria food, and that's when I remembered Sarah's comment about my eyes being dilated. So she had seen it too. It wasn't just a hallucination. That didn't make sense though, surely Sarah's reaction would have been stronger if she had seen glowing blue pulses of light travelling over my skin. Was it possible that she couldn't see the pulses, but only the strangeness of my eyes? This theory was certainly supported by that fact that I couldn't see the pulses in my reflection in the mirror. Was it possible that the change to my eyes was allowing me to see the particles on my body?

This idea didn't bring me much comfort. I was still seeing things that shouldn't be there. In all likelihood I was simply going crazy. But at least the unbearable pain had gone. I had to be grateful for that at least.

I threw some more water over my face and made my way back out into the quadrangle. I got about half way there before another strange feeling came over me. It was as if I was wearing a wet suit or a thin layer of PVC over my skin. I could kind of feel the blue lights on my skin moving across my flesh. It was an uncomfortable feeling. I made it to the row of benches outside the toilet block before I had to stop as my legs had become rubbery and difficult to control. I took a few deep breaths and steadied myself.

As annoying as this was, I much preferred this to the headache, as at least I could open my eyes now.

"Mr Wills, is there a problem?" A curt voice broke me out of my reverie. Crap, Saunders! I looked up to see him bearing down upon me with a determined expression upon his face. He'd obviously come out of one of the classrooms.

"No, sir… No problem," I replied, trying to avoid eye contact.

"Sitting there staring at your hands is not the best way to gain an education, young man." He smiled smugly as if he'd just made the funniest joke.

"No sir, I'm feeling a little woozy," I mumbled, keeping my eyes downcast lest he noticed my eyes.

"Why aren't you in class?"

"I had to go the bathroom."

"And yet you've been sitting there for at least five minutes, are you planning on spending the rest of the class sitting on this bench?"

"No sir," I replied, still desperately trying not to stare straight at him.

"I don't believe you, I think you were planning on

skipping class." Out of the corners of my new eyes I saw him smiling at me, his hands turning to lock around behind his back, his pose a classic 1950s old English schoolmaster. "Maybe even the rest of the day too."

I didn't respond as I was desperately trying to decide what to do, anything further said on my part would probably result in detention. I could almost feel his eyes penetrating into the top of my head in an obvious attempt to assert dominance. He was just waiting for me to say something so he could increase my days in detention. I remained silent.

"Look at me when I'm talking to you," he barked.

I cringed as I tilted my head to look at him, awaiting the inevitable explosion as he noticed my crazy eyes.

"Two days of detention, Mr Wills."

I didn't say anything. Had he noticed my eyes? He wasn't acting funny though – what the hell was going on?

"Have you nothing further to say for yourself?" he said.

"No sir," I said, eyes cast back down, my mind working in circles. He must have seen my eyes. How could he have missed something like that?

"Then off to class with you," he ordered, and he turned and headed back to his classroom.

I watched him go until it was safe to run back into the toilet block. I had to find out what was going on. I was relieved to see that my eyes had returned to normal when I checked back in the bathroom mirror.

What the hell was going on? I could still see the lines on my body that were now faintly pulsating across my arms. I made my way back to class desperately trying to avoid looking directly at my glowing skin. By the time I got back Mathematics had all but finished. Mr Cromby frowned as I sat down but didn't comment. Science class was next and it was not my favourite subject, but on the upside it was one of the few classes that I shared with Tony.

* * * *

"You what?" Tony growled. "Detention for two days? Well, that sucks!"

"Yeah, Saunders sucks alright," I replied, face down in my textbook. Biology was a subject that made me a little uncomfortable. Mrs Dowling, our Science teacher, was a dominating old bag who ran her class with a controlling iron fist. She looked like she was in her fifties, but she could have been much older. She was stick thin and incredibly small yet somehow carried an expression of mild violence and menace that seemed out of place given the fragility of her small frame. I would not even contemplate horseplay in her class. Tony however was not as subdued as the rest of the class or as cautious as I was.

"Well don't worry. We'll see that you're not lonely!" Tony avowed, his face alight with imagined mischief. I could literally see evil plans in his eyes as he contemplated what he was going to do.

"Speak for yourself," Garry replied. "I'm in enough trouble with Dowling as it is."

Abruptly Tony got to his feet. As he made his way to the back of the classroom unnoticed, Garry and I looked at each other with bemused yet tolerant expressions. Tony was usually unpredictable especially when he had something up his sleeve. The grin on his face foretold that this would certainly be interesting.

Tony parked himself at the far end of the room. Picking up a telephone directory, he flipped through the pages, idly raising his feet and placing them jauntily in the middle of the table. A look of intense concentration crossed his face.

"Hmm... discreet and exotic!" he said loudly enough to cause everyone to look towards the back of the room in alarm.

"Beautiful and professional, ooh... that sounds good, I want me some of that!" he continued, his finger running down the directory.

"Mr Ward, what do you think you're doing?" Mrs Dowling demanded, a ruler held in her hand like a riding crop.

"Is this Biology class or what?" Tony said. "I'm looking up escorts. I figure I'll flunk the written so going all out for the practical."

"Detention! For a week!" Mrs Dowling practically shrieked, the ruler still vibrating as she whacked it across the table while the classroom dissolved in laughter.

"Silence!" Mrs Dowling scowled at the class, her ruler

now like a sword – jabbing at any student who dared to defy her. Silence immediately fell upon the room.

"Oops, overshot," Tony smirked to me as he returned to his seat. "I only wanted two days."

The class resumed its lesson. Eventually the students returned to their usual level of noise and the class began to feel normal again.

"Nice one," I whispered to Tony.

"Now *you* owe *me* three *days*!"

Tony had cheered me up and distracted me but when the alarm bell went off and we all filed out I found myself staring again in wonder at my hands with the small particles of lightly slowly roaming across my knuckles and up my wrist.

I couldn't for the life of me think of any illness that would lead to hallucinations like the one I had had in the toilet block. If my flesh wasn't still glowing I would have probably shrugged it all off. However when your fingers are sparkling blue it tends to stick out in your mind.

Detention proved to be as stimulating as I had feared. Saunders hushed anyone who dared to open their mouths so Tony and I sat in complete silence, staring at Saunders' forehead the whole time.

"Last time I do a favour for you," Tony said out the corner of his mouth as we headed for the door.

"Same time tomorrow, boys," Saunders smirked, holding the door open for us as we hurried to the school gates.

Tony lived around the corner from Mum's place, so we usually walked home and hung out for a bit before he went home. Tonight, however, I begged off, explaining that I felt a little off and would just crash. Tony took this with good grace and headed home without argument.

My room was the same as any other teenager's. In the far corner there was a pile of clothes in desperate need of cleaning. My prized possession, my roller-blades, hung up in the corner by the door with my hockey stick resting below them. I used to go rollerblading with my father when he and my mother were still together. We didn't go blading much anymore. He was always too busy working now.

My desk was overflowing with sheets of paper, books and magazines. My bed had a comforter lazily draped across its surface but mostly on the floor. Flipping my laptop on I hopped onto the bed and began to search the internet for a reason for my blue sparkly problems.

The internet wasn't much help. Hallucinations were apparently quite commonplace and were caused by a variety of reasons. The most common reason being drug use, but this obviously wasn't the cause. I had eaten mushrooms in a stir-fry about a week or so ago, but unless Mum's shopping trip was a little stranger than normal I seriously doubted that they were the cause of all this. Despite Sarah's claim, I didn't believe for a second that this was alcohol-related from last weekend. There was a listing on a web page about a migraine or coma hallucination but that was also usually linked to unconsciousness and I couldn't remember passing out.

I started researching migraines. I supposed my splitting headache today could have been a migraine. If the other effects were also caused by a migraine then I should go back to normal soon. So I simply sat on the side of my bed, twiddling my fingers and watching the blue particles work their way from my fingertips up my arms. I noted that the effect appeared to be less severe than this afternoon. I took that as a good sign.

Maybe the whole thing would just go away?

No such luck, if I thought I had had trouble sleeping before, this night set a new bar. My body just couldn't seem to make up its mind. I was either burning up in my sleep, or freezing. By 2am I had kicked all the covers off my bed and was curled up in the centre of the bed cursing the mythical mushrooms that I couldn't remember eating, the magical marijuana that I hadn't smoked, and the crazy concussion I didn't have. It was a long time before sleep finally claimed me.

By 3am the quickening beat of my heart snapped me awake. I could feel the thudding against the insides of my chest. It sounded like a symphony with the gentle clicking of my pulse acting in staccato. The sound of my breath drawn from my body in short gasps almost acted as lyrical accompaniment. I turned and looked into the mirror and noted that my eyes had taken on the strangeness again.

I gripped the sheets, causing light particles to zig-zag across my fingers. These particles were far brighter than before, but now I noticed in the darkness an unusual fact. The light from the particles was not being reflected onto the walls.

I could see the source of the light on my skin, but not shadows that would be caused by them. With the intensity of the light emanating from my body my room should have looked like a disco. It instead looked like those action movies where they show you the night scope. I could see the particles flowing across my body like pulses, not following the conventional lines of my veins. They seemed to dance across my body in random swirling patterns, twirling around my arms and presumably onto my back in time with my breathing.

There were about twenty particles across my flesh as best I could figure but trying to count them accurately had proved an impossible task. After a few minutes of watching I discovered that there was a pattern, an erratic one, but a pattern nonetheless. If I actually was on drugs this probably would have been vastly entertaining; however, it seemed that sleep deprivation didn't seem to have quite the same buzz as alcohol.

I didn't sleep for the rest of that night. In fact, I didn't sleep very well for the rest of the week. My days and nights blurred into one long waking nightmare. When I did sleep it didn't seem to refresh me; my temperature steadily rose until I felt I was burning up. I couldn't eat, food tasted like ash and gave me no sustenance, but I was always hungry. After a while my friends began avoiding me after I'd snapped at them on several occasions for no good reason. It was the longest week of my life, although I can't remember any details except that I was more irritable and exhausted than I'd ever been. It was as if my body was under some great pressure – I felt ready to snap in two at any moment. I struggled to react to anything, my whole body moved sluggishly and it seemed to take the greatest amount of effort to perform even the smallest task.

I should have gone to see a doctor or the school nurse, but I was hesitant to do so. For one, they might not believe me; and two, they might believe me and send me to hospital. I was going out with Tony at the end of the week and I wasn't going to miss that. It was the one thing that had kept me going, through all this. I could survive until then. If I was still feeling like this next week then I'd go see someone. It couldn't be that serious, could it? Besides, it came and went throughout the day. Sometimes I was fine, other times I wasn't. Maybe it was just growing pains? The more I thought I about it, the more I was able to rationalise it away.

It wasn't until much later that I realised how much danger I actually was in, not just to myself but also to those around me. There is no greater threat in this world than unchecked power in the hands of those who will not control it or those who are simply unable to do so.

CHAPTER TWO

"Are you ready, man?" Tony slapped me on the shoulder and knocked my backpack off my shoulders. I'm sure that had been his intention, he was kind of a jerk like that, but he did it in such a good natured way that you couldn't really hold it against him.

"Yeah," I grumbled as I yanked my backpack onto my shoulders.

"Cheer up bud – it's Friday!"

We both walked from the locker hall into the gloomy Melbourne evening. Every Friday I took the train into the city to stay with my father. I had already arranged for Tony to stay the night with me and Dad earlier that week.

I really didn't like spending time at Dad's place. He was hardly ever there and apart from the huge TV there was precious little to do by yourself in the city. I'd much rather spend the time at home with my mum and friends nearby. The only thing I looked forward to was a morning ritual where Dad would get up early to walk down to the bakery and purchase the crispest loaf of bread he could find. He would then come home and cook bacon and eggs. You can't beat waking up to the smell of bacon and eggs in the morning. Lately, however, Dad had taken to offering cornflakes and excusing himself immediately after breakfast and heading back into the office. I then usually finished my breakfast in silence and found some way to entertain myself for the remainder of the day.

The Sunday breakfast tradition dated back to my dad's father. It was something that we'd done for as long as I could remember. Among my earliest memories were waking up weekend mornings to the smell of cooking bacon, a side of tomatoes and over-easy eggs. Despite divorce and three changes of jobs for Dad, we had still kept our little Sunday morning ritual – until now it seemed.

Dad's apartment was a short walk from Flinders Street Station, almost right in the centre of Melbourne's business district, just off Elizabeth Street. Sarah had arranged to meet us at the gig at 9pm. Her brother was driving into the city that night anyway and could easily drop her off and pick her up again later. I'd met her brother only a few times and hadn't really formed an opinion. He was pretty quiet whenever I was around at Sarah's but he seemed cool enough. He worked as a mobile mechanic and spent much of his time on the road.

It was dark by the time we got to Dad's apartment, and as I had predicted Dad had left a note indicating he'd be working back late in the office. Tony and I hung out at Dad's for an hour or two until it was time to go.

The journey to Fitzroy was uneventful. It was only a ten-minute tram ride, followed by a short walk. We didn't have trouble finding the gig either – there were flyers all over the place. The place looked kind of rough though. Two thug-like bouncers stood outside the doors, scowling.

This would be the first time I'd used my ID to get into a club and I was nervous. I didn't have my driver's licence. I had my learner's permit but I'd lost the actual card and had never replaced it. I'd brought along my passport, which I'd heard was valid ID. I hoped this would be okay. No line had formed yet outside the club. The bouncers looked down at me with their condescending gaze and I wanted to curl up into a ball and hide. I tentatively presented my ID to them and they grunted and waved me in. Well, that was easy.

There was a small booth just inside the door with a bored lady behind the counter. Tony passed the young lady cash through a small slot and she pressed a small ink stamp against each of our wrists, which proudly proclaimed "Paid", and gestured towards the door to our right.

The club was divided into two sections with a large stage area dividing them in the centre of the room. The sound of the band currently playing drowned out all conversation as we walked in. The band consisted of three guys, two on guitars and the other on drums. I couldn't quite make out the lyrics over the insistent whine of the guitars. I can't say I was overly impressed, though maybe if I could have actually heard the singer it might have been different.

Tony wandered over to the bar, ordered some drinks and directed us to a booth. The band was obviously nearing the end of their set as both guitarists had a thick sheen of sweat covering their foreheads and both looked pretty beat.

Tony sat back with a contented grin as he turned to look at the band. I had a beer in one hand and my foot was tapping in time to the music. It suddenly hit me – this was the best I'd felt all week. The pounding in my head had long gone. I hadn't slept too well last night but I wasn't actually feeling all that bad.

Maybe all my issues had just been related to stress? Now if I could just figure what I had been stressed about. I wasn't completely healed though – I could still see the blue lights pulsing through my flesh but I'd had all week to get used to that. I was quickly developing the ability to ignore it. It's kind of funny how given practice even the most strange things can be made mundane. The effect was a little more frantic than usual this evening, but it came and went in intensity throughout the day so I wasn't worried. I couldn't really figure out if there was a pattern to it or not. Hopefully that too would disappear in a few days, or maybe it was just something I'd need to learn to live with.

For all I knew, hundreds of people could see blue lines on their bodies, but no-one ever spoke about it. No, probably not, but the thought was a little comforting nonetheless. Smiling to myself I pushed all such thoughts out of my head. I was going to have fun tonight and worry about my magically glowing skin later.

I gestured to Tony a thumbs up. Conversation was out of the question as the music drowned out everything. I saw Tony get to his feet, grinning broadly, and wave to Sarah who had just walked into the bar. She was dressed in a slim black shirt and denim jeans, and I've got to admit she looked pretty hot. I nodded in way of greeting as she joined us at the table. She casually looped her arm through Tony's and slid in next to him.

"Thank you, Melbourne!" the singer with the Mohawk shrieked. It was the only time I got to actually hear his voice. I guessed he was hoarse from trying to sing louder than the guitars and not suffering from a six-day-old throat infection, which is how his voice sounded.

The house music returned as the band began packing up their gear. It seemed like a lot of effort for about forty minutes of playing. I watched them lug their equipment off the stage and out a side door. The house music was softer than the band and we could hear the dull murmur of multiple conversations fill the club.

"I'll buy you a drink," I said to Sarah. "What would you like?" This would be the first time I'd ordered something and I was dying to use my ID. I'd brought it from home specifically for this.

"House red?" She smiled back, getting out her purse.

"This one's on me." I got to my feet and headed towards the bar. Since we had gotten in, the crowd had almost doubled in size. It was getting kind of hard to make my way through them. We were lucky to have our booth now. It took me some time to work my way through the crowd to get to the bar.

"House red and two beers," I shouted as I finally attracted the bartender's attention, frantically waving my ID at him.

He pushed my ID, but seemed to get some amusement from my eagerness to present it. Seconds later he produced our drinks. Working my way back to our booth required more skill as the place was filling up fast. I sat down just in time to watch the next band begin to set up.

"These are them," Tony proclaimed, pointing at the band as I set our drinks down on the table.

This band was much larger than the previous – two guitarists, a drummer, a lead singer and a keyboardist. It was actually pretty amazing how quickly the band was able to set up all their equipment, considering the complexity. Then again I suppose that you'd get pretty good at it once you'd done enough gigs.

The lead singer purred loudly into the mike and began to pump her foot on the ground. The keyboardist lay down a complex series of notes and seconds later the guitarist broke in, weaving the guitar around the keyboard. It was intoxicating. This band was good – really good. I wasn't surprised – Tony was normally pretty skilled at picking the good bands.

I was stunned into silence and sat and watched as the singer finally began to sing. Her voice pierced into my head with startling clarity and I found myself sitting mutely as the crowd around me burst into cheering, clapping and singing along. I had goose bumps all up and down my arms and that feeling you get when you're listening to really, really good music.

The songs were dark, deep and vibrant and far better than the usual level of pub band rock. Their music had a taint of Goth but without all the melodramatic suicide references. The singer's voice had that husky quality to it that I found appealing in women's voices.

"Wow, these guys are good," I finally stammered.

"Yeah, I told you!" Tony shouted back, his hands clapping in time.

The band played three songs and a ballad and I sat stock still through the entire set, intoxicated by the sound. The guitarists and keyboardist broke into a complex instrumental that wove complicated melodies around each other. Each note built into a crescendo of sound that washed over the audience and led to more cheering and screaming from the crowd.

"Wow," I mumbled again, unable to find the words to express myself.

Sarah snickered and punched me on the arm, bringing me back from my stupor. She'd obviously asked me a question that I'd missed.

"They're very good," I repeated. "How'd you find them?"'

"Saw them play at a pub a few weeks ago," Tony replied glibly, turning to face me. "By the way, you're being checked out," he grinned, gesturing behind me.

I scowled. This was typical of these two whenever we went out. They'd usually try to hook me up with someone they spotted. I think it was some sort of game between them. I turned and glanced at Sarah, expecting her to laugh and nod agreeably.

"I dunno," she said thoughtfully. "She doesn't look that interested." This was unusual, usually she'd agree with Tony even if the woman appeared to want to throttle me.

"She looks a bit old for him and she seems pretty angry," Sarah said. "Do you know her?"

"Well, she's been staring at Devon pretty much constantly since she got here!" Tony said.

I'd gone through this on several occasions with these two. Normally they'd encourage me up to the point that I'd build up the courage to chat to the woman in question. My track record wasn't that good – they normally always turned me down. I'd been starting to suspect that Tony and Sarah were intentionally sending me after women who they knew weren't interested.

I turned to look at her and my jaw dropped.

She was standing on the other side of the club, a drink resting on the bench next to her. She had long, dark hair and Sarah was right, she was older than me, much older, maybe mid-twenties. She was pretty in a neo-Goth kind of way: she was wearing a cropped black top that exposed her stomach. She finished the effect with oversized military-style boots and black jeans.

None of this attracted my attention until much later. What did attract my attention was a small blue halo of light particles dancing in small circles in the centre of her chest, just above her breasts.

Tony and Sarah were right. She was staring at me and she looked worried. That look changed to annoyance as I got to my feet and made my way over to her. I couldn't hear the music or the noise of the crowd. I couldn't even really see the crowd around me anymore – all I could see was the small circle of light lazily dancing across her chest.

"My breasts are a little lower," she said dryly when I finally got into earshot. Her voice was amazing, I couldn't quite pick her accent, but it definitely wasn't local. She was staring at me strangely as I stumbled about for a suitable response.

"I'm sorry," I stammered, desperately trying to compose myself. She was still staring at me and it was making rational thought kind of difficult.

"You're sorry for not staring at my breasts?'" she enquired, her mouth twisting into a mocking curl.

"Umm… yeah, I guess," I continued, still at a loss for words and she wasn't making it any easier.

I kept working it over and over in my head. What did this mean? Did she know she had glowing pulses in her body? Why were hers different to mine? Could she see mine? What would happen if I touched her?

I so desperately wanted to touch her, to kiss her, to be with her. I'd never believed in love at first sight before, but I was starting to re-assess that belief now. I could feel my body respond, the pressure building again. I couldn't see the particles of light frantically rising in tempo in my body, but I could swear I could feel them racing across my flesh with manic intensity.

"You're quite the conversationalist…" she began, then her eyes narrowed and her mouth twisted in a snarl. "What the hell do you think you're doing?"

"I'm trying… to…talk… to you?" I stammered, confused.

She had backed away several steps, glancing around seeking an escape.

"Don't go," I begged.

She didn't say anything. She just glowered and turned and made her way quickly to one of the side doors.

I had to follow her. I had to have an answer. I wasn't sure if it was love, lust or a simple need to understand what was happening to me, but I was desperate for an answer from her. I couldn't just let her get away. I needed some answers about this! I'd just about written off my condition as delusion and now here was someone else with the same effect. It couldn't be just a coincidence.

The next band had started playing as she stormed off and I was quickly blocked by dozens of people heading towards the stage. I saw her run past the crowd and slip out the side exit. It took me a little longer, and by the time I'd made my way through and out into the street she was almost at the end of the alley.

"Wait," I shouted. "I need to talk to you!"

"Leave me alone!" she snarled, turning to face me. I could see her eyes glittering from the light above her. Her irises were wide and threatening and her face was twisted into an indecisive grimace.

I started towards her; I couldn't let it end like this. She had to tell me what was going on – she simply had to!

"Please!" I began, but I was interrupted before I could finish.

With precision the girl tensed up her body and lashed out her hand in my direction in a sweeping motion. I saw with clarity the blue lights in her chest dance down her arms and flick out from her wrist. With startling accuracy a whip cord of blue particles burst from her outstretched hand and hit me on my right side with stunning force.

The impact sent me reeling, knocking me into the air in a spin. I hit the wall behind me, and promptly dropped onto the dumpster below it with a dull thud. My whole body went numb from the impact. I didn't feel any pain but knew with certainty that I was more hurt than I felt.

I looked up with disbelief – she still stood about ten metres away. She hadn't moved since she'd attacked me. She'd made no move to run. She was simply looking down at me with a strange expression on her face. I couldn't get a read on what the expression meant. There was definite fury there, contempt too, but there was definitely something else as well.

"I told you to Leave. Me. Alone!" she declared finally, biting off each word.

I gasped for breath. I was pretty sure I had cracked some ribs, as every time I inhaled pain lanced across my chest. I made it to my knees as black spots began dancing across my vision. Each breath I took was a harsh lesson in further pain.

"What's happening to me?" I moaned as I collapsed back to the ground. My vision was going blurry and I felt like I was going to throw up.

"Shit," I heard her say as the darkness set in.

* * * *

When I came around my chest still hurt and each breath felt like I was breathing fire. My wrist was throbbing painfully too; I must have sprained it in the fall. It took me several seconds as it all came flooding back – the woman, the lights in her chest, the alley, the flick of her wrist, the pain. And now here we were, seated together back in the club.

"I wanted to make sure you were okay," she murmured. "I thought you might have a concussion."

I couldn't find a suitable response. She looked even more beautiful than before and my eyes were dazzled, although that may have been the concussion's influence.

"…How?" I simply mumbled.

"Well, doctors say that when you hit your head…" she began dryly.

"No, not how do you get a concussion. How did you do that to me?"

"You really don't know?" she asked, her expression going from guilty to horrified and then back to irritated. Her eyes bore into me imperiously. "Look, I'm sorry I hit you so hard. I thought you'd be able to defend yourself."

"How do you defend yourself against that?" I grunted, remembering the particle whip lashing against me and lifting me into the air. She didn't answer my question.

"If it's any consolation it probably saved your life. The build-up of energy you were displaying could have been life threatening."

This wasn't exactly the answer I was looking for. I looked down at the particles of light pulsing throughout my skin and noticed that they had lessened. Before they were very bright and jittery, but now they were lighter and sluggishly pulsated across my skin.

"You absorbed the worst of my attack," she commented. "How long you have been a…?"

"I've been seeing blue lights all week if that's what you're asking," I answered, holding my head back in my hands. I had a pounding headache again – though that probably had more to do with the concussion.

"A week? One week!" she said.

"Keep your voice down," I grumbled as her shrill voice rang through my throbbing skull.

"One week," she finished glumly.

"Is that bad?"

"No, not bad, just unusual, you're what… seventeen, sixteen?"

"No, I'm eighteen," I corrected somewhat defensively.

"I was five when it first happened to me. Fortunately my grandfather was there to tell me what was going on."

"Your grandfather?"

"Yeah, he's like us too."

I could tell she was choosing her words carefully. There was something she wasn't telling me. What does that mean?

"Why did you attack me?" I asked, not quite sure I wanted to know the answer.

"I wasn't sure what you were doing and our kind don't normally get along too well." Her face went dark. "I thought it might have been an attack," she confessed.

"You thought I was going to attack you?" I pressed, confused.

I'd never been called threatening in my life. It was a complete shock that anyone would consider me dangerous. I didn't know how to respond.

"I didn't realise you were simply out of control," she said sharply, as if in some form of reprimand.

I didn't have an answer to that either. I wasn't even sure what it meant. How was I not in control? I wasn't surprised by the accusation, I'd been accused of being out of control by a string of high school teachers for years.

I was pondering the implications of this when I had a sudden feeling that someone was standing right behind me. I've always had a nervous twitch in my shoulders, especially when someone is standing behind me. My nervous shudder was unusually strong this time, causing my whole body to jump, which in turn caused me to shudder in pain as my ribs shrieked in complaint.

The person turned out to be a busboy who just wanted to collect the empties.

"Smooth," the girl said, once the guy had left. "What's with the twitch?"

"Always had it," I replied. "Dunno why."

"My name is Renee by the way," she said, offering a handshake across the table.

"Devon," I replied, flipping her hand over and kissing it lightly. I did this gingerly as every movement on my left side felt like a knife in my ribs.

"Wow! You are a smooth one, aren't you?" Her eyes softened for the first time since we'd met. The change made a huge difference to her whole face. If I thought she was beautiful when she was mad – well, when she was smiling she was breathtaking.

"It's a pity you're not older," Renee continued.

Renee was twenty-four, had her own apartment in the city and was studying Film Studies at Melbourne University. Her grandfather apparently came in from time to time to check on her, but other than that she was pretty much her own boss. I learnt all this by asking direct questions and receiving very short answers. Renee wasn't exactly forthcoming with information. She was really making me work for any personal information. I had the feeling that she walked away knowing a lot more about me than I did about her.

I could feel her eyes drilling into me during our

conversation. It was like she was taking me apart and learning how I worked – taking my secrets and making them hers. It wasn't an unpleasant feeling as such but it was a little confronting. Most of her questions seemed related to the blue particles and how I'd come to possess them. At first she had seemed angry at my vague answers, but she soon obviously came to the conclusion that I was too witless to lie and genuinely didn't know more than I was saying.

There was urgency in her questions and a brisk harshness. She was desperately trying to find something out about me and I could tell she was getting more frantic the longer our conversation went. I wasn't quite sure how to broach the subject so I just went for plain brutal honesty.

"So can you teach me to use this… thing?" I gestured with my hand causing a flash of particles to spark. "You obviously know how to use it."

"I could." She smiled devilishly. The smile never reached her eyes though. There was fear in her eyes – I've never seen fear like that. It was quickly replaced with her twisted grin, but I saw enough to recognise it for what it was – terrified fear. Renee was desperately afraid of something and didn't want anyone to know about it.

"…but I'm not going to," Renee finished lightly.

"I thought your grandfather taught you!" I complained.

"Yeah, he did," she said disarmingly, "…but we don't really have time and besides your friends have found us."

Tony and Sarah had just walked through the doorway from the stage area, heading our way. I cursed under my breath.

"Dude! Do you have any idea how long we've been looking for you?" Tony boomed as he walked towards us. "You totally ditched on us."

I mentally tried to tell Tony to take a hike.

"Yeah, sorry," I grumbled. "I got… distracted."

Renee's eyebrows shot up in response. I desperately wanted to ask Renee more questions, but I couldn't with Sarah and Tony around. I think Renee knew that too; in fact I'm pretty sure she was counting on it. She didn't look at Tony or Sarah.

"Well, if you'll excuse me, I've got an early start tomorrow," she said. "It was nice to meet you, Devon." She smiled as she rose to leave. "I'll just leave you here with your friends."

"Okay… See you," I said sullenly.

Renee gave me a piercing look, grabbed her bag and headed for the door. I sat there in stunned silence for a few seconds before I leapt out of my chair after Renee.

I wasn't going to let this opportunity get away from me.

I caught her by the time she'd reached the street. In a daze of teenage hormones I caught up to her and pulled her to me, pressing her against my chest as I pulled her in close, she wrapped her body around mine and I felt her hands wrap around my neck and pulled against me in turn.

Our lips met with stunning force and I could feel

the blue halo particles in our bodies collide. My breath disappeared in an instant as I was sucked into the oblivion that was our kiss. Intention, thought, desire were all swept away with the single fact of our lips pressed firmly against each other's.

I could almost feel the blue particles in our bodies entwine and form a pattern around our bodies, joining us, binding us, and jumping from body to body in pattern. I could feel our bodies unite in a single purpose, I could feel her under my skin through the blue lights and I knew she could feel me too. She was inside me now and I was inside her and there was nothing that I wanted more. When we broke, there was a dull silence. The loss of the connection to her filled my soul and I was weakened by it, my essence drained – incomplete.

"You're cute, but you're much too young and you're really not my type," she whispered, her eyes twinkling with mirth.

She was trying hard to keep things light-hearted, but I could see the loss reflected in her eyes too. She covered it up well but I noticed that she hadn't let me go yet.

"Can I at least have your number?" I pleaded shamelessly. I breathed a sigh of relief as she disengaged from my arms to draw a pen from her purse and scrawled down a number on an old receipt.

"See you, Renee," I murmured as I watched her turn to leave.

"See you, Twitch," she called back, and then she was gone.

I returned to the table with a look of pure ecstasy mixed with stunned shock on my face to apologise to my friends. Sarah and Tony glanced nervously as I approached the table. It had been obvious that I was limping slightly. I sat down on the table with a noticeable exclamation. Sarah's face immediately crinkled in concern.

"Are you okay?" Sarah asked gently.

"What? Oh? Yeah, I just fell down earlier," I replied quickly.

"Oh."

Tony and Sarah exchanged glances again. I didn't take much notice though, I was too lost in my own thoughts of Renee. I wondered if it would be too soon to call her tomorrow morning or if I had to wait the whole three days after the date thing?

* * * *

"Ullo, is Giuseppe's Pizza! Can I take your order?" A fake Italian accent boomed down the line with startling volume.

"Uhh… hello… is Renee there?" I hesitantly asked, already knowing that the answer would be no.

"No, is no Renee here, only pizza!" the voice returned. "You order now, no?"

I switched off my phone in disgust. She had given me a fake number. Who does that? And a pizza place? If I wasn't so invested in this woman I'd have been howling with laughter.

I had woken up about twenty minutes before and tentatively inspected myself in the mirror. I hadn't had time to do it properly last night when we had returned home. I'd definitely sprained my wrist. It was horribly swollen and was starting to throb uncomfortably. Complete with the wrist I also had bruising all down my left side – deep purple bruises that started on my chest and spread around my lower back.

It hadn't looked like it was this bad last night. On the upside it didn't appear that I had actually cracked any ribs – they were just bruised. Painfully bruised, but not broken. That was lucky at least. It was no longer painful to breathe, only slightly uncomfortable.

The smell of cooking bacon slowly wafted into my room and brought me staggering out into the living room. I hurriedly threw on a T-shirt to cover the bruising. I was greeted by the sight of my dad standing over the stove with Tony sitting on the table next to him, chatting amicably. Tony and Dad had always gotten along famously.

"Morning Dad." I groaned as I limped over to a chair and tentatively sat down.

"Rough night?" he inquired, looking me in the eyes.

"Yeah, I fell down a flight of stairs," I lied quickly, nodding to Tony to collaborate in the lie.

"Stupid bugger, he saw some chick he fancied," he said.

I gave him a sharp warning look.

My dad smiled as he began dishing up. "I always had a soft spot for ladies I shouldn't have."

I said nothing in response. I wondered if he was referring to Mum.

"So what do you boys have planned for the day?" Dad asked.

"I've got to be home relatively early in the afternoon," Tony stated in between mouthfuls. "Got this family thing this evening, I've got to look my best."

"That'll take some doing," I muttered under my breath, although of course everyone heard.

"What about you, Devon?" Dad turned to me.

"Nothing much, Dad, just thought I'd hang out," I replied.

"I'd like you to come to dinner tonight. There's someone I'd like you to meet."

Great, this meant one of two things: either Dad had another date he wanted me to meet, or he was career hunting for me again. Either way, it meant a painful night. Dad must have picked up on my lack of enthusiasm because he didn't press the issue further.

"Well, boys, on that note, I think I'll see you later. I just need to pop into the office for an hour or so."

That meant Dad would be gone for the rest of the morning and probably most of the afternoon too. Tony left shortly afterwards. I offered to walk him down, but changed my mind after considering how much trouble I had getting to the door. I'd only slow him down.

"How are your ribs?" he asked. He gawked when I pulled up my shirt to show him the bruises.

"Shit," he breathed out.

I stared at him.

"What happened?" he asked. "Did you fall down a flight of stairs like you said?"

"Yeah," I mumbled. It was obvious I was lying.

Tony slowly nodded. It was the first time I had kept anything from him and I felt a little sick at the idea of starting now. I'd have loved to be able to tell him what was going on, but that required something I didn't have – an understanding of what was going on.

"Well, see you, dude. I'll see you at school."

I'd usually go wander around the city for a while when I was bored. But I couldn't really leave the apartment in my current condition. I'd already seen all of Dad's movies on numerous occasions so I didn't really feel like watching a movie.

And I was too distracted anyway to focus on a movie. I couldn't stop thinking about Renee. Every train of thought led me back to her. I imagined her when I closed my eyes and I could almost still smell her fragrance on me. I remembered her lips on mine, the way it felt to hold her against me.

I pictured her standing there outside the club smiling at me. Then I remembered her in the alley with her hands held forth and blue particles whipping out to strike me down.

Could I do that?

Surely not?

Why not?

I wouldn't want to attack anyone with it, but surely

it could do other stuff, move things? Lift things? That sounded pretty cool. My face twisted into a curled grin at the thought of all the fun I could have with that kind of power.

My sprained wrist disrupted my train of thought with a violent throb. I looked down and began to lightly stroke it, trying to massage away the discomfort. That only partially worked, but it did make me feel a little better.

Once the pain subsided in my wrist I began to contemplate the lifting stuff concept more. Renee had technically lifted me when she had attacked me – so therefore it must be possible.

With my logic figured out, I tried to visualise how she had actually got the particles to come from her hand like she had. I went over the scene in my mind again and again until I could almost see the scene on the inside of my eyelids.

She had flexed her fingers and the particles had run down her arm to her hand. The more I thought about this the more I could feel the particles buzzing up and down my arm. It was as if they were preparing for something.

Time to give it a go.

I reached out and wiggled my fingers – nothing happened. Okay, I hadn't seriously expected that to work anyway. I tried pointing my forefinger and said, "Abracadabra", half thinking something might happen. I felt very foolish but no-one was around so I concentrated and tried something else I had seen in movies. There was an empty glass on the table about two metres away. I focused on it and thought about it moving as hard as I could.

Nothing, not even a twitch.

It took me a good hour before I could even get the blue particles to move with any degree of control, and even then I had to calm myself and breathe steadily. Fortunately I had plenty of time to practice.

I kept focusing on my breath while observing the particles of light.

In.

Out.

In.

Out.

Eventually, I could feel the particles begin to move in a pattern of sorts, with a degree of control. I could force them to slowly slide down my arm and then back up. It took about another hour before I felt I had it. Yet no matter how hard I tried I couldn't get them to leap from my hand into that whip-like thing that Renee had used.

Okay, this was getting frustrating. I reached out my hand, straining against the couch, focusing intently on the glass. Zip. Nothing. Infuriating.

I strained with my fingers stretched to their apex. I could see the particles swirling down my hand and across my fingers. Try as hard as I could, I just couldn't get them to leap from it.

Then it happened. On the out breath – when I had expelled everything.

It felt as if I'd reached my hand through a wall made of water. It gave way before me with laughable resistance. I watched with glee as the particles trailed out from my fingers a few centimetres, curling in on themselves into a tight spiral.

It snapped back and dissipated almost immediately – but I now knew it could be done and that was enough.

I tried again.

It was easier this time. The particles crept from each outstretched finger on my hand, slowly forming something akin to a backbone of particles. They were always in motion, swirling in a circular pattern outwards from my palm. It was so slow at the start but then gained more speed. The particle slivers merged into one solid thread – similar to what I'd seen Renee use, although far less impressive and painfully slow. But it was a start.

With a grunt I snapped my arm forward while flicking my good right wrist and saw the particle whip flow from my fingers. The thread almost immediately dissipated and I felt a shock ripple up my arm. The pain wasn't too bad, certainly nothing compared to the bruises I was currently sporting on my left side. The shock of the sensation running up my arm was more disconcerting, however. It had caused my arm to go rubbery and limp for a few seconds.

I instinctively recoiled, which caused my back to spasm as it was pulled and led to more complaints from my bruised back muscles. This wasn't going well. Giving myself a few minutes break, I leaned back down on the couch to rest. I watched intently as more particles spread down my arms towards my wrists. They were slowly circling in tight ovals around the joint of my wrist and then around down into the palms of my hands. Taking a deep breath to ready myself I thrust my hand with a quick flicking motion, palm up at the glass.

It worked! The particles immediately formed a thread of light that lashed from my hands and out several metres. I'd done it! Speed appeared to be the critical component here. This was going to make it difficult to control, but it must be possible! After all, Renee had done it. I tried again.

Damn it! I had missed but I had the distance about right. It took me several more tries before I clipped the glass by accident, causing it to wobble and then eventually fall over. The glass rolled over and threatened to fall off the edge of the table. It was at this point I realised that I could potentially cover the floor with shards of broken glass. Cursing myself for my own stupidity, I went and grabbed a plastic mug from the kitchen.

It took me several more minutes to repeat the success of my previous attempt. The particle whip now leapt from my fingers with a reliable ferocity and smacked the cup firmly, causing it to fly from the coffee table and smack with a resounding thunk against the window on the far side of the room.

It took even more time to try to slow the particle whip to a speed that I could control without slapping the mug off the table. It was infuriating – if I made the particle whip move too slowly it would dissipate, too fast and I wouldn't be able to control it.

I was so frustrated with the mug flying off the table that I ended up fetching several more mugs and placing them in even intervals. This way I wouldn't need to get up quite so often as I telekinetically scattered mugs about the apartment.

I was up to my fifth and final mug when finally I managed to slow the whip enough to wrap it around the mug. I was promptly greeted with a shrill shriek of complaint as the plastic mug simply collapsed in on itself as the particle whip tightened around it. The shards of the mug scattered out in an explosive pattern across the surface of the table as the mug exploded under the stress.

Damn, that wasn't even close to what I was trying to do.

I leaned forward to pick up one of the other mugs and tightly squeezed it with my fingers, trying to get it to crack. It wasn't even close to snapping in my hands. I felt the plastic flex beneath my fingers but it was nowhere near breaking limit. I simply could not apply the necessary pressure with my fingers to get the mug to even crack, let alone shatter like the other one had.

How much pressure had I been able to exert before?

The sound of keys in the door brought me back to reality. Damn, Dad was home. He walked in with his usual after-work expression: slight annoyance and tiredness.

"I trust you didn't forget dinner tonight," he grumbled as he saw me on the couch, then his eyes narrowed with curiosity. He didn't say anything but I'm sure he was wondering what I was doing with four mugs and a smashed one, lined up in a row on the coffee table.

"Nope," I said, getting to my feet to clear up the mess. "Give me five minutes to get changed and I'm ready to go."

"Okay. Wait a minute though, I want to talk to you first," he called before I could head into my room.

Great, this was definitely a pre-meet-the-woman-I'm-dating speech. I was a little sick of these – they never went well and the women Dad dated never seemed to hang around that long anyway.

"Have you given any thought to what you're doing next year yet?" he started, taking me a little off balance at the unexpected direction. "Your mother says you are only just scraping by in all of your subjects this year."

Thanks Mum. Of course both my parents and the school were adamant that I'd go to university. "I've looked at a few courses," I grumbled.

That was true at least. I had looked at a few courses, but couldn't muster up any enthusiasm for any of them. All of my friends had a calling. Garry was kind of a jerk and was failing a lot of subjects even worse than me, but he was brilliant on the guitar and aced Music class – both theory and practice. Tony could play at being the fool but his grades were better than mine in every class, apart from Art. Sarah got the best grades in English and had won the year level's poetry prize. I didn't seem to be very good at anything much at all and certainly had no idea what I wanted to do with my life.

"That's what you said last time," Dad reminded me grimly. "Life is not a free ride, Devon. You have to earn what you want. You're going to have to take some responsibility and make some serious plans for the future."

"I know, Dad," I groaned. If this was the preamble before the dinner then the actual dinner was sure to be as fun as a root canal.

"I've arranged for you to meet with a friend of mine. He works for a graphic design company. He's got a proposition for you."

This was unexpected – and I wasn't sure that I liked where this was going.

"Well, even if you're not interested, at least be polite. I've known Martin for a long time and I will not have you being rude to him," Dad finished.

Dinner turned out to be a pleasant surprise, causing me to re-evaluate the powers of perception my old man possessed. Martin Boyd ran a small graphic design company that my father regularly used. The offer was to work for a year after I finished my finals, and get some real work experience. I don't know what favours Dad had called in for this offer, but this sounded like a much better offer than studying for three or four years at a university.

Martin was very sure of himself but friendly enough.

He and Dad got along very well, which surprised me as I had never heard of Martin before and I thought I knew all of Dad's close friends. I suppose thinking about it, I didn't have that much to do with Dad's professional life. I guess I never asked.

After a light dinner and some after-dinner drinks I was feeling like things had just fallen into place. I finally knew what I was going to do with myself after high school. I was going to work for a year and not even think about university.

I was gazing out of the restaurant window feeling excited when I saw Renee. Her bright blue light particles caught my eye. She was standing across the road, leaning against a wall and looking directly at me. I rose so quickly I almost knocked over my bourbon and Coke. She winked at me and walked briskly away.

I sat back down and turned my attention back to Dad and Martin. She may have given me a false phone number but she had also tracked me down. Perhaps I could learn to track her down just as easily.

* * * *

Mondayitis had come with its usual doom and gloom, made worse because it was a particularly wet and miserable morning. Tony and Garry met me at my house as they usually did and we all walked to school together.

School turned out to be as intellectually stimulating as ever. I'd already sat through English with Saunders and the bloody *Heart of Darkness* and was now enduring a Maths class. Maths should be outlawed in the afternoon.

I was bored and the subject matter didn't appear to be offering much in the way of entertainment. That was okay, I could make my own entertainment. I'd had this stunt up my sleeve for about a month but I just needed the right moment to attempt it. This looked like it.

I took the small screwdriver that I'd always kept in my pencil case to my calculator, gently removing the four small screws that held the back plate on. I had to do it discreetly, using my books to cover what I was doing. Fortunately Mr Cromby was in the middle of a lecture about something to do with angles so he wasn't paying attention to what I was doing.

With a small clunk the calculator came apart and the rubber mat that held the keys and the battery pack were exposed. Using a small cutting knife from my pencil case, I gently cut the plastic numeric mat and very carefully placed the keys back in order, except backwards. The nine key was now in the position of the one key and vice versa. It took me several minutes to get the calculator back together and, jiggling to make certain it was okay, I turned my attention back to the class. Mr Cromby still hadn't noticed my lack of attention and had just about finished his lecture.

"Mr Cromby!" I tentatively put up my hand. "I can't seem to get the same result."

If truth be told – I had no idea of what the equation was, let alone what the result should be, but I would bet that it definitely wouldn't be the answer my calculator would give.

"Sit down, Devon." Mr Cromby sighed wearily, waving me away.

Damn it! Mr Cromby wasn't going to fall for it. He must have spotted my expression or seen me tampering with my calculator. It was of course possible that he just simply knew me far too well after three years of teaching me to fall for anything.

Well, at least it had kept me entertained for a half hour or so.

The rest of the class passed with too much preamble – of course I couldn't do the actual work now. I'd tried at first but the mental math of figuring out where the keys on my keypad should be made the calculations even harder. I had just about given up when the class bell rang.

"Fix your calculator before next class too, Devon," Mr Cromby called as I walked out the door.

I couldn't help but grin to myself. Mr Cromby might not be the flashiest teacher but damn the man was smart. I'd have to come up with something more devious next time.

"What's wrong with your calculator?" Garry asked as we entered the hall.

"Nothing much," I smiled back, passing it to him. "What's nine plus nine? Try it."

"Two?" Garry murmured. "How'd you do that?"

"Magic," I smirked as I enigmatically waved my fingers about in his face.

"You're an idiot!" He smiled and threw my calculator back at me.

I had a free period that afternoon which I spent in the library looking up any reference to magic that I could find. Unfortunately other than fictional references to magic users, magicians and sorcerers, I came up with very little.

I somehow doubted that figures such as Gandalf, Harry Potter or Merlin would be useful as role models anyway. I needed a non-fiction book – a how-to book. Fictional stories didn't go deep enough into how these guys controlled their powers – and it was advice about control that I was desperately seeking. Unfortunately they don't have *A Dummies Guide to Magic* in our library. The internet too had proved to be a complete loss. There were a variety of groups that claimed to have magical powers, but I doubted that they had anything like this. I couldn't imagine anyone wanting to advertise that they were this different from everyone else. They would instinctively hide. They would have had to, otherwise everyone would know about it.

No. After several hours of useless web surfing I came to the inescapable conclusion. There was only one person who could help me. I just had to find her and convince her to teach me what I needed to know. If I was honest with myself I'd probably have admitted that I might have had other reasons for wanting to see Renee again.

"Devon?"

I glanced around to see Tina Higgins gazing at me.

She had a pile of books in her hands and a nervous expression. Tina and I had History class together. She was one of the nerdy kids who sat up the front of the class. She was also one of Sarah's friends, but I hadn't really spent that much time with her. I didn't know her that well at all actually. She had curly dark hair and wore tight wire-rim glasses on her freckled face. She wasn't one of the popular kids, but I wasn't exactly going to win any competitions for class president either. We had sat together and worked on several group projects, but we weren't exactly friends.

"What are you searching for?" she asked as she logged into the computer terminal next to mine.

"Just something for English." I shrugged as I quickly minimised a webpage on Gandalf. "You?"

"History," she groaned. I didn't even know we had something due for History. I really should start paying more attention in class. We sat in uncomfortable silence for a few more seconds.

"I like your new contacts," she began. "I didn't know you needed glasses."

That statement had come out of nowhere. Contacts? I wasn't wearing contacts. Where had that come from? I frowned at her in confusion, searching her face for any sign that she was making fun of me. If she was – I didn't get the joke.

My silence couldn't have been helping with her nervousness as she began nervously twiddling with her hair.

"I was thinking about getting those coloured lenses too," she stammered, "but I didn't think the school would allow them. They're making your eyes very blue."

It finally struck home: she couldn't see the blue particle lines, but she could see that something was strange with my eyes.

"Has anyone told you off?" she asked.

"Not at all. I need contacts for reading," I said. "I got red eyes from the contacts at first," I continued.

I was making it up as I went along and was amazed that it actually made some kind of sense. I've always been a bad liar but it looked like Tina was being taken in.

"I thought the blue contacts would help hide the red-eye," I finished lamely.

"Well it seems to have worked." Tina smiled, gazing into my eyes with a strange expression on her face. "Your eyes are completely free of red!"

"Yeah," I said, getting nervous. "I'd better go now." I shut down the computer.

"Yeah," she agreed. "Well, see you later Devon…" she murmured uncertainly as her sentence kind of trailed off.

The rest of the day finished without too much grief. No-one else mentioned my eyes. That was good. Mum had phoned me to say she was going to be late and that I'd have to sort my own dinner out. Mum was studying a business course at night school and so every now and then I had to fend for myself. I didn't mind it actually – it was kind of nice to be self-reliant.

I fried up sausages for dinner. It was not the most appealing meal, but it was safely within my cooking repertoire. After I finished eating, I did the dishes and went outside. Our house was the rear unit in a lot of three, so I had plenty of privacy. I'd never get a better time to get some more practice.

I vaguely thought about getting out some more mugs to practice on but it had been pretty obvious from my earlier attempts that I needed to try something different.

In a burst of inspiration I hurried into the garage and rummaged through the storage boxes. It wasn't long before I found what I was looking for. It was an old horseshoe game. It was something that I'd played as a kid. I think it was a gift from my grandmother for one of my birthdays. I hadn't played it in years.

I sat down on the concrete floor in the garage, a ring held balanced on my palm while I slowly let the particles wrap around it. I didn't have much trouble looping the thread through the hole and around the ring. I didn't need anywhere near as much control. The family cat looked at me, annoyed that I had disturbed it when I had been looking for the horseshoe game.

There was a noticeable creaking noise and an indent on the ring where the thread was gripping it. The ring didn't break, but it did look like it was undergoing an enormous amount of pressure. I held the ring in one hand and had the particle whip around the other. All I needed to do now was remove my hand.

The ring fell to the ground. The particle whip had

stretched from my hand to accommodate the distance. I tried several more times before I figured out the trick. I focused the particles from both hands into one thread, trapping the object between my two hands. The ring hovered in mid-air. I could cause it to rise and fall by altering the pressure from either hand.

Brilliant!

The cat and I exchanged brief amazed glances at the ring floating in mid-air. It didn't take long before I figured out how to get the ring to rotate and turn in the air, but I soon grew bored of this. What I really wanted to try was throwing the ring at the post telekinetically. My eyes narrowed with concentration as I tried to gently throw the ring onto the wooden pole about three metres away. 'Gently' being the operative word. The results were spectacular. I applied what I thought was a little amount of power as I attempted to launch the ring at the post. I hadn't even really aimed at the post. Anywhere close to the post would have been fine.

The ring left my hands with a speed I hadn't anticipated and disappeared with a shower of leaves as it tore through the bushes on the far side of the yard. There was a dull thunking noise as it hit the brick wall that separated our houses. The cat glanced at me with curiosity before heading over to inspect the damage.

Investigating, I found it had gouged a chunk out of the brick wall. The impact had wrecked the rope ring. Now that it was broken I could see that the rope had been wrapped around a small metal ring.

The metal was also snapped neatly in two. I stared at the ring in disbelief. I had broken it in two by doing nothing more than throwing it. I investigated the chunk missing from the brick wall and realised that the only way I'd normally be able to do this kind of damage was with a sledge hammer. It was frightening, awe inspiring and so totally cool all at once. I needed to try again, but I'd take a little more care this time and avoid throwing things at the wall.

I grabbed another ring from the collection and tried again. It was a little easier to wrap the particles around it this time. I was so elated by my supposed improvement that I lost control of what I was doing and ended up jerking the particles to one side.

With a metallic shriek the ring tore itself into two. The first piece imbedded itself in the ground inches from my foot. The second piece shot straight up past my face. I felt the air whoosh past me and my hair flutter in its passing. It took several seconds before it returned back to the ground. There was a horrible crash as the piece returned to the ground right through the garage roof, leaving a fist-sized hole.

Damn. That would be hard to cover up, I concluded as I inspected the damage. My God, what if that had hit me on the way down? This was too dangerous to continue. I could seriously hurt someone. Perhaps even kill them. I needed help with this before I continued. I could tell from the way that the cat was nowhere to be seen that he agreed with me.

Fortunately Mum didn't comment on the damage to the garage or she never noticed. If she did notice she must have assumed something else as it wasn't the type of damage that she would normally attribute to her eighteen-year-old son. The next week was subtle torture. I now knew that I lacked the necessary control to experiment on my own. I needed to find Renee more than ever. I resolved more firmly to track Renee down and insist that she teach me what she knows.

Friday seemed to take forever to come around. I had called Dad earlier that week and said I would be busy Friday night and that I'd crash at his place at around twelve. He didn't comment other than a curt acknowledgment, so I figured he must have been busy with work.

That meant I'd have the whole night to hunt for Renee. I figured that I'd start at the Fitzroy pub where I'd first met her. She was there last Friday so it wasn't totally out of the question that she'd be there again.

* * * *

I arrived very early to the club and it was pretty much empty. Tony had wanted to come but I hadn't let him – I wanted Renee all to myself without Tony getting in the way.

The band that was playing was simply awful. It sounded like a mixture of screeching and droning. I'd heard Tony comment that the good bands didn't come on until after nine. He was obviously right. I resolved to sit and wait for Renee to turn up.

I sat through three torturous bands before I finally lost my patience. All the while my eyes scanned the almost empty room for the tell-tale sign of a particle halo. Every new face that entered the room was examined and Renee's face was definitely not among them. I was so frustrated. By the time I decided to leave the club was starting to get busy and the bands had notably improved but I didn't care.

On a whim I decided to check the alley where she had thrown me down. Yes, the alley was pretty much as I'd remembered it, but Renee wasn't there. I nodded sourly and returned to my seat inside. It had been a long shot anyway. Why would she be hanging out in an alley?

The fourth band was just setting up when I resumed my seat.

"Hey, Twitch!"

My stomach lurched in fright. Finally. She was wearing a tight black dress and I wanted to kiss her again straight away, but that probably wouldn't have been a good idea.

"Where have you been?" I exclaimed.

"About," she muttered noncommittally. "I wasn't sure I was going to come."

"You're avoiding me?" I asked, hurt.

"No, I came looking for you," she said. "Come on, I know a place where we can talk quietly – unless you came here for the music?"

She smiled at me, her expression smug. She knew what I had endured waiting for her and obviously found it funny. It was both endearing and infuriating all at once. We left the pub and she took me to the smaller and quieter sports bar on the corner. It had very few patrons and no-one appeared to pay us much attention as we settled into a booth in the far corner.

"I see you haven't fried yourself yet," she said grimly once we had sat down. "That makes things more difficult."

"Fried? Difficult?" I stammered. What was she talking about?

"Yeah, I'd hoped you'd charcoal yourself and then you wouldn't be my problem," Renee said. I could tell that she was forcibly trying to keep her tone light.

It was charming the way that she'd put that with the emphasis on the word "my" as if this was something I was doing to her.

"Given the way you looked last time we met I was sure you'd be a cloud of ash right about now," Renee continued lightly.

"I guess that means you owe me a Coke," I said.

"You don't understand, but you will," she continued, unabashed. "You've obviously learned some level of control."

"Control? No, not really, I just can't seem to control anything."

She raised her eyebrows.

"I tore a hole in my mother's garage roof," I announced guiltily, then snickered involuntarily.

"How?" Renee's voice had taken on a dangerous quality, her eyes had narrowed and I could see her irises had taken on the 'stranger's look' as she gazed at me. It was unsettling.

I glanced around the bar nervously. I was reassured by the fact there were witnesses about. Although, I reflected grimly, if she wanted to be rid of me, I doubted the presence of the other bar patrons would present much in the way of resistance.

"I threw a metal ring through it," I said, deciding that it was best to opt for truth.

"Threw?" There was a small facial twitch. She was having trouble not grinning.

"Like you threw me into that wall, last week."

The grin disappeared.

"You saw me do that and now you're attempting it?" Her voice went deadly quiet.

"Is that not normal?" I asked carefully.

"No, none of this is normal. Firstly, our kind usually manifests long before eighteen and secondly they don't see other spells and then figure them out on the first try."

"Hey, it took me all afternoon to figure it out!" I protested.

"What? It only took you an afternoon?" she hissed. "Please." She leaned in close and stared daggers into my eyes. "You're not supposed to be able to learn spells simply by watching them!" Her voice had a hint of hysteria.

"Whoa, wait… calm down," I pleaded, taken aback by her ferocity.

Renee's eyes flashed angrily. "Eventually you're going

to kill yourself or, worse, you'll end up on the nightly news! Which will bring your trouble down on me!" she yelled. "And you think I should be calm about it?"

I didn't say anything. I was scared I would drive her away.

"I can't tell if you're telling me the truth or not," Renee whispered darkly.

"Everything I've said is true!" I protested weakly.

"I wasn't going to give you this, but I can see it's no longer my choice." Renee pulled an older style floppy disk out of her pocket and passed it over to me. She passed me the disk as if she was passing on something very dangerous.

"It's a treatise on mana," she said carefully, "written by my grandfather. It will help you."

"Mana?"

I'd read about mana when I was researching magic at school. It was the term used for the magical force that powered the spells that wizards used. I supposed, looking down at the blue particles lining my arms, it seemed as good a term as any.

"This old disk is a spell book?" I asked as I slowly rolled the disk over in my hands.

"What were you expecting? A gold-plated, engraved, tome of a book bound in human flesh? That can only be read by moonlight?" she said.

I wasn't sure what I was expecting, but a piece of technology small enough to fit in the palm of my hand definitely wasn't it.

"What would have happened if I hadn't learned some control?" I enquired. I wasn't sure if I wanted an answer.

"If you were still as jazzed up as you were last week, I would have let you go," she said. She looked a little guilty to be admitting it.

"And what would have happened to me?"

"The mana in your body would have burned you out and you would have died." Renee refused to look me directly in the eyes.

"I could have died because of this? And you didn't tell me?"

"Hey, I'm telling you now, alright? So just drop it!" she demanded. "Besides, I would have done you more harm than good last week anyway!"

"You were going to let me die," I repeated, staggered.

"I said I'm sorry already!" she snarled back, despite the fact that she actually hadn't.

We sat in silence, staring at each other. My anger kept me silent and I'd like to think her guilt kept her quiet.

"Thank you," I murmured when my anger had subsided.

"For what?" she said defensively, her arms folded across her chest.

"Well, for not letting me die for one, and for your grandfather's treatise for two," I said. "Can I have your proper number this time?" I asked.

"You didn't like the pizza?" she laughed.

"You use that place a lot?" I replied, dumbfounded. I had just thought she had picked a number at random.

"Yeah, they stiffed me on a pizza once," she continued.

Amazingly, she made no move to leave and I was able to ask her more questions. She was a little more open with me now. I wasn't sure if she'd decided that she could trust me, but she was a lot more forthcoming with answers about her life. Renee refused to discuss anything further about the mana though, imploring me to read her grandfather's writings, saying it would explain it far better than she could, but we chatted long into the night.

"So you didn't answer me earlier," I said as the night drew to a close. "Can I have your real number this time?"

"No," she said.

"No?"

"I'm not going to give you my number today – that would be too easy."

"Easy?" I was becoming a parrot.

"If you can find me again, I'll give it to you." She smiled. "And I'll know that you've understood my grandfather's work."

"How am I supposed to find you?" I asked in desperation.

"Read my grandfather's work!" Renee repeated smugly. "See you soon, Twitch!" she said as she walked away. "Don't keep me waiting too long."

I just stared at her with longing.

"Oh, and keep that disk safe. I want it back when you're done."

CHAPTER THREE

I didn't sleep well again that night. I twisted and turned in my sleep, unable to switch off. Renee's words repeated over and over in my mind: "I see you haven't fried yourself yet."

I could have died. I wasn't prepared to use the mana until I knew how to use it properly and I couldn't learn to use it properly until I read the information on Renee's disk. Unfortunately my dad's computer didn't have a three and quarter inch drive, neither did my laptop. The only place I knew that still had them was the computers in the school library. I'd have to wait until Monday. I hate waiting.

After three days without using mana I began to feel my temperature rising. I still wasn't sleeping properly and my dreams were troubled. The whole experience had introduced me to a new concept – being eager to get to school. This was a new feeling and one that I didn't like.

I left for school very early on Monday morning, leaving a note for Tony or Garry on the front door telling them that I'd gone ahead to finish an assignment. I'd hoped to catch a half hour or so in the library where I could look at the disk uninterrupted. The library is always open before school, so that kids can finish homework before class. I tore into the school at high speed, kicked open the doors into the library and burst inside. I ignored the outraged expression on the librarian's face and her indignant demand to slow down and settled down in front of a computer terminal. After logging into the system I hesitantly placed the disk into the slot and waited for it to load.

The discordant sound of the floppy disk loading was unusually loud in the quiet library. I looked around guiltily but the librarians had gone back to their morning duties. There were about a half dozen documents on the disk and I selected the one entitled "Basic Principles". That document seemed like the logical place to start and it also had the earliest creation date.

It was a large document – very large. This was going to take some time to work my way through it all. I tried reading several paragraphs but to be honest I couldn't really focus on the text. Key sentences kept jumping off the page, drawing my attention to them, but for the most part it was gibberish.

> ...*at the heart of the process is the chemical reaction caused by the conversion between mana energy (Vis Viva to use the Latin term) and other forms of energy. It is the conversion of Vis Viva to other energies that gives a mage his power. Kinetic, sound, light and heat – these are all forms of energy in their most visible form. Converting one to the other*

is possible as seen in basic physics – heat to light, light to heat and kinetic energy to heat or sound.

This was really dry reading. I may as well have read a Physics textbook. I had no idea what Renee's grandfather was trying to tell me. I could see the mana particles in my arms, but I still had no idea how to draw upon them. At times it almost was like the mana seemed to know what I wanted to do, but it wasn't through any conscious order.

How can that be?

When I tried to lift something I could see the particles trail down my arms towards my hands. How did it do that? I had yet to read anything that led me to believe that the magic was consciously aware.

…It can be theorised that as with other forms of energy conversions, no energy is lost in the conversion process. It can then be stated that the average human being must contain an unparalleled level of energy in mana. This would explain the amount of kinetic energy that can be produced by even the most untrained mage with the simplest of telekinetic spells.

This was making me sound like I was some form of human nuclear power plant and that thought did not bring me much comfort. Why couldn't the book just get to the point and tell me how I needed to gain control of this thing?

... The crux of the issue is the human ability to generate mana. Once a mage begins generating mana, a hormone is released into the bloodstream. This effect in turn releases a series of endorphins which creates a general feeling of euphoria when the mage is actually using mana. The hormone also stimulates the production of yet more mana. The cycle of mana production becomes directly linked to the amount of mana expenditure and soon enough the human body will suffer withdrawal symptoms if the mana is not generated. Therefore the more mana one uses, the more one will crave it and the more mana energy one will be able to generate and the more powerful one will become.

This last sentence made me pause. Something important was being said here. The more I used my powers, the more powerful I would become? That sounded good. Although that wasn't really telling me anything I didn't already know. If you practice something of course you're going to get better. I didn't realise until much later that the actual importance of that sentence was not about 'generate', it was the word 'crave'.

I didn't manage to get through the whole of that particular document – it was far too long. There was a second, shorter piece titled "Kinetic transference" that I spent most of my time pondering over. I was pretty sure that it was what Renee had used in the alley that night.

The frustrating thing about this 'book' was that there

didn't appear to be any spells as such. It wasn't like I could memorise a string of words to weave my magic. There were no secret words or base enchantments. Renee's book was trying to get me to understand complex principles and theories. It was a little strange reading a book that read like my Physics textbook but discussed the most un-scientific topic I could imagine.

Renee's grandfather had even included some test notes in footnotes, claiming to be able to lift up to 500 kilograms, but theorised that with intensive use, there was probably no limit to how much weight could be lifted.

…The spell of telekinesis relies heavily upon the principle of extension or the ability to draw the mana from your body into a mana thread. It is a difficult challenge and one that usually takes several weeks of practice. It is difficult at first to maintain the thread as it will often attempt to dissipate once outside the confines of your flesh.

Apparently Renee was right, I had done something unusual. I had learned the basic control within an afternoon. To be fair it wasn't complete control, but I certainly hadn't had any great issue with the mana thread dissipating. It wasn't until I got to the following paragraph that an important truth dawned upon me.

…It is important to understand the relationship between mana and mind. Mages attempting to

protect themselves from a fire could do so in several ways. First, one could suck all the air away from the fire, thereby suffocating the flame. One could employ a hydrant to the fire thereby dousing it. One could cause the flame to increase in intensity thereby burning itself out before reaching its intended target. It is important to realise that this is not a conscious decision on behalf of the mage – the mage merely wishes the fire out.

It is the unconscious mind that determines the result of the endeavour. Only in understanding the way in which we interact with the world around us can we become more precise and less wasteful of effort. This in turn makes the mage more powerful: knowledge is the key – power itself is irrelevant.

I re-read that paragraph three times before I finally understood what I was being told. This explained why I couldn't lift up an object with any precision. I was trying to do what Renee had done!

I had seen Renee use this technique as a weapon to knock someone down in an attack. An attack can't be used to lift or move things! There was no subtlety in Renee's attack thus there could be no subtlety in my use of the technique either. I sat back from my chair in a daze, my mind trying to assimilate what I'd learned. I could feel the excitement building within me. It was not my lack of control that was leading me to failure, it was my unconscious intent.

I was sure that I could do it now – but I needed

to practice and I obviously couldn't do that here. The library was far too open and I had run out of time. I had about five minutes before my first class.

I packed up my stuff and ejected the disk from the computer. If I had been thinking more clearly I would have copied the files from the disk so I could look at them later, but it didn't occur to me until after I had already left the library.

Tony and Garry were waiting for me at a long string of benches where we usually hung out. It was our unofficial meeting place as we usually gathered there before going to class or walking home.

"Morning," Tony greeted as he saw me approach. "Forget our homework, did we?" He seemed friendlier than last time, but there was still something off.

"Yeah," I mumbled back sheepishly.

"Yeah, well, if you get detention again, don't count on me to help you out this time."

"Help me out! How did you help me out?" I said in mock outrage.

"Hey, I kept you company!"

"Kept me company? As I recall we just sat there silent for the whole hour!"

"Yeah, well… I didn't have anything to say."

"That explains why I was so quiet then – I was stunned into silence at the thought of you running out of anything to say."

Tony laughed then looked at me seriously. "So, what's going on, mate? Did you see her again?"

"Yeah." I didn't want to pursue this line of conversation at the moment, but Tony wasn't to be put off.

"What's this? You met up with a girl?" said Garry. "Get anywhere?" he smirked lewdly.

"No, well she wanted to…" I grinned, playing along, "…but I had a headache and had to wash my hair."

"You do have such lovely hair," Sarah interjected from behind me – I hadn't even heard her approach.

"Wash, rinse, repeat," I said, quoting an annoying shampoo commercial.

"What technique, you must be a fantastic lover." She smirked back, poking her tongue out at me.

"I don't get any complaints," I said. Actually, although I had kissed a few girls, I had never had sex. But Sarah didn't need to know that. Fortunately for me the bell rang before anyone was able to comment further.

English class again. Mr Saunders' monotonous voice filled the room, only broken by the squeaking on the white board. I wasn't paying attention. Instead, my mind was fixated on what I'd learned in the library. I was sure I could do it now. I definitely couldn't practice in class. It would be too obvious and unfortunately Saunders would never let me go anywhere. If I asked for a toilet break, he'd probably come looking for me after five minutes.

I'd have to sit through English and wait until my next class. I scanned my timetable, History next. That wasn't too bad. I could easily get away with ducking out of History class for a few minutes without causing too much disruption.

Because I was so tired from the sleepless nights I actually dropped off to sleep for a moment and Saunders woke me with a question. Strangely he didn't seem that angry about it. What the hell? I would have thought he would have torn me a new one. He seemed to let it pass and English class drew to its thankful conclusion and we all marched in a line to the class door.

"Devon, a moment please."

Resigned, I turned and walked back into the room.

Mr Saunders waited at his desk. "Sit down," he said.

I did. Great. I was going to get detention for sleeping in his class. This was more like the usual Saunders that we all knew and loved.

"I want to talk to you." He peered over his glasses at me.

"Yes, sir?"

"Is… everything okay at home?"

Wow. Saunders actually looked nervous. "Yeah… sure it's fine," I stammered. We looked at each other, confused.

"You haven't been looking well recently."

"Everything's fine," I assured him. "I've just been having some trouble sleeping at the moment."

"Stress with the workload?" he suggested. "We have that essay on *Heart of Darkness* coming up next week."

Shit. I hadn't even started that yet. That was going to cost me.

To my surprise, he gave me another week without even prompting. Something was definitely going on here, but I decided not to look the gift horse in the mouth.

"Get some sleep," he called as I left the room.

This was unexpected. I wouldn't have thought Mr Saunders would even notice if I wasn't feeling well. Sure, I'd fallen asleep and I hadn't been actively trying to make his class a laughing joke recently – but I can't have been that out of it. Why was he being so nice? Is it possible that I'd misjudged him?

I caught up to Garry who gave me a questioning look about being called back by Saunders. I ignored it. "I'm going to cut History," I announced. "I need to finish some homework – I'll see you at recess."

I waited a few minutes around the corner before heading towards the toilets. The bathroom I'd selected was a remote one, unlikely to be used during class time. So it was unlikely that I'd be interrupted. I made sure there was no one in the bathroom and quickly locked the door behind me. I turned and looked at myself in the mirror and saw the 'stranger's eyes' taking hold of me as I took a deep breath. I could feel the mana in my body react – almost as if it knew what I was about to do. I turned and placed my bag on the far side of the room. I breathed back out and held my hand in front of me. I flexed my fingers and watched with glee as a tendril of mana surged from my hand and with perfect precision wrapped around my school bag and brought it floating back to me.

An intense wave of euphoria washed over me, one that had nothing to do with endorphins. I grinned to myself as I felt the unfamiliar wave of pleasure as the mana washed over me.

This was the control I sought – I had perfectly dictated the movement of the bag. It was not like I was fighting for control with myself any longer. The wild uncontrolled thrashes that had previously been the limit of my control were gone. This was perfect. I hadn't even rumpled the sides of the bag as my telekinetic chord wrapped itself around it.

It was a single perfect moment. My bag was floating about two feet in front of me. I leaned back against the wall and watched transfixed as the mana particles slowly pulsed from my outstretched hand to the corners of the bag.

I had done it! I had achieved the desired level of control and I had achieved it in the most ignoble and inglorious of places – a high school toilet block.

I had a reasonable wait before recess. I had thought about returning to class, but decided against it – instead I chose to go to the library. I needed to copy across the documents from the old disk anyway.

The library was relatively quiet when I arrived – but then again it's always quiet. I selected a computer terminal and loaded up the disk again.

I opened up the last document I'd been looking at and scrolled down until I reached where I was up to. I also took the time to copy the files to my USB drive so I'd be able to read them later on my laptop. There wasn't that much more on telekinesis left.

The next section was entitled "The Principle of Detonation". It detailed how to get particles of mana to leave the body in a tightly wound ball and then prompt them to explode. This would send particles scattered out in every direction. I had no idea what the potential benefits of this might be. Renee's grandfather talked about the technique as if it were a standard practice and used quite commonly; however, I didn't see the benefits. You couldn't use it to lift anything as the thread would be far too sudden and uncontrolled. You might be able to knock something over with it, I supposed. I just didn't get it.

It wasn't until Renee's grandfather began detailing a new spell entitled "Awareness" that I saw the point. This wasn't about getting things to move. The awareness spell was fairly simple in intent. It would send out mana rocketing in each direction over a wide area. When the mana came into contact with human life it would burn with a luminance making people easier to see. The mana would pass through walls with little difficulty allowing the mage to see people that were out of sight or in other rooms. That seemed kind of cool.

> ...*with intent the mana vortex will expand and cause a reaction in the mana particles, the centre cannot hold and the resulting reaction will cause the particles to expand outwards. When they collide with the human force in the bloodstream they will recoil and burn upon themselves creating a light source that is visible from some distance away.*
>
> *Mana is a form of energy and thus can travel through solid objects, coming in contact with life on*

*the far side of walls or columns. With practice a wide
area can be spanned.*

"Hi Devon," a familiar voice called out from behind me.

Tina was standing behind me. How did she keep sneaking up on me like that? She had a pile of books casually tucked under one arm and a curious look on her face. If she were here then it must mean that History class was over and it was now recess. It's amazing how easy it was to lose track of time when you're reading this damned book. She quickly pulled up a chair and sat down next to me.

"What's that you're reading?"

"Nothing much," I replied quickly as I closed the window with Renee's grandfather's document.

Tina actually looked a little nervous and bit her bottom lip. I was eager to return to my research, but also curious. "What's up?" I asked, attempting to draw her out.

"You roller-skate don't you?" Tina began.

"Blade actually," I corrected.

"Do you think you can teach me how?"

"Sure," I said. "Do you own a set of skates?" I was pretty cocky about my skating abilities. I wouldn't say I was the best skater in the world, but I was pretty good.

"No, I thought I'd hire some," said Tina. "From the skating rink."

I had pictured teaching her on the streets. "Yeah, sure… when were you thinking?" I said.

"What about this Friday? I'll pick you up," Tina suggested shyly.

"Umm, that could be difficult. I need to go to my dad's on Fridays."

"I can drop you back there or at least to a train station afterwards," Tina assured me.

"You're sure? It's a long way."

"It's no problem. My dad bought me a car for my birthday," Tina stated proudly.

My dad had talked about buying me a car for my eighteenth but I don't think he was ever really serious about it. I was happy enough with the laptop he had bought me instead, but a car would have been awesome. I didn't have my driver's licence anyway – so a car would have been wasted on me.

"Sure, I'll ring my old man, and let you know tomorrow," I replied. " Who else is going?"

"Umm… I'm not sure," Tina said.

"I'll invite Sarah and Tony?" I said.

"Great!"

"See you then, Tina," I called as she got up to leave.

I got back to the documents with an eagerness I'd never shown to my text books. It was dry – but it was relevant. I badly needed somewhere to practice – somewhere where I wouldn't be interrupted. I pondered going back to the toilets, but quickly dismissed the idea. I really didn't particularly want to hang out in a dingy bathroom for any extended period of time.

I needed somewhere remote, somewhere no-one

would go. I quickly scanned the timetables in the entry hall to the library and quickly realised that there wasn't going to be such a place – I'd have to wait till I got home. Mum wouldn't come home until late tonight as she had her night classes.

The rest of the day passed pretty slowly as I worked the concepts that I'd learned over in my head. I still wasn't sure that I completely understood all the specifics of how the Principle of Detonation varied from the Principle of Extension.

I went straight home after school, telling Garry and Tony that I still hadn't finished my homework. Tony gave me a funny look as if he didn't believe me but let it go. I moved into my bedroom and began by re-reading the section on the Principle of Detonation. The document was getting easier to read the more of it I read.

I began with the breathing techniques that the document had recommended. The awareness spell required a high level of focus as I forced the mana particles to leap from my fingers into a swirling vortex between my hands.

It took me a good hour or so to get the mana to leap from my fingers and not form a thread. I hadn't seen this performed before so I didn't really know what to expect. I had just about given up when a mana particle fell from my fingers and hung suspended between my two hands.

It dissipated almost immediately, but I was able to duplicate the effect afterwards. The next challenge was getting more particles to join the first.

I forced more and more particles into the mana vortex and watched it grow in size. It gradually grew to the size of a basketball. Once the vortex reached a certain size I could see that I was losing more particles than I was gaining. I'd obviously reached the limit of what I was able to use. I knew from my previous attempts that if I tried to make the vortex too big it would collapse in on itself. Nervous about making a mistake I attempted to detonate the mana. Nothing happened. Once I had stopped pumping in more mana, the vortex quickly dwindled in size and quickly disappeared completely.

I had no idea how to get the vortex to detonate.

The document wasn't much help as it didn't give any specifics. It had said that the amount of mana required was minimal. Maybe I had used too much and that was the problem? I tried a second with much less mana this time. This didn't make any difference as the vortex still faded and vanished. Frustrated, I returned to the document and re-read the relevant section.

There just weren't enough details on how to perform the technique. It was as if the document was written for someone who already practiced the basics of mana, not someone as completely untrained as me.

This probably was the case, I reflected ruefully.

I began to wish that the document was indeed written as an incantation, simply recite the words and the spell would work. It always looked so easy when they did it that way on TV shows.

Tired and frustrated, I returned back to the document

and kept reading. Eventually Renee's grandfather moved on to further points, but it wasn't until I got towards the bottom of the document and read the following section that I discovered another interesting point.

> ... *The aura of a mage is different from a human. It is darker, soaked with the residue of expended mana. Those capable of reading auras will determine that the aura is that of a particularly creative or passionate person, however this is not always the case. When using the awareness spell the luminance provided by one with a mana-soaked aura is far greater – as the effect is intensified by the mana in the aura. Mages can be seen via an awareness blast at a far greater distance and with far greater clarity.*

Great, the one spell I couldn't figure out properly was the spell I was supposed to use to find Renee. Brilliant! I hadn't seen the point of this spell until now. Subconsciously I hadn't really wanted the spell to work. I was blocking myself but not consciously. It was amazing how often I was doing this to myself.

Reinvigorated, I attempted the technique again, my legs crossed on the bed, my hands held outstretched with a small vortex of blue mana slowly revolving in the gap between my fingers. I gently flexed my fingers.

Boom.

With a burst of bright light, the vortex exploded sending particles spinning in various directions, most were quickly absorbed back into my body, but several made it as far as a metre away before dissipating.

Well, it was a start. But unless Renee was hiding behind my wardrobe I doubt I'd be able to find her using this technique. Pleased with myself, I resolved to test that again later and finish reading the document. At the bottom of the document was a footnote: a comment left by Renee's grandfather.

...mages must always hide their power from the world around them, our kind does not exist in the fabric of society and society MUST be protected from our existence. Should they discover us, one of the two must end, either we will be hunted into extinction, or we will destroy that society in an effort to control it.

The world is changing around us now and becoming smaller. The mistakes of our kind cannot exist in a world dominated by the media. You must always be careful, my student, and remember that we practice what we learn in the hope that we never need to use it.

Others of our kind are our only threat and in them we face our greatest challenge. Too many of our kind fall prey to arrogance of their powers. Too many claim godhood and declare themselves all-powerful. They always fall.

I urge you with humility to learn from my mistakes, from the consequences of my actions. We are not gods, we are but men with a man's weakness and faults.

It is folly to assume that with great power comes the authority and maturity to exercise that power responsibly. Too many of our kind have fallen along that path and been destroyed.

Victor Whittlesea

1992

This just raised further questions. What mistakes had Victor made? Who was this apprentice that Victor had left notes for? Was it Renee? This didn't seem like the kind of message you would leave for a grandchild.

I pushed the laptop away from me and suddenly became aware that I was very weary. It was the kind of fatigue that sneaks up on you. My body was jazzed and I could feel the energy coursing through it. My leg was twitching slightly and my fingers kept moving nervously almost of their own accord. I had a slight headache and my temples began to throb. It's funny how you don't really notice a headache at first, but once you do it seems to increase in intensity. I flicked my laptop closed quickly and walked into the kitchen. I went and took some aspirin, saying hello to my mum who had just returned home and was unpacking groceries.

The headache stayed with me all night.

* * * *

I was in English class again the following morning. There were exactly twenty-three people in the room with me. This was obvious and I could have learned this without any mystical assistance by simply looking around the room. What I couldn't have known though, was that there were exactly twenty-four people in the room next door.

My awareness spell had worked. It had only covered this classroom and the two next to it – but it had worked.

I could still see a faint residue of their auras swimming across my vision. The awareness spell had gone off flawlessly. It had been a calculated risk to attempt a spell around people without drawing attention to myself.

I quickly realised that telekinesis would be impossible due to its very nature. I couldn't hide what I was doing as things moving around the room by themselves would naturally draw attention. This was unfortunate as it could have been used to achieve the most entertaining results – and Tony would love it. But this would give me away and I had taken Renee's warning to remain off the radar seriously. I didn't want to do anything to anger her. My instincts told me that angering her would be amongst the last things I ever did.

All in all, my test had gone fairly well, no-one had seemed to notice anything. My heart still pounded in my chest and I expected at any moment someone to turn to me and exclaim, "What the hell is that?"

I had slowly built the mana up in my fingers using my book as cover. I tentatively glanced around before I released the blast. I gasped softly and watched with wonder as the wave of mana passed across everyone bringing a faint blue aura to everyone's shape. Although I knew what to expect I was still shocked as the wave passed through the wall and ghostly blue halos began to appear in my vision. I could see the wall, but I could now make out the shapes of people behind it. It was awesome.

"Are you okay?" Garry whispered from behind his book.

"I'm fine," I hissed, a manic grin still plastered on my face.

The double vision of the mana auras made my eyes water and made it difficult to see. I noticed with some discontent that the text on the book inches below my face was practically unreadable.

Garry kept taking furtive glances in my direction when he thought that I wasn't paying attention.

I tried to estimate the distance that I had seen into the other room. Assuming that the classroom was full, I had probably only been able to extend the area of effect about five or six metres into their room.

This distance was still a far cry from what Renee's grandfather had claimed was possible, but this was a good start. After a minute, my vision returned to normal and I could no longer see the auras of those in the other room, and my ability to read small text returned soon after. The lines on the page slowly sharpened back into focus.

While it was amusing to see people in the other room, it was not overly productive. Until I could extend the area of effect, I couldn't see the spell being overly useful in my search for Renee. I tried several times again but I just couldn't seem to get the effect to continue out any further than the next room. I didn't know if it was because I was trying to be inconspicuous or because I merely didn't know what I was doing.

It wasn't long, however, until the end of class bell rang and I had run out of time. Grumbling to myself I began to pack my books.

"Well that was fun," Garry commented as we got to our feet to leave the class.

"Quiet reading beats loud work," I replied glibly.

"Yeah, I noticed you weren't really reading," Garry said, his voice tense.

Before Garry could elaborate on his strange statement we were interrupted by a call from Tina who was struggling to make her way through the crowded corridor.

I turned to Garry. "I'll see you later, mate." I was glad that we hadn't been able to continue our conversation. He nodded back as I turned to walk towards Tina. Damn, I had forgotten to check with Dad about Friday. Not that he'd notice my absence – he would probably be busy that night in the office anyway.

Tina appeared to be a little out of breath. I can only assume she had to run to catch me. Garry usually set quite a fast pace. He wasn't one to amble from place to place.

"I wanted to see if you were still okay for Friday," said Tina, still trying to catch her breath.

"Yeah, it's okay," I smiled back as she moved in a little closer.

"Which rink do you want to go to?" I asked as Tina fell into step next to me.

"I thought we'd try the Caribbean Markets one. I've heard it's good."

It was the closest rink to us and pretty large. I used to go there regularly before I realised I enjoyed street skating more.

"No worries." I smiled back. "Haven't invited Tony and Sarah yet – but I will. Who else is coming?"

Tina laughed nervously and placed a hand on my arm. I stopped and got out of the way of moving traffic.

"I thought it would be just us," she said, trying to gauge my reaction.

In many ways I would like to think that I'm quite intelligent, alert and perceptive of what was going on around me; however, in this one case I'll admit that I was a clueless wonder.

"Oh? You want to make sure that you can skate before you invite your other friends along? I understand." I laughed, oblivious to the fact that her face fell a little at my response.

"Yeah, that's it," she agreed readily. "Pick you up at seven?"

"Sounds great!"

* * * *

Friday night came quickly. I was sleeping better this week and was feeling pretty good when I found myself startled by the honk of a car horn outside my house. Tina's red hatchback was parked outside. I saw her peering at me through the window waving at me. I quickly grabbed my skates and bid goodbye to Mum and headed for the door.

"Hey!" Mum's voice caught me in midstride.

"What?"

"Is this a date?" She gestured a thumb towards Tina's car.

Even though Tony had already teased me, the realisation came crashing down around me at this point and I'm pretty sure that Mum must have seen the expressions change on my face as I tried the idea on for size.

"Uh, no, I don't think so, no," I stammered.

"Good," said Mum, "because it's customary for you to pick her up, not the other way around."

"Uhh, no we're meeting up with friends, she just lives closest to me," I lied.

I'm pretty sure Mum probably had more of an idea of what was going on here than I did, but in her typical fashion drew her own conclusions without making me look too foolish. Yet at the same time she gave me that enigmatic mother look that implied, "I know what's really going on here young man, but I'll do you the favour of not saying it out loud. Remember this next time I need you to do something."

"Well, have fun, darling."

"Thanks Mum."

Tina smiled as I loped up the driveway. "Hi!" She grinned.

"Hey." I smiled back. "Thanks for the lift by the way."

"Don't sweat it. You can pay me back later. By not laughing at me when I fall over." Tina laughed.

It was about a fifteen-minute drive to the skating rink from Mum's place. Tina and I chatted easily about school, teachers, roller-blading and Sarah. It was the first time I had really talked to her and she wasn't that shy or quiet after all. To my surprise she was amazingly easy to talk to.

When we arrived she said, "I've got to come clean here. I've never actually skated before so you're going to have to teach me from scratch."

I laughed inwardly. That wasn't quite where I thought she was going, especially after the ideas that Tony and now my mother had put into my head. I wasn't sure if I saw her that way but I was going to go with the flow.

It wasn't packed. A DJ was playing disco pop, but not too loudly. Tina had plenty to space to perform a move that all rookie skaters begin with known affectionately as the two-footed shuffle. This is where the skater tries to propel themselves forward without moving their feet, their knees or any form of motion that might unbalance them and cause them to fall over.

Either from natural skill or my expert tutelage, Tina soon found she could move around the rink with some degree of ease. She was still understandably unsteady on her skates but confident enough to attempt more speed.

"Enjoying this so far?" I said as she shuffled around a corner.

Tina had an expression of intense concentration on her face and replied without looking up from her feet. I'd had to subtly guide her around three corners already because of this. When you're skating around in a circle you really shouldn't glue your eyes to your feet as corners are an inevitable and unavoidable reality.

"Want to get a drink?" I asked, noting that she could probably use a break.

The look of gratitude on her face said volumes as she nodded back. We slowly made our way over to the café. I was guiding us over to the exit as Tina fixated on her skates.

"What would you like? It's on me," I said.

"A Coke, I guess."

"Me too. Won't be a tick."

I returned pretty quickly with our drinks and sat down opposite her.

"Do you do this often?" she asked.

"Drink Coke? Yeah sure, I love the stuff," I said.

I'd never seen anyone so skilfully pull off a "you're a loser" look whilst still attempting to look interested in what I had to say. Most people usually don't bother with the second part of the look.

"I used to come here often but I prefer skating on streets now," I explained. "One, there's no charge and two, it's a little more challenging with hills."

It added a degree of danger to the experience and

taught you very quickly to control your speed. If you lost control and went too fast you'd fall over and if you fell on the streets you were going to get hurt. Fortunately I'd only had several small accidents leading to only scrapes and bruises but no lasting damage. The most serious of injuries that I'd had would have been the blisters on my feet from breaking in new skates.

"Are your feet sore?" I asked. Tina had taken her skates off.

"Umm, it's not too bad." Tina rubbed her feet.

I noticed the clock. "Speed skating is going to start in a bit!"

"Are you going to go?"

"Maybe," I said, unsure of the convention here. I'd heard somewhere that it was bad form to abandon your date but on the other hand I really wanted to show off.

"You should, I'll happily sit out."

It didn't take too long before the DJ started up the speed skating. There were about a dozen or so other skaters on the rink and we pretty quickly formed into a line. This happened often as the line was usually broken up into two groups. The speed skaters who knew what they were doing and those like me who just liked to go fast.

I stormed into the rink with a burst of speed and pulled in behind the last skater. I leant forward to pull up more speed and fell into a circular pattern with the other skaters. The skater in front of me was very good and I would have had trouble catching him if I hadn't been caught in his slip stream.

I'd heard other people talk about this effect before and previously I'd been sceptical, but it really was true. It took less effort to follow closely behind someone than to try to keep pace next to them.

The music played during speed skating was invariably fast dance music. It got the heart racing and the blood pumping. I could feel myself getting caught up in the music and noticed with some alarm that the blue particles that were flexing down my arms were getting more and more noticeable as I gained speed. I wasn't sure if it was in relation to the speed, the build-up of adrenaline or something else. It was becoming quite distracting though. Actually it was becoming too distracting. It is a universally accepted fact that a speed skating rink is a bad place to lose one's concentration. I started wobbling as I took the last corner and realised with some small degree of panic that there was little I could do to prevent an eventual fall.

Now, there are two things one can do when one is about to fall – panic or attempt to control the fall. I'd fallen over enough times to know what to do. The basic technique they teach you when you start skating is to attempt to fall forward on your hands and knees to prevent smacking your head. The impact of course can be quite hard and you will invariably hurt your elbows, wrist or knees. In practice you'll usually hurt all three.

I didn't much think that this was such a good idea at the speed I was going. My ego had much to say on the subject – if you're going to embarrass yourself on a date then you'd better make it seem intentional.

Using the last bit of my control over my feet I attempted to sweep my feet out into a slide and aim myself roughly in the direction of the exit. You know what they say, if you've got to go, go out with a laugh.

This was all right in theory, my legs collapsed under me and I slid over onto my side. I landed with grace and I soon found myself sliding at high speed towards the exit. I had one arm behind me attempting to direct my travel the other waving cockily at the crowd as I departed the rink. As the surface of the rink was quite smooth, I hadn't notably slowed down by the time I reached the edge of the circuit.

I realised my mistake at about the same time I realised that there wasn't much I could about it. I was aimed directly, feet first, at the carpeted floor beyond the rink exit. Now carpet is usually pretty soft right?

Wrong. When you're sliding across it at high speed it's actually pretty rough.

I hit the carpet while I was still going pretty fast. My natural showmanship with my unorthodox exit had served me well as the crowd of skaters had vacated the exit and were laughing at my tumbling act.

The funny thing I've noticed whenever I've hurt myself is it's not so much the act that hurts it's the moment just afterwards. I didn't feel a thing as my arm shredded along the rough carpet, nor as my shirt was pulled back and my lower back exposed to the same treatment, I didn't feel anything until I came to a standstill and carefully got to my feet. Carpet burn is a harsh mistress.

Wincing, I watched as Tina made her way over to me with a look of concern across her face. She placed a tender arm around under my shoulder as she helped guide me back to the cafe. I played down the pain I was actually feeling. People were patting me on the shoulder as I passed them by – everyone loves a good laugh.

I sat down looking calculatingly at the burns along my arm. It wasn't too bad actually, it hurt like blazes and looked awful, but I wasn't bleeding and I wasn't too badly bruised. All in all I'd live. I didn't particularly want to inspect my back, especially in front of Tina as I suspected that it would look worse.

"Are you sure you're okay?" Tina asked, gazing at my arm.

I waved her off nonchalantly, attempting to suppress a grimace at the pain that shot down my back from my grazed side. Forcing a smile I shrugged.

"Forgot about the carpet." I grinned cheekily at her. "You want to go again?" I gestured towards the rink.

"Uhh... No. I think that's enough for one night." Tina smiled back.

It was almost closing time anyway so we weren't missing much. Tina waited for me to remove my skates and we headed for the door. Already I was feeling a little better and could walk normally without wincing. I also noticed with some surprise that the mana in my body had dulled and was now lazily circling throughout my body.

"Where do you need me to drop you?" Tina asked as we got back into her car.

"Any station is fine. I'm going into the city. Thanks again for this."

"Thanks for teaching me how to skate."

"Well, actually I think I showed you how not to do it."

"Well, that too. Are you sure you're okay?"

"I've done worse." I smiled as Tina put the car in gear and drove out of the rink car park.

It was a strange ride to the station. The station wasn't overly far from the rink and we pretty much drove in silence. Tina was very quiet; I couldn't help think that perhaps I'd done something wrong or I'd offended her somehow. It wouldn't have been the first time I'd inadvertently offended someone with a witty comment that had turned out to be incredibly offensive, stupid or both.

The train hadn't arrived at the station when we did and Tina offered to wait with me. I told her that wasn't necessary as she'd already helped me out enough. She smiled politely enough and pulled the keys from the engine and opened her door.

It wasn't that late, but the station was pretty much abandoned. It clearly wasn't a commonly used station. There were only a few cars in the car park illuminated by the overhanging lights from the station.

"Well, thank you for a lovely night out," Tina stated quietly.

"No, thank you, it was your idea." I tilted my head in

mock salute, which brought a tentative smile to Tina's face.

I was just in the process of trying to think of something witty to say when she quickly leaned forward and planted her lips on mine. I was so shocked at first that I didn't quite know how to respond.

Wow, she was kissing me. I attempted to pull my arms around her but before I could act she was gone. She rushed back to her car with her head down. I thought I heard her mumble something like "Thank you for a good night" before disappearing into her car.

I stood stunned as her car quickly took off into the night. I touched my lips. Then I immediately thought of Renee.

* * * *

The train didn't take too long to arrive, for which I was grateful. I had neglected to bring a jacket and I was starting to get cold. I had checked out the carpet burns on my back in the station bathroom and they weren't too bad either, although in the cold they were starting to sting.

The train ride back was pretty uneventful. It was late in the evening but not late enough that people would be returning home. I had the carriage all to myself and sat watching as the cityscape outside gradually became more built up as the train entered the city proper.

Housing gave way to factories, factories gave way to offices and before I knew it I was entering Flinders Street

Station. I took the side exit from the station and not the main entrance. I vaguely thought about getting some food as there were numerous fast food places available at this hour when something caught my eye – a spark of blue mana out of the corner of my eye.

It was only there for a second and then gone – but I was sure I had seen something. I was so sure that I sent off an awareness spell. It had happened so quickly I can't consciously remember the decision to use it. It had just happened, almost of its own accord.

A wave of mana particles flowed outwards from me across the busy station, highlighting the people already visible and those below me that I couldn't previously see in the tunnel walkway that led over the river next to the station.

As the wave of mana washed over the platform my vision was immediately captured by the silhouette of a figure running down the stairs behind me back into the walkway. The figure was practically glowing with mana particles. The mana issued forth from it like smoke and danced around it in wide circles.

It was like a bonfire for my senses and I could see it almost more clearly than the aura of someone standing three feet in front of me.

Renee. Who else could it be? Mages were apparently easier to see with awareness.

My hunger forgotten, I quickly turned and barrelled back towards the station platforms. I could see from my enhanced vision that Renee had now reached the far side of the tunnel and was probably about to reach the bridge that led across the river and to the casino.

The tunnel walkway was quite busy and I had to push my way through. By the time I had made it to the bridge I couldn't see her and had to resort to another awareness spell. The second wave showed me a mana signature racing across the walkway towards the casino – how the hell had she gotten there so quickly? It seemed impossible.

I raced across the bridge only to see the figure disappear into the casino. It took me several minutes to follow. It was quite a distance.

I was out of breath as I burst into a massive entry hall of the casino. Two bouncers looked warily at me as I pushed my way into the hall. I could see the figure at the far end of the hall about twenty metres or so away, obviously waiting for me. I couldn't see her clearly, but I was sure that it was Renee.

There was definitely something strange about her but the shape was obviously female. It looked like I was right in my assumption that it was Renee. I could see the shape of her body through the path that the mana particles left across her skin, but I couldn't see flesh tone, clothes or anything. She had to move on several occasions as people drifted into the space she had been standing.

She'd made herself invisible! There could be no other explanation for it! No-one was looking directly at her. People seemed to walk right through the space she'd just vacated. Yep, she'd somehow made herself invisible. I was just about to reach her when she flicked her arm out and I saw a familiar tendril of mana particles lance from her outstretched hand. I cringed expecting an attack but she hadn't aimed the thread at me. She had aimed at the roof.

I watched in bewilderment as her mana thread latched onto the topmost level of the entry hall and she launched herself into the air, spinning gracefully and landing poised on the handrail of the top level.

She had just gracefully leapt up three flights of stairs. Well that explains how she had managed to get to the other side of the river so fast.

I was even more out of breath by the time I reached the top level of the casino entry hall. I really needed to get more exercise. There was only one door on this level, which looked like it led into a popular casino night club.

She was obviously inside.

Once I got into the nightclub I couldn't see anything. The place was packed with people from wall to wall. The lights were strobing and flickering from colour to colour, making it difficult to see clearly.

I couldn't see Renee in the crowd, but there were too many people on the dance floor to be sure. I'd have to get closer. I looked from side to side as I moved through the crowd trying to catch a glimpse of my elusive prey, but it was hopeless. I'd have to use awareness again.

Attempting awareness didn't have quite the effect that I'd hoped for. The combined light of the particle auras of so many people in such a confined place mixed with the strobing effect from the lights blinded my vision to the point that I was physically reeling. I quickly fell backwards with my hands held across my eyes as the shock of the effect hit me.

"Hey! Watch it!" A rough shoulder pushed me away from the man I'd just fallen into. Unfortunately this knocked me into another couple who deftly moved out of the way letting me stumble forward to my knees.

The music pounded into my head and my vision was still blurred – I couldn't even make out vague shapes. I'd effectively blinded myself. That was clever.

Someone whom I could only identify as a shining blob pulled me to my feet. They had obviously thought that I'd had too much to drink. They patted me on the shoulder and pushed me in the direction of the bathrooms.

As my vision slowly regained its clarity I could see the white light faded into distinct shapes. I could now see the individual auras of those around me but they still blurred into one another as they danced. If I focused I could differentiate them but it was hard work.

I scanned the room and with a small smile, I saw her. I couldn't see anything else clearly, but I could see her. Renee's mana glow was easy to pick up in the crowd. I could barely make out the people around her as mere shapes blurred into indistinct blobs, but her mana signature was clear.

I could see her moving through the crowd and watched as people moved out of her way – she must be visible again. People wouldn't have moved out of the way for an invisible person. She was keeping her distance, moving through the crowd but still trying to keep away from me. I'd move towards her causing havoc as I still hadn't regained full use of my vision and couldn't easily navigate through the crowd.

However, when I got to where I'd last seen her, she'd be elsewhere. This was quite a large club and she had plenty of space to keep her distance. It was obvious that she was playing with me. It was infuriating. I could see her only through awareness, but every time I employed that I was physically blinded again to the real things around me. When I didn't use awareness I couldn't see her through the crowd.

Renee must have tired of this game as I spotted her leaving the club by the far entrance. It took me some time to get to the other side of the club and found that the doors led out into a gaming area. My eyesight was still blurred from extended use of awareness. I couldn't really make out any of the details of the room as the halos of the gamers pretty much blurred into one another as I ran past.

I set off another awareness blast and noticed with some degree of surprise that in only a short time my skill with awareness had increased. The distance this blast went was much further than I'd thought my previous limit was. I didn't really have time to measure it properly as I saw Renee making her way out the far exit to the gaming room.

She was certainly making this difficult. I raced through the gaming hall leading to more shouts of outrage and commotion. Fortunately I hadn't attracted the attention of any security guards yet though I knew if I kept creating such a hassle that they weren't going to be too far away.

Renee had gone into a closed shopping precinct. Row after row of retail shops led into the distance, each bolted and shut down. There is something creepy about a shopping centre when all the stores are closed.

I could see Renee making her way down the corridor just past a hair salon; fortunately she had slowed up some. I was relieved to be gaining on her. I saw her look quickly over her shoulder at me, obviously judging the distance between us. With a mocking wave and a grin she took off through a second set of double doors. I followed her several seconds later.

I found myself in a multi-level car park. I was on one of the middle levels. The car park was pretty much empty. Looking around quickly I spotted Renee land gracefully on the hand rail of an adjacent building's car park level. There was about a ten metre gap between the two buildings.

"You'll have to jump!" Renee called across from the other side as she walked nonchalantly across the handrail of the car park on the other side.

Behind me the double doors were smacked open and I could hear the calls of security guards in pursuit. Great, I hadn't got off as scot-free as I thought I had. Renee tilted her head towards me and shrugged – her message was clear, either jump or go with the security guards. I had no desire to leave myself to the tender mercies of the security guards – they looked pissed! I pulled my backpack that contained my roller-blades more firmly against my back and then turned to face the gap.

I breathed in.

I let out the breath.

I breathed in again.

I ran. If Renee could make the jump, so could I.

My breath was jolted from my body as I jumped over onto the guard rail of the car park and leapt out into the void. I heard with startling clarity the shouts of the security guards turn to alarm.

Then the ground came into stark focus. It was a five-storey drop and there was no way I was actually going to make the distance. It was simply too far for anyone to jump. I saw Renee's expression turn from approval into bewilderment and then anger.

Anger that was most obviously directed at me and my stupidity. I felt a hard shudder as the motion of my body was suspended and then completely stopped. I felt hard tendrils of mana wrap around my body. Two tendrils wrapped along my torso and one around each leg. My body was twisted horizontally and I was pulled forward as with cold precision as Renee directed me with less than a gentle thump onto the car park floor behind her.

Due to the speed at which I was travelling I slid forward across the cold concrete floor and deeper into the car park. The carpet burns from earlier in the evening screamed in complaint as I slid across the car park and down a ramp that led to the lower levels of the complex.

When you are sliding head first down a car park ramp, hoping to the heavens that a car isn't about to come the other way, your life decisions really come into question.

I hit the base of the car park and slid to a halt several metres from the base of the ramp.

"You tried to jump? What are you, an idiot?" Renee snarled as she reached the bottom of the ramp.

I stared up at her in bewilderment. Renee was staring down at me with a look of bemused anger on her face. I must have looked a pretty pathetic sight.

"Ouch," I stated dryly in way of complaint as I leaned up into a sitting position.

"You should have used your powers to propel yourself across the gap."

"I realise that… now," I said as Renee pulled me to my feet. "However, I'm still not quite sure how you did that!"

Renee looked me up and down considering this as if it hadn't occurred to her.

"Okay, maybe that last bit was a little hard," she conceded, "but you were doing well up until then."

"It wasn't easy," I replied. "Did you turn yourself invisible?"

She nodded curtly as we began the short walk down the ramp to the base of the car park.

"That's a neat trick."

"It has its uses. Though it's difficult. It's probably what I'm best at though," she continued quickly.

"How do you do it?"

"Oh no. Learn how not to fall off buildings first and then we'll discuss invisibility."

* * * *

"You obviously read my grandfather's work," Renee commented later as we were sitting in a café some distance from the casino. We had given the security guards from the casino the slip, though I doubt they'd tried hard to look for us.

They'd just seen someone leap across a ten metre gap and unlike me they weren't stupid enough to attempt it themselves. At least I hoped they didn't – we didn't see any ambulances arriving outside so it was safe to assume that they were okay.

"Yeah, didn't understand most of it though." I nodded back. "So, why did you want me to chase you?" I asked, nervously twisting the napkin in my hands.

"Hey buddy, I didn't ask you to chase me, I just wanted to see if you would," Renee snapped back with a grin.

"I caught a glimpse of you out of the corner of my eye. I got curious," I replied.

Renee laughed somewhat mockingly. "Yeah, well I wasn't exactly being subtle."

"What?"

"That spell I was using, it only makes us invisible to non-casters; for people like us we're lit up to the beacons. I'd have been surprised if you didn't see me."

"Leading me into that nightclub was a rotten trick though." I grinned.

"Hey, you followed me in." Renee laughed, her eyes twinkling in evil delight.

"Were you waiting for me at the station?"

"Actually, no I was returning home, it was just luck that I spotted you across the station line and I wanted to see how much you'd learned."

There was a grudging respect hidden behind her statement. It was heavily covered with sarcasm but it was there nonetheless.

"Eloquent test," I grumbled under my breath.

"Relax, you passed with flying colours!" Renee laughed, tousling my hair. Her fingers felt like light electric shocks. "So what do you want to do now?" she purred.

"Kiss you," I said without thinking.

There was an awkward pause. I may have over played my hand. Renee stared at me as if I'd said something horribly offensive.

"Well, actually I'd like to learn how you did that swinging trick at the casino," I quickly blurted out.

That obviously wasn't the follow-up she was expecting, but she shrugged with good grace.

"I know just the place to teach it."

It was a short walk back into the city. It was starting to get late so the streets were quite crowded with clubbers. Renee led me deep into the city away from the clubbing and retail district. This side of the city was old and consisted mainly of large office block buildings.

We rounded a corner and I saw we were making our way to a locked gate at the side of one of the buildings. The building was surrounded by construction awnings and safety fences that had bill posters pasted onto them.

"Keep an eye out," Renee hissed at me suddenly as she turned to pay attention to the lock on the gate.

"For what?" I asked stupidly.

Renee didn't answer and I heard a click as the lock opened in her hands. She stepped inside and gestured for me to follow.

"This is a worksite," I commented with my usual skill to state the obvious.

"Nothing gets past you," Renee commented. "Come on."

Glancing nervously around I followed her into the hollowed-out building.

"This building used to be offices, but it's been condemned," Renee announced. "I think they're going to build apartments."

I looked around to see that all the internal floors of the building had been ripped out. This left girders and solid concrete posts in a shell of the building. I could see all the way up to the solid roof. It was at least four stories high.

"Okay." Renee nodded, looking around. "This will do, the surface here looks soft enough." She smiled, indicating to the solid concrete floor beneath us.

"Yeah, snug," I grunted, stamping my foot slightly in the cold.

"Do you want to learn this or not?" Renee smiled back.

"Alright, you see that girder up there on the second floor?" Renee gestured upwards into the darkness.

"Barely," I nodded.

"Reach out if as if you're going to pull it down, but don't actually attempt to pull it."

Flexing my arms I reached out and wrapped a tendril of mana around it. There was a crunch and some grinding and the girder snapped off from the column.

"Ah okay, maybe a little less force." Renee cringed. "You're obviously not a soft touch. I'm glad I didn't let you kiss me," she smirked.

Irritated, I glanced quickly at her. Jokes were not appreciated.

"Now, try again, Twitch," she ordered, business-like again. "Maybe that one a little further away, and remember you're not trying to bring it to you."

With a loud clang I let the previous girder drop to the ground and tried again. It fell a good ten metres or so. The noise when it landed reverberated throughout the building.

"Quietly!" Renee admonished.

"Sorry," I replied sheepishly.

It took me several more tries before I was able to

latch my mana thread over a girder without pulling it out, but eventually it seemed solid enough.

"Alright, now picture wrapping the tendril of mana round your wrist as if you're going to swing across a rope," Renee instructed as she pulled herself in behind me and wrapped an arm around my waist.

A second tendril of mana shot out from Renee onto a girder above me.

It was intoxicating to be so close to her, I could feel her breath on my neck and the tickle of her hair on my cheek. I could smell her scent in the air.

"Relax, Twitch," she whispered. "Ready?"

I watched her hand as it curled in on itself, her slender fingers forming into a fist. I did the same thing and saw the particles in my hand mirror the same effect.

"Now, imagine pulling on the thread like a rope," Renee ordered.

There was a loud snap and suddenly the girder was flying at high speed towards us, with a strangled shriek I attempted to regain control over what was essentially a piece of fast moving shrapnel coming right at us, but I was unable to do so. With a laugh Renee threw her weight forward and both of us stumbled out of the way.

The girder imbedded itself a foot deep into the concrete where we had previously been standing. If that had hit us we'd both be dead.

Renee got back to her feet with a small chuckle.

"Did you do that on purpose?" I demanded as I jumped back up.

"No, Twitch, that was all you." She laughed. "Now try again."

When I attempted again either nothing happened or I snapped the girder out of the concrete again. It was infuriating.

"I think you need some motivation," Renee purred after watching me for several minutes. "I tell you what, if you can follow me up – I'll give you a reward."

Renee latched a mana thread onto the top floor and with a small leap was gliding up into the darkened building. Seeing the technique in action actually helped quite a bit, but I wasn't going to criticise her teaching.

In the end the trick turned out to be a lot like roller-blading. A lot of the trick to skating is the ability to move one's centre of balance from one foot to the other. This was similar except that I was moving my centre of balance from my feet to my arms, almost like doing a handstand.

I began tentatively at first with a small leap and let my arms take my weight. I was relieved that they did. I was now floating several metres above the concrete floor with my feet dangling uselessly below me. I could hear the sound of clapping echoing from the rooftop.

"That's not helping!" I yelled up at Renee.

"You're doing very well." Renee's mocking voice floated down. "Now you're stuck in mid-air, try again!"

With a grunt I landed back on my feet and immediately tried again, this time I leapt further now secure in the knowledge that it was possible. It wasn't that I was no longer feeling gravity, it was simply as if I was security fastened in a harness as I was slowly rising up to the girder. It was a strange sensation.

I held my breath all the way to the top and came to rest on the edge of a girder. With some effort I was able to pull myself onto the first floor of the building. There had to be a more elegant way of doing this.

"That's one!" Renee called down from the darkness. "There are four more floors."

I'd had about enough of this game. I latched a mana thread securely onto a beam on the roof of the building and used it to swing across to another part of the same floor, testing myself, and once I was sure that I was secure, I attempted to climb to the next level. I've never been scared of heights but this was something I've never experienced. Every other time I've looked down over a tall building or off a bridge, I've always been secure in the knowledge that my feet were firmly placed on solid structure. Looking at the ground several metres below through a gap between your feet is another sensation entirely.

It wasn't scary but it was definitely sobering. Still, as I found myself hanging in mid-air by a mana thread, I felt completely at ease – I was in control. This must be how birds feel when they take to the air. I didn't bother with the second, third or even fourth floors. I ascended straight to the roof.

"Clever boy," Renee complimented sarcastically from the darkness.

She was obviously out of direct line of sight because I couldn't see her mana signature. A quick awareness spell told me she was on the far side of the level. This particular floor was a maze of girders and beams.

Latching back onto the roof I made my way across the beams. Renee immediately dashed out from behind a column and dived down into the gap. She gracefully twisted mid-flight to level herself out and glide with accustomed ease into the darkness below me. Damn she was graceful, I felt like a bumbling ox by comparison. I shrugged and stepped out into the darkness and felt my body begin its fall as gravity took hold. I smiled as I willed my descent to slow, allowing me to come to a halt on the same level as Renee.

Renee was crouched on the far side of the gap about five metres across from me. She smiled impishly and I could see her readying to take flight once more. I had an idea. It was risky. It would be something Renee wouldn't expect. I waited until Renee had launched herself and then I reached out with a second thread. I wrapped my power around Renee's waist and pulled her towards me. She let out a shriek and startled curse as she inevitably began to swing towards me as my body now acted as ballast as I stepped out into the void to meet her. This was the first time I had tried multiple threads. Renee's grandfather had talked about mages being able to handle dozens of threads at any given time but I found it disconcerting merely to focus on two.

Reaching out as she swung past, I pulled her into

an embrace, hanging there mid-air by two particles of mana. She laughed as our bodies entwined and I felt her hands reach around to pull me in tight.

"Well, that wasn't the way I thought this would go," she whispered. "But…"

Breaking off mid-sentence she pulled me into a fervent kiss. I instantly went slack as the mana left me and my mind filled with desire. All awareness of where I was and what I was doing was swept away with that one desire to kiss this woman in my arms. I could the feel the mana in our bodies once again react and boil into a frenzy. The mana danced across our bodies like liquid fire drawing me in. It was intoxicating and I wanted more, fortunately for both of us, Renee was not quite so distracted and her mana thread held us in place. We slowly descended to the ground on her mana thread alone. Mine had long since dissipated.

CHAPTER FOUR

The air bristled through my hair as the road stretched out before me. My skates clacked against the road as I accelerated to match the speed of the car in front of me. The ability to pull myself into the air with a gesture had a very dramatic and obvious effect on my skating skills. No longer was I concerned about controlling my speed, sudden stops or even passing cars. It brought about a sense of invulnerability that would have bordered on suicidal insanity had I not had my powers.

Last year I would have never attempted the route before me. It would have been my death. The road was a sharp decent onto a major four-lane highway. There was no room to manoeuvre and even less to safely slow your speed. Get it wrong, and you're roadkill.

There is a certain amount of grim joy to be gained from a close encounter with death. The feel of adrenaline flowing through your veins as your brain shuts down and your knees go weak. It makes you feel alive. I reflected on this sombrely as I sat down on the edge of the road at the base of the descent, my skates still slightly spinning as I gently lowered myself on to the sidewalk. I missed that feeling. There was no rush. There was no thrill. There was no fear. The mana had ruined all that, the rush was gone, the excitement vanished. At the mere extension of my hand I could now slow myself down or and even pull myself air borne if required. It happened so instinctively that I almost had no control over it at all.

Bugger.

Skating just didn't seem to have the same buzz. There was no thrill, because the moment I became concerned or even had the slightest inclination that I was likely to fall, my mind would instinctively take over and slow myself down. With this sad fact in mind, I rose to my feet and began the trip home. There didn't seem to be much point continuing skating if it was going to be like this. Up until now I hadn't previously considered that there might be a down-side to my new powers. It takes a certain kind of pessimistic mind to turn a simple fact – "The mana won't let me maim myself into roadkill" and turn it into "The mana is a buzz-killer".

It takes a special kind of stupid to create that kind of logic.

There were of course compensations, in that I could gain more speed and more control over my movements. I could change my direction and speed at the merest flick of the wrist. Last year I would have begged for a taste of those skills.

My school life also suffered. Nothing mattered, nothing counted. No-one could teach me anything that compared to the mana. It was mysterious and intoxicating. I found myself using it when I didn't need to – to do small things, petty things. When no-one was looking, I would move a pencil or snatch a paper from a book. Last week, these things would have taken intense concentration. Now it was almost effortless.

I had to be careful not to be observed. There was some danger involved in this as I had to direct the power with a hand motion. Most times, it didn't matter as no-one would notice the slight twitch of a hand or wave. I didn't seem to have the urge to target anyone in particular, which I suppose, speaks highly of me as I could have used my powers to make someone's life miserable.

Renee's grandfather's work had insisted that the hand motion wasn't necessary but I couldn't seem to summon the power without some form of gesture. It didn't seem to matter how pronounced the movement. The slightest twitch of a finger would be sufficient but I couldn't summon the power by thought alone.

I suppose in the end that's what I really wanted though. It wouldn't have been anywhere near as much fun without the risk, however slight.

* * * *

Tina grinned nervously as she looped her arms through mine at the cafeteria table. I had totally forgotten about her – I had been so wrapped up in thoughts of Renee all weekend. Tony smiled wolfishly at me and Sarah just nodded approvingly in a slightly condescending way. Tina noticeably relaxed as I looped my arm back and leaned against her. I hadn't realised how tense she'd been.

This was the first time we'd seen each other since Friday night when she'd dropped me at the station. I had been nervous about seeing her after our kiss.

"Hey you," she whispered in my ear.

"Well, this is new." Sarah smiled back from across the table.

"About time," Tony grunted approvingly placing his feet on the table. The cynic in me noted that he took the time to scan the room for teachers before doing so.

"How did it happen?" Sarah asked, skilfully ignoring Tony's boorish behaviour yet at the same time managing to knock his feet with her elbows from the table. Sarah also appeared to be blissfully unaware of what she'd just done.

"Umm… I'm not sure," I mumbled back. "We… ah kinda… kissed when she dropped me at the station."

Sarah nodded expectantly, her face screwing up with disappointment when neither Tina nor I appeared forthcoming with any further information. Obviously she had already learned that.

"Details Man! I want details!" She playfully banged her fist on the table.

I coughed nervously and looked at Tina in a panic. Girl talk was not my strong suit and there could be no mana-assisted wizardry to get me out of this one. I'd seen that look in Sarah's eyes previously when she found something she really wanted.

"Well… are you boyfriend and girlfriend?" Sarah

pressed firmly in a no-nonsense kind of way.

They say in some moments of danger that time slows down allowing you to see the danger with stark clarity. Right up to the point that the aforementioned danger clouts you cleanly between the eyes. This was one of those moments.

I gulped and was very aware of the fact that Tina was sitting right next to me and was yet to say a word. I was also aware that my answer now would be very important. My response would be taken and dissected for further analysis by both Tina and Sarah. I had no idea how to get out of this one. Tina was nice – but she wasn't Renee.

I'd have given anything to possess Renee's invisibility right now. It would have been so nice to be able to just fade into the background of the chair and escape this. But there was no help for it. I was trapped – caught in my own indecision. I nodded very carefully.

Tina breathed out. I hadn't even been aware she'd been holding her breath. Sarah smiled and nodded slightly as if she was silently approving, like she was rewarding a correct decision. I shot her a quizzical look and turned to Tina.

Tina was beaming at me, her arm pulling me in a little tighter. Great, I now had a girlfriend. Brilliant. The only problem was that she wasn't the girlfriend that I wanted. The girlfriend I actually wanted though didn't want me back. She had told me so, and then she had kissed me. Talk about sending mixed messages.

So I wasn't cheating on Renee but it sure did feel like it. I still barely knew Tina and our conversation now felt stilted. Fortunately Tony and Sarah were there to cover up the awkwardness. They were discussing some band that they wanted to go see in the city next weekend. But apparently Tina's parents were strict and wouldn't allow her to go. Roller-skating at night at a nearby rink was one thing but there was no way in a million years they would let their daughter go into the city on a Saturday night.

"Devon? Are you going to come with us? You're not busy this weekend are you?" Tony drawled.

"Uhh," I replied, then noticed the strange look on Tina's face. "Better not," I said, noticing Tina's expression relax again.

"That's right!" Sarah finished for me. "He's going to spend some time with Tina."

Well, it was decided. I would spend some time with Tina this weekend. Sarah could be quite pushy when she wanted to. Before Sarah could decide any more of my plans we were distracted by an apple in a crowded cafeteria and a student who thought he was funny.

"Hey, John!" a voice yelled out across the hall. "Catch!"

An apple was thrown at high speed with poor aim. It happened so fast. I reacted without thinking.

With a casual flick of my hand I reached up and sent a mana thread at the apple. With no conscious thought I wrapped the thread around it and brought it soaring back into my outstretched hand.

A stunned silence descended over the cafeteria.

Everyone looked slack jawed at me. I shrugged slightly and forced a cheesy smile to my face.

"You're an awful shot, Rob," I began lamely.

The silence was broken by smatterings of halting laughter. Rob was standing there with a stupid expression on his face and a wary look in eyes. He hadn't meant to throw the apple at me. In actual fact he hadn't thrown it anywhere near me and he knew it.

"That's quite a curve ball you've got there," Tony called out again, causing the people in the hall to break into laughter. I breathed out a sigh of relief. I could always count on Tony to lighten the mood.

I sat back down and casually tossed the apple over to John, who promptly dropped it.

"Nice catch, Dev." Tony grinned as I resumed my seat, a raised eyebrow prominent on his face.

Tony had seen exactly what I'd seen. The apple had changed direction after I had reached out. There was an expectant look on Tony's face as he resumed his seat next to me.

"Just lucky I guess." I smiled at him.

"Yeah… lucky," Tony finished. He wasn't convinced. He was still staring at me expectantly.

It's amazing how people so easily accept what they can't explain. What they had just witnessed was solid proof of the unknown. Witchcraft, sorcery or whatever you wanted to label it had been performed in their presence. Yet within moments everyone in the room had somehow managed to discount the idea or rationalise it in their minds.

It was impossible that I caused the apple to change direction mid-flight. No-one can do that. So therefore logically I didn't. Rob must have thrown the apple with a strange spin or a gust of wind had caught it. There were any number of other facts which might explain it away rationally. The fact that the apple ended up in my hand could easily be explained through either luck or good sportsmanship on my part.

Tony scowled when I didn't appear to have anything more to say and shoved his chair back and threw his feet on the table. Sarah in her usual fashion casually leaned forward and knocked his feet back onto the floor.

Conversation soon returned to normal in the cafeteria. I thought everything had returned to normal except for Tony. Tina and Sarah obviously hadn't noticed as they were deep in a whispered conversation.

"What do you want to do this weekend?" Tina nudged me.

I'd drifted off into my own worried little world and hadn't noticed that everyone was now looking at me.

"No idea," I stammered. "Anything you like I guess, I'm pretty easy."

"Yeah… I've heard that about you," Sarah snickered.

"You could go pick apples," Tony suggested darkly, his eyes narrowing as he leaned forward.

I remained silent for the moment, studying his face. Signs of confusion, hurt and betrayal clearly lined in his features. I'd have to do something about this. I was not prepared to alienate my best friend.

"How about a movie?" Tina interjected.

Much to my relief, the suggestion lowered the tension level around the table. I wasn't sure if Tina was aware of the tension or was merely saying something in an attempt to change the subject. The end result was the same. It gave me the out I wanted.

"That sounds great." I smiled and stood, looping one arm around Tina and pulling her up with me.

"Well, catch you later guys," I called back as I led Tina away. Tony's eyes glittered as he watched me leave. Something was definitely wrong there.

"How did you catch that apple anyway?" Tina asked as we walked down the corridor to class.

"Luck," I replied dryly, not really expecting her to believe it.

"Well, it was very impressive."

I'm an idiot sometimes, I really am.

* * * *

I couldn't concentrate on my classes for the rest of the day. My mind kept fixating on that damn apple from the cafeteria at lunch. It should have exploded! There was no way that I had the control necessary to exert that kind of control at that speed without crushing the apple into pieces. Only three days ago I was accidently tearing down metal girders. How does one get to a new level of

131

control without even trying? I hadn't even had a chance to practice that much. I hadn't even really used the mana in any noticeable way in days.

My powers were growing and what was even more disconcerting was that I wasn't aware that they were growing. The thrill that I was getting more powerful was finally tempered by the feeling of dread in my stomach.

"That's a neat trick." A curious voice cut into my reverie. It was Josie Macintosh from the seat next to me in History.

Oh no. That's when I realised what I was doing. I was spinning a small coin on the tip of my finger, using the mana to hold it in place and gently rotate it. I guess I must have liked the way the light glanced off it or something because I certainly wasn't focused on it. Josie was staring at my face and her features twisted into one of concern, a slight twinge of fear.

"What's wrong with your eyes?" she gasped, trying to back further into her chair.

"What?" I stammered, caught off guard. I immediately pulled the coin into my hand and stopped the mana thread. I knew once I stopped using the mana that my eyes would return to normal.

"Nothing, why do you ask?" I replied, trying desperately to keep my voice calm.

"Oh… I must have imagined it," she continued, unsure of herself now and looking behind her to see if there was anything that might have caused a strange reflection on my face.

"You're weird." I smiled back, attempting to throw the conversation back onto her.

"It's still a neat trick though. Where'd you learn it? That coin was spinning for ages. It was like you weren't even trying!"

"My uncle," I lied quickly, trailing off. "He taught me..."

"Oh, well. It's cool," Josie said hurriedly.

I was getting sloppy. It was unacceptable. I couldn't afford to slip up like that again. The most disconcerting thing about this encounter was that unlike the apple, which I could easily discount as instinct taking over, this was something I genuinely hadn't been aware that I was doing. I wondered darkly how far this could go. Could I be sitting in English class tomorrow thinking about the weekend whilst unconsciously levitating every chair in the room? The thought terrified me. What was the use of having this power if I couldn't control it properly?

Examining the coin in my fingers, I noted with some degree of satisfaction that there were no divot marks around the corner, no grooves that would have been created by overpowering force. I nodded thoughtfully to myself. I was definitely getting more powerful, the problem was that I still wasn't learning control.

I glanced furtively at the direction of my classmate only to notice her glance down quickly to her book. She'd been looking in my direction, and I don't think she was looking for the good reasons. It didn't overly matter I suppose, what was she going to say? I saw Devon with demon eyes? Hardly anyone would believe her. The problem was that if enough people starting noticing strange things, it'd soon get out of hand. The last thing I needed was a witch hunt, especially when I would be the witch.

I needed to learn some control. I also desperately needed to talk to Tony. I really didn't like the way I'd left things with him. I missed my friend. Things hadn't been right with Tony since I had first met Renee.

I left the classroom shortly before the end of class. I simply just packed up my books and left, I don't think the teacher even noticed me leave. I was going to talk to Tony. I knew what class he was in so I simply waited outside the classroom door. Pretty soon, the bell rang and a stream of students fled out the room.

"We need to talk," I said as soon as I saw him.

"Don't sneak up on me like that," Tony grunted angrily.

"I wanted to see what's up with you?" I blurted out.

"What's up with me?" he said, his voice going shrill.

I hadn't expected the level of anger he had displayed and it took a few seconds for me to recover.

"What's up with you?" Tony retorted angrily.

I'd never seen this side of him before. He looked thoroughly unimpressed with me. People in the corridor hurried around us as Tony stood there, arms crossed, eyes narrowed in anger.

"I don't know if I can tell you," I faltered.

"Since when?" he barked. "Since when have you been

unable to tell me anything?" His eyes bored into mine.

"I want to tell you everything, Tony," I pleaded. "I just need some time. Or – just not here, not at school."

"Take all the time you want," he snarled and stormed off, smacking open the doors at the far end.

That didn't go as I'd hoped. I didn't follow him. There was no point. There was no talking to him when he was in that mood.

* * * *

Tony wasn't waiting for me at the usual spot when school finished. In fact no-one was. We had always walked home from school as a group, as we all lived relatively close to each other. Something was very wrong.

I waited for a few minutes until it became obvious that no-one was coming. I suppose that in hindsight I had left my last class a little late. I'd been daydreaming and hadn't noticed that the final bell had gone off. But surely they'd have waited for me. They used to wait for me. I nodded glumly to myself and I resigned myself to the inevitable and began the walk home alone. It was the same path as always. I walked across the road from school through the shopping centre and then down the hill and up through the park. It wasn't very long, but the walk always seemed longer when you were alone. When I walked this way with my friends it didn't seem to take any time at all.

It was a cold and lonely walk home. I am sure that

the shopping centre was packed with people, but I didn't notice them. I'd taken my time as I had no particular need to be home and I was not in the mood to hurry.

The final leg of the journey was to walk through a reserve that led to my street. Trees lined the reserve on both sides and thus it was always a little dark inside. I'd always liked this part as it reminded me of walking through a forest, something that in the suburban landscape we didn't do all that often.

I made my way through the shopping centre and made my way down the hill towards the little reserve that led to my house. It was nice little reserve through a residential block. It probably cut about ten minutes off the trip home, but I probably would have gone that way even if it were longer.

I was about half way through the reserve when I felt a thud on my backpack. I turned around only to see a figure dart behind the trees to my right. My shoulder hurt slightly and I looked down to see a rock at my feet behind me. Someone had thrown a rock at my back, but they hadn't thrown it very hard. This wasn't about hurting me.

Was this another of Renee's games? If so, this was awfully obscure. However, making me chase her halfway across the city had seemed pretty odd at the time too. I looked around the reserve and I couldn't see anyone. I was completely alone.

A quick burst of awareness told me otherwise, there was definitely a figure hiding behind a tree to my right about ten metres away. The figure definitely wasn't a mage however as there was no mana aura. It wasn't Renee.

"Come out," I demanded angrily.

I was feeling very sure of myself. If this was someone trying to mug me then they would come out very poor from this encounter. I could see them crouched against the far side of a tree, glancing furtively in my direction.

"Catch the rock, Apple Boy!" a familiar voice yelled back. "The next one will be aimed at your head!"

Tony.

He quickly spun out from behind his tree and lobbed a rock in my direction. He had no idea that I could tell exactly where he was due to my earlier awareness blast. I could see him lurking behind another tree a little distance from his original hiding spot.

Without my mana sight I would have been hard pressed to see into that dark thicket of wood. I smiled grimly. This was another useful trait of awareness even in this limited range. The rock wasn't even thrown properly. It was thrown as if you were skipping a rock across a pond. He obviously had no intention of hitting me, only coming close enough to make me think he was serious. The rock landed a few metres to my right.

"That was hardly my head," I said dryly.

"Don't force me to do it," Tony yelled as he leaned/ leant forward to scoop up another rock.

"Force you to do what?" I replied, getting annoyed.

Tony moved positions, swiftly moving behind the

trees. God he was fast. I turned slightly to face his new direction. This must have disconcerted him somewhat as nothing was said for a few seconds.

"This is stupid," I declared abruptly. "I'm going to go home now. If you could kindly not take my head off when I leave, that would be great."

I was about to turn to leave when Tony emerged from behind a tree, his face grim and a small stone held, ready to throw, in his hand.

"Don't make me do this," he repeated.

"I'm not making you do anything."

"How long have we been friends?" He was almost pleading now.

"About five years, long enough for you to know my aversion to having rocks thrown at me," I said. He still hadn't thrown the rock yet; however, he had yet to put it down.

"Long enough for you to trust me?" he asked.

"Hard to trust you when you're throwing rocks at me."

Damn him, he was going to do it, I could see it in his eyes. He knew it, and he knew that I knew it too. Damn him.

With an exaggerated movement, he drew his arm back.

The whole thing was so stupid. It was like one of those moves you see baseball pitchers use where they ham up the move to get the audience more hyped. It was exactly like that. In any other situation it would have been funny, except it wasn't. Tony was plainly telling me he was going to throw a rock at my head and I needed to do something. The stone left his fingers and hurled towards me. Unlike his previous throw this one was true, if I did nothing, it would probably hit me right between the eyes. Strangely enough I wasn't angry and I wasn't shocked. I wasn't even particularly scared. Time appeared to slow down into moments. I saw the resignation in Tony's eyes and saw his muscles tense. The stone left his fingers and began its inevitable journey towards my head. I sighed to myself and raised my hand to telekinetically grab the stone.

I stopped the stone in mid-air and kept it floating slowly between us. It was amazing how quickly it all happened and how easily I had intercepted the rock. I could have dodged or I could have thrown myself to the ground. I could have even let the rock hit me. However, in the end I'd chosen to do what Tony obviously wanted me to do. There was something in his expression, a desperate need – he had needed this from me and that perhaps was why I had capitulated. He was my best friend and he had needed this. I couldn't deny him.

"I knew it!" he whispered in awe.

I let the rock fall to the ground with a dull thump, which probably sounded louder to my ears than it actually was. I nodded grimly to him as he approached and turned to leave. There would be no more thrown rocks. He caught up to me several seconds later, pulling up beside me with his usual ambling gait.

"You can now justify my trust in you," I stated without looking at him.

"We'll never speak of this again," he replied, grinning.

"Good, because this could end me," I replied somewhat coldly. This was exactly what Renee had told me not to do. But I was positive that if there was anyone I could trust it was Tony.

"Can I ask you some questions though?" Tony pressed.

I nodded.

"How long?"

"Since my birthday."

"Where did you learn it?"

"It's not something you learn, it's something you are," I said.

"Does this have anything to do with that girl from the club?"

I turned to look at him silently. He'd obviously been thinking on this for some time.

"I keep forgetting how damned clever you are," I replied. "But I can't talk about that – it's not my secret to keep. No matter how many rocks you hurl." I ended with a smile.

"Fair enough," he replied.

"Now some questions for you," I said. "What gave me away?"

"I saw you pull a pencil across the desk the other week, without seeming to touch it. I thought I was imagining it or it was some trick, but then after today with the apple in the cafeteria, kind of hard to explain that."

"Yeah, that was stupid," I agreed.

"Wouldn't have expected anything else from you." He laughed and suddenly the tension was gone and everything was back to normal.

"You should have told me though," Tony said when we had finished laughing.

"I wanted to. But I was told that no-one can know."

"Is it that dangerous?" he asked.

"Life threatening – almost died, still might," I replied callously.

He nodded slowly, his expression unreadable; however, I knew then with certainty he would never betray me and that he would, true to his word, never speak of this again. He knew now how serious this was. And I felt so relieved to have my friend back. Hopefully things could now return to normal – or at least as normal as they could be with this power.

* * * *

The next morning I awoke refreshed, more invigorated than I had felt in a long time. Meeting up with Tony and Garry on the way to school was just like old times. We joked and laughed on the way to school and made the obligatory donut stop at the supermarket.

I realised just how much I had missed this. I had been focused so much on the mana recently that I had alienated my friends. I resolved not to do so any longer. I smiled gently as Sarah and Tina walked through the school gate and lazily threw my arm around Tina as she snuggled next to me.

"Well, Devon." Sarah smiled. "You look very comfortable."

Her eyes twinkled with delight as Tina and I snuggled against the wall together with our knees side by side.

"I feel very comfortable."

"He is quite comfortable actually," Tina quipped, giggling slightly as she nestled into my shoulder.

"Aww man, that sounded like one of Devon's jokes!" Tony drawled loudly. "You're catching his sense of humour."

"Soon, there will be two of them…" Garry intoned in an eldritch voice, "…and the world will be damned forever."

"Join us …braaaains," I groaned, my hands stretched forward like a zombie. My impression was disrupted as Tony threw his bag at me.

We dissolved into laughter and just like that everything was alright until I noticed that Sarah was sitting off to one side, a calculating look on her face. She stared straight at me with the strangest expression on her face.

My gut went cold. What had Tony told her? She had obviously known that something was wrong. The two of them obviously spoke regularly. Had he told her? I glanced at my best friend, my eyes shifting slightly. He was still laughing as he recovered his school bag.

Could he have told her?

I turned to stare back at Sarah, watching her face change from a look of calculation into concern and then into confusion. She brushed her hair away from her face then she quickly turned her head to look away, unable to meet my gaze. She knew! How could he have told her?

Tony was talking away to Garry about something else, but I wasn't listening. I turned my attention to Tony and noticed he was oblivious that anything was going on. Sarah turned and gestured across to the other seats about ten metres away.

She wanted to talk.

I took her meaning and quickly excused myself from Tina and carefully made my way across to her. I'm not sure what the others thought as we both went off and I didn't care.

"What happened with you and Tony?" Sarah asked as I approached.

"Nothing," I said.

"Tony was pretty upset with you yesterday, but now everything seems fine."

"It is fine. Nothing to talk about now."

"What was it?"

"Nothing, it doesn't matter."

"I've never seen you guys fight like that," Sarah pressed. "It must have been something."

"It's a guy thing," I stated, getting desperate.

"Do you really expect me to believe that?"

"Umm… no, I guess not," I stammered. "But trust me – it's better if we just leave it alone."

"Tony wouldn't tell me either!" Sarah pouted.

He hadn't told her. I immediately felt my shoulders relax and my breath come a little easier.

"Just let it drop... please?" I said.

Sarah didn't say anything, just stared silently back at me.

"Please?" I repeated.

"Okay," she whispered back eventually.

"Thank you." I smiled and pulled her into a quick embrace.

"Hey! That's my girl you're mauling there, buddy!" Tony's voice called out from across the path.

I smiled back with genuine mirth – trust Tony to lighten up a tense moment.

"I'm done with him now," Sarah loudly declared, playfully pushing me away. "You can have him if you want him!"

I laughed and she grabbed my arm.

"Tina's my friend," she said solemnly. "And she's never had a boyfriend before. She really likes you." She stared in my eyes. "Don't hurt her, okay?"

"I don't plan to," I squeaked, and coughed, looking at my feet.

"Do you actually like her?" Sarah pressed.

There was a pause and we locked eyes.

"Let's go back," I said.

We walked back to the group silently.

CHAPTER FIVE

There is a theory that time is relative. It was quite a popular theory in its day and it is indeed true. Anyone who has experienced the joy of an afternoon maths class will be able to testify to this.

Time plays havoc on the mind, making a forty-minute math class seem like it has lasted for three weeks. Seconds drag into hours as you watch someone scrawl semi-legible markings onto a white board. Minutes turn into weeks as you struggle keep your head aloft with a look of semi-intelligent concentration plastered onto your face. All the while your eyes keep flicking across to a clock whose hands never seem to move but made angry ticking noises nonetheless.

The ticking of the hands on the clock reverberated across the room in relative loudness defying the actual noise. Each 'tick' was followed several seconds later by the inevitable 'tock'. The room quickly became a cacophony of 'ticks' meeting 'tocks' as soundwaves met bouncing from wall to wall. After a half hour of this, which seemed like a week and a half, my brain had shut down and my mental processing capabilities had slowed to the speed of a bowl of pudding. When the bell finally rang I didn't react immediately as I mistook it for a particularly loud 'tock'.

I knew with experience that it would take at least twenty minutes to wake up again after the class.

"Do you want to go to the pub tonight?" Tony called out as I turned into the locker bay.

He had already packed away his books and was waiting for me, in the five minutes it took me to get to the locker bay.

"It's Thursday," I replied in way of disagreement.

"What? Are you afraid you'll miss your beauty sleep?" Tony drawled back, punching me in the arm. "Besides, tomorrow is a public holiday!"

"Well, I am feeling pretty ugly today," I quipped, mockingly flouncing my hair and pretending to preen myself.

"You're lucky," he replied, deadpan.

"Oh why?"

"You don't have to look at you," Tony replied dryly.

"Fair enough, see you at the pub." I laughed and punched him in the shoulder.

The pub in question wasn't too far away from either of our houses. It was the local for Tony's older brother, Greg, who was a bit of a boozer, but I'd never been there myself. I'd need to go home first to get changed.

Tony was already at the pub when I arrived. He was chatting with Greg by the bar. There were several bored looking barstaff serving drinks and a stereotypical looking barman lurking behind the bar.

"Devon," Greg greeted as I approached. "Does your mother know you're here?"

Greg was a good three or four years older than us and had picked on us both quite unmercifully when we were younger. Now that we could hold our own and were getting of a similar size and strength, the teasing had degenerated into taunting and childish insults. This isn't to say that Tony and I didn't like spending time with him. He was often a good source of entertainment when we were growing up.

"Does your parole officer know where you are?" I retorted.

"Nice." He grinned. "Get this man a beer, and put some lemonade in it, he's only twelve!"

"Going to need to see some ID there, son." The barman nodded at me.

I'm not sure if Greg's comment had made him nervous or if he genuinely felt the need to card me. I produced my passport and passed it to him. He seemed a little amused that I was using a passport, but let it pass.

"I'll assume the lemonade was a joke," he commented gruffly as he passed over a glass.

"Kinda strange to see you two in here," Greg commented as I took my first sip.

"Why?" Tony laughed back.

"Well, it's kind of like you're stealing my local," he replied, grinning.

"No, it's not stealing. We're just borrowing, like those magazines of yours Tony borrowed when he was fifteen,"

I insisted, smirking back.

"Yeah… The difference is… I didn't want those back afterwards." Greg chuckled.

"Ha ha, shut up, the both of you!" Tony chuckled, finishing his beer.

The bar was relatively quiet. It hadn't quite gone six o'clock so most people hadn't finished work. There was the occasional worker like Greg who worked just around the corner and the pub was a short walk on the way home, but the main evening rush hadn't started yet.

There was a TV mounted on the wall broadcasting horseracing , but other than that it was quiet. In actual truth I was getting a little bored.

"Want to play some pool?" Tony suggested, gesturing towards the vacant tables.

"Sure."

We moved to one of the pool tables and racked up. I've never been very good at pool. I was a strong proponent of the 'whack them really hard and hope one of them accidently falls in the pocket' technique. This tactic wasn't the most effective other than allowing me to pull off some really fantastic shots once every blue moon. I maintained hope that one day it would miraculously turn me into a brilliant pool player. Tony on the other hand was a very good pool player. He had spent years honing his skills against his brother. We were playing winner stays on which basically resulted in the majority of the matches being Tony versus Greg. Greg had a long running joke that to lose without potting a ball would result in having to run around the pool table with your pants down around your ankles. I couldn't tell if he was being serious or not but wasn't prepared to risk it.

"Well kids, I think that's it for me tonight," Greg said after our third game. "I've got an early start in the morning."

"You're working on a public holiday?" asked Tony.

"Who said anything about working?"

"We'll hang around for a bit longer, right?" I asked Tony. I wasn't sure what the convention was.

Even though I was losing I was actually having fun. Maybe it was the mixture of booze and pool that had loosened me up but I was having fun for the first time in ages and wasn't about to let it go.

"Sure, no worries." Tony nodded back.

"Try not to wake me when you get home." Greg waved a mocking finger in front of Tony's face. "And if there's a tie on the door…" He winked.

"It'll mean he's picked up a businessman on his way home," I interjected.

"Yeah, right Devon," Greg chuckled and we said goodbye.

I'm not sure how much we had drunk at this stage. I definitely wasn't sober but I wasn't having too much trouble walking and playing pool either. In fact if anything I was getting better. There is a theory that the drunker you get the better your pool playing skills get. There may be some grounds to this as my game had improved dramatically over the past hour. I was now at least giving Tony some competition before he beat me. I'd much rather rack this up to alcohol because it couldn't have possibly been attributed to the several hours of pool practice I'd just had. That was crazy talk. I was leaning forward over the table with my arms lined forward holding the pool cue like a rifle before me. This shot would determine the game. I gently tapped the white ball carefully towards my desired target and with the most gentle of "thunk" noises my ball gently tilted forward into the pocket. This also knocked one of Tony's balls out of the way. It couldn't have been more perfect if I'd planned it. There was no way in a hundred years I'd have normally been able to pull off a shot like that. The only reason now I was even attempting it was because I was snookered everywhere else. Tony stared at me with a quizzical eyebrow slightly raised and a contemplative expression on his face.

"Are you cheating?" he asked, tentatively wiggling his fingers about in a random pattern.

"What? How the hell do you cheat at pool?" I retorted, confused.

"Uh, you know," he replied, waving his fingers around.

"Oh… umm. No," I replied, inwardly cursing myself. Why hadn't I thought of that?

That would have been fantastic. Every jibe Greg had ever directed at us would have been returned in one fell swoop. Let's see him try to wiggle out of running around the table with his pants down around his ankles.

"Hmm – well, good then," he replied. "Sorry I asked really."

"Don't get me wrong, I would have been if I'd thought of it." I smiled back.

"… Right, so, too honest to lie, too stupid to cheat," he continued dryly.

"That's me." I nodded as I potted the final ball, winning the game. This was probably the first win I'd had against Tony in years.

"Rack 'em up," he grunted.

I felt it was a little uncharitable of him to fail to comment on my uncommon and definitely comment worthy win. Tony didn't feel the same way. I'm not sure if Tony had something to prove now or was merely trying to make up for lost ground but he absolutely creamed me next game. By the time I had potted my first ball he'd already racked up four. It came to no surprise to anyone when he potted the final ball and won the game.

"Maybe you should start cheating." He grinned as his last ball slid into the pocket.

"I can if you want; wouldn't exactly be sporting though now would it?" I said.

"Give me some competition though." He laughed.

We were halfway through our next game, which of course I was losing, when a gruff voice interrupted us. Tony had just leaned forward to take his shot and was tentatively lining up the white ball with his intended victim.

"Are you two ladies done with this table yet?" the voice demanded.

We both turned to face the newcomer. He was a rough

looking tradesman wearing paint covered overalls and sporting a three-day growth. He was leering at us with a beer in one hand and an intimidating smirk on his face.

He was probably in his mid-forties and looked just a little bit worse for the drink. He had that jowly cheeked and bulbous red nose look attributed to people who spend half their lives glued to bar stools.

"There are other tables," Tony replied calmly, finishing his shot apparently unfazed by the interruption.

"I don't want to use another table." He snorted.

You could tell he thought he was being incredibly funny but the amusement never quite reached his eyes. They had the look of a predator swooping down on its prey. Behind him there was another tradesman who was a lot younger, probably the older man's apprentice. He was about our age or perhaps just a little bit older. He had a stringy, lanky look to him and looked ill at ease in the bar room. He kind of reminded me of myself about two hours ago when I first entered the bar – before the drinks.

"Well, as you can see, this one's taken," I said firmly. "We'll move on when we're finished, game's almost done."

"No rush ladies, I enjoy a good pool game," he grunted, chuckling to himself at his own humour as he parked himself on a stool overlooking the table.

"Though what you're doing hardly qualifies," he finished.

The delicate sound of pool balls clinking together

and the satisfying sound as they fell into pocket became a steady rhythm to the rise and fall of the game. The background noise had seemingly disappeared as both Tony and I were more focused on the game. We tried to ignore the lewd and mocking chuckles from our unwelcome onlooker. He would cackle to himself when one of us missed a shot and snort in derision when we did drop a ball. This game seemed to take much longer than the rest of our games.

I was about ready to call it a night when our less-than-welcome observer abruptly got to his feet and grabbed a pool cue from the stand behind us.

"I'll show you a little something about the game."

The words "No thanks" were on the tip of my lips when Tony grunted "Sure", deciding the matter for me. He popped in a couple of coins into the table causing the balls to drop into the catchment. Well there was nothing for it – we were committed now.

I think Tony had reached the point where he'd had enough of snide backhanded comments and wanted the opportunity to take this lout down a peg. I wasn't sure I was up for this, but after his rude interjections I was kind of looking forward to seeing Tony take him down too. I probably wasn't going to be able to contribute much towards this goal, but it would be nice to watch nonetheless.

"I'll break," the lout announced and moved to the far end of the table as Tony set up the table.

As he broke he grunted slightly, as if the exertion of

playing pool was almost too much. It was a good break though, he didn't pot anything but it was a good, solid break nonetheless.

Tony took his turn. We had already determined between us that he would go first and quickly potted several balls. I was watching our opponent and his glittering eyes smirked as he watched the play unfold. His face never showed the amusement that twinkled in the light behind his eyes.

His apprentice upon order took the cue next and dutifully potted one ball and narrowly missed a second. He did set it up for an easy pot next round though, and then it was my turn.

I had a choice here. I could take the easy shot – the red ball into the close pocket, or the difficult one, which would put us in a better position for later. I decided the former. Sink the balls available – after all with my limited skills it was probably going to be better to assist in a small way rather than none. A small chuckle escaped our opponent as my white ball gently clinked off my intended target and rolled to a halt, both balls mere inches from the pocket.

"Laugh away," I grumbled with somewhat poor grace.

"This merely means you're snookered now," Tony interjected with some degree of satisfaction.

This outcome was better than my potting a ball, as Tony would make far better use of the two shots he would obtain when my opponent messed up his turn.

"Shows what you know," the guy grunted.

I'm still not quite sure how he did it but he managed to reflect the white ball off two surfaces to gently knock against one of his balls, grinning mockingly at me he tilted his cue in my direction.

"Nice," I grudgingly said.

As much as I didn't like the guy, that was a sweet shot.

"Won't make much difference though." Tony smiled and with casual and long honed skill sent another two balls into the depths.

Surprisingly enough, even this didn't seem to faze him. I've always prided myself on being a good judge of character and something was definitely wrong here. For someone who was three balls down in a game he was awfully smug.

His apprentice didn't fare much better than me. He obviously didn't have much more skill than I did. That is to say we both had the ability to move balls around the table with reliable frequency to not sink anything. I also had a nagging suspicion that he wasn't enjoying himself too much either.

After my next shot it had become more obvious that the game was actually only between two players and that didn't include the apprentice and me.

"Want to make this a little more interesting?" the guy grunted as he stepped up for his next shot, sloshing his beer against the table as he clonked it down.

"What did you have in mind?" Tony smiled back. I'd seen that look in his eyes before and this didn't bode well.

"Say ten dollars?"

"You're still down mate, but I'm not going to say no to taking your money though." Tony grinned back, deciding the matter for both of us.

"Each," he snapped. He cut off the last word with menace, gesturing towards me.

"Take your shot," Tony stated as I nodded the affirmative.

Something definitely wasn't right here. Perhaps my intuition was wrong as over the next few rounds he did indeed pot a few more balls and close the gap. The final round saw him two balls down and us sitting on an easy shot for the black.

"And that would be…" Tony started as he leaned forward. In one fell swoop he adroitly tapped the black, sending it ever so gracefully rolling towards the pocket. "…Game," he finished as the black dropped gently into the pocket.

There was a stunned silence around the table, partially thanks to Tony's obvious show boating. I stood offside, watching our opponent and trying to gauge his reaction. He was a cool one though as the smile never left his face. I had expected some form of abusive or insulting outburst; however, he remained quite still, the smile frozen on his face.

His eyes, however, glittered with unexpressed violence.

"Seems you boys can play after all," he said. "Another game," he commanded. He wasn't asking. This was an order.

"Money upfront!" I demanded. "You guys owe us twenty bucks."

My demand was perhaps delivered somewhat undiplomatically as even Tony turned to give me a strange look.

"Small change boy, we'll settle up when we're finished," he grunted at me, deftly putting more coins into the table and racking up a new table.

"Since you boys obviously know your stuff – let's make this one count," he continued, laughing. "See how you handle yourself under some real pressure."

"What did you have in mind?" Tony asked with a raised eyebrow.

I felt a sinking feeling in my gut. This definitely wasn't going to end well.

"One hundred," the sot grunted.

"Each?" I balked – if we lost I wouldn't be able to cover it I only had about fifty dollars on me, which included the ten I was now owed.

"Each," he confirmed with a nod. "What's the matter, princess, too rich for you?"

"I can't cover that," a soft voice interjected. I turned with interest to note that it was the voice of the apprentice.

"You're covered," our opponent interjected, gruffly cutting off whatever the poor guy was going to say next.

Tony looked at me with a quizzical expression and then with a devilish smile that I knew all too well shrugged and smiled. "It's your money."

"It's your break," the older man grunted.

"You go." Tony nodded to me.

I've never been overly fond of breaking. There's a

smaller chance of actually being able to sink anything as nothing is setup for an easy shot. I didn't embarrass myself too badly as my shot broke the balls from their formation at the centre of the table into a wide arc. It was a decent break but I didn't manage to sink anything, which was a little disappointing.

Smiling broadly our opponent stepped up to the table and leaned forward to take his shot, casually potting one ball and setting two others up for an easy sink later in the game.

I breathed in a deep breath and heard Tony mutter under his breath. He took his next shot to set up another two balls into place. He now had four of his balls in positions where they would be easy to sink. It seemed pretty obvious he was trying to go for a trick shot, setting up the shot and then sinking all the balls in one fluid motion.

"Your turn, ladies." He smiled.

Tony looked somewhere between worried and angry. I wasn't sure what his finances were like at the moment but I doubt he could afford the hundred dollars any more than I could.

"We're being sharked," he hissed into my ear as he passed to take his shot. "The bastard set us up."

In hindsight it seemed pretty obvious that that's what he was doing. He had been preying upon a couple of young and obviously inexperienced pool players. He'd been building us up to up the ante.

A cold dread filled my stomach. I didn't have the

money to pay my debt and he didn't look like the type to extend credit. There was nothing for it, I'd have to cheat. I could see Tony's eyes narrow with anger as he leaned forward over the table to take his shot. A narrow bead of sweat slowly made its way down his brow. It was obvious that he was nervous.

This would be difficult. I'd never been able to summon my power without some form of hand motion but I didn't want our opponent to have any idea that something untoward was going on. I'd have to be careful.

I'd heard of a technique called misdirection that stage magicians use to draw the audience's attention away from what their other hand is doing. I'd have to look into these techniques, but for now I'd have to wing it and hope for the best. I could see the shot Tony was trying to go for. It was a delicate and difficult shot and normally I had faith that Tony could pull it off, but under these circumstances I had my doubts. Fortunately for Tony, however, I had other ideas.

I built up a mana thread and gently intercepted the white ball as Tony took his shot. I'd been forced to keep my back against the bench to keep what I was doing hidden from sight. This had the quite unintentional effect of looking as if Tony had clipped the white ball rather than hitting it directly on.

This caused a loud guffaw from our opponent who charmingly sprayed beer out of his mouth mid laugh as he watched the event unfold.

"Nice one, sunshine." He chuckled, moving forward

to take his shot watching as the ball took off in a direction other than the one Tony had intended.

Tony had a look of confusion on his face that quickly turned into anger. He must have been sure that he'd hit the white ball dead on. His look of anger turned into one of bewilderment and then shock as the white ball casually careened into another of our balls gently potting it. Tony now had a second shot.

It had taken all my skill to do this and even I was amazed at the results. It hadn't taken more than gentle pressure to break Tony's shot and send it in the direction I wanted to go. Timing had been paramount but it was well within my skill level. My only concern was subtlety.

Our opponent stood slack jawed, his eyes glued to the table as if he couldn't believe what had just happened. His pool cue was still in hand as he had moved forward to take his shot.

"You might want to wait to the end of his shot before you make further comments." I smiled disarmingly back at him.

"Luck!" He cursed back at me, his look turning cold and for once the patronising amusement had finally disappeared from his face.

"Take your shot," he snarled at Tony.

"Hey, Tony, whack that blue one in at the far end of the table as hard as you can," I advised.

Tony looked at me quizzically as this type of shot would normally have resulted in one of two things. Either both balls would be knocked out or the opponent's ball would be knocked in. Neither result was too appealing to Tony. He shook his head briefly as if to disagree but then I winked and he smiled in understanding.

Tony moved to the other end of the table. With what could only be described as exaggerated showmanship he took his shot, sending the white ball off at high speed. This was pretty much what I'd expected and I gently placed a mana thread around my opponent's ball to steady it and prevent it from being knocked in by the impact.

It only took a quick flick of the wrist to arrest the motion of the white ball, sending it knocking into the blue ball and causing it to flick deftly into the pocket with a satisfying clunk.

The white ball was sent ricocheting off the padding, knocking our opponent's ball out of the way and sending it sliding across the table knocking another of his balls out of position. This had the effect of leaving our opponent with only one ball still set up for an easy sink.

Tony nodded professionally as if this had been his desired outcome. Our opponent simply stared daggers into the back of Tony's head.

"What do you recommend now?" Tony drawled as he walked past me grinning in a mocking fashion. Our opponent was getting a little red in the face and looked worried. His eyes darted nervously from side to side. He obviously couldn't believe what he was seeing.

"I think maybe the red ball in the middle pocket," I called to him with a smile.

"Okay." Tony nodded back, spinning the cue in his fingers with ninja-like skill.

Tony would have probably been able to handle this shot without my assistance but I wasn't about to let this opportunity go to waste. Tony didn't even take the time to aim. He simply leant forward and took his shot. Unfortunately this caught me off guard as I'd expected more show boating from Tony. Fortunately the white ball was at least heading in the right direction. It didn't take too much correction for me to guide it towards our desired location.

With a subtle clink it bounced against the red ball, sending it tumbling down into the pocket.

I took this moment to walk past Tony, pretending to get a better view.

"At least look like you're trying," I hissed to him as I passed.

Tony just chuckled to himself and moved to the other side of the table to assess the remaining balls on the table. I'm pretty sure that I saw our opponent's eyes narrow in anger at our display, though I doubt he heard us, especially over the bar room noise.

It didn't look good; even using mana it was unlikely we were going to be able to pot another ball this round. I think Tony knew that too or he had counted on me to alter events. I had decided, however, that it might perhaps be more fun to sabotage our opponent's shots rather than sink more of our own balls.

It also allowed more opportunity as he had almost

twice the number of balls left on the table than we did. Tony's next shot went wild and I suppose in some way I should have informed him of my intentions as his ball went fiercely into a cluster of balls. Tony had obviously counted upon me controlling the course of the ball into a desired direction. A slow hiss escaped his mouth and he glared up at me in anger.

I wasn't quite sure what to do. It was obvious that Tony had looked at me when his shot went wild. I now had both tradesman and apprentice looking quizzically at me. I shrugged nervously and gestured towards the apprentice to take his shot.

"That would be two shots," our antagonist commented dryly, not taking the opportunity for a cheap shot. Something was definitely wrong here.

I wasn't interested in embarrassing the apprentice so I left his shots alone. He was obviously nervous and I could tell that the pressure was getting to him. It was at this point that I realised that he probably couldn't afford the money any more than Tony or I could. This was unfortunate but better it be his problem than ours.

The apprentice took aim at the remaining ball that was setup and with a casual skill that undermined his nervousness calmly potted the ball into the pocket. This wasn't a great loss as we were still far ahead. His next shot went wild as he used too much force and bounced his desired target from a good position into the centre of the table.

I nodded to him and went to take my place. I had

some doubts that I would be able to use mana and focus on the pool game as well. Fortunately I didn't need to, as the white ball had been placed in a fortuitous place almost directly in the path of one of the balls we had set up earlier.

With a deep breath I attempted to take the easy shot, but misjudged the force required. I hit the ball but all I did was simply move the ball closer to the corner pocket. This wasn't a bad outcome all things considered as the ball would be easily potted later.

Again our antagonist chose not to say a word, merely moving into position to take his shot. It was pretty obvious from the outset what he intended to do. He was going to attempt to knock my newly placed ball out of position and sink his own in its place.

I had no doubt that with his degree of skill he would be able to accomplish this feat. Unfortunately for him I had another outcome in mind. Slowly wrapping a mana tendril around my ball, I strengthened it against the table.

When the inevitable impact occurred, even I was slightly surprised by the noise. The noise of the two balls crashing together created a loud "thwock" that reverberated around the table. As expected my ball didn't budge an inch. Our opponent's ball, however, was sent ricocheting across the table and it didn't require too much modification from me to cause it to accidently knock another one of our balls into a convenient pocket.

"That would be two shots," I commented dryly. I had

matched my mannerisms to his comment from before. I had expected him to curse and swear at me.

He jerked himself up from his leaning position over the table his fingers curling into fists and I seriously thought he was going to throw a punch at me. This stunned me slightly. I hadn't expected him to actually resort to physical violence. I was more than capable of defending myself if he actually punched me but I just hadn't expected it. I had no doubt he would have been able to catch me with a sucker punch that would have floored me. Fortunately he must have spotted the bouncer. He took several deep breaths and appeared to be in control of his anger.

"Your turn," he snarled at Tony, turning away from me.

It was at this point that I'd decided enough was enough. You can only push someone so far. It was time to end this. Better to end this quick. We had only two balls and the black left to pot. One of these balls was already set up so it wouldn't be too hard to finish this.

Tony seemed to have the same idea as he took aim at the more difficult shot. The shot required a rebound off the far cushion to hit our desired target. This was fortunate as it was quite easy to redirect the ball from the cushion and send it rolling towards its target. This left the ball balanced delicately against the edge of the pocket.

I thought about tipping it in; however, I quickly realised that this wouldn't be necessary. Tony had a second shot and possessed the skills necessary to pot both balls.

All I needed to do was make certain that the white didn't disappear down the pocket with it. No further meddling was required, as with accustomed skill Tony sent the white smacking into its target and rebounded to place itself within easy reach of its next target, setting him up for an easy sink. The sound of the last coloured ball dropping into the pocket was greeted with silence as the four of us acknowledged the end of the game was near. We had only the black ball and they still had five balls on the table.

Tony moved into position and I noticed with some degree of relief the look of weary resignation cross our opponent's face. With a noticeable 'thunk' it hit the black, sending it arching towards the far pocket. Tony's aim was true. The black ball dropped into the pocket leaving the white to bounce harmlessly against the side cushion.

"That would be game, gentlemen," Tony drawled, looking up and grinning slightly.

The apprentice looked helplessly at his elder and threw down a couple of twenties on the table.

"That's all I've got," he said helplessly, looking at us.

"I said you were covered," the older man stated.

I nodded agreeably as Tony recovered the money from the table. "You still owe us one hundred and eighty dollars," he said.

I noticed that the older man cringed slightly as he heard the amount.

"Good luck getting it, ladies," he said.

"You have to pay!" I insisted.

He nodded, almost eagerly. "Money's in me van," he said.

Tony and I escorted him out into the car park towards a van parked on the far side of the car park. It had gotten quite dark by this time and I realised with some degree of concern that I had no idea what time it was. I hadn't intended to stay out this late.

Our opponent pulled the keys from his pocket and turned the keys into the back sliding door of the van. Tony and I stood several metres away from the car nervously watching as we heard the rummaging noise. We both took a step back as he returned with a crowbar held firmly in his meaty fist.

The apprentice cursed to himself and took several steps back, a look of fear and slight disgust on his face. Any thoughts I had harboured of him being in on this were instantly dispelled. He looked positively sick at the thought. In fact he looked more scared than Tony or I did.

"You're going to turn around and walk away now," the tradesman commanded slowly, gesturing at us with the crowbar.

Tony looked at me nervously and then back to the loutish tradie. There were two of us and one of him. We could probably take him but that crowbar looked like it would take either of us down without too much trouble.

"Sure," I replied, stalling for time. "But after you pay us what you owe us."

"You've got balls kid, I'll give you that." He laughed and for once I heard genuine amusement in his laugh.

There was something strange in his eyes, almost like grudging respect. This statement had fortunately given me the chance to throw a mana thread out and wrap it around the crowbar. The crowbar was no longer a threat. Unfortunately our opponent didn't know this.

"Just pay us," I entreated nervously, walking forward with my hand outstretched.

"Sorry kid," he snarled, "it's not personal."

"Don't," I whispered.

I was aware that it was already too late though. He had pulled the crowbar back, ready to bring it smashing down onto my skull. They say in times of stress and terror the mind shuts down all higher activity allowing you to assess and act far quicker than your rational mind would allow.

I remember seeing the crowbar descend and a look of rage cross the tradesman's face. There was a hurried shriek from the apprentice behind us and Tony leaped forward to pull me back out of the way.

Then I reacted. In a swift motion of my arm I used the mana thread to sweep the crowbar from his grasp. I tore the crowbar easily from his fingers as if he were no more than a baby and sent the crowbar sliding across the car park.

A gasp of pain escaped my attacker's lips as he turned to look with stunned shock at his weapon now sliding from his reach. The look was replaced by one of stark horror as my backswing sent a thread into his torso catching him just under the ribs on his right side. I heard a sickening crunch.

Time seemed to slow down even more as the reality of this sunk in. The impact hit him hard and lifted him off the ground for a few seconds. I saw his face scrunch up and grimace in pain. His eyes clenched shut and his teeth clamped down as the air was forcibly expelled from his body.

He fell down to his knees holding his stomach. With each cough he winced in pain as the cough racked across his shattered chest. Blood oozed from the corner of his mouth as he fell to his knees before me. He made no attempt to flee – in fact I doubt he even could have. He simply blinked twice and looked up at me, his eyes widening with horror and fear.

I knew he couldn't have seen the mana thread that downed him. But I also knew that he would have seen my eyes staring unmercifully down at him. He would have seen my irises alight with the mana and seen my face turn into the cruel stranger.

I knew this because I could see my small pupils centred in a cruel and merciless face, reflected in the whites of his eyes. I was ready to end this. I wanted to end this. I wanted it with every fibre of my soul. It scared me how much I wanted to complete my dominion over this wretched man.

Fortunately for both my victim and myself I never had the chance to complete the act.

"Run," Tony hissed in my ear pulling me away. At first I fought against him but the red haze lifted from my vision and I realised that he was right.

I turned to the apprentice who had backed away in fear against the far side of the van.

"You saw nothing!" I commanded harshly.

I took a half step towards the poor guy who flinched in terror.

I heard the muffled thump as the body of the tradesman finally collapsed to the ground behind me.

"I saw nothing!" the poor guy uttered, his voice quaking with fear as his eyes darted down to the fallen body of his employer.

"He was hit by a car!" Tony hissed at the apprentice as he pulled me away.

My last image of that night was a horrible one. The body of the tradesman collapsed in on itself. The apprentice was staring at our retreating figures with terror in his eyes. The worst part was the wild look on Tony's face as we ran from the car park.

* * * *

"I can't forget the look on his face," I murmured into my hands.

"Don't think about it," Tony advised as he passed me a bottle of whisky.

It was about twenty minutes later. We were sitting at one of the local parks as neither of us really wanted to go home just yet. Tony had stopped in at his place on the way here to collect a couple of jackets and the booze from his brother's stash. There'd be hell to pay later but I don't think he cared at this point in time.

"This can't have been the first fight you ever got into, is it?" Tony asked.

"The only other fight I've been in was when I was ten! And I lost that one!" I retorted mournfully.

"Well you're now at a 50 percent batting average now." Tony grinned cheekily.

I couldn't help but chuckle even though I didn't really want to. "It's not really the same," I replied darkly.

"I know." He nodded. "Still, if it's any consolation, you probably saved both our lives. He was going to hit us with that crowbar. He wasn't messing about."

"We wouldn't have even been there if it weren't for me," I objected.

"Well, by that argument we wouldn't have been there if it weren't for me either!" Tony retorted.

As much as I hated it I couldn't fault his logic.

"I felt it," I mumbled, taking a swig of the bottle as it came past again. I cringed as the liquid slid down my throat. It burned uncomfortably.

"What?"

"I felt it, you know, when I hit him," I repeated.

"You can do that?" Tony's eyes were wide.

"I didn't think it was possible, but I definitely felt something, there was a crunching kind of feeling when I hit him."

"There would have been more than a crunching feeling if he had whacked me over the head with that crowbar," Tony retorted.

It was an obvious point. Except that the crowbar wasn't aimed at Tony. It was aimed at me.

I was the one standing to the front. I was the one who didn't back down. I really had goaded the tradie into it. I was so confident in my ability to handle the situation. I handled the situation just brilliantly – the poor wretch was probably lying in a morgue somewhere right now. I shivered at the realisation.

I may have just killed someone.

Tony saw the look on my face and nodded slightly. He obviously saw what was going on in my head. He had a habit of being able to do that.

"You're an arrogant bastard. You do know that, don't you?" he hissed angrily at me.

"What?" I turned, slightly alarmed.

"You're going to take responsibility for his actions, aren't you?" he accused, his eyes narrowed. "He's an adult and responsible for his own actions. He chose to start something he couldn't finish. End of story."

The accusation hit me hard and fast and what's more, it was true. But I also knew without a doubt that I was responsible. There was no shirking that responsibility.

"What the hell!" I snapped back. "That's supposed to cheer me up?"

"You want to be cheered up – go to a woman!" He snickered cheekily, dropping out of his angry routine.

"I'm all about tough love," he continued, grinning at me in the darkness.

"Yes, I've heard you're into that kind of thing," I snapped, then chuckled.

"That's better. Now gimme that bottle."

"You think he's alive?" I tentatively asked after a few seconds.

"Don't know, don't care," Tony muttered nonchalantly.

But he was lying, I could tell that he did care. It was all he was thinking about, it was clear from his expression on his face. you didn't have to be a mind reader to see the events playing again over and over behind his eyes. I knew this because the same events were going over in my mind.

"I think I'd like to find out," I whispered.

"I know." He nodded and got up. "Come on, it's getting late. We should go."

It was a cold and lonely walk home alone. I didn't get any sleep that night and I doubted Tony did either.

* * * *

It had been several days since my encounter in the pub car park. I hadn't realised it or consciously made the decision, but I'd stopped using the mana and it was beginning to show. I had become nervous and jittery again. My eyes darted nervously and I jumped at any sudden noise or movement.

I'd returned to a pattern of not sleeping properly

again. I became more and more anxious and impatient with those around me. Once again I'd alienated those closest to me. Tina in particular was quite upset by this. I couldn't really blame her either as I wasn't trying with her at all, but this was something I needed to work through on my own. I hadn't gone to Dad's last weekend. I feigned sickness to get out of it although it wasn't really all that much of a lie. The night of the incident I didn't sleep at all. I simply went home and sat in my room gazing out of the window into the darkness of the backyard all night. I didn't sleep the following night, although I did try. I lay in bed cursing at myself to sleep but sleep eluded me. Eventually I gave it up and got up.

School the next day wasn't much better either. Tony and I met before school and he told me that the guy was alive. I nearly cried with relief. I wasn't a murderer. Then Tony said he was in hospital in a coma and I felt lousy again. I'd calmly and coldly told him to remain true to his promise to me and never talk about this again.

True to his word he didn't bring the subject up again but he did place a newspaper cutting in my hands the next day. The article was about a hit and run accident at the local pub car park and that police were making inquiries, urging anyone who had seen anything to come forward. Obviously the police hadn't made any progress with the case or were treating it as a road accident.

This didn't have the desired goal of calming me, in actual fact it agitated me further. It wasn't that I was worried about the police finding me. It was kind of reassuring to note that the man's apprentice had kept his mouth shut about what had actually happened. Then again when you examine it in the cold light of reality – the poor guy didn't really have much choice. He couldn't very well tell them the truth.

Tony's brilliant spur-of-the-moment excuse about the man being hit by a car had explained everything. I was still a little in awe about how he had come up with that so fast. I'm certain that I wouldn't have been able to lie as well in his position. I would probably just have made more of a mess of the situation than I already did.

The logic behind this did little to comfort me. It simply drew me towards one inescapable fact. It had been so easy to do this and there would be no repercussions of my attack. My guilt was the only thing preventing me from losing complete control.

I cannot logically explain the strange sense of dread that this thought invoked in me. There is truly nothing scarier than knowing that there is no safety net and I realised then that there would be nothing to stop me should I lose control completely. It would be so easy to believe myself effectively above the law now.

Actually this wasn't entirely true: there was something or rather someone who could stop me – Renee.

I should probably come clean and tell her everything that had happened. The only problem with that was that I still had no way of contacting her apart from using that spell and roaming all around Melbourne. Even worse, I would then have to explain the situation to her which

175

would reveal yet another of my lies. I had told Tony about the mana and any retelling of the events in the car park would obviously include Tony.

This meant that I had either used mana in front of someone or worse yet betrayed Renee's trust. She would be furious with me in either scenario.

No, I couldn't go to Renee. In this, I was alone.

I'd been sitting at the cafeteria looking out over the oval. My thoughts were miles away. I wasn't even totally sure if it was recess or lunchtime. In actual fact I would have been hard pressed to tell anyone what day it was.

"You've been avoiding me," a small voice said from behind me.

I turned to look at the newcomer, already well aware of who it was.

"No Tina," I replied resignedly. "I haven't been avoiding you."

She had a defiant look on her face as she sat down next to me. We both looked at the oval where kids were playing and running around. I was jealous that they could live their lives being perfectly normal. They didn't have to put up with being like me. They'd never have to deal with this. I had a sudden sense of loss for that. I couldn't explain it. It seemed wrong. I needed normal. I needed to make it work with Tina. She could be my link to the normal and I really felt that I needed normal right now. My life was spinning out of control and I had no idea how to stop it.

"What do you see when you gaze off into the distance like that?" Tina asked me.

I didn't have an answer for that. I wasn't sure what I saw anymore. I didn't answer her.

"Do you mind if I at least sit with you or should I leave you alone?" she demanded as her anger flared up at my lack of response.

"No," I whispered. "Don't go."

"What's the matter with you?" she asked softly, placing her hand on my arm. "Something's been bothering you all week."

"Something happened last week. Something bad."

It felt better to just say this.

"What?"

I could tell that she was genuinely concerned by my response and she moved in a little closer. I couldn't tell her everything. That would definitely be wrong of me. She didn't deserve to be dragged into all this. But that wasn't the reason I didn't tell her. I was selfishly concerned that once she discovered the truth about me and what I'd done, she'd leave me. And she should, a voice accused in my psyche. I would deserve it.

"I hurt someone," I mumbled to Tina. "There was a fight."

"Badly?" she whispered, her eyes seemingly searching across my soul, desperate for the answer and yet at the same time dreading it.

"Bad enough." I nodded.

"Why?"

"I'm not sure how it started," I lied guiltily, "but I know that I didn't start it."

This at least was true. I hadn't started it – I had merely finished it.

"Where did this happen?"

"I was at a bar with Tony," I began, already aware of how this sounded. "Tony wanted to go." I'm not sure why that was important.

"What was it over?"

"A guy thought we were cheating at pool when he ended up owing us quite a lot of money,"

I could tell that she was confused. It was probably better that she didn't understand.

"What happened then?"

"He led us out to his van. He told us that the money was in it. When we got there he threatened us with a crowbar."

Tina sucked in her breath at this, her eyes wide. "What happened then?" she repeated breathlessly.

"I'm not sure," I lied again. "I think he swung the bar at us but somehow dropped it. And then I hit him." My voice was beginning to crack up and tears welled in my eyes.

I relived this event over again in my mind. I could see the look of horror on his face as I pulled the crowbar from his fingers. I again felt the crack as my mana thread slammed into his chest. I heard with clarity the cracking noise as the wind was expelled from his chest and saw the look of disbelief as he fell to his knees.

"Oh Devon," Tina whispered and pulled me into a tight embrace.

"He went down so quickly," I murmured brokenly into her hair.

My body was wracked with quiet sobs. She held me as I unashamedly cried onto her shoulder. I was sure that we were creating a scene in the canteen; however, at that point I was beyond caring.

There is no escape. We pay for the violence of our actions. One way or another – we pay.

CHAPTER SIX

My conversation with Tina actually did make me feel a little bit better. I was still consumed with guilt, but I was coping with it better. I guess being able to get even a little bit off your chest does help. My afternoon classes were strangely disjointed. I could see people taking tentative looks at me out of the corners of their eyes and then hurriedly look away as I'd turn to face them. Obviously my outburst during lunchtime had been noticed and had done the usual gossip rounds.

It would have been interesting to have known just what the gossip network said was the cause of my outburst however upon reflection I found that I didn't much care anymore. I'm sure in my previous life I'd have been mortified at the prospect of becoming a social outcast.

I was getting ready to leave school later that day. I'd just left the locker room when a sneering voice broke across the hallway towards me.

"What was the matter at lunchtime, Devon? Your boyfriend breakup with you?"

I turned to look at the source of the voice even though I knew who it was.

Mark Constance.

I'd had several run-ins with him over the years and I didn't like him very much. Fortunately I didn't have too much to do with him. Mark was considered one of the 'cool' kids. He and his cronies didn't usually bother me too much as I wasn't much of an easy target. Except for today.

There was a reason why guys don't cry in public at school. Guys like Mark were the reason. They would zone in on weakness like vultures and I'd obviously provided them with a target too tempting to resist. He was lounging against the wall on the far side of the corridor surrounded by several of his friends. He was never alone. They were cackling loudly to themselves at Mark's joke. Although I didn't see any humour in it.

"Yeah, Mark, he did," I replied with a sigh. "He said you were better in bed."

It was a childish retort, but considering the audience it was perfectly suited and delivered with – if I do say so myself, perfect timing. Immediately the cackling stopped and the cronies looked fearfully at Mark and then back at me. They expected some form of cutting rejoinder from Mark that would put me in my place. This wasn't the way the script was supposed to go. Mark stood silent, as he obviously couldn't think of a suitable response.

I almost felt sorry for him.

I shrugged slightly and grinned at him disarmingly. I pulled my backpack over my shoulder and moved to walk down the corridor. Mark immediately moved to intercept me. He was quite large and noticeably stronger than me. He loomed over me in a threatening pose. In my other life this would have been terrifying. Now, however, it seemed like pointless posturing and his failed attempt at intimidation appeared a little silly. Pulling up short I looked up at him with a resigned look on my face. I really didn't want to do this now.

"Get out of my way, Mark – I don't have time for this," I said, and roughly pushed my way past him.

He stumbled back several steps to the side as I forced my way past him. Mark gasped behind me – obviously he'd expected some form of back down. Maybe even a slight show of fear. But I'd given him nothing. I could hear the stunned silence as I walked away. That probably could have been handled better, I was sure that I'd pay for that later; however, at the moment I didn't much care.

The truth was that I was indeed terrified. It wasn't of Mark – but of me – and what my reaction might be should he really push me. I didn't trust myself and that was the worst feeling.

What the hell was wrong with me? I'd just finished a fight with one guy and now I was baiting someone else for another? I couldn't afford to lose control over something as stupid as this. I was jittery enough without Mark agitating me and I had no idea what I might be capable of in my current state. I hadn't used mana consciously in almost a week and I could feel the build-up in my gut and see the mana particles visibly agitated along my arms and legs. There was nothing for it. I came to a quick decision. My conversation coupled with my encounter with Mark had convinced me that I could no longer just swear off mana. That would be irresponsible. I'd need to blow off some steam tonight. I had the perfect idea of just what to do. I just had to wait until nightfall.

Night couldn't have come any sooner. I had a quick dinner and did a little bit of homework while waiting for it to get dark enough. Mum wouldn't be home until very late as she had some stuff she needed to do for her course. She'd left a packet of sausages defrosting in the sink.

This suited me as I'd be home again before she was and hopefully rested enough to sleep. I hadn't really been able to focus on Saunders' assignment either. He'd kindly given me the extension and I still hadn't started it.

The cat grumbled to himself, his dull purr rumbling across his chest as I playfully scratched under his chin.

"What's new, pussy cat?" I mumbled to him. I didn't really expect an answer of any kind from him. Cats are kind of jerks like that. True to form he simply ignored me and rolled over onto his back so I could scratch his stomach. It must be nice to be a cat.

It was strangely peaceful, sitting on the front porch. I had a soft drink in one hand and my other was petting the cat. It wasn't quite dark yet, although it was definitely twilight. The only sound was the sound of an occasional car in the distance, the sound of crickets and the loud purrs of a thoroughly contented cat.

Once I determined it was late enough and there wouldn't be too many people about, I set off. I pulled my roller blades onto my feet and tucked my keys into my pocket. I scratched the cat under the chin once more and took off. The cat grunted, annoyed that the patting had stopped and rolled back onto his side to watch me go.

It felt good to be active again, I hadn't skated that much in a while and I'd missed it. There's nothing like exercise for sorting out a troubled mind, but that wasn't the point of this exercise. I turned the corner from my house and began coasting down the hill to the highway. I soon stopped skating and just let my momentum keep me going. I was quite nervous, but I needed to be certain I could draw upon my powers uninhibited. I hadn't used my powers in at least a week and with what I had planned ahead for tonight, I needed to be sure that they would come when called.

Breathing a deep sigh I readied myself and with a slow extension of my arm I sent out a mana thread. I need not have worried. The mana drew forth from my hand with ease.

I felt a small shudder run up my arm as the mana thread took form and a wave of euphoria flushed over me, making me slightly giddy. I used the mana thread to pull myself around the corner in a controlled arc, actually picking up speed as I threw my weight into the curve and used the momentum to throw myself out of the corner.

It was fun in a small way, but it still didn't give me the

rush that skating used to. Hopefully that would change tonight.

I used my momentum to pull myself further into the street. My final destination was the local shopping centre. I'd figured that by this stage it would be mostly empty as trading hours were long over. The shopping centre was a huge multi-level complex and although there was a supermarket open at the other end of the complex, I shouldn't be disturbed if I was careful.

I quickly put on a burst of speed to get myself up the on-ramp and onto the top level of the car park. I wasn't even out of breath. I reached the top level and sure enough it too was empty.

I grinned slightly to myself in the darkness and readied myself. There was something particular that I wanted to see if I could do. This car park was divided into two sections with a gap between them that dropped several levels to the centre's entrance below. A single walkway of several metres spanned the gap.

I wanted to see if I could vault the gap between the two car parks. It was perfect! My blood was pumping and I felt the slightly sick twinge of excitement that I hadn't felt in a long time. I pulled up just before the gap and looked over the railing down to the ground. I wished I hadn't done that. It almost destroyed my resolve. It was an awfully long way down.

I breathed in. I could do this.

Turning sharply I skated away from the edge giving myself a good run up to the gap. I breathed out. I could do this. I was going to do this. With a sudden burst of speed, I took off. I could barely feel my feet as the skates danced along the ground. I had never gone this fast before and I was approaching the car park chasm at high speed. There was no way I could stop in time even if I wanted to.

At the last moment I threw the power down at my feet, setting a mana thread into the ground below and forcing myself into the air. I hadn't expected it to work this well. I cleared the gap between the two car parks with ease and covered almost half the length of the other car park as a bonus. I can't say I landed with perfect grace. In fact I completely mucked up the landing, but I did make it.

I threw a mana thread at the ground to steady myself before my skates touched down. Unfortunately my timing was way off and my legs collapsed under my weight as I landed back on the concrete. I found myself sliding along my side to the car park, but surprisingly I wasn't too badly hurt. I grinned to myself as I recovered my footing. I was pretty sure what I had done wrong. Next time I'd do it properly.

I geared up to go again when the sound of a siren with flashing lights caused me to turn with alarm. There was a security patrol car tearing up the ramp to this level of the car park at high speed.

A security guard leaned out the side window gesturing at me to stop. At this point I wasn't exactly sure how much they'd seen or what they wanted, but I wasn't about to wait around to find out.

I immediately took off in the opposite direction. There was no way that I could outrun a car trying to catch me but fortunately I didn't have to. All I had to do was to get to the ramp before them. I could also jump over any obstructions on the pavement that they'd have to go around. This gave me a distinct advantage.

I heard the security guard curse and attempt to bring a spotlight to bear on me. I easily leapt over several embankments and managed to keep out of the light. The car screeched off in close pursuit.

I was about halfway there when I realised that I was pretty much going at my full speed and I wasn't even really breathing that hard anymore. I should have only been able to maintain this kind of exertion for a few minutes, but I felt completely fine.

I'd made it to the down ramp when the security car was about half way across the upper level. I quickly grappled my way around and slid down onto the next level of the car park.

The regular poles that held the roof up dominated the second level of the car park. This meant that I could use these poles to avoid my pursuers. I was about half way across the car park when I heard the squeals of the security car as it made its way down onto this level.

I decided to change plans slightly and made my way over to the far side of the car park and attempt to hide behind one of the poles. I figured that they'd think that I'd already gone down to the next level. I could then go back up to the top level and escape down the ramp I'd come up.

I pulled myself to a sudden stop and hugged close behind a pillar at the far side of the car park. It was very dark here, making it obvious when the security car had come down, as the headlights played across the walls behind me.

The car descended the ramp and I watched as it slowly pulled to a halt in the centre of the main roadway of the car park. Two security guards exited the car and walked in opposite directions, shining their torches around the abandoned lot.

Damn it! They obviously didn't think that I could have gotten down the opposite ramp so quickly and must be hiding here somewhere on this level. Damn it!

I cursed my rotten luck. Who were these security guards? In the movies the car would have simply kept going down the levels, leaving the hero unhindered and free to go about his business.

I'd have to do something pretty soon. If I stayed here the guard closest to me would soon spot me. There was nothing for it. I'd have to make a dash for it. The only problem was I couldn't make it to the down ramp. One of the security guards was in my way.

I glanced about in a panic and saw a stairwell not too far away. I could make a dash for that. I exhaled nervously and waited for the security guard to be focused on another area of the car park when I made my dash.

"Hey! Kid! Stop!" the guard called almost immediately as I left the cover of the pillar. He quickly followed in pursuit.

One of the interesting things about rollerblades is that a running man is actually faster over small distances than someone on blades. Fortunately I was much closer to the doorway than the guard and made it there first.

The door was closed. This didn't prove to be a problem as when I was few metres from the door I sent a mana thread barrelling into it and forcing it open. I had originally planned to slam the door shut behind me to prevent the guard's access but I now had bigger problems.

Another of the interesting things about rollerblades is that they don't work too well on steps. Yet here I was barrelling at high speeds into what was essentially a very small room with lots of steps in it.

If I didn't do something I'd probably end up breaking my neck. My instincts kicked in and I was able to loop a mana thread around the stairwell handrail above me and pull myself into a horizontal flip over the handrail. I landed with a small degree of inelegance on the floor below. I quickly pulled open the door as I heard the guard burst into the stairwell above me.

"Who is this kid?" he exclaimed as I disappeared onto the roof below him.

I took off at high speed towards the car park complex exit. I wasn't out of the woods yet though. While one guard had pursued me, the other had returned to the car and I could hear it making its way down the ramp onto this level. It was now a race. It was a race I couldn't win.

I was only one level above the ground. I could see

the park area just over the barrier on the far side of the car park. If I could reach there I'd be free. They couldn't bring a car into that area and I doubt they'd chase on foot for any distance. Once I got up to speed there was no way they could catch me anyway. The only problem was getting there. I swiftly changed directions and headed directly towards the barrier. If this were a race that I couldn't win – then I wouldn't race at all.

The security patrol car followed in close pursuit. I wasn't exactly sure what they planned to do as the driver was driving way too fast. I vaguely wondered if they intended to ram me against the barrier. I didn't think I'd annoyed them this much. I grinned slightly to myself; when I wanted to I could certainly antagonise people. It was a gift.

I had no intention of slowing down when I reached the barrier. If anything I increased my speed and leapt into the air. I had to tuck my legs in tightly to my chest. I cleared the barrier with ease and was now literally flying over the car park below me.

I heard the screech of brakes behind me as the security car pulled to a halt. I casually latched a mana thread onto the ground to control my descent and with a graceful crouch I landed onto the ground level car park. Now THAT was a rush! I turned back and saw I had effectively just done a jump from at least ten metres onto solid concrete. I couldn't help grinning to myself. It hadn't occurred to me that if I'd mucked up the landing I would probably have broken my skull. The security car didn't pursue me any further but I think I saw one of the security guards give me an astonished look from the first floor car park.

Well, that was less than subtle, but I consoled myself in the fact that they would have no idea who I was. It was also doubtful that anyone would believe their wild tale of a flying skater in the car park. I made for home. I'd had enough excitement for one night. I had even raised a fair bit of sweat.

I had timed it well. I arrived home about five minutes before Mum. I greeted her as she walked in the door. I had the cat on my lap and an expression of disarming integrity on my face. In hindsight this was probably what clued her off that I'd been up to no good.

"Okay, what did you do?" she demanded as she saw my expression.

She was in full on mum mode. Nothing would get past her. I had to play this carefully, give her the impression that I'd been a dutiful son. That I'd been sitting here all evening with the cat for company and not out at the shopping centre being chased by security guards.

"Nothing," I exclaimed, forcing a wounded expression onto my face.

"This isn't like the time you set the oven on fire is it?" she asked with a wry smile on her face and glancing around the house with mock alarm.

"The oven is fine and besides, that wasn't my fault!" I declared, my face taking on that of the terminally misunderstood.

"How was that not your fault?" she enquired curtly.

"It's an oven," I insisted. "It's supposed to be able to handle heat! It's the manufacturer's fault really, not mine!"

"Most people don't cook their toast until it's glowing charcoal," said Mum.

"Maybe that's the way I like my food." I smiled cheekily.

"Then you definitely got your cooking skills from your father and not me!" Mum retorted.

"Hey! I cooked the sausages without setting off the alarm!" I was the wounded party here. My culinary skills had been questioned. I got to my feet to defend my honour and right the slur against my name.

"You didn't use the microwave did you?" Mum asked suspiciously, glancing around the kitchen. She must have noticed the frying pan in the kitchen sink – which would have attested to the fact I hadn't used the microwave.

"Sheesh, that was only one time I did that!" I grinned back.

"They were like pencils." Mum shuddered with remembered distaste.

"Well, it was better than the time I tried to make mashed potato in the microwave," I reminded her.

"Yes well, I'm still not sure we got that all cleaned out properly." Mum nodded to me, screwing up her nose. I'd spent several hours cleaning out the microwave after that attempt until Mum had grudgingly declared it clean.

"Yes, I've learned my lesson – mashed potato is not a food to be cooked in a microwave," I replied solemnly. "Even if you can buy it in microwave packets."

"That's right." Mum nodded agreeably. "We'll make a cook of you yet. Good night love, don't stay up any later." Mum smiled as she turned to head towards her bedroom.

"Oh, and if you're going to go skating out late, put on a helmet next time," she called back from her room.

I chuckled softly to myself. There is one absolute constant in the universe – there is no chance of pulling the wool over my mother's eyes. She must have spotted me on my way home. Fortunately she didn't know where I'd been.

* * * *

The following afternoon we had a school assembly for the final year students. They had cramped us into a common room designed for half the number of students. The Year Twelve coordinator was a small Chinese lady renowned for having a fearsome temper and carrying a bright yellow flyswatter. She would use the flyswatter on students whose crimes included having their shirts untucked or walking across the pavilion grass.

I had felt its cruel lash on many occasions and I had no desire to cross paths with her again. It was incredibly embarrassing being bullied around by such a small woman. I suspect on some level that this was her desired goal. It wasn't like she actually ever hurt us with the fly swatter and even if she did accidently hit us. It's a damned fly swatter. How much would it have possibly hurt? It was damned embarrassing though.

I realised that I'd once again managed to drift off into my own thoughts and I had missed most of the assembly. Normally this wasn't a bad thing as they were pretty boring but this assembly had begun with terrifying words written across the white board – Mid Year Exams.

I breathed a sigh of relief as the assembly merely appeared to be an exercise in pointing out the importance of these exams. I wasn't too concerned as I already knew that I wouldn't be going to university next year anyway and had thus managed to avoid the whole drama.

I waited behind after the assembly to allow the majority of students to fight their way out of the small doors to the common room. I had no interest in attempting to push myself through the hundred or so other students who were attempting to do the same thing.

"Do you need something, Devon?" Mr Saunders boomed at me from across the room as he noticed me still slouched against a chair.

I grinned back at him and hiked a finger towards the doors as the commotion of students and smirked.

"Just waiting to avoid the rush," I replied.

I could see Mr Cromby standing behind Mr Saunders and smiling slightly at my response, but Mr Saunders just grunted and muttered, "Get to class."

I shrugged and got to my feet to join the end of the queue.

The rest of the day went quickly. I was the last of our little group to arrive at our after school meeting place. The others were waiting for me. Garry was standing impatiently off to one side with a scowl on his face. "You took long enough," Garry grumbled as I walked out of the school gates.

"Sorry," I replied.

I was not really that sorry at all. Tina looped an arm through mine and pulled me next to her. She looked pleased to see me at least.

"Hi!" she chirped and kissed me on the cheek.

"Sorry I'm late," I shrugged. This time I was a little more sorry.

"Not a problem," she replied. "I'm happy to wait."

"Well at least someone was," Tony chipped in. "The rest of us were going to ditch you."

"Shut up, Tony." I chuckled, as we went on our way.

Our destination was the local shopping centre food court. We'd stop there occasionally after school, when enough of us had money. It wasn't something the school approved of, in fact we'd been instructed on several occasions to go home first to change out of our uniforms. We politely ignored this mandate. It didn't seem to make much sense for us to walk all the way home and then to walk back. The shopping centre had recently just been overhauled and the food court was incredible. We gathered around one of the tables to chat. Sarah and Tony went off to order some food.

"Oh, I've got something for you." Tina smiled as she started rummaging through her bag. She eventually drew out a small folder and passed me a folded piece of paper. I unfolded the note and read it. In neat little rows in Tina's immaculate handwriting was my entire mid-year exam timetable. She had even included the class, exam time and even the exam room. Tina had recorded everything I'd need for my exams.

"Where did you get this from?" I stammered, a little confused. I didn't remember this information being given out.

"They gave it out at the assembly," Tony informed me with a slight grin on his face at my confusion.

"I knew you weren't paying attention!" Tina laughed. "Someone needs to look out for you!"

"Thank you!" I breathed gratefully, studying the timetable. It looked pretty doable, except for that three-hour English exam. That sounded pretty rough.

"You're very welcome!" Tina replied, smiling as I kissed her on the cheek and pulled her chair in a little closer to mine, pulling her into a close embrace.

"Keep your hands above the table there, buddy-boy," Sarah snickered as she returned to the table with her food and saw the two of us cuddling.

"Who are you talking to there?" Tina laughed cheekily, thrusting her own hands below the table and placing them on my knee. I grinned and began to make mock moaning noises with a dopey expression on my face. Tina immediately pulled her hands away and glanced worriedly around the food court.

"Too far?"

"Just a little," Tina said.

"It's nice to know where that line is," I said.

"It's usually about three feet behind you," Garry snorted.

"All part of my charm."

"You have charm?" Tina turned to look at me in mock amazement. The rest of the group broke into laughter.

"Nice," I grumbled as I got to my feet. "I'll be back. I'm going to get a drink."

"You're supposed to cuddle her afterwards you fool!" Tony called out before being elbowed in the ribs by Sarah.

I returned with my drink several minutes later, and walked into a discussion on the exam timetable. Tina and Sarah in particular were quite concerned about the seriousness of the exams. A bad result could affect our final marks for the whole year.

"Change of topic," I announced, retaking my seat. Tony and Garry looked relieved at my suggestion. The girls just looked a little annoyed.

"Well what do you want to talk about then, Devon?" Sarah asked sarcastically.

"Absolutely anything else," I breathed theatrically.

"Amen," Tony agreed, drawing Sarah's ire towards him.

I leaned back on my chair looking for a suitable response when I noticed another group of students from our school sitting at one of the other tables. Sitting at the head of their table was Mark Constance.

He was looking in our direction, in particular towards Tina and me. He had a look of raw hatred on his face. I ignored him, turning back to my friends. You know that feeling you get when you know you're being watched and it's really creepy? I had that uncomfortable feeling for the remainder of the conversation. After about five or ten minutes of this I could no longer stand it and I decided to leave. Which was fortunate because everyone else looked about ready to go.

"Well folks. That's it for me," I announced. "Walk you to your car, Tina?"

I offered her my hand and pulled her next to me. I noticed as I did this that Mark had also gotten to his feet and was making his way towards the exit. Tina and I walked hand-in-hand only to have Mark run up from behind us to move in front to block the doorway.

"I don't like you two going out. 'You're a fucking loser!" he blurted out as he flexed his fists against his sides nervously. I wasn't sure what he was so nervous about but it was obvious from his stance and facial expression that something was bugging him.

"I don't recall asking," I snapped and simply moved to one side. He didn't respond or make any move to follow us. He just watched us as we made our way back into the shopping centre.

"What a tool," I murmured to Tina as we were out of earshot.

"He used to tease me unmercifully during lower school. He made my life a living hell," Tina said.

Upon later reflection it was obvious what the problem was with Mark. He had a thing for Tina and he had absolutely no idea what to do about it. I thought I was bad with women, but I could have taken lessons from this guy on how to repel girls.

* * * *

Tina pushed me away breathlessly as her lips pulled themselves from mine. Her eyes glittered as they pierced into mine.

"Will you miss me this weekend?" she asked in a husky voice, keeping her body pressed against me.

"Definitely," I said, still a little out of breath from our efforts.

Tina had waited until we were in the lower car park of the shopping centre before throwing me against a wall and launching herself at me.

"Miss me?" I whispered, still trying to gain my breath back.

She nodded agreeably, her impish face alight with mischief.

"Maybe I'll call you Saturday night," she whispered, her hands trailing through my hair provocatively.

"Maybe I'll call you Saturday night," I whispered back.

"No, better not, my parents will be home Saturday night," she said, becoming sombre for a second. "They don't know I'm seeing anyone. I'd rather not give them any clues just yet, at least until I'm ready for you to meet them."

I nodded. Tina's parents were crazy-strict and had forbidden her dating anyone during her final year of high school. I'd met them once when they'd picked Tina up from one of Sarah's birthday parties. They didn't look like the type you wanted to get on the bad side of.

"You do want to meet them, right?" Tina asked.

I didn't think it was worth mentioning that I'd already met them. I knew what Tina meant. It wasn't so much a matter of meeting them, but of them meeting me.

I nodded the affirmative grimly.

"Come on," Tina urged. "Walk me to my car."

"At your service." I bowed and leaned forward offering her my arm. "This way if you please, ma'am."

Tina's face glowed with amusement. "You really are an idiot sometimes, you know that don't you?" she murmured as she took my arm. I simply nodded with a cheesy grin on my face. I was starting to really like her. Sure, it wasn't fireworks like with Renee, but it was nice, it was easy. I felt good when I was around her.

"Oh, and you need a haircut," Tina said.

"I thought I'd grow it out, tie it back into a pony-tail maybe," I said.

"Not if I'm going to introduce you to my parents you're not."

"Would you like me to put on a suit as well – with a tie?" I grimaced.

"That would do nicely," Tina replied thoughtfully.

I sighed. This wasn't going to be easy. I don't normally make very good first impressions and Tina's parents appeared by all expectations to be a very hard crowd to please.

"Anything else?" I muttered, despondent.

"Only that I'll make it up to you," Tina whispered provocatively, kissing me quickly on the cheek before dashing off laughing.

I gave chase and didn't have too much trouble catching her, although in all fairness I suspected that she wasn't really trying that hard to elude me.

* * * *

After dropping Tina off at her car I made my way home, picked up a change of clothes and caught up with Tony and Garry at Garry's house. Garry's mother answered the door when I knocked and led me into the back living room.

I quite liked Garry's mother and despite my previously mentioned lack of skill at making good impressions for some reason Garry's mother quite liked me too. Mind you she appeared to like everyone so I wasn't overly sure that it counted for much.

"What are we doing this afternoon?" I flopped myself down on the couch.

"Dunno," Tony grumbled, "we were just talking about that."

"We could go to the pub," Garry ventured.

Tony and I looked at each other quickly and in unison blurted out, "No!"

Garry looked suspiciously at the two of us, his face turning from person to person, face to face.

"What the hell is going on?" Garry demanded.

"We just don't want to go the pub," Tony drawled, doing his damnedest to appear disarming and nonchalant.

"No, that's not it," Garry said. "Something happened, and I want to know what it was."

Garry turned to look at me, correctly concluding that I'd be an easier mark to give away information. If this were a normal situation, he'd have been right.

"Had a bad time the last time we went," I said. "Besides I'm pretty broke right now."

As far as lies go, that wasn't a bad one. In fact it was almost the truth.

Fortunately, before Garry could interrogate us any further, his mother entered the room with a tray of drinks and a bowl of chips.

"I can heat up some food, if you boys are hungry," she offered graciously.

"No, Mum," Garry grunted. "That's fine."

Tony and myself echoed, "Thank you Mrs Fisher."

"Well, just make sure you clean up after yourselves."

"Yes Mum," Garry promised as his mother turned to leave the room.

"How about a game of table-tennis?" Tony suggested.

Garry was the undisputed king of table-tennis and rarely knocked back an opportunity to let everyone know it. There wasn't a better solution to getting Garry off our cases about a visit to the pub.

Table-tennis, due to the speed at which it was played, was probably one of the few games that I'd be unable to interfere with the play telekinetically. I wasn't sure if that's what Tony was worried about, but he needn't have worried anyway as I had no intention of cheating.

I wasn't too bad at table-tennis. I was nowhere near Garry's level of proficiency, but I could at least give him a run for his money. I usually won maybe one game in three.

I saw Garry glance speculatively from Tony to myself during the game, but he didn't bring up the subject of going to the pub again. He probably had guessed that neither Tony nor I would speak any further on the subject. Either that or he was simply enjoying beating us at table-tennis.

After a few hours it was time to go.

"Well, it's dark," Garry noted, redundantly, as it was quite obviously dark outside.

I probably should have gone home, but my mum wouldn't have been home anyway so I wasn't in much of a rush.

"What? Does that mean we can switch to hard liquor?" Tony grinned.

"Shh!" Garry smiled back.

He was unsure how his parents would react. They were kind of funny about Garry drinking. Garry's eighteenth had been a sombre and dry affair compared to mine. I was beginning to suspect that Garry's father may have had a drinking problem at some time or simply was one of those who condemned the consumption of the grape.

"No, it means it's time to go home," Garry said.

"Fair enough." I grinned, smacking Tony around the head.

"We're done being beaten by you anyway," Tony grumbled as he headed to the door.

"See you Mrs Fisher," Tony and I called out in unison as we left.

"Careful boys, it's dark outside," she called as we left.

We promised we would be careful as we buckled our rollerblades and headed out onto the street. Tony's house was on the way home from mine. It wasn't far out of my way so I took the time to drop him home. I felt like the company. As we pulled into Tony's street we saw Greg's legs on the front nature strip – sticking out from under his car where he was tinkering under the street lamp.

"Car trouble again? Sucks to be you," Tony teased.

Greg came out from under the old car. "Hi Devon," he said, ignoring his brother's comment.

"Hey."

"I believe you owe me a bottle of Jack!"

"Hey! Tony stole it!" I retorted, watching Tony grin at me.

"He said you drank it!"

"Hah! He ratted me out? That bastard!" I snickered as I threw a half-hearted punch towards Tony. Tony simply allowed himself to roll backwards on his skates out of the way. "I'll give you the money," I said.

"Sure," he grunted, turning back his car.

"I've actually already replaced it," Tony said as we skated up towards the house.

"Oh damn, I was really looking forward to writing the phrase 'bottle 'o' jack' on the IOU."

* * * *

The school bell rang with its usual degree of disdain for the hopes and dreams of the school populace. It's a universal constant that the school bell rings when it's damned well ready to ring and not a moment before.

It was at the end of a long and tiring Friday filled with boring subjects and the annoying prospect of going back to the city to see my father in the evening.

I wasn't in an overly good mood to begin with as Garry and I made our way towards the locker bay. We were amicably discussing some TV show that we'd both recently gotten into. Garry had just unlocked his locker and I was leaning on the far side of the locker bay waiting for him.

Garry was extraordinarily disorganised so it always took him longer to pack his bags for home. Tony would probably already be waiting for us at the school gates. I was getting a little impatient but resigned in the fact that this was pretty much the norm on Fridays.

While cursing Garry under my breath and silently entreating him to hurry up I noticed Mark Constance and his cronies saunter into the locker bay. I really didn't want too much to do with him right now. He grunted at me as he pushed past me and went to his locker – which was only two lockers down from Garry's. Garry was still muttering on about the TV show and I was still really wishing he'd get on with it.

Mark nudged one of his friends in the ribs and grinning casually, looped an arm around the locker and pulled Garry's keys from the door, quickly pocketing them. I started, not quite believing what I'd just seen.

"You'd better put those back," I grunted at Mark, straightening up.

"What?" Garry asked, thinking I was talking to him.

I gestured towards Mark and grunted to Garry, "Your keys."

Garry's keys had his house and his parent's car keys on the loop so it would be incredibly difficult to explain how and why he'd lost them. Garry's eyes narrowed as he pulled the locker door closed to look for the missing keys. His eyes widened again in rage as he turned to look up at Mark.

"Give them back," I ordered in a grim voice.

"It was only some fun," Mark protested obnoxiously in his nasal voice. His hands were held high in mock defence, yet he made no move to return the keys.

"Not for me, it's not," Garry replied evenly.

Garry had a reputation for being slightly unstable and being prone to angry outbursts when provoked. Mark visibly gulped and I could see him turn to assess the situation. His friends were standing well back from him and wouldn't be much use in a fight if it came. He turned to stare back at Garry, his face going slightly paler. He obviously believed that Garry might just be stupid enough to attack him.

The tension in the room was palatable.

"Just give him his damned keys back," I shouted at Mark, losing my temper.

Mark visibly sighed and pulled the keys from his

pocket, tossing them onto the ground at Garry's feet.

"Now leave," I ordered.

Mark flashed me a quick look of anger as he quickly unpacked the rest of his locker into his bag and turned to leave. As he passed me his shoulder intentionally bumped against mine pushing me to one side.

"What a dick," Garry commented as we left the bay. "He always has been ever since we were in primary school."

"Yeah," I agreed.

Tony and the others were waiting for us as we reached the school gates, noticing immediately that something was wrong.

There was another reason I wasn't looking forward to going to Dad's this weekend. I was freaking out about running into Renee again and although it wasn't probable that I would meet her again unless I really looked for her, I worried that I would just see her in the city one day.

Thinking of Renee made me feel longing, desire, hurt and embarrassment. Plus I would have to tell her about Tina – now that I'd made that commitment. Even though Renee had made it clear (in words, if not actions) that she didn't want to go out with me, I knew she would not be impressed. And truth be told I felt like a bit of a heel. I still wasn't really sure how I felt about Tina and didn't relish the thought of having to explain all that to Renee.

I was deep in thought when a shout rang out from behind us. We were in the middle of an alley headed over to the shopping centre near the school and I turned to see an angry Mark Constance storming down our direction.

"Where do you think you're going?" he snarled as he approached.

I didn't quite know how to answer that question. I turned to look at Tony and Garry who both similarly shrugged.

"Home?" I said.

"You've been pissing me off all week," he declared, thrusting his face aggressively into mine. I noticed with some degree of amusement that he had chosen to pursue his grudge with me rather than with Garry. Presumably because he assumed I was the easier target. I smiled with wry humour – if only he knew. With a flick of my wrist I could send him smacking into the far wall of the alley. Not that I would do that of course.

I was just in the process of trying to think up a clever response when a dull thud resounded through my skull and a flash of red light filled my vision. I felt the sensation of heat on the left side of my face and heard a resounding smacking sound.

Time seemed to slow down as I felt myself falling backwards, a throbbing ache resounding across the left side of my face. I fell down to my knees gazing upwards in disbelief.

He'd punched me. The bastard had punched me.

A red haze dropped down over my vision and I watched with some degree of satisfaction as Mark took several steps backwards, his hands falling into a defensive fashion as I rose in fury. His two friends who normally followed him around took several steps back too.

"You're a dead man!" I snarled, then my anger turned into shivering enjoyment as the mana rushed from my chest and flowed with sickening ease down to my clenched fists. The pleasure of this action took me by surprise as it formed a stark contrast to the slow throbbing pain now occupying my face. My surprise was probably the only thing that had saved Mark's life.

Tony shouted out and jumped in front of me. At first I thought he'd taken a swing at Mark until I felt his arms pull me to my feet and hold me back.

"Run," Tony hissed at Mark.

I was still struggling as Tony and Garry held me back. I cursed at them as I watched my prey run from the alley. I wanted nothing more than to strike back at the bastard who had dared to hit me. Tony and Garry held my arms firmly away, and I couldn't bring my power to bear. It wasn't until I glanced to one side and saw the horrified faces of Sarah and Tina and began to calm down.

"Thanks," I mumbled to Tony as I regained my senses.

"No worries," Tony replied glibly. I could tell he was worried though and now that I'd calmed down a cold clamour of dread came over me. I'd come so close to lashing out at Mark.

"One thing I don't understand," Garry interjected.

"What?" said Tony.

"Why did we hold him back? Mark's a jerk and deserved any thumping Devon gave him," Garry said, only half-joking.

Tony and I looked at each other with grim stares, the answer was obvious to us: Tony had held me back because, if I'd hit Mark, I'd probably have killed him.

Garry glanced backwards and forwards between us before nervously snorting, "Sheesh guys, it was only a joke."

"Yeah, I know," I replied darkly.

"Since when did you get to be such a tough guy?" he demanded.

I ignored him and rubbed my cheek until the heat sensation started to wear off. It was replaced by a dull ache and a slight throbbing sensation. This wasn't an improvement.

"It's a funny feeling, isn't it?" Tony murmured conversationally. "It doesn't actually hurt when you get hit, but it hurts afterwards."

I nodded agreeably, but inside I was still deep in thought. This must not be allowed to happen again. Once again my emotions had gotten the better of me and I'd allowed my anger to almost cause a catastrophe. I glanced nervously between Tina and Sarah's shocked faces and I realised with shame that they'd almost seen everything. If it hadn't been for Tony's quick thinking they'd have seen me strike down Mark in a mana-assisted rage.

I shuddered in apprehension. Something needed to

be done and soon. I was becoming increasingly reckless and it was inevitable that eventually those around me would notice something that I wouldn't be able to explain away. I couldn't let that happen.

Tina and Sarah shared nervous glances between each other for the rest of the walk. Nothing was said, but I could tell that Tina was uncomfortable. I wondered if she would leave me, and I wouldn't blame her if she did.

CHAPTER SEVEN

The city was unusually busy by the time I got there that evening. Usually traffic had died down as most people had either already left the city or were busily heading back home. The nightlife of the city wouldn't really ramp up for a few hours until the nightclubs opened.

It took me longer to get to my father's place than normal as the sidewalks were packed. I'd bought a cheap set of sunglasses to cover what now appeared to be a rapidly darkening black eye. I could tell that people were glancing at the idiot wearing sunglasses at night, but I was embarrassed about displaying the fact I had a black eye. If truth be told I was having trouble seeing.

I stopped in briefly at Dad's place to take a look at the eye. It didn't actually look that bad. Sure, it was obviously blackened but in really poor light I couldn't really even notice it. I hoped it wouldn't get any worse. I finished getting changed and went back out into the lounge room. As usual Dad had decided to work late that evening so I enjoyed a quiet dinner alone while I waited for it to get dark enough to go out to begin my search for Renee. Before I left the apartment, I left a note on Dad's kitchen table indicating that I'd be home later and that I was meeting up with friends.

I was going to complete my search for Renee and confess everything: My assault on the tradie at the bar, the uncontrollable desire to kill Mark Constance, Tina... Hopefully she'd know what to do. I needed help and Renee certainly didn't seem to have any problem exercising restraint over her powers. Or did she? That stray thought chilled me to the bone.

When I'd first met Renee she'd almost killed me with a mana thread on the premise that she thought I was going to attack her. I certainly had had no intention of doing so and believed that I never gave the appearance of wanting to do so either. The misunderstanding was entirely hers. Perhaps she didn't have the iron bound control over her own powers that I had assumed. After soul searching I concluded that despite any misgivings, coming clean to Renee was still the right thing to do.

It was still too early to search the bars as I knew from experience that Renee wouldn't turn up until later. I'd begin my search at the bars in Fitzroy where we had first met. She might have a local that she frequents. It seemed like the people at the club where we had first met had known her. I tried to use the time on the tram ride to Fitzroy to determine just what I was going to say to Renee. By the time the tram reached my stop, I still had no clue. It was late enough by this point and clubs were now opening but they obviously hadn't been open all that long. It had taken about a half hour to get into the club where we'd first met. I was sitting patiently in the club as I listened through the assortment of bands. I ordered a beer and sat down where I could see both entrances to the pub. I looked up as each person entered. The first few bands confirmed my previous conclusion that they got better as the night went on.

I had parked myself on the edge of the bar where there was a nice little niche off to one side. I could easily see the band from here but more importantly I could also see both entrances to the club. I'd ordered several rounds of drinks before I concluded grimly that she wasn't coming.

"Who are you waiting for?" a sultry voice said behind me.

I turned to see a hot blonde spilling out of a neon blue dress standing behind me. Fortunately there was a lull in the music so we didn't have to shout.

"No-one," I lied. I wasn't sure why I had lied. I had nothing to hide.

"You seemed to be looking at the door quite a lot for someone who's not waiting for anyone then," she concluded with a teasing grin.

I grinned as I knew that I'd been caught in a lie. Actually it technically wasn't a lie as I actually had no idea if Renee would even be coming tonight.

"My friends and I figured that you'd been stood up," she said, gesturing towards a group of young women at the other end of the bar. One of them, a cute pixie-haired chick, waved back at me with an impish grin on her face.

I half-heartedly waved back and grinned sheepishly at the blonde. Now that I'd had the chance to look closely at her I saw that she had a pretty face too, to go with the long hair and the curves. She had bright green eyes and dimples. I liked dimples. Yep, she was very attractive.

"...and then I said that you seemed too cute to stand up." She smiled.

This had never happened to me before! I'd approached women with the intention of asking them out but they never approached me. I wasn't entirely sure how to act. Take the jokes and one-liners out of my conversation and I tend towards the idiotic.

"My name's Devon." I smiled as I introduced myself in way of an opening line. It seemed to work. She smiled back. Easy.

"Natasha," she replied. "If you're not here waiting for anyone, would you like to come over and join me and my friends?"

"Actually I am waiting on someone," I said, with an apologetic expression on my face. "At any other time I'd have been delighted though."

"I knew it! You are on a date!" she said cheekily.

"You should dump her though," she went on, with a twinkle in her eye, "it's really not nice to keep you waiting so long."

"Actually it's not a date as such," I said. Wow, when did my love life suddenly get so confusing to explain. "But I do have a girlfriend."

"Pity." She gave me a wink and I watched her walk back to the other side of the bar, greeted by catcalls of laughter from her friends.

I couldn't help but grin to myself. It doesn't matter how grim things can get there's always something, somewhere that can put a smile back on your face. It's almost always the last thing you expect too.

I figured that I'd spent enough time here and that tonight Renee was a no-show. I waved down the attention of the bartender and slipped him some money.

"Can you send a glass of whatever that blonde girl is drinking down to her table, compliments of Devon."

He nodded at me, a dry grin on his face and a slightly bored expression in his eyes. He obviously didn't find this as entertaining as I did. I'd always wanted to do this. They made it seem so classy in the movies and it was actually kind of fun now that I'd done it.

I winked in Natasha's direction as I made my way to the door and listened as Natasha's group broke into laughter as the bartender delivered my line. I turned and made a hat tipping motion in her direction, which brought more giggles as I left. I couldn't help but enjoy that. Sure it hadn't gotten me any closer to my goal of finding Renee – but that had been a lot of fun.

My search was getting frustrating. So I walked the streets. Using the awareness spell helped a little, as I was able to see into bars and clubs without paying an entrance fee. I'd probably saved about fifty dollars from my quickly dwindling savings. I grudgingly arrived at the conclusion that Renee wasn't in the area and determined that a better place to search would be the Central Business District and the Casino complex where

I had also run into her. The tram ride back into the city was quiet. In fact I had the section to myself. Once I got into the city it was a vastly different situation. Swanston Street was packed with people, as late night shopping hadn't quite wrapped up yet.

You could tell from the strained expressions on some of the storekeepers that closing time couldn't come quickly enough. I walked from Flinders Street Station up Swanston Street trying to avoid knocking into people. It was chaos. There was no way I was going to find Renee on these streets.

I tentatively sent off an awareness spell when I finally reached a moderately secluded spot, only to be greeted by the huddled mass of light as the awareness spell simply merged the shapes of everyone in the crowd into one amorphous blob. There were simply too many people in one place for the spell to really be effective. What I really needed to do was to get up higher and look down on the street. At the moment Renee could be on the next street across and I'd never find her.

I needed to get up onto the rooftops.

There was no way I was going to be able to get up higher on the main street without drawing attention to myself. I had no doubt that Renee would be furious at me if I got caught on a bunch of mobile phone videos. I'd need to get off the street. This part of the city was mainly buildings of about three or four stories tall. I needed to find a back alley or somewhere where I could work unhindered.

It didn't take too long to find a suitable alleyway. A

quick awareness spell indicated that there was no-one already in the alley. It appeared to be a loading bay for several of the retail businesses on the far side of the building.

Excellent. This was just what I wanted.

In my haste I hadn't noticed that I had been followed. It wasn't until I was already in the alley that a sneering voice brought me spinning around.

"You lost, kid?"

As I turned I could see a rough-looking looking man saunter down the alley. He was wearing one of those stupid blue beanies over his head and a blue tank top and scruffy trench coat, his hair matted to the sides of his head in dreads under the beanie.

"Yeah," I answered. "I thought this alley might have gone through to the other side."

"Well it doesn't." He smiled grimly.

It was obvious that he'd positioned himself in the centre of the alleyway to prevent me from getting past him.

"In fact, it's pretty much a dead end," he continued, "which is bad news for you."

"Why is that?" I asked, not liking his tone of voice.

"Because once you're off the main street," he gestured behind him, "there's no-one to help you."

I could see people walking down the street in the distance. Unfortunately they were some distance away and unlikely to get here in time even if they were inclined to help.

"Why would I need help?" I asked, playing stupid to gain some time.

"Look buddy," the man grumbled, finally getting annoyed. "Just throw over your wallet and mobile phone and you won't get hurt," he demanded, pulling a knife from his coat.

"Listen mate," I sighed, drawing extra emphasis on the word 'mate'. "I've already been in one fight today. I really don't need another."

He balked at me slightly. This show of defiance obviously wasn't the reaction he'd expected from a little kid like me.

"You see the knife, right?" he said in a raised voice, taking a step forward. This obviously wasn't going to his script.

"Yeah, I see it," I confirmed, "and if you take another step I'm going to take it off you."

"Big talk for a small kid," he snarled.

He took several more steps forward, obviously about to attempt bodily harm.

"I'm going to enjoy wiping the smile off your face," he sneered as he rushed forward.

There was a good ten metres or so before he'd get close enough to strike but I obviously didn't intend for him to get that close.

My encounter with Mark Constance that afternoon had taught me one thing – don't let an opponent get close enough to hit you. This is actually a fairly fundamental truth in hand to hand combat. I had taken several martial arts classes through school. The main thing they always tell you is that if someone attacks you with a knife then you need to do whatever you have to do to get away. No matter how good you think you are – you're going to get cut. Your skill just determines how bad that cut will be.

The technique I've been told is to wrap your jacket around your arm and use it to attempt to take the first swipe and then hope like hell that you're faster than his second strike.

Fortunately I had other options.

With a quick flick of my wrist I sent out a mana thread around the blade of the knife. I quickly pulled it effortlessly from my assailant's fingers. He had obviously not expected any kind of resistance as the knife slid free. My assailant let out a startled curse. He obviously thought he'd dropped the knife by accident.

His curse turned into a strangled yelp as the knife slowly curved its downwards motion and flew into my out-stretched hands. I stepped forward to meet the blade as I reversed its direction and allowed the blade handle to slide into my hand.

My assailant at this point became a victim to the laws of physics. It's impossible to simultaneously rush forwards to attack someone whilst at the same time flee in terror. With a horrified look he fell on his back with his knees scrambling as he attempted to pull himself away from me.

I continued my steady walk forward, which caused him to scramble crab-like against one of the alley walls.

He frantically pulled himself up and attempted to press himself through the wall behind him. He looked terrified.

His eyes widened, glued to the knife that I now held lightly in my fingers. I opened my fingers with a mocking smile. I heard a sharp exhale of breath from my foe as I used the mana to direct the knife, point first, towards my terrified attacker who was now paralysed with fear.

He let out a horrified gasp as the blade of the knife pressed slowly against the side of his throat.

"You were saying?" I murmured, allowing my head to tilt slightly in a mocking fashion. I still stood about four or five metres away, my hand held up before me and a quizzical expression on my face.

His only response was a slight croak, his eyes darting wildly between the knife point and me.

"Speak up!" I demanded.

He jerked slightly at my raised voice with his hands pressed firmly against the wall behind him. He looked frantically down the alley towards the main road. He was obviously looking for someone to help him.

"It's as you said to me before," I confirmed with some satisfaction. "There is no-one to help you."

"Are you going to kill me?" His voice raised slightly higher as he realised that he might not want to know the answer to the question.

"That depends," I replied. "Why should I show you the mercy that you wouldn't show me?"

"Don't hurt me!" he pleaded as tears began to stream from his eyes.

"You were going to stab me," I pressed, feeling little sympathy. "You followed me into this alley with the express purpose of stabbing me."

"No! I just wanted your money! You have to believe me! I wouldn't have stabbed you!" he pleaded, his panic finally giving him the power of speech beyond a hushed squeak.

"I have trouble believing that." My eyes were cold.

"It's the truth, I swear!" he wailed. "I just wanted your wallet and phone! That's all!"

"Okay," I shrugged, "let's say I believe you, what do you think I should do with you now?"

He didn't answer, just looked at me with pleading eyes. Fear was literally pouring off him now and tears were freely running down his face.

"Drop your phone and wallet on the ground," I ordered harshly.

He looked up at me hopefully and began to rummage through his coat pockets. To my amazement two wallets and three phones dropped to the ground.

"I have trouble believing that all those phones are yours," I stated dryly.

He croaked again as I slid the knife slowly up his throat – forcing him to raise his head. Then I placed the tip of the blade just at the joint between his jaw and his neck.

"They're not mine," he whimpered pathetically. "Please don't kill me."

"I don't know if I can afford that luxury," I whispered,

just softly enough so that he could hear me. "After all, you've seen my face."

"I saw nothing!" he promised. "It's dark here! There's no way I'd recognise you again!"

"If you tell anyone what happened tonight, I will find you and make you wish that I hadn't. Do you understand?"

He squeaked another affirmative.

"Just let me go, man," he pleaded, trying to simultaneously talk but not move his jaw at all.

"I'm still not sure I should, and I'm sure at least three other people would agree with me," I continued, gesturing to the pile of phones and wallets at his feet.

"If I get out of this alive, I'll never mug another person again in my life," he swore. "I promise."

In truth I really didn't want to hurt him. But I also really didn't want him to blab about what had happened here to anyone.

He shook his head very gently from side to side, which was actually kind of impressive considering he really couldn't move his neck that much.

"You will never speak of this and you'll never mug anyone again?" I asked, as if I was trying to make up my mind.

"I swear," he whispered far too quickly.

"You have to mean it," I hissed as the stress of the situation finally got to me. I wanted this over and I wanted it over now.

"I swear! Just let me go!" he repeated, louder this time.

I let the knife fall to the ground and took several steps back, allowing him a clear path to exit the alley.

"Then, go," I ordered. I kept my eyes on him in case he tried anything stupid.

I had a mana thread raised and ready to smack him back into the wall should he attempt anything. I didn't particularly want to use it though as if I did hit him, he'd probably not survive an attack at this range.

To his credit he didn't even look at me. He simply ran as fast as he could down the alley. I left the knife on the ground but recovered the wallets and phones. I'd deposit them at a police station, claiming I'd found them in the trash.

I took a few seconds to calm down before I attempted my next move. I grinned to myself with some degree of dark amusement. If my assailant was watching the alley waiting for me to come out then he'd be disappointed as I did not intend to leave the alley that way. I didn't think it was likely he was waiting. It was more than likely that he was still running.

I could have had quite a career in law enforcement with these powers. In fact I wondered if this was how superhero crime fighters in comic books felt when they first began their careers. I shook my head sadly as I realised that this wasn't a comic book and I was most definitely not a superhero.

I had no inclination to ever place myself in a situation like that ever again and I'd question the sanity of anyone who would knowingly seek out such situations. I was no hero – I saw no reason to risk my life for others too stupid to avoid situations like this.

I latched a mana thread onto the roof of the building in front of me and launched myself into the air. I quickly gained momentum and latched myself onto the roof. I was amazed at how easy it had become. I pulled myself on to the roof and turned back to see if anyone had noticed my ascent.

Confident that I hadn't been spotted I took a moment to look around. From my vantage point I could see the street below and watched as people walked past, unaware of the fact that they were being observed. In actual fact I could see most of the block.

There were several larger buildings further down the street that would allow me an even better view. It took several more jumps before I was in what I'd considered to be an ideal position. I was perched on top of Flinders Street Station.

The view was amazing.

I could see far along the river line and down across the casino and waterfront areas. The view facing towards the city was a little more restricted. If it weren't for the buildings directly in front of me I'd have had an unobstructed view of pretty much the whole city. Fortunately direct line of sight wasn't required by the awareness spell. The point of the spell was to be able to see through walls in the first place.

Yes, this spot was perfect.

I took a few seconds to ready myself. This was going

to be very interesting. The largest awareness detonation I'd accomplished so far was only about fifty metres. I'd had thought that large enough at the time. This time, however, I wanted to make it as large as possible to increase the chances of catching Renee within its reach.

This was going to dwarf anything I'd attempted before.

I breathed in as I built the mana within me. The feeling of mana intoxication washed over me and pulsed from my chest and down into my arms. I built the mana into a small but potent ball of power in front of me. I filled the sphere with more energy. I watched with satisfaction as it grew in size. I noted with pride that I was having no trouble with the stability of the sphere as I enlarged it. It was already twice the size of what I'd previously thought was possible. This isn't to say that it wasn't causing me some strain. Keeping the mana flowing from my body in such a fashion was taking a heavy toll. I was sweating profusely and my breath came in gasps as I struggled to maintain the vortex of power before me.

The best way to describe the strain I was under would be to compare the process to attempting to blow up a balloon underwater. It's a delicate balancing act between power – your breath, and the external force – the water.

I'd reached the apex of what I considered to be my limits when I released the mana. The shockwave of the blast sent me reeling backwards. I hadn't expected such force from the charge. I watched the mana charge as it absorbed the street below and then the next street. It didn't look like it was slowing down much as it made its way through the Melbourne streets. The wave passed over the street and people going about their night's activities. As the wave passed over each person they began to glow with an unearthly blue light.

It was fortunate that only my kind could see the light created by the mana or I would have created chaos on the streets. I watched with increasing curiosity and amazement as I could now see several people far below the street level. I guessed that they were standing on a train platform in one of the city loop subway train stations. Several couples were obviously in conversation as they took the escalator down to the platform. I noticed with amusement that a discreet couple were making out in what I assumed to be a broom closet.

The mana charge still showed no sign of slowing and I watched with flabbergasted disbelief as the charge quickly consumed several more street blocks. If anything it appeared to be gaining in momentum.

In a few more city blocks it would have consumed the entire CBD. I was giddy with elation as I watched the mana charge expand, my eyes searching out for the tell-tale sign of a mana user within the charge. I had found no-one yet. I waited for a few more seconds as the mana charge did indeed consume the entire Central Business District and felt the first tremors of doubt. I couldn't see her. Renee wasn't in the city. This made the whole exercise a little more than an elegant and excessive waste of time. I watched with amusement as it impacted the sides of the apartment buildings and allowed me a voyeuristic glimpse of people in their homes. I could see them sleeping in their beds, watching their TVs and going about their everyday lives.

The wave passed across the CBD in seconds and out into the inner suburbs I watched as streets, buildings and then whole city blocks were made visible by the detonation. Everywhere I looked I could see the pulsating signatures of people going about their everyday lives, they looked normal – there was nothing that would have led me to believe that they were anything special. I was just about to give up as the mana wave reached halfway into Carlton. Renee was not in the CBD. The mana charge was impressive though – it had consumed the entire CBD area and was now taking a large chunk out of the surrounding suburbs too.

Then I saw a brightly glowing blip on the third or fourth floor. It must be Renee! I'd found her. She stood out like a beacon to my senses shining with all the radiance of mana assisted brilliance. She just wasn't where I had expected to find her. The immediate way the figure leapt to its feet convinced me that it could see the mana charge that had just barrelled through its walls and into its home. I could see how this would be distressing if you didn't know it was coming or knew what it was.

The figure within the building appeared to be doing something odd with mana as they moved to sit into a bowed position on what I'd assume was a chair or bed. I could see the mana react as the figure drew upon the mana. This had the effect of making themselves even more spectacular in my mana enhanced vision.

Without any warning I saw a thread of mana arc out from the figure and move with great speed out across the sky obviously following a search pattern. It immediately became obvious that they were looking for the perpetrator of the mana. It took only a few seconds for the thread to locate me, as it simply needed to zone in on the centre of the mana charge.

I examined the thread once it got close enough. It didn't look like a standard mana thread as I understood them. It didn't appear to have any strength or solidity to it at all. The thread obviously couldn't be used to lift or move anything. If it wasn't for the awareness blast I probably would have had trouble even seeing it.

It had a strange element to it that caused the hairs on the back of my hair to stand up. I was pondering the nature of this thread when a frightening idea dawned upon me. What if this wasn't Renee?

What if I'd stumbled onto another of our kind? How would they react to an invasion of their privacy? This might be an attack! I might already be in the target sights of some mage staring down the mana equivalent of a bazooka rocket. I was just about to flee when the mana thread changed form yet again, solidifying a few metres away from me. I raised my hands and drew the mana into the arms readying for an attack.

I noticed with panic that very little answered my call. There were only a few dozen mana particles that had worked their way down to my hands. I'd obviously used most of what I could muster in my awareness spell.

A loud clapping noise filled the air without warning, as the mana thread simply disappeared and in its place stood a very bemused looking Renee.

"You certainly got my attention," she said.

"I got your address too!" I grinned back, unable to help myself. I was giddy at the expenditure of so much mana and relieved that this wasn't some form of attack.

"That you did. You got the whole damned city." She rolled her eyes.

I couldn't help but grin back at her again.

"There's going to be some really intense paranoia tonight," she snickered, shaking her head with mirth.

"What do you mean?"

"You know that feeling where people say that they feel like someone's standing on their grave?" Renee explained. "Or that feeling you get when you know you're being looked at?"

"Yeah," I answered, not really getting her point.

She simply gestured around us to the glowing people going about their business.

"Not everyone, of course," Renee amended, "but those with sufficient sensitivity can feel it when mana passes through them. You've probably just freaked out a whole bunch of people."

I couldn't help but chuckle at the concept.

"Did I earn your phone number yet? Or should I just send flowers to your flat?" I joked.

"You're just lucky that there are no others of our kind in the city. No-one could have missed a display like this," Renee continued, ignoring my question.

"Yeah," I commented ruefully. "That thought occurred to me too – but only after I'd already sent off the charge. Whatever you did to get here so quickly scared the life out of me."

"Well then, mister, we're even. That mana charge must have taken three years off my life when it came bursting through my kitchen wall." Renee snickered.

"Most people call." I nodded, chuckling, "I prefer the more personal touch of a mana charge."

"Personal?" Renee asked with a raised eyebrow. "You probably just touched over several thousand people you letch!"

"Yeah, but I was thinking of you!" I grinned, playing along.

"Still, I suppose I never said we couldn't see other people," Renee concluded jokingly.

"We can see all the other people," I said, gesturing the panorama left in the wake of the mana charge.

I knew from experience that the effect caused by the awareness blast would last a few minutes at least; however, given the strength of the charge I'd used I wasn't able to predict when exactly the charge would end. I took Renee's hand and held it. She allowed it for a moment and then took it away.

"What did you want anyway?" she asked after a few seconds of silence as we both observed the display below.

"Actually, I wanted to talk. I've been having some trouble and I wanted to ask you for help."

"What kind of trouble?"

I didn't know what to start with. "I almost killed one of the jerks at my school this afternoon. He punched me and I just lost it. I can't seem to keep a handle on my temper," I explained tentatively.

"Killed? How?"

"Mana thread," I concluded grimly. "Fortunately I had some friends that held me back. I was just overcome with this rage. I couldn't control it, is there some trick mages use in dealing with it?"

"That's not a mage thing," Renee replied gently, placing a hand on my shoulder. "That's a teenager thing."

"Mana doesn't affect your personality, at least not directly," Renee continued. "It doesn't make you more unbalanced or out of control – that's just normal teenage hormones."

Renee had just lied to me. I didn't know it then and to be fair she probably didn't either. Everything she had just said was a lie. Power, any power, is corrupting, and absolute power such as the power given by mana is absolutely corrupting, there is no escaping that universal fact. Those with power become changed by it, and those without it crave it once they become aware of it. It's unavoidable, it's human nature.

"No, what you've got is standard run-of-the-mill teenage pent-up aggression and mood swings," Renee finished with a mild grin. "Do you want my advice?"

"Sure." I nodded tentatively. This really wasn't what I wanted to hear.

"Write some angsty poetry, eat a lot of junk food and hate your parents. That seems to be the way most teenagers deal with the problem."

Renee flashed a cheeky grin at me.

"That's not a lot of help," I concluded. "What do I do if I get into another fight at school?"

"Don't," she advised gruffly.

"It's not like I'm starting them," I sighed. "The problem is I can't keep wanting to telekinetically smack anyone who chooses to start something with me. I need to learn some restraint."

"Actually, from what you've told me you've already shown a lot of restraint with your powers," Renee said, then glanced to the slightly glowing city surrounding us.

"Tonight aside," she amended with a slight chuckle as she gestured towards the city still in the arcane grip of my mana charge.

"You know what I mean," I pressed.

"Okay," Renee continued. "Sounds to me like you simply just need a response other than telekinetic assault."

"I'm listening." I was a little unsure of where she was going with this.

"Okay, what I'm about to show you is a little more advanced, so if you get lost stop me and we'll go over it again slower."

I nodded eagerly.

"Right, so you know about mana threads and mana charges. I don't think the stuff I gave you from my grandfather mentioned mana fields at all did it?"

I shook my head. "What's a mana field?"

"Pretty much what it sounds like," Renee stated. "It's drawing the mana into a field around you. It's a pretty useful technique."

"Okay, show me."

"Alright, what I'm about to do is create a mana field around me. It won't do anything, but it will give you the basis to see how it's done."

Renee took a deep breath and flexed the fingers on both hands. The mana slid from her centre and began to form into a strange pattern.

This was far different from the pattern that was formed when you built a thread. The mana began to swirl into tight loops around each other. They were almost forming small links of mana that were sliding across her body. The mana spread down from her chest, across her breasts and down her legs and arms before it completely enveloped her.

"Done," she concluded with a degree of satisfaction. "I've never tried to do that so slowly before. It was more challenging than I thought it would be."

I walked around her fascinated as I inspected the effect. Each mana link had looped around several of its companions and had formed a rough weave of mana. The whole field pulsated slightly across her flesh as it moved.

"This is what I saw you doing when you made yourself invisible at the casino," I guessed eagerly.

"Yep." Renee nodded.

I took several circles around her before I asked, "Okay, how do I do it?"

"You know how to form a mana thread," Renee explained. "It's like that, only smaller and with less strength."

"Less strength?" I asked, not quite understanding.

"Yeah, the power comes from the unity of the whole field, not the strength of the individual links," she continued. "Okay, now you try it."

I concentrated and felt the heady rush as mana rushed down my arms and slowly pulsated in my unclenched fist. It took me several seconds before I could force the mana into the swirling pattern that I'd seen Renee use.

"No, too much – think smaller," Renee interjected critically.

I immediately discarded that attempt and tried again, this time using less power. A small thread of mana appeared in my palm. It didn't appear to be doing anything.

"Okay, that's serviceable." Renee nodded. "Now try forcing the thread back down upon itself forming a small circle."

A contest of wills began as the thread didn't appear to want to turn in upon itself. I didn't really know how to do it properly, but after what seemed like several minutes of effort I finally managed to get the mana thread in a U-shaped configuration.

"Okay, that's almost it," Renee confirmed. She moved forward and brought her own mana field down as she moved into a sitting position in front of me. She took my hand in hers and pulled me to the ground. We sat facing each other cross legged with my hands in hers.

"Okay," she said, bringing one of her hands across mine.

"Do as I do," she commanded, and I felt the strange draw as we both worked mana together. A small mana thread formed on her outstretched palm. She looked up at me expectantly and then smiled as I duplicated the effort.

This part was easy.

"Now look closely," Renee ordered.

I peered down at her palm as I watched the mana thread slowly turn on itself. Now that it had been pointed out I noted that the thread didn't appear to be actually bending but reforming into the new shape.

I nodded with understanding. My thread was too solid, too much like a telekinetic thread. I tried again and nodded with satisfaction as my mana easily turned into a link, a small circle of power rotating lazily on my palm.

"Good, very good." Renee nodded. "That's better than you have any right to be. Now for the hard part."

"That wasn't the hard part?" I muttered.

"Not even close, now pay attention," Renee said. "Repeat the process while maintaining the original thread."

I watched with fascination as Renee slightly flexed her fingers and two more threads appeared to loop around themselves and link into the original field. It took me several tries before I was able to duplicate this feat. On my first attempt my original thread dissipated but on my third attempt I was able to have three mana threads looped around each other.

"That's it," Renee encouraged with a smile and a squeeze of my hand.

"This barely covered my palm," I objected with a grumble. "How many links would I require to cover my whole body?"

"No idea." Renee smiled back. "You're thinking too much on the individual activity. Remember it's not the thread, it's the pattern."

With those simple words understanding came crashing down very quickly. In many ways Renee was quite a skilled teacher. With one simple sentence she'd explained the entire process.

It wasn't the actual creation of the threads that was the key. It was like in a dance routine, once you understand the basic steps you don't need to concentrate on the individual movements. You just focused on the pattern. I attempted to draw upon my newfound understanding and found that once I'd started I couldn't seem to stop. Links upon links were forming across my palm and then arcing up my arms, across my chest and down my torso. I felt a slight shudder as the field completely enveloped me.

"Wow," Renee gasped. "I didn't expect you to be able to do that."

"Then why teach me in the first place?" I grumbled.

"You don't tell a student that you think they'll fail," Renee retorted. "You're good! You've never done this before?" Her eyes narrowed in suspicion.

"No," I reassured her. "This feels funny having this field around me."

"Yeah, I like that slinky feeling on your skin." Renee replied.

"Kind of like a wetsuit." I agreed. "But without the constriction."

"Yeah, damn that's impressive," she said, admiring the mana field around me. "It took me six months to get something even remotely close to that, you've even closed off the threads."

"How did I do that?"

"You don't know?"

"I just did as you did!" I retorted.

"Well, you did it right then," Renee concluded.

"Great, now what do I do with it?"

"Okay." Renee released my hands and stood up. "You can let down the field now, as I seriously doubt you'll be able to do what's required next with the field up."

"Done," I announced as I got to my feet.

She moved to stand about five or six metres away from me and with a quick flick of her wrist brought a mana field up around her. This field was a little different though.

"Wow," I uttered, moving in to inspect the field. The links were arranged in a more clustered fashion. "Okay, that's pretty, but what's the difference?"

"Attack me with a mana thread," Renee ordered. "As hard as you can."

I shook my head vigorously from side to side.

"I seriously doubt you'll be able to hurt me with this up. It's the strongest I can make." She gestured to the field around her.

"Okay," I conceded grudgingly. "But for the record, I think this is a bad idea."

I drew forth a mana thread and held it before us, before nodding and whispering, "Ready?"

Renee nodded the affirmative and I quickly struck, bringing the mana thread down into a vicious downward strike.

The mana thread impacted, eliciting a slight gasp from Renee. The field around Renee did its work in lessening the force of the blow but she staggered and was forced down onto one knee.

"Are you okay?" I rushed forward to assist her.

Renee seemed okay and had regained her footing by the time I got there.

"Sorry! I didn't mean for that to happen!" I said, taking her arm.

"Holy fuck, you're strong! I don't think I could have summoned a more powerful thread," she whispered as she gazed at me. "Neat field huh? Without it I'd be dead now."

I agreed breathlessly, impressed despite myself. "That didn't hurt at all?"

"A little," she admitted ruefully, waving me off before I could apologise again. "Think you're ready to try it yourself?"

I nodded wordlessly, still a little unsure myself. Renee walked around me, twice inspecting the field I raised before reaching out gently and slapping me. Her slap went straight through my field and caused bright sparkly explosions as the field dissipated. Her palm connected and left a stinging sensation on the left side of my face. Why was it always the left side of the face? It was feeling quite abused.

"Okay," she snapped. "What did we do wrong?"

"I'm not sure – I think that was exactly how yours looked."

"That field of yours would have worked fine against a mana thread, but that wasn't what I did," she announced gruffly. "Look again and pay closer attention," she ordered as she raised her shield again, far quicker this time.

I inspected the field again, this time looking for subtle differences in the pattern. It only took me a few seconds to notice what I had done wrong and raise another shield using the correct pattern. I'd obviously gotten it right as Renee gave a quick smile to indicate her approval and whispered, "Ready?"

I nodded and watched as Renee calmly took several steps back and flicked her palm in my direction sending a powerful mana thread in my direction. I couldn't help but to flinch as the impact slammed against my shield. True to my predictions the field held, but the impact forced me to take several steps backwards.

"Good enough." Renee smiled as she approached. "You'll need to watch your speed though. You're raising your shield far too slowly for it to be of much use if you're taken by surprise."

It was hard to argue with that.

"I must admit." She continued. "That shielding isn't really my preferred use of this theory. I much prefer invisibility."

"That did look pretty cool," I said.

"It is." She replied simply. "Do you think you're ready to try something different? Maybe test that speed of yours a little?"

"What did you have in mind?"

"Okay, stand forward with your shield down. I'm going to punch you in the face and if you can't get the shield up in time, you're going to get whacked," Renee announced.

"This is because I made you fall down earlier isn't it?" I smirked.

"You got it." Renee winked.

"Why does everyone I know want to punch me in the face?" I groaned.

"Just your charming personality," Renee grinned.

"You do realise that if I do get the shield up in time you'll probably break your wrist?"

"I hadn't considered that," Renee agreed ruefully.

"Thus, the student becomes the master?" I murmured cheekily.

"Oh? Is that so?" Renee replied in mock outrage, "Then defend yourself master!"

She was still smirking as she launched a mana thread at me, catching me off guard. I was barely able to get the mana field up in time as her first thread belted into the side of my shield. The impact knocked me over, sweeping my feet out from under me as I slid across the rooftop. I rallied quickly, jumping back to my feet and rushing at her. Renee was merciless, and with a quick sideways slash she swept my knees out from underneath me again and brought me crashing back down onto my back.

"Don't get too cocky." Renee smirked.

This had all happened before I could even consider launching a counter attack.

"Okay, okay," I protested, getting the point. I was seriously outclassed here. Renee was still grinning at me as she walked over to me and offered me her hand.

I gratefully took her hand and felt the electricity of her touch as I always did. I let her pull me to my feet. With a quick pull I found myself in her arms as she wrapped her body around mine and leaned in to kiss me. I wanted nothing more but something made me pull away. This was wrong, I scolded myself. I was with Tina now. I couldn't kiss Renee like this. As much as I wanted to kiss her I couldn't, and I really, really wanted to. Renee immediately tensed up and I felt her question before it came.

"What's wrong?"

"I have a girlfriend now," I whispered back, wishing I didn't. "It wouldn't be right."

I saw a multitude of expressions cross her face. It was the look of hurt rejection that surprised me the most. The expression flicked across her face and was just as quickly replaced by cynical detachment and then finally a look of friendly affection.

Renee delicately extracted herself from my arms with a cheeky grin on her face.

"So? Lil' Twitch is getting some now then, eh?" she teased in her usual impish fashion. She laughed as I flinched at her accusation and then ruefully grinned back.

"Can we still be friends?"

"Of course." Renee smiled and leaned forward to kiss me on the cheek. "For what it's worth, I appreciate the honesty. Besides," she said, "you're still far too young for me. I'd ruin you for other women."

"Can I have your phone number at least? It'd be easier than setting off a mana charge and freaking out the city every time I want to talk to you."

"Sheesh, you know where I live, what more do you want?" Renee laughed.

"Hey! There are a lot of apartments in that building block. I can't remember who lives where."

"Fine," she grumbled with mock gruffness. "Get out your phone."

I rummaged through my pockets pulling out several phones. I was having trouble determining in the dark exactly which one was mine.

"How many phones do you have?" Renee asked with a quizzical expression as the mobile phones played hide and seek in my coat pockets.

"Long story," I replied as I finally found mine and programmed in her number.

"Well, I should really get going," Renee announced. "Keep practicing that shield spell. If you get good enough you'll find yourself using it without realising it when you're in danger. It's quite useful."

I promised her I would.

"How are you going to get down?" Renee asked.

"Same way I got up," I replied. "You?"

"I'll just teleport home," Renee replied dryly, as if this wasn't a big deal.

"Teleport?"

"I don't do it that often, it's really difficult." Renee shrugged. "My grandfather showed me how to do it last time he was here. I can show you one day when you're a bit better with fields."

"Definitely."

"Night, Twitch." She smiled and gave me a casual salute.

"Good night Renee." I really wanted to kiss her but forced myself to smile casually.

I watched as she closed her eyes and concentrated, sending forth that strange mana thread over to her apartment and then with a clap of thunderous noise and a slight rush of air she was gone. I took a more traditional route back to Dad's, by jumping off the roof.

CHAPTER EIGHT

"Ello. You ring Golden Dragon Restaurant. You order now?"

"Wrong number," I replied dryly, hanging up. Somehow I was less than surprised. I couldn't help chuckling as I realised that Sarah would now have a new restaurant to try out. She quite liked the Italian restaurant that Renee had used in her last prank number.

Still, it wasn't like this was a complete dead end. I now knew where she lived in Carlton. I didn't know which flat, but that wouldn't take mana to find out.

I hadn't had a chance to drop the additional phones and wallets to the police station last night, so I took the opportunity in the morning. It was a strange feeling walking into the Melbourne City Police Station attempting to return property that had been stolen at knife point.

The police man at the desk looked a little bored as I approached and in a dull voice intoned, "How can I help you?"

"Yeah, hi, um, I found these in a trash bin on Latrobe Street and I wanted to turn them in."

He perked up a little as I dropped the phones and wallets on the desk.

"Where did you say you found them?" he asked as he began his inspection.

"In a bin," I repeated, a little confused. I hadn't been prepared to be interrogated on that part.

"That's a little odd, there's still money in these," he commented as he placed the items into a zip lock bag. "Can we get your personal details for our records?"

"Sure," I nodded.

I filled in the paperwork and passed it through to the cop on the other side of the desk. He looked quickly over them and nodded.

"Thanks," the cop mumbled, "you may be contacted if there are any problems."

I returned to Dad's after I left the police station. I had ducked out early before Dad had gotten up concluding that he'd assume I'd gone out to get supplies for breakfast. I stopped in at the supermarket to get some bacon, eggs and the other stuff for our morning ritual. I'd just walked in the front door of the apartment when Dad grumpily emerged from his bedroom.

"You were gone awhile" Dad said as I dumped the shopping on the bench. He'd obviously already been awake for some time.

"Yeah, the line at the supermarket was hell," I said. I didn't much relish the thought of explaining to him that I'd been to the police station. Fortunately he let it go at that.

"Right, so what do you have planned for the day?"

I knew that when Dad asked that, it meant he'd have to go into work.

"An essay for English," I replied.

He nodded but didn't say anything as I began to cook breakfast.

"So when are you going to tell me about how you got that black eye?" asked Dad.

I tenderly probed the bruising under my eye. It had gotten worse overnight.

"Yeah, had a little disagreement with someone." I chuckled, trying to play the incident down.

"Problems at school?" he asked with a raised eyebrow.

"No, it's all under control," I confirmed, not wanting to go into more detail.

"As long as you're sure," Dad said.

"Yeah, I'm sure, everything's fine," I lied with more confidence than I actually felt.

"Does your mother know?" Dad asked sternly.

"Sure," I said. The last thing I wanted was another discussion between my parents about me. Dad didn't pursue the subject and we lapsed into a stilted silence.

I texted Tina on the weekend – out of duty more than anything – and the conversation was stilted and awkward. She had asked me about my Friday night and I had lied about having an early night. I didn't want her to see the black eye on Monday, but there was nothing for it. I don't know what she was thinking of me right now anyway.

My thoughts of Tina inevitably led me back to thoughts of Renee. It was strange how that happened. It shouldn't be happening. I was haunted by the look of rejection on Renee's face when she had moved to kiss me. What the hell did that mean? In a million years I doubted I'd ever understand women.

I wanted to go and try to find her flat today, but I wasn't sure she would see me or what her response would be. In the end I determined that it probably wouldn't be a good idea. I should probably just finish my homework.

Although I really wanted to see her again, a number of excuses raged through my head as to why it wasn't a good idea. I'm such a coward sometimes.

* * * *

School that week took a decidedly frantic turn as our mid-year exams began the following week and the pressure was on to try and cram as much knowledge into our heads as possible. It was even starting to affect me and I normally didn't pay too much attention to exam pressures. I normally didn't even care about good grades. The last good grade that I had received was in primary school.

My attention to my studies was probably due to my relationship with Tina. For Tina getting good results was a necessity due to her strict parents. I guess I was trying to keep pace with her and several teachers noted the increased attention to my studies. I don't think the extra study was helping much as I didn't feel any smarter. I privately wondered why people went to the effort, but I kept this musing to myself.

"How does it feel to be the guy who got punched in the face?" Mark sneered as he walked past us in the halls before my morning class.

"At least Devon didn't run away from a guy who just got punched in the face," Tony called back, which had the effect of causing Mark to shut the hell up for the rest of the day. That alone was almost worth the punch to the face, I reflected with some mirth – but only just.

"Thanks man, that's very helpful." I grinned sarcastically as we both watched Mark storm off. "How's the study going? I've actually finished the English assignment," I said, almost proudly, eager to change the subject. "Where are you up to?"

"Don't ask." Tony sighed. "I guess we're just not cut out to be academics."

That was nice of Tony. I knew his grades were fine – they always had been. Tony had an annoying ability to get fantastic grades without putting in much effort.

"No, I guess not," I concluded with mock sorrow. "So what are we cut out to be?"

"Dole bludgers?" Tony replied glibly.

"No." I shook my head vigorously. "Do you know how much work those guys have to do now to keep the payments coming in? It would be almost easier just to get a job."

"So you're basically saying that we're too lazy to lie about working?"

"Yep," I concluded with a grin.

"That's practically Zen."

"I thought you'd like it." I grinned as we moved towards our lockers.

I watched with some degree of caution as Mark stormed past us and out of the locker bay. I hurriedly moved to one side to allow him passage past. I didn't particularly want to annoy Mark any further. I didn't really know how best to handle him right now.

The shielding spell that Renee had taught me was all very well and good. I just couldn't really see how it offered me any long-term solution. I wanted Mark humbled and humiliated to the point that he'd leave me alone. This was the only way to deal with this kind of bully. The problem was that I had no idea how to do it without giving myself away and doing something magical that would be very hard to hide. I hadn't even considered that I might be able to resolve this without using my powers.

School was its usual monotonous drone for the remainder of the day. The only ray of hope in my otherwise grey and hopeless world was that Sarah had announced that her parents had allowed her to have a party after the exams. I was really looking forward to it. Sarah didn't throw too many parties but when she did they were always fun. Sarah had a large pool in her backyard, but it would probably be too cold to use at this time of year. There had been several pool parties over the summer and I'd had quite a good time at each of them. I'd cleared the event with Dad so he wasn't expecting me until the following morning. I planned to get drunk and crash at Sarah's. Tina had also announced that her parents had grudgingly let her go too – but not to stay the night. All in all it was looking to be a good night.

It had been some time since I'd let my hair down and with everything else going on in my life I was really looking forward to letting off some steam. Fortunately, the rest of the week went by pretty quickly. I had gotten the best mark I had ever received in English class for the essay too. Saunders had written "Well done, Devon" but then proceeded to tear it to pieces of course. Still, I think he liked it. I got a D+, and considering all the marks taken off, that was a damn good result.

I had shown Tina the essay and she had liked it. "The thoughts are there," she had told me, "you're just expressing them really clumsily."

Tina had obviously decided that I couldn't be trusted with my own studies and had had insisted that we study together at my place. To be fair she was probably right – if she hadn't insisted I doubted I'd be studying right now.

"You're not even trying!" Tina exclaimed, throwing her book down.

"It's hard!" I disagreed. "I can't focus."

"I don't see how I can explain it any other way," Tina stated impatiently, tapping her finger on the section of text that we'd just gone over.

"I'm just not motivated enough," I sighed.

Tina nodded darkly.

"You could motivate me?" I grinned. "You know, make a game of it."

"What? Strip-studying?" Tina laughed back. "I don't see it taking off."

"Hah!" I chuckled. "I was only after a kiss, but nice joke!"

"What joke?" she smiled, looking a little confused.

"Not seeing strip-studying taking off," I prompted.

"Oh, that was unintentional," she stated, adjusting her glasses in a businesslike fashion.

"Now, where did we land on that kiss?" I pursued with a smile.

"Not until you at least finish the chapter," Tina scolded with a smile.

"Okay, now I'm motivated," I concluded dryly.

"Shut up and study!" Tina grinned as she leaned forward to plant a tender kiss on the end of my nose before sitting back down and resuming study.

"This can't be good for your studies," I argued. "I must be slowing you down."

"You won't be if you'll just be quiet for ten minutes!" Tina shot back.

"My mouth is sealed, milady," I uttered solemnly, attempting to focus back on my work. This worked for a little while.

* * * *

I didn't end up going to Dad's the following weekend. I had originally intended to but had gotten side tracked by all the studying that I was supposed to be doing. It's time-consuming work pretending to be busy. It takes even more effort than the actual studying would have been in the first place. I'd come to the conclusion that it didn't make much difference if I studied or not. There was no way I'd need all this pointless knowledge that we were cramming into our heads. In truth I was getting a little annoyed at the way everyone was acting about these tests. These exams surely can't be as important as everyone was treating them.

I was an exception anyway. If Renee's grandfather was to be believed, only one in a multitude had the skills I possessed. If that didn't exclude me from having to participate in certain mundane activities such as study then I don't know what does. The exams when they arrived were as anti-climactic as I'd feared they would be. We were hustled into the main gym where they had set up row upon row of tables and chairs. Mr Saunders was monitoring the exam and had given a stern lecture about how we were not to bring any notes or electronic devices into the exam. We were assigned seating and I was seated next to Sarah, which made me feel a little better.

Flicking briefly through the exam paper I was struck again by the single overwhelming thought. What good was any of this going to do me? There was nothing in here that was even remotely practical for everyday use.

I struggled through the three hour-long session. Mr Saunders spent his time marching up and down the rows of tables with his hand clasped behind him like a commandant of a prisoner of war camp. He'd occasionally loom over an unfortunate student, peering down at them.

"Move along, nothing to see here," I whispered as he tried the same trick on me.

I grinned at him cheekily.

"No talking!" he hissed back, but to my relief he did move on.

For three long hours I stared alternatively between the paper on my desk and the clock on the wall. When I did attempt to answer a question I wasn't sure that my answer was accurate – or even sane.

When Mr Saunders finally announced that our time was up, I gleefully placed my pencil on the table and rose to my feet along with the herd of other students heading towards the door. I can't speak for the other students as they shuffled from the gym but I was feeling quite relieved that the exam was finally over.

"How'd you do?" Sarah asked once we were far enough away where we could talk without Mr Saunders telling us to be quiet.

"Not bad," I concluded with a slight grin. "It was easier than I thought."

"Right." Sarah smiled, seeing straight through my lies, "only you seemed to be doing quite a lot of watching the clock and not much writing."

"You noticed that, eh?" I grinned.

"Yeah." Sarah nodded, concerned.

"It's a Zen kind of thing, working myself up into the right mood for it." I chuckled, discounting her concern.

"What? Hypnotise yourself into being a better student?" Sarah scoffed.

"Yep." I grinned back.

"You'd better get really good at it then," Sarah concluded. "You'd better get really good, and really quickly too."

"Thanks." I smiled as Tina darted through the crowd and launched herself into my arms.

"I think I've aced it!" she gushed exuberantly as she kissed me on the cheek.

"I'm sure you did!" I agreed.

"How'd you do?"

"Oh, I think I did alright." I hesitated nervously. I couldn't hold either Sarah or Tina's gaze for very long.

Tina nodded happily. I could tell she was only partially listening to me.

"What did you write your essay on?" Tina asked, still in full-on academic mode.

"Do we really need to discuss this?" I grinned. "I'd much rather forget about the whole exam thing."

"Sounds good to me." Sarah nodded agreeably.

I could see that Tina definitely wanted to compare notes, but she nodded sadly as she saw the determined looks on both our faces and allowed us to change the subject.

"What's the plan for tonight?" I asked, changing the topic of conversation.

"Don't know," Sarah responded. "Tina and I are heading back to my place straight from school. Do you want to join us?"

"Sure." I nodded agreeably. "as long as we can make a quick side trip so I can get changed."

My place was on the way between school and Sarah's place and I didn't particularly want to go to a party in school uniform.

"I'd like to get some wine or something on the way. Do you have your passport on you?" Sarah asked, my passport still a running joke.

I really needed to get my driver's licence so at least I had some form of proper ID.

"Ha ha, it's not like I carry it around with me."

"What and you don't need a passport to get through the school doors?" Sarah mocked. "Maybe we can convince Tony to go."

"Convince Tony to go into a grog store?" I grinned. "You're joking! He'll never go for it!"

"Yeah," Tina piped up. "The hard part will be convincing Tony to leave!"

"Leave where?" Tony boomed as he appeared suddenly through the crowd of other students leaving the school gates. He had obviously only arrived in time to overhear the last sentence of our conversation.

"The grog shop," I stated with a grin still plastered on my face.

"Why would I ever want to leave?" Tony chuckled, casually throwing one arm around Sarah.

"We wanted to pick up something for tonight," Sarah interjected, slipping out from Tony's hug.

"No problems. I've already swiped a bottle of Jack

from my brother for tonight," he commented. "I left an IOU that was signed 'Devon.'"

He grinned, punching me lightly on the arm.

"Nice, like he wasn't already pissed enough at me already."

"Yeah, now it's two bottles you owe him," Tony snickered maniacally.

"This isn't going to end well," I predicted gloomily.

Sarah's parents had made other plans for the evening, which left Sarah's brother in tentative control of the household. He was pretty cool and stated that as long as we didn't burn the house down or interrupt him too much he promised to leave us to our own devices.

It wasn't long before Tony and I had the barbeque fired up and the delicious aroma of meat cooking filled the air. The weather hadn't turned out to be too bad at all. It wasn't warm enough that we would consider swimming but warm enough that we were comfortable hanging out by the pool without jackets and coats. Sarah had connected her iPod to an outdoor stereo system and was pumping music over the pool and barbeque. Sarah had invited about twenty or so people from school and it wasn't too long before we were all having a really good time. It was nice to laze about and not think about school for a while.

"How'd you think you went on your exams?" Tina asked me quietly. We were both lazing on some deck chairs by the pool. We both had half-finished meals on the side table and were nursing drinks.

It was obvious that she'd been dying to ask me this question all night.

"I really don't want to even think about it," I replied honestly, taking another sip of my drink.

"Oh," she said in a soft voice. I could tell she wasn't overly impressed by my lack of interest.

"Come on, it's just school!" I joked. "It's not like it's real life or anything."

"Just school?" she protested, her eyes glittering dangerously.

"Yeah." I nodded, not noticing the warning signs.

"You really need to take this a little more seriously," Tina whispered. "It is important. It determines what university you'll get into next year."

"Actually, I'm not going to university next year," I replied. "Dad has arranged for me to work at a graphic design company. I'll go to uni the year after next or so."

"How are you planning on getting in?" Tina asked.

"Oh, come on," I said, a little angrily. "It's not like my life is going to be over if I never go to university. There are other options."

"You've never shown any interest in graphic design. You're not even taking it as an elective," said Tina. She was now refusing to make eye contact.

"Look, I'm sorry, school and work are just not that important to me right now, is that so bad?"

"No, no," Tina sighed. "I just wish we had more in common. I guess I assumed that you were a little more ambitious."

"Well, I'm not," I replied. "I'm happy just being who I am."

"You don't want to better yourself at all?" she pressed.

"Well, yes, but I don't think that university is the only way to do that," I argued.

Tina didn't respond. It was obvious that she was never going to see my point of view. Maybe we were just too different. She had the whole academia thing ahead of her and I'm sure she would land herself a brilliant job, probably in medicine – as that was what she wanted to get into. As for me I had no idea what I wanted, let alone how to get it. That kind of makes it difficult to create plans around. I sighed wistfully and returned to my drink. I did not enjoy the rest of the party. Tina replied only in curt one-line answers to any questions I asked and didn't appear to be overly interested in talking at all. It took the buzz out of the whole evening.

I remained behind after the party to help Sarah clean up. It was quite a mess and I'm sure she appreciated the help. Bins had been provided but most people had left their empty bottles wherever they had finished them. It was quite a task hunting down the elusive bottles and binning them.

"Who leaves a bottle in a drain pipe?" Sarah cursed as she pulled the offending bottle and threw it in the bin with a loud clink.

"Got me," I said with a shrug.

Sarah's verbal tirade degenerated into a string of unintelligible swear words as she located a bottle that had been sucked up into the pool catchment area for the filter.

"I think that's it," I concluded, looking around the yard for any stray bottles. Tony had gone out the front to fill the bins.

"Yeah, looks okay," Sarah agreed grumpily. I could tell she was still a little steamed about the bottle in the pool.

"Last time I throw one of these," she grunted.

I chuckled dryly. I knew that as much as she cursed about it she loved playing host and come summer there'd be many more of these parties.

"Are you okay?" Sarah asked, placing a hand on my shoulder.

"Yeah, I'm fine," I shrugged, not really wanting to talk about it.

"Tina?" Sarah smiled. I often forget how intuitive she can be.

I nodded vaguely and grinned, hoping she'd change the subject.

"Well, I'm here to talk if you need," Sarah smiled. "But don't say anything too mean. She's my friend after all and I don't need to know any bedroom details either!" She snickered, tousling my hair.

I genuinely chuckled at that. Sarah really knew how to lighten the mood.

"You always know just how to make me feel better."

"It's just the way I smile," she said. Her face turned into a frown as she spotted another beer bottle. This one was lodged in a tree. The three of us kept drinking and laughing into the night. I was having fun again but I decided not to stay the night. I'd give Tony and Sarah some alone-time. I could tell Tony wanted it. It was a quiet skate home. The funny thing about skating at night is that you always seem to be going faster at night than during the day.

It was relatively flat from Sarah's place to mine so it wasn't exactly a challenging skate. Not that that was really an issue anymore, I didn't get the same buzz from a steep decent any longer – not with the ability to pull myself telekinetically to a halt at a thought. Skating had now simply become just another mode of transport and not the source of entertainment and excitement that it used to be.

It's sad how life can change the simple pleasures into routine – it's kind of a bitch that way.

* * * *

On the train ride out to the city next morning, I determined that I would break up with Tina and see Renee again. I'd been a little concerned about how she would take another intrusion, but figured that she'd managed to draw this out long enough.

This time I'd get her damned phone number too.

Dad had left a note at his apartment that he would be busy for the most of the day so I scrawled a note at the bottom of his indicating that I'd be busy too. This was a regular pattern, it wouldn't be questioned. Dad and I would catch up on Sunday morning.

It was late afternoon when I got off the tram in Carlton. I knew roughly which building Renee lived in but it was difficult to locate it from the ground. It's quite different seeing a building in the distance and then trying to locate that same building on foot. The tram dropped me off a little way off the main strip in Carlton and it was a short walk to the shopping precinct. I thought Renee's building was just on the other side of the shopping strip. I spent some time wandering past the shops. I'd never come out this way before.

It seemed that every second shop was either a pizzeria or a gelato store. I'd have to come back here at some point for dinner as some of the restaurants looked quite appealing. Several shop owners tried to tempt me inside with offers of free garlic bread as an incentive to lure me in but I waved them off.

The building I thought was Renee's turned out to be fairly easy to spot in the distance several blocks away. It didn't take me too long before I turned off the main street and down a side street that I guessed would take me to Renee's building. To judge from the houses on this street, this was quite a wealthy area.

I was standing outside the building that I believed to be Renee's when I encountered my first problem. There was a security door preventing entrance into the building and a series of buttons each relating to an apartment number. I had no idea which apartment Renee was in.

I was almost positive that this was her building but had no way of proving it.

"Twitch?" Renee called out suddenly from behind me. I jumped in fright as I was so focused on the building that I hadn't been paying attention to the street. I turned to see Renee behind me. She looked slightly out of breath as if she'd recently run somewhere.

"What are you doing here?" She smiled, her lips twisting into a slightly mocking curl.

"I was in the area and wanted to see if you wanted to get a coffee?" I stammered back a little lost for words. I hadn't actually thought what I'd say to her. This was typical of my brilliant planning skills.

"I've just had a coffee," Renee replied straight-faced.

"Okay, can I reimburse you for that one?"

Renee tried to keep a straight face, but slowly cracked into a grin. "You're an idiot." She smiled, pushing past me and unlocking the door. "Come on in."

"So, this is your house then eh?" I asked, secretly pleased with myself.

"Yeah." Renee nodded as we walked up the steps towards the top level. There were about twenty or so apartments in the building. Renee's apartment was right at the top.

"Wow, this place is amazing," I murmured as she opened the door to let me in. "You live here alone?"

I couldn't believe the size of the place.

Renee's apartment was an open plan lounge/kitchen set up with several bedrooms off the main entrance. She had a large sofa couch along the far wall with a massive

TV and entertainment system on the opposing wall. Interesting old film posters covered the walls and she had a bookcase overflowing with books. There were also some large and colourful canvasses. I didn't know much about art and I couldn't work out what they were depicting. Renee shrugged and threw her bag onto an armchair and curled up on the couch. She gestured towards one of the armchairs next to the couch.

"Well, actually this is my grandfather's house," Renee explained. "But he's overseas at the moment, he travels quite a lot."

"That's kind of a cool set up," I said, "having the place all to yourself."

"He checks in on me from time to time," Renee continued.

"What does he do for a job? I assume he travels for work."

Renee gave me a funny look but smiled back. "I'm not actually sure what he travels for – he certainly doesn't work. Well, not that I know about anyway."

"Mysterious," I teased. "Maybe he's a spy."

Renee ignored me and I turned around to examine her apartment a little more. There were three violins on display on the sideboard near the kitchen.

"Do you play?" I asked, gesturing towards the violins.

"No, they're my grandfather's."

"Not interested in music?"

"Not really." Renee nodded. "Never really had the knack. I think my grandfather was a little disappointed at that. I paint and I make films." She pointed to the stack of canvasses in the corner and on the far wall. "What about you? You play anything?" Renee continued.

I felt embarrassed. Renee had hobbies, interests, ambitions. I had nothing. Should I tell her about roller-blading? Does that count as a skill? "No, I don't, but not through lack of trying," I replied. "My mother is musical, she spent quite a lot of time trying to teach me."

"Didn't stick?"

"Not as such," I concluded sourly. "I think I had more music lessons in my childhood than most people have in their lifetime – piano, guitar, trumpet, drums." I quickly rattled off the full list.

"And you can't play any of them? Not even a little?"

"Not even to save myself," I said.

"Music's not your thing, eh?"

"Actually, that's not quite true – I love music," I argued. "I guess I was just a little undisciplined as a child."

"Ever think about taking something up now, or are you undisciplined as an adult too?"

"Nice." I smiled, a little hurt by her intimation, however correct it may be.

"Coffee?" Renee asked, after a few seconds of awkward silence.

"No thanks, never developed a taste for it," I declined hastily.

"Coke?"

"Sure." I nodded back as Renee got to her feet and went into the kitchen area.

"So, you were just in the area for a coffee, you said?" Renee passed me the drink.

"Dunno, just wanted to see you I guess." I smiled nervously.

"Well, aren't you sweet," Renee stated back dryly. "You didn't think to call first? I may have been busy or had plans."

"You keep giving me fake numbers," I protested "This is your fault really."

She gave me a sharp look. "Shouldn't you be hanging out with your girlfriend?"

"Why? Did you have plans?" I asked tentatively.

"No, not as such."

"Then why…?"

"I just wanted to mess with you a little bit," Renee said. She threw herself back onto the couch and pulled a newspaper from the table in front of her.

"Are you into horoscopes?" she asked unexpectedly. Renee had a habit of jumping between topics without warning.

"Not really," I replied, feeling a little uncomfortable. I wouldn't have thought Renee would be interested in something like that – it seemed a little too hippy for her.

"I mean, I'll check them if I see them, but wouldn't say I go out of my way to read them," I continued.

Renee nodded agreeably.

"That means you at least believe in them," she concluded with a satisfied smirk.

I didn't answer her. I was still running her faulty

logic through my head when she interrupted my train of thought.

"What's yours?" she asked, ruffling through the paper looking for the right section.

"Aries."

Renee chuckled as she read my horoscope. "Looks like a new romance is on the cards."

I felt my face go hot.

"Best not tell that to your girlfriend," she teased with her smirking half grin on her face.

"No, probably not a good idea." I agreed. "I wouldn't have imagined that you believe in all that horoscope stuff?" I wanted to steer the conversation away from any mention of Tina.

"Oh, I don't." Renee replied. "But you obviously do!"

"I do?" I stammered.

"You must believe them since you make some effort to read them," she said.

"What? How does that make any sense?"

"I never check my own," Renee continued, "but I'll check other people's."

"Why?"

"Because it's handy to know what their expectations of their day are," Renee finished.

"What?"

"No, seriously, think about it," Renee said.

"How does knowing my horoscope in any way help you?"

"Well, it doesn't help me as such. It gives me an

idea of how you think your day is going to be," Renee explained. "So I know what to expect from people. I don't like getting surprises."

"That sounds a little manipulative."

"Possibly," Renee conceded grudgingly. "It's just something I do."

"Anything else in there I need to know about?" I asked, cursing myself at the inevitable mocking that would come from my question. Renee would no doubt jump on the opportunity.

"Oh? So you are interested in your horoscope for today then?" Renee retaliated triumphantly.

"Just read out the damn horoscope."

Renee went back to reading the paper. "It says in here that you need to be careful sharing confidential information today as you may hurt someone's feelings."

"Wow? Really? That's kind of specific," I said, a little surprised.

"No, it's pretty much the usual garbage that they usually dole out."

"Now look who's suddenly an expert in horoscopes," I teased.

"Shut up," Renee laughed. "I told you I never read my own."

"Pass over the paper then," I grinned, sliding myself onto the couch next to her so I could read over her shoulder.

I was immediately overpowered by the aroma of her perfume and the heat of her body next to mine. I was very conscious of the fact that her leg was pressed against mine as I leant forward.

"Okay, what's your sign then?" I demanded nervously.

"Like I'm going to tell you!" Renee laughed, either ignoring or not aware of my obvious discomfort.

"What are you afraid of?"

"Who says I'm afraid?" Renee snapped instantly, her eyes flaring at the implied insult.

"Well, come on then, tell me your sign."

"Aries," she sighed grudgingly. I was pretty sure she was lying.

"Ha!" I snapped, instantly taking advantage of her lapse in judgement. She shouldn't have selected Aries as her star sign.

"What?"

"You did read your own star sign before!"

I was a little proud of myself that I'd managed to pull one over Renee.

"No, wait, what?" Renee stammered as she realised she'd been caught out.

I burst into laughter at her expression. At first her eyes narrowed dangerously but she shrugged and joined in.

"You're not really an Aries are you?" I enquired once we'd stopped laughing.

"No." She smiled. "And don't bother asking me either. To be honest, I actually don't know."

"You don't know your own birthday?" I asked with a raised eyebrow, all hilarity immediately disappearing from the conversation.

"No, I don't," Renee snapped. "Can we just drop it?"

"Sure, no worries," I replied. "It's just unusual."

"There's a reason why I live with my grandfather and not my parents," Renee continued, her tone turning sharp again.

"I'm dropping it, I'm dropping it," I protested, not wanting to antagonise her further.

"So, you don't celebrate your birthday at all?" I asked after a few seconds silence as my curiosity finally got the better of me again.

"Is that dropping it?" Renee asked acidly.

"No, I guess not. It's kind of sad though."

"Not really." Renee shrugged. "I don't feel like I'm missing out on anything."

"Fair enough." I nodded, still not convinced.

"So, what did you have in mind?" Renee asked with a slightly upraised eyebrow and a smirk even though she was obviously just trying to change the subject.

"In mind about what?" I asked. "To be honest I haven't given any of my plans much thought."

"Well, that figures," Renee replied dryly.

"What are you implying?"

"Oh, nothing much," Renee chuckled. "It's just that you look like the type to barrel into situations with no idea of how you're going to get out of them."

"What do you mean?" I asked.

"Well? You invited yourself over here and intruded into my time," she continued with a mocking smile on her face. "Entertain me."

I couldn't tell if she was serious or not. I couldn't help but notice her hand had moved from the table and was now resting on my knee.

"What do you want me to do? Dance for you?" I joked back, attempting to focus on anything other than her hand resting gently on my knee.

She must know she'd put it there. It's not like you can accidently place your hand on someone's knee without noticing.

"Can you dance?" She grinned.

"Umm… No?"

"Then, yes."

"You want me to dance for you?"

"Yep." Renee nodded.

"Umm." I gulped.

"Sit down." Renee chuckled as I made a motion to move myself from the couch.

"I wasn't going to dance. I was just getting more comfortable."

"Sure." Renee nodded. "Boy, you really do have no shame do you?"

"So, what do you want to do tonight?" I asked, ignoring her question and trying to change the topic of conversation.

"I don't have any plans." Renee smiled.

"You didn't have any plans, and yet you thought it would be fun to grill me on disrupting them?" I shot back.

"Yep." Renee chuckled. "It was more fun than I thought it would be."

"You're very welcome," I replied sarcastically.

"Well, you do make it very easy."

"So, after all that," I grumbled, "did we actually decide what we're doing tonight?"

"Nope." Renee smiled. "Who says we need to do anything?"

"You brought it up."

"Yeah." Renee nodded. "But I was only teasing you."

"I guess."

We both lapsed into a nervous silence. I made slight tentative glances at Renee who smiled back at me as I focused in on my drink.

"How is your girlfriend anyway? How are you guys going?" Renee asked innocently.

"Good, good," I replied a little too quickly. Renee's eyes flickered at my outright lie.

"Really?"

"No, not really," I replied, deciding to come clean.

"Oh," Renee replied.

"No, we're just not getting along, you know?" I continued.

"Yep." Renee nodded sharply. "So break it off then."

"It's not that easy," I disagreed. "It's complicated."

"No, it's not," Renee argued. "It's actually very simple, if it's not working then it's not working."

"It's that simple, eh?" I mocked sarcastically.

"Yep." Renee smiled. "That's all there is to it. If you're not happy then most likely she's not either. You'd be doing both of you a favour."

"What a remarkably pessimistic philosophy," I said a little petulantly.

"Call it what you will."

"What about yourself?" I pressed. "Any boyfriends on the scene?"

"Not at the moment," Renee replied. "Just came out of a serious relationship a few months back though."

"Oh? Got difficult did it?" I snapped peevishly.

"Yep." Renee shrugged, ignoring my jibe.

"What happened?"

"He was a jerk," Renee continued.

"Was he normal or was he like us?"

"Yeah." Renee nodded. "One of us."

"What happened?"

"He was a jerk," Renee repeated.

"That's not overly descriptive."

"I know, didn't mean it to be," Renee replied. "Relationships between our kind don't often work out anyway."

"Oh? Why not?"

"Something about two strong personalities at odds with each other eventually turning the relationship into a power struggle I guess," Renee mused.

"I can see how that would be a problem."

"To be honest, when I first met you, I thought you were him," Renee commented.

"What? He looks like me?"

"No, but what you look like can easily be changed. You could have been doing anything with the state you were in at the time."

"Anything?"

"You were projecting a lot of mana. It was coming off you in waves. It's a technique sometimes used by mages to hide what they're actually doing under a blanket of magical noise."

"Magical noise?"

"Yeah, I can't really explain it any better than that," Renee continued.

"Like waving your hand to hide what you're doing with the other hand? You know that trick stage magicians use, what's it called? Misdirection?"

"Kind of." Renee nodded. "That's why I attacked you in that alley. I wasn't sure if you weren't going to attack me first and didn't want to risk it. You could have been doing anything behind all that static."

"Oh."

That made sense.

I had wondered why Renee's immediate response had been one of attack when we had first met in that alley. It had seemed excessive at the time and a little out of character, now that I knew her better.

"So all that crap about it being life threatening? Was that a lie?"

"No," Renee replied. "It's true you were at a dangerous level – if you continued like that you would probably have burned yourself out, but I didn't know you weren't faking it."

"Burned out?" I prompted.

"It's more like immolation but by the time that

happens you'd probably have been unconscious for some time. You probably wouldn't have felt anything."

"Small mercies eh?" I grinned, attempting to make light of it.

"Have you ever heard of spontaneous combustion?" Renee continued.

I nodded. I had heard of it, It was a term used when human bodies were found half burned to cinders yet the surrounding area was untouched. People had been found burned to ashes sitting in their armchairs and the only damage to the chair was a slight charcoaling of the leather or fabric. It was one of those great unexplained mysteries of the world, like ghosts or UFOs. Of course I'd always discounted it as fiction.

"It's caused by mana?"

"It's where the body is unable to cope with power being released and burns itself, from the inside out," Renee nodded back.

"Sounds nasty."

"I've never seen it, but my grandfather described it once. He said it was amongst the most horrible things he's ever seen."

"So, tell me about your ex then," I prompted, changing topics. "What was he like?"

"I'd rather not discuss it," Renee cut me off. "It didn't end well."

"Fair enough." I shrugged. Renee obviously didn't want to talk about it. "You brought up relationships though…"

"Tell you what, if you let this drop, I'll teach you that invisibility spell you asked about last time."

I leaned forward eagerly. I had been looking forward to learning this. I nodded as Renee moved herself over onto one of the armchairs on the other side of the coffee table.

"Okay," Renee began. "It's really quite a simple technique. Although mastering it takes some time."

Renee held out her hand over the table and I began to watch as she skilfully threaded a mana field across her hand.

"This is close enough to what the weave should look like," Renee instructed.

I mulled the thread over in my head. It didn't look that different from the thread field that we were using for the shield spell, but I could spot some differences.

"Okay, I'm going to start now." Renee nodded, getting to her feet. "I have to project the field around my whole body or the thread won't hold."

I nodded in understanding as Renee flexed her fingers. The thread expanded up her arm, along her sides and wrapped around her body. The mana flared once and then she simply faded away.

I could still see her mana of course but I realised with some degree of understanding that I was now looking at the mana weave across her body, not her actual flesh.

I wasn't looking at the details of her body as the shape had become a little indistinct and there was certainly no colour. All the details were washed out into the pale blue spectrum of the mana particles.

As I watched I could see the field pulsing with power as the mana threads in the weave reacted to the mana particles flowing across its surface. It left a small blue shadow of her silhouette as it travelled across its path.

"Okay, the theory behind it is," Renee explained, her voice appearing crystal clear from the figure in front of me.

It was a little disturbing that I couldn't see her lips move or discern any kind of facial expression as she talked.

"The mana weave bends the light around it," Renee continued, ignoring my obvious discomfort.

"Bends light?" I asked, not understanding.

"Okay," Renee clarified. "As I understand it what you see around you is caused by light reflecting off objects and being picked up by your eyes."

"Yeah." I nodded back. I understood — that was eighth grade science stuff.

"What the mana field does is to cause that light to be bent around you. This means that the light never reflects off you and this is what renders you invisible. The light simply passes around you."

"But," I began before I was quickly cut off.

"Just take my word for it," Renee snapped, irritated.

I grinned and didn't pursue it. I couldn't really formulate my question into words yet anyway.

"You think you've got the weave now?"

"I think so." It had been relatively simple.

"Okay, give it a go then."

I placed my hands in front of me as I slowly

concentrated on the thread. Once I was sure I had the thread right, I began to duplicate the effect without trying to focus too much on what I was doing. I'd learned from the shield spell that the trick was to focus on the pattern and not the thread.

I flexed my fingers and began. I watched with satisfaction as the field worked its way up my arms and across my chest. Immediately my world was plunged into darkness. This wasn't just night, or being in the dark. This was a complete lack of light. Complete darkness. I shivered slightly and it felt as if I'd walked into a walk-in freezer.

I must have shouted or gasped in fright, because I heard Renee chuckle. "Everything go black?"

"Yeah," I replied shakily. It was starting to get uncomfortably cold.

"I think it's getting colder."

"Yep, it'll do that, absence of light," Renee confirmed. "It's not dangerous."

"I don't like this," I stated. It was getting quite uncomfortable.

"Yeah," Renee whispered. "It's quite disconcerting."

"I don't see how this is in any way useful," I grumbled.

"Oh, it's not." Renee chuckled. "Not like that anyway – you're doing it wrong."

I immediately dropped the field around me and was bombarded by the sensation of light and heat washing over my body. I had to clench my eyes shut. When I at last opened my eyes I couldn't see properly. Everything was blurry and my eyes stung a little as they filled with tears. I began to blink rapidly, trying not to let them fall.

"You let me keep that field up all that time before telling me that I was doing it wrong?" I accused darkly.

"Don't worry. We all do that the first time," Renee explained. "You were making the weave too tight."

"What?"

"You have to let some light through."

"What?"

"You need light to see," Renee explained, breaking off each word as if speaking to a child. "Let some light through your field."

"But then I won't be invisible," I argued.

"Not completely, no," Renee agreed. "That's not the point though. You don't need to be completely invisible."

I tried it again, this time ensuring that the threads were a little looser. The field enveloped me and it was if a veil had been thrown over my eyes. It was weird, the veil moved and pulsed across my vision and made areas of the room fade into a greyish haze and then become visible again.

"This is weird."

"You're doing it right then," Renee confirmed. "Go into the hall and have a look, there's a mirror."

I stumbled across the room, accidently catching my shin on the edge of the couch that I couldn't see properly.

"Watch for the vase," Renee yelled out, reminding me of its existence just before it flashed into my vision and then immediately disappeared.

"How do you get around like this?" I called back.

"The better you get at the technique, the easier it becomes to see. I'm almost at the point where my vision is hardly impaired at all," Renee explained. "You'll get better with more practice."

"If I don't accidently walk off a cliff first," I murmured ruefully. My shin still hurt.

It took a little bit of time to make my way across to the mirror.

"Hey! I've been meaning to ask you. Why can't I see mana in the mirror?"

When I looked directly at Renee I could see the mana field surrounding her. Even through the invisibility field I could clearly make out the mana writhing across her flesh. It shimmered into my vision with an intensity that was impossible to ignore. I couldn't help but see the mana when I looked at her. However when I looked at her through the mirrors reflection, I just saw a woman sitting on a couch – there was nothing unusual about her.

"It's got something to do with light frequency and refraction. I didn't quite understand it when my grandfather tried to explain that to me either. But it's in one of the documents."

I looked at my own reflection in the mirror. It was very strange. I could just vaguely make out my outline. It was infuriating as the veil across my vision didn't exactly stand still long enough for me to inspect the mirror properly. A blurry haze would pass before my eyes and

I'd have to wait several seconds before it passed and I could see again.

When I could see my reflection, it was like I'd become insubstantial. I could definitely see through myself to the wall behind me. There was a pulsating distortion around my body though that created a fuzzy blur. I found that once I moved I could make out the outline of my shape through the blur. It was possible when I wasn't moving, but it was much harder.

"I still can't see this being overly useful," I commented. "I just can't see well enough."

"Practice," Renee stated simply as she moved to stand next to the mirror.

"This is probably what I'm best at," Renee explained. "It all comes down to how much light that you let through the field. The ability to move around relatively undetected has been quite useful." Renee said.

"Breaking into banks?"

"Actually, escaping boring lectures," Renee shot back.

I chuckled as I took another glance around the mana-veiled room. This would be useful to get out of school.

"It would be a pretty slow escape for me right now." I laughed. "I dare say that I'd accidently barrel straight into a teacher without seeing them."

"Motion appears to be more visible through the haze," Renee commented.

"Haze?"

"It's what my grandfather called the greyish blurring effect caused by the field."

"Good word." I conceded thoughtfully.

"It's something to do with the human ability to recognise movement. You won't necessarily see the shape or details but you'll definitely notice movement," Renee explained. "He said it was something to do with the way in which the human eye interprets motion."

"What does it look like when you're good at it?"

"Take your field down," Renee ordered and nodded as I did so. I watched as my reflection suddenly blurred into view in the mirror. It was quite an interesting effect as I phased into visibility.

"Close your eyes," Renee murmured.

I could see Renee's mana field move closer and I closed my eyes.

I felt Renee's body against mine as she wrapped her arms around me from behind. I shivered as her slender arms slid under mine and pulled me in close.

I could feel Renee's breath against the back of my neck and heard her whisper in my ear.

"Open your eyes," she instructed.

I opened my eyes and looked about. There was a slight rippling effect across my vision as I looked into the haze.

Renee was right! I could see everything clearly but it was as if I was looking through a sheet of slightly frosted glass. The details were there but they were indistinct and I had to intensely focus on them to see them.

"Wow," I muttered. "This is quite a difference."

"Practice makes perfect." Renee whispered from behind me.

"Just out of interest, why are we hugging?"

"Why do you think?" Renee smirked.

"Was it because you couldn't keep your hands off me?" I grinned, wiggling myself around within her grasp so that I was facing her.

"Yeah," she grinned dryly. "You got me, I jumped on the first excuse I could get. You're just too much man for a girl like me to resist."

"Right," I murmured back as I hugged her closer. I knew she was only joking but it felt good to hear her say it. I wrapped my arms around her and pulled her in close. She leant forward and rested her head on my shoulders. We stayed that way for a long time. The only sound was the energy in Renee's mana field making a slight buzzing noise around us.

I didn't want this moment to end.

CHAPTER NINE

"It's not working out," I blurted, focusing on my feet, unable to look Tina in the eyes as I said it.

I'd been dreading this conversation all weekend after I'd left Renee's. Renee and I hadn't done anything more than hug but I still felt guilty. I needed to end things properly with Tina first. I owed her that much at least.

I had been obsessing about it all day. I'd arranged to meet Tina at a coffee shop at the shopping centre. I hadn't meant to but I'd arrived late and found Tina was already waiting for me. She had a look of resigned patience on her face.

I threw myself into the seat across from her and blurted out my line. I didn't even have the common courtesy to say hello first. I cursed myself. Sometimes I really am an idiot.

I was butchering this.

Tina looked livid. "What?" she demanded.

"It's not working out," I repeated. This still wasn't going any better.

The look on her face was both hurt and angry. I began to nervously fiddle with the small packets of sugar on the table, unable to look at her directly.

"Why? Is this about the party on Friday?" Tina asked, struggling to get control of her voice. "Because I was going to apologise for that."

"We're just too different," I continued, still unwilling to look at her in the face.

"Is it because I was pushing you to be more academic?" she continued. "Because, I don't care about that anymore."

"No," I mumbled. "It's not that at all."

"Then what is it then?" Tina said, her voice wobbling.

"It's just not… working… you know?"

"That's just repeating the same sentence in a different way."

"It's not um… fun, anymore."

"Fun?"

I nodded silently.

"Relationships aren't always supposed to be fun," Tina snapped. "It's something you have to work at."

"It's too hard."

"You mean you're not willing to try," Tina said, with a flinty element entering into her tone.

"No," I whispered. "I guess not."

"Then I guess that's it then," Tina stated, her voice taking a softer quality.

"I'm sorry," I whispered, and I was. I felt wretched. I should never have gotten into the relationship in the first place. I thought of Renee's comment yesterday: "You barrel into situations with no idea of how you're going to get out of them" she had said. She was right.

"Can we still be friends?" I asked.

"That's just something people say when they break up," Tina snapped. "It never actually happens."

I nodded back briefly. I wasn't going to argue that point with her. I took a deep breath and looked at her face. She looked sullen and angry, but that wasn't surprising. She was rubbing her tear-stained cheek with her sleeve.

"I'm sorry," I repeated.

"I'm sorry too," she replied and immediately got up and walked away.

I watched her go. I waited there for some time as I didn't want to run into anyone I knew. It was a long lonely walk home where I had plenty to time to mull over just how much of a jerk I was. I hate walking by myself.

Sarah turned up on my doorstep about an hour after I got home. She arrived with a prelude of furious knocking on my door followed by a smack over the face when I eventually opened the door.

"You dumped her?" she hissed at me.

"What?" I mumbled, rubbing my face.

"You just dumped her?" Sarah repeated. "Just like that? That's harsh – no talking, no trying to work it out?"

I opened my mouth to begin to defend myself when Sarah cut me off again.

"I knew you guys were having some problems, but that's cold, man!" she yelled, jabbing me in the chest with her finger.

"You never even tried to work at it, or… you know, or even discussed it with her!"

"I…" I began, but finished with the suffix of "I'm sorry".

"You should be!" Sarah continued. "She deserves better, and quite frankly I expected better from you! Jesus, Devon! You're not a jerk! What could have possibly caused you to do this to her?"

Sarah didn't even wait to let me to attempt to get a word in.

"So? What was it? What was this mystery thing that caused you to dump her?" Sarah demanded. "What could have possibly prompted you to make such a hurtful and mean decision without consulting anyone?" Sarah's voice bored into me, "are you seeing someone else?"

"Err," I stammered, sounding a little unsure.

"Not even that woman from the club? What was her name? Renee?"

"No," I argued. "It's not like that. I was with her last weekend, but we just talked. I didn't cheat on Tina!" "Renee said that if things weren't working with me and Tina it's the best thing to do for both of us," I continued.

"Well that's a pretty crappy piece of advice," Sarah thundered. "Relationships take time and effort. You don't just bug out the first time things get difficult. Why the hell are you listening to this woman?"

"What she said made sense," I began, before being cut off again.

"Why didn't you talk to me, you numbskull?" Sarah demanded. "I even offered!"

"I didn't feel comfortable talking about this with you. You're one of Tina's friends," I said. "And you and Tony were so happy that we were going out…"

"Keep talking," she ordered as I'd drifted off into silence, expecting to be cut off.

"I didn't think it was right to discuss my relationship problems with you as you're her friend."

"Why not? She does!"

"Tina talks to you?"

"Of course Tina talks to me," Sarah said. "So you've been too gutless to talk to anyone about this, and now the poor girl has no idea why you've even broken up with her."

I looked down, unsure of what to say next.

"Fix this," Sarah hissed at me. "Fix it now."

I didn't say anything as Sarah turned on her heel and stormed away from me. She slammed the door behind her on the way out. She was right – there wasn't much else to say. The problem was I didn't know how to begin to fix this. I wasn't sure if it was even possible.

School holidays passed without too much comment. Dad was away on business overseas so I didn't end up spending much time in the city. This was good as I wasn't sure how I felt about seeing Renee again. I was conflicted between an overwhelming desire to see her again and on the other an overwhelming guilt about that same desire.

I ended up calling up Tina and attempting to make things right, but it didn't go well. It was a horribly stilted conversation in which I apologised again and told her that I should have handled matters better.

In the end I repeated the old "it's not you, it's me line" and immediately cursed myself. Tina was gracious about it, however, and didn't call me on the fact I'd begun to talk in patronising clichés. She listened to my excuses and didn't get angry. Still, I could tell she didn't want to be talking to me. We promised we'd try to remain friends but I think it was an empty promise on both our parts. But I suppose it might have made a difference. Especially since we were both friends with Sarah and wanted to remain that way. When I hung up, apologising again, I didn't feel any better about the situation and I suspected that neither did Tina.

Tony had spent the holidays working with his brother at the garage and although nothing was said I knew he and Sarah were avoiding me. I can't say I blamed them but it hurt nonetheless. I saw Garry from time to time but for the most part I spent the holidays watching movies, skating by myself and being alone with my thoughts.

I took the time to practice the invisibility field that Renee had shown me. I showed some improvement but I was nowhere near as good at it as Renee was. I was able to generate a field where I could see most of what was going on around me, but it was still blurry. What I was doing was actually kind of risky. The only way to test the principle properly was to intentionally reveal my powers to strangers and hope that I had gotten it right.

I had attempted it only once publicly before but found that I didn't have the stomach for it. The mana field didn't make me completely invisible and as Renee said the human eye is unusually good at picking up movement. I was fine if I remained completely still, but the moment I moved I panicked, fearing that I had been seen. In less than adequate lighting it was relatively safe. In good lighting more people would turn to see where I'd been than I was comfortable with.

It must have looked funny as people would jerk their heads in my direction. Usually they would then screw up their face thoughtfully as they looked around as they tried to determine just what they had seen. I was only caught out once, but I wasn't sure if the woman was paranoid or just more perceptive than everyone else. She was an older lady who had seen me and she began to immediately shriek about seeing a ghost. She became so distraught that her daughter had to step in to try to quieten her down. The ability to bring old ladies to hysteria soured any entertainment value inherent in the activity. I consoled myself by checking my progress in a mirror from then on. I concluded that I'd be able to make myself invisible when I needed to, but I wasn't good enough yet to get away with it without danger of being spotted.

At the end of the day it just wasn't worth the risk.

* * * *

I finally caught up with Tony and Sarah towards the end of the holidays. They had arranged to have a barbeque at one of the local parks and Tony had sent me an invite. I was a little nervous about going, as I didn't know who else was going. I didn't particularly want to spend time with Tina. When I arrived it was as I feared: Tina was there. I noticed that Tony and Sarah were both making what I assume they thought were covert glances in our direction.

"Hey you." Tina smiled fake-brightly. There was a tension behind her eyes that was never there before. She wasn't as breezy as she seemed.

"Hey." I tried to smile, hoping it looked natural and at ease.

So as not to keep talking I busied myself with the bag full of chicken sandwiches I'd brought with me, organising them onto plates at the nearby table.

Tony waved at me vaguely but he was in the middle of what appeared to be a losing battle with the barbeque. I could see that already several sausages had lost the battle of attrition and were cast to the side. The sausages at this point were little more than smouldering carcasses made into brittle husks of charcoal.

They now stood as a grim warning to the dangers of barbeque inattention.

Garry nodded at me as he went over to assist Tony. He was a fantastic barbeque cook and understood that barbeques have more than one heat setting.

Damn, it meant I had to keep up appearances with Tina.

"Hey you," Tina repeated as I moved over towards the table.

"Hey." I nodded, slinking into a seat on the other side of the table. "What did you get up to on the break?" I began. Even to my ears it sounded lame.

"Oh, I studied, finished some assignments," Tina replied. "I've got a good head start on next term."

"Why am I not surprised?" I teased.

"You?" Tina asked politely, ignoring my jibe.

"Oh, nothing much," I replied. "Didn't seem to get much accomplished at all."

"Why am I not surprised?" Tina retorted, mimicking my exact tone and phrasing before breaking into a slight giggle.

I couldn't help but join her. We both giggled nervously.

Tony wandered over with a plate of cooked meat, which he placed tentatively on the table.

"Some survived, eh?" I joked.

"Shut up, it's harder than it looks," Tony grunted.

"No, you just need to learn to turn the heat down once in a while," I commented as he headed back into battle.

Now that Tony had gone, it was just Tina and me again and an increasingly uncomfortable silence.

"Tina," I began, "I'm sorry about everything."

"Just don't," she cut me off. "Let's just let it go."

I shouldn't have mentioned it. And perhaps I had apologised enough. I didn't know what to say or how to change the subject. The uncomfortable silence returned, louder than ever. Tina was either unwilling or unable to fill the silence either so we simply just smiled politely and attempted to look at anything other than each other. It was excruciating.

Luckily Sarah must have spotted this or been waiting for it as she swooped in and plonked herself down next to us.

"Looking forward to school next week?" She asked with obviously forced brightness.

"Not really."

"A little," Tina mumbled at the same time. We'd managed to sync up our replies almost perfectly in time. This caused us to look at each other and slightly chuckle again.

"Well that certainly shouldn't have been a great surprise to anyone, from either of you," Sarah commented.

"Drinks, anyone?" she asked as she grabbed a bottle and gestured towards us both.

"Sure." I replied as she poured me a glass of coke.

"My family has been coming here for years," Sarah commented. "Perfect for picnics and barbeques."

"Yeah, it's pretty nice," I agreed as I looked about.

It was a relatively nice day too, for a Melbourne winter. It was pretty good weather for a picnic. There were a number of people who'd had the same idea.

"I'll have to remember this place," I added.

"There are bike paths that lead from here. They go pretty much all the way to your house," Sarah explained.

"That would be an interesting ride."

"Yeah." Sarah nodded. "Some bits are quite pretty".

"How're you doing anyways, buddy?" Tony drawled as he placed another plate of mostly burnt food on the table and threw himself onto the bench beside me.

I nodded agreeably and began to search for a sausage that wasn't too badly burned. I eventually selected one and threw it swiftly into a curled up slice of bread. It was still slightly burnt, but I expected that.

"How was working with your brother?" I asked between mouthfuls.

"Pretty much sucked," Tony grumbled. "The bastard sent me to get a box of sparks on the second day."

"A box of sparks?" I grunted, "just how stupid does he think you are?"

"Showed him though," Tony continued.

"How?"

"Well, I took several hours getting them and then when I returned I said that they were all out of sparks at the corner shop." Tony grinned.

"Sounds reasonable."

"Only problem was," Tony said, "he'd actually asked me to get a box of spark plugs."

"Oh." I grinned. "That's not good."

"No, it kind of put a downer on the rest of the week to be honest." Tony chuckled.

"At least he didn't ask you to get a left-handed screw driver," Tina interjected. "That's one of the classics isn't it?"

"No, well, they tried that one on the first day," Tony grumbled, "which was why I thought the box of spark plugs was a joke."

"What did you do?" Tina laughed.

"Just handed them a normal screw driver," Tony replied, straight-faced.

"Oh?" I asked in a raised tone. I was pretty sure I knew where this was going.

"They complained, mind you. They said it wasn't a left-handed screwdriver," Tony continued, but I could tell he was having trouble keeping it together though. There was a slight twitch on the corner of his mouth.

"So I…" Tony began.

"…told them to turn it the other way," we both finished in unison.

Tina and Sarah both rolled their eyes.

"What? You've heard that one before?" Tony exclaimed in mock outrage.

"Did that really happen?" Tina asked. "Or is there a book of bad jokes that you guys both have?"

"There's a book," I confessed.

"No, it didn't happen, I actually had a lot of fun," Tony continued, ignoring my comment. "I think I might become a mechanic when I grow up."

"If you grow up." I grinned.

"I can't believe it's school tomorrow," Garry groaned.

"Please don't remind me," I grumbled.

"Well, cheer up. School's more than half over!" Sarah commented.

"Exactly half," Tina corrected.

"Not if you count the holidays."

"Who counts the holidays as school?" Garry argued.

"Well, aren't we 'Mr glass is half empty' today," Sarah mocked.

"You're the kind of person who claims that the week is half over Wednesday morning?" Garry shot back.

"Yep," Sarah agreed readily.

"That's stupid!" Tina interjected. "Wednesday night maybe."

"No, no," I argued back. "I can see her point, the worst part of school is getting up early. So therefore by school time on Wednesday morning you've already gotten up three times so the worst is over. It's only two more times you need to do it before you can sleep in again," I continued.

"I knew I liked you for some reason." Sarah grinned. She was obviously grateful for the support.

"What? That doesn't make any sense!" Garry snapped. This led into a more ridiculous argument. It got so silly that I got to my feet and wandered over towards the drinks at the other end of the table. Sarah joined me several seconds later.

"That's not nice, you know." I smiled at her.

"What?"

"Starting an argument like that and then legging it and leaving them to it."

"Hey, you're just as guilty of that as I am," she commented. "And besides, Garry started it."

We both turned to observe the argument.

"You've got to love Tony." I grinned. "It's nice how he can take an argument like that and just run with it."

Tony had obviously taken up Sarah's cause in her absence and was vehemently arguing her case.

Tony was pretty renowned for doing that. He also commonly argued long past the point that he'd already lost the argument. It didn't seem to faze him much and he never seemed to have any hard feelings about it when he inevitably did concede defeat. You really did have to admire him for that.

"Yeah, he's really sweet." Sarah smiled. "How are you doing anyway?"

"I'm good."

"I'm sorry about – going off at you the other day, you know," Sarah began.

"No," I said, "you were right. I could have handled it much, much better."

"Still," Sarah said, "you never did actually give me a reason."

I thought of Renee. "It just didn't feel right. Can we leave it at that?"

"Well, I suppose so," Sarah reflected sadly. "I just wish I understood. I was the one who suggested to Tina that she go after you and now I feel kind of bad."

"Oh." I didn't know that, but in hindsight it wasn't too surprising. Sarah did love playing matchmaker.

"You're sure it's not that girl? Renee?" Sarah asked about as subtly as a brick.

"I really don't know what's going on there."

"But would you like something to be going on there?" Sarah prompted.

"I don't know." I reflected as I thought about it some more. "Maybe, kind of… yeah."

"Maybe, kind of, yeah?" Sarah grinned with a raised eyebrow.

"She kind of scares me," I confessed.

"Scares you? How?"

I looked at Sarah gratefully. Sometimes she was so easy to talk to. "I don't know, but I just can't seem to keep away from her."

"It's like that sometimes." Sarah nodded.

"Look who's suddenly an expert," I teased gently.

"I'm more of an expert than you are buddy boy," she snapped, playfully punching my shoulder.

"True."

"Does she feel the same way?"

I could only shrug. I had no idea what Renee was feeling or thought.

"Sounds like you need to ask her then. Then at least you'd know," Sarah replied simply. "That'd be something at least."

I nodded. She did have a point.

"Well, it looks like the argument is finally winding down." Sarah grinned, gesturing towards the others. "Want to wind another one back up?"

"Sure," I nodded. "Politics? Or religion?"

"Neither, I'd like to go home before midnight and don't fancy spending the rest of the afternoon in an argument." Sarah shuddered.

"It'd be guaranteed to start one though."

"Overkill," Sarah commented back. "You're such an amateur."

"Well, I can't argue with that. You're the one that started an argument over if Wednesday is the middle of the week or not."

"I did not!" Sarah grinned, biting off each word. "That was Garry!"

* * * *

The following morning I awoke groggily to find Tony sitting on the edge of my bed.

"Sleep in, did we?" He smirked.

"What time is it?"

"Eight-ish."

"Give me five minutes," I groaned and rolled over, attempting to pull the doona over my head.

"Oh, no. We're not playing that game. No snooze button here, buddy," he declared as he threw my school uniform over my head.

"I meant get out for five minutes while I get changed," I lied as I resigned myself to my fate.

There was nothing for it. I'd have to get up.

"Oh, right." He grinned as he tossed one of my shoes into my lap as he exited the room.

When I emerged from my room I found Tony and Garry sitting on the couch.

"Morning sleepy-head." Garry grinned. "Have a late night?"

"No, not particularly," I grunted as I moved over towards the kitchen. "How did you guys get in anyway?"

"Your mum let us in before she went to work."

"Nice of her to wake me," I grumbled.

"Apparently, she tried," Tony protested. "She asked me to pour cold water on you if I couldn't wake you."

"You wouldn't?" I chuckled. I noticed with some degree of alarm a half filled jug of water on the sink.

"Let's just say that you're lucky you got up first time," Tony called back as I poured myself a glass of orange juice for breakfast and made ready to leave for school. I wasn't sure what I was expecting from the second and final semester of my last school year. The school didn't seem any different, but there was an unspoken promise that all this would soon be over.

Our teachers delivered our final end of year assignments with stern warnings that they would make up a good portion of our marks and that we couldn't simply attempt to rely on doing well during the end of year exam. We had another lecture shortly after lunch on the importance of university and how best to choose one that suited your needs. I was kind of glad that I'd chosen not to bother with the whole thing after the first half hour. It was quite tedious. After the full hour I had begun to lose feeling in my legs and by the end of the second hour I'd completely lost all hope for my future.

Why did they have to make it so hard? Why was it so important to get into a good university course straight out of high school? Why did the decision of what you wanted to do with your life have to be made now? It didn't seem fair.

"I see you haven't applied for any courses next year."

I looked around and saw the condescending visage of Mr Saunders staring down at me.

"No, sir," I replied meekly. I just wished he'd go away. "I've decided to work for a year first."

"Have you considered deferring from a course?"

"Deferring?" I asked.

"You sign up for the course, get accepted and then defer the course for the following year," Saunders explained.

"Oh." I hadn't even known that was an option. I suppose if I had been paying attention to the lecture or the several others similar to it earlier in the year I would have known all about it.

"I don't really know what I want to do," I said lamely.

To my everlasting surprise, Mr Saunders just nodded.

"That's understandable," he agreed. "It's an important decision though. Think about it – there's still time. For what it's worth though, young Devon, you do have some skills in creative writing. You might want to consider that for a career."

"Really, sir?" I was stunned. That had almost sounded like a compliment.

"Don't act so surprised," Mr Saunders continued. "You have quite a lot of potential and you know what they say – there's a novel in everyone."

"A novel?"

"Sure," Mr Saunders advised. "Just don't make yourself

the main protagonist and you'll do fine."

Wow. That was surreal. I watched Mr Saunders as he walked away. I didn't believe it. It was almost like he was a real person. He was being supportive and everything. Writing a novel sounded hard though. I had no idea what I would write about. Knowing me it'd end up being some tacky science fiction about something so nerdy that after twenty pages most people would have lost interest.

Still, it was something to consider, in the meantime I'd look into a course to defer – maybe a creative writing one. Maybe Saunders was right, I could be a writer. By Friday I had it narrowed down to three courses, none of which I was one hundred percent sure about. It was a good start though. I was planning on discussing them with Dad this evening.

I was half terrified and half anxious with excitement about going into the city that night. I had a premonition that I'd run into Renee again and this time I wasn't sure what was going to happen. It seemed to take a long time for the school day to be over and my evening start. I breathed a sigh of relief when the train pulled into Flinders Street Station. The station was as busy as it normally was at this time. It was filled with people struggling to get home after a long day's work.

I almost had to fight my way through the crowded station platform. This crowd was impressive in size, even for a Friday night. It was mostly made up of business people, all suited up and looking thoroughly miserable. It was depressing that this was their whole life. They were merely corporate monkeys working for corporate Australia. I had hoped not to become like them, however, if I ended up working for Martin's graphic design company next year I'd be among them. It wasn't a happy thought, so perhaps university was preferable.

I was able to move more freely once I cleared the platform area and made my way to Dad's to drop off my school bag and get changed. Dad hadn't left a note on the bench, which meant that he'd be home for dinner.

This meant I had about an hour or so to fill in.

I didn't much feel like hanging out in the empty apartment so I made my way back down into the streets. There was an arcade at the end of the block that had gaming machines. This was a good way to kill some time. It was, as Dad put it, a criminal waste of money but I didn't mind.

My favourite game was one of those shooter games. The kind where you need to point the gun controller at the screen and shoot the zombie before it gets you. Tony and I would occasionally play it after school in an arcade closer to home.

I'd never been good at these games. Tony had always been much better than me at this kind of stuff. I always ended up with a respectable score, though in the end the zombies always got me. Say what you like about the living dead – they're persistent. I was doing well this time though, I must have killed at least three dozen zombies before I was interrupted. I let out a shriek as two hands suddenly snaked over my eyes and a voice whispered in my ear.

"Hey, Twitch. Are you avoiding me?"

I grinned as I recognised Renee's voice.

"Is a zombie eating my brains now?" I asked, ignoring her question, gesturing towards the screen with the gun controller.

"Yup." Renee informed me. "Nice girly scream by the way."

"Damn," I grumbled, ignoring her jibe. "I was going really well that time."

"Eh, small loss." Renee chuckled, finally removing her hands. "You won't miss your brain, you hardly use it."

"Well, that's nice." I said. "It's good to see you too."

"You didn't answer my question," Renee reminded me as she casually threw some money in the machine and picked up the other gun.

"No, not avoiding you," I explained. "Dad was travelling for work. I was at Mum's."

"Oh," Renee replied as she skilfully shot two zombies. Seeing her play made me realise just how bad I was at this game.

"Nice," I commented, referring to her skills in zombie eradication.

"Eh, these games are designed for two players." Renee shrugged as she dispatched two more.

"Are you using my character as zombie bait?" I asked suspiciously after a few seconds.

I was already down to half health on my brain shaped health meter.

"No, I don't think you can do that, but it's a good idea though."

"I thought you'd like it," I replied dryly.

Several minutes later we were both ambushed and consumed by zombies.

"So much for your bait plan." I murmured as we both looked at the game over screen.

"Hey, they got you first," Renee retorted. "Play again?"

"No, I think the zombies have been well enough fed for one day."

"So, what are we doing tonight?" Renee asked as she threw an arm around my shoulder and gently ushered me away from the machine.

"We?" I smirked. "What if I've already got plans?"

"Then you'll change them," Renee replied, straight-faced.

"Well fortunately, I don't have any plans."

"Very fortunate," Renee agreed.

"Are you stalking me?" I teased as I suddenly realised that Renee had turned up out of the blue.

"No." Renee smiled. "I saw you as I was walking towards the tram stop. We do tend to stand out in a crowd." She gestured towards the mana circle of power on my chest.

"Thanks, I think you're pretty too." I grinned cheekily.

"Not what I meant, but I'll take the compliment." Renee laughed. "I take the tram every Friday back from university."

"It's strange that we haven't run into each other before."

"Who says we haven't?" Renee replied innocently.

"You have been stalking me!" I accused half teasingly.

"No! Not at all," Renee disagreed. "However, before you came into power I doubt you'd have stood out in a crowd to the same degree. I'd also bet that although you probably stare at women all the time, you don't remember their faces."

"Hey!" I protested loudly. "I remember faces! I'm good with faces!"

Renee laughed at my protest. I had to grudgingly agree that it was possible that I'd already seen her in the past but I hadn't noticed her.

"Came into power?" I asked after a few seconds. The term seemed a little odd.

"It's a term my grandfather uses for when you can first see mana," Renee explained.

"It sounds a little cheesy."

"What would you call it?"

"Dunno."

"Then don't pick on my terminology."

"Awoken?" I suggested.

"Were you asleep before?" Renee pointed out acidly.

"No, I guess not," I reflected. "Ascended?"

"Too arrogant," she scoffed.

"There must be a word for it," I argued.

"There is! It's a phrase and it's called 'came into power'," Renee replied dryly.

"I'm not going to argue the point," I conceded. "Want to get something to eat?"

I gestured towards one of the cafés we were walking past.

"I'm not going to say no." Renee shrugged. "But not there."

She scowled slightly at the café. It didn't look that bad, but Renee obviously didn't like it. She grabbed me by the arm and led me into a lane way. We entered into a small series of little arcades of cafes and shops. I didn't even know this place existed. Small alleyways and arches weaved their way through a series of main buildings and skipped across side streets.

It looked as if you could walk all the way down here to Flinders Street Station.

Renee smiled as she ushered me into a Chinese Tea House. A waitress who was wearing a dark coloured kimono greeted us at the door. She bowed graciously as we entered and shuffled forward and led us up some stairs to a table that overlooked the arcade below.

"Tea?" I asked quizzically when we were seated.

"They've got food too," Renee assured me as she passed over a menu.

I glanced over the menu until the waitress returned.

"Oolong," Renee ordered.

"Make that two," I replied as the waitress turned towards me. Renee also ordered a plate of dumplings before the waitress shuffled off towards the kitchen.

"Not a tea drinker, huh?" Renee smiled from across the table.

"What gave me away?" I smiled.

Renee shrugged by way of an answer.

"How's your girlfriend?" Renee asked unexpectedly.

"We broke up," I replied sombrely.

"Yeah, I thought you might. You sounded like you'd already come to that decision when we last spoke," Renee commented.

I nodded in silence.

"Better the dumper than the dumped though, right?" She grinned.

"Not particularly, no," I grumbled sourly.

"That was a joke."

Our waitress arrived with our order before I could respond. She deftly placed two empty cups, a pot of tea and the plate of dumplings in front of us. The tea was quite bitter, but I found I liked it.

"You like?" Renee asked.

"It's quite strong, but good," I replied. "My only other experience with tea was black tea and I wasn't a fan."

I took another sip.

"Yeah, Chinese tea is really much better." Renee nodded.

We made small talk over the tea and finished off the dumplings, both avoiding any subject of substance. The dumplings were amazing. I'd have to remember this place. I desperately wanted to ask her out, but had no idea how to even approach the question let alone gather the courage to voice it. Renee had a way of turning me into a nervous moron unable to express myself properly. There was nothing for it – I'd have to just bite the bullet and do it.

"Have you been practicing with the invisibility

field?" Renee asked before I managed to get my thoughts together.

"Not as much as I probably need to," I replied sourly. I felt that I'd missed my chance to ask her out.

"Want to practice now?" asked Renee.

"I never know what to say when a woman says that to me." I chuckled.

"I'm serious," Renee laughed.

"What did you have in mind?"

"A game of tag," Renee explained with a smirk on her face.

"Aren't we a little old for Kiss-chasey?"

"Who says you get to kiss me if you catch me?" Renee replied with a raised eyebrow.

"Oh, I'm sorry – I just assumed you'd get to kiss me if you caught me!" I grinned with a mock air of hurt indignation.

"Well, seeing as how you didn't catch me last time we played I think the point is moot." Renee smiled.

"Last time?"

"At the casino."

"Oh."

"Hey! I did too catch you!"

"You threw yourself off a building and I had to rescue you," Renee retorted with a snort.

"No-one said we had to play fair!" I grinned. "What did you have in mind anyway?"

"You know that statue of the guy on the horse at the top of Swanston Street?"

"Outside the State Library, yeah?" I nodded.

"First one to get there, wins," Renee suggested.

"That doesn't sound that challenging."

"You've got to be invisible the whole way," Renee reminded me.

"Oh. Well, that does give you the advantage."

"Well, we'll make it fair then," Renee offered. "I'll give you a head start."

"How long?"

"Say a half hour?"

"Half an hour? I could walk that in half that time," I exclaimed.

"Fifteen minutes then."

I nodded.

"Okay, then. Go!" Renee ordered as she adjusted at her watch.

"Wait, what? Now?"

"Fourteen minutes, fifty-five seconds," was Renee's only reply.

I fumbled with my wallet and threw some money down on the table as I got to my feet.

"Don't forget the mana field," Renee called out as I cursed inwardly. I hadn't considered getting down the stairs with the mana field surrounding me.

I took a deep breath, flexed my shoulder muscles and summoned the field. The familiar creep of mana flowing across my body made me shiver with pleasure as the field slowly enveloped my vision and my world turned into the blurry grey void of the haze. I tentatively made my way forward, dodging chairs and tables as I blundered towards the stairwell.

Each table had small lamps on it, which created a conflicting cacophony of shadows and lights that danced around the room when anyone moved. As there was no overhead lighting in the room this meant that most of the room was bathed in shadow. Renee must have chosen this place for precisely this reason.

"Fourteen minutes, thirty seconds," Renee called out.

I had made it to the stairwell in what seemed like five minutes. This wasn't going very well. At this rate I'd only get to the front door when my time was up. I now had to tackle the stairway down into the shopfront. Unfortunately the lighting in there wasn't good. This made navigation all the more difficult. On the upside though that would probably also lessen my chance of being detected by anyone as I made my way down. I tentatively took my first step down the stairs, feeling a vague sense of relief as my foot found the step below it. If you've ever tried walking down stairs in the dark you'll know that the steps can sometimes seem a lot further down than you think.

I was three or four steps down, when immediately, the waitress burst into my vision and then immediately disappeared. She was coming up the stairs!

Crap! Crap! Crap!

I immediately threw myself against the wall. Fortunately it was quite a wide stairwell so there was plenty of room for the waitress to pass. I must have held my breath as she walked past as by the time she had gotten past me I was quite out of breath.

I don't think she noticed me, but she was kind of jittery as she walked up the stairs. She kept glancing in my direction with a concerned expression on her face. She didn't appear to be scared at all but it was rather as if she was trying to work something out.

I breathed a sigh of relief once she had passed by. I immediately regretted this as it brought her head snapping around to stare in my direction. She had definitely heard something. Fortunately Renee came to my aid.

"Can we please have the bill?" she called out, attracting the waitresses' attention.

The waitress turned and made her way over to the table and began clearing up the dishes. This gave me a few seconds window to make it down the remainder of the stairs. I almost threw myself down the final few steps as they floated into view and made my way across to the closed door. This was my next challenge. How could I open the door without people noticing? Renee certainly hadn't made this easy.

The door opened inwards, so it would be very obvious. I'd have to wait until someone left and then follow on their coat tails. It was definitely risky. I wasn't sure I could pull that off and the chance of discovery was too great.

In the end I decided to simply ignore good common sense and make a mad dash for the door. I almost threw myself at the door handle and pulled it open with a jerk. Almost every head in the room immediately snapped around to look at the door that opened by itself.

By then I was already in the alley outside.

I glanced back and watched as one of the waitresses walked over to the door and quizzically began to inspect the hinges. This distraction almost led me to disaster. There was a solid thump on my right side. Someone had walked into me.

I heard a gasp and a curse and had to throw myself to the ground to avoid the probing hand that shot in my direction. The person who'd walked into me groped around as he tried to figure out what they'd just walked into. I scooted myself against the wall of the alley hoping that the shadows against the wall would be enough to completely obscure my presence. I waited and watched warily. The person who had walked into me was an old man. He appeared to be scowling and looking around for someone to abuse.

He eventually hobbled off, cursing.

I'd learnt from my experience with the waitress in the restaurant not to give myself away with a sigh of relief. I got to my feet and continued up the alley. I realised about three steps in that this wasn't going to be easy. The alley was crowded with people going to and from restaurants.

If I were visible it would have been easy to navigate my way to the end of the alley, as people would move out of my way. However, as I was now invisible they hopefully wouldn't see me and thus I was the one who was forced to move.

While I was weaving through traffic I ended up knocking into a few people, fortunately as it was busy most people just assumed that someone had bumped into them and moved on. There were several people, however, that began to look around in a panic as they realised that there was no-one close enough to knock into them.

The whole process was infuriatingly slow. It must have taken me at least ten minutes to get here and I hadn't even made it half way up the alley.

I must have been slower than I thought because a bright flash of mana caught my attention as Renee came leaping out from the upper balcony of the restaurant and into the alley. With a quick flick of her wrist she secured a mana thread onto one of the buildings and with a deft hand she pulled herself onto the building.

I couldn't see her features due to the invisibility field but I could imagine her mocking grin as she turned and looked down at me. She gestured towards the rooftop just above me. Shit, why didn't I think of that? That would have solved everything. I didn't need to bother with the crowds if I'm on the rooftops. The only issue with this was that this would require me to keep a field and a thread active at once. I'd never tried that before. But I had handled multiple threads – that wouldn't be much different would it? Well, no time like the present to find out.

This was my first attempt to do this and I mistakenly assumed it would be easy. I was able for short times at least to handle multiple mana threads without too much difficulty. This was much more difficult.

The mana thread I sent out was a feeble one and immediately dissipated as soon as it reached my desired target.

"Relax, let the mana field just continue doing its thing," Renee's voice suddenly whispered in my ear.

I glanced about nervously but she was still on top of the building. She'd somehow projected her voice down to me. It was kind of creepy as she had sounded like she was right behind me.

"You can do this," Renee urged.

I tried again. This time I focused more on the mana thread and to my satisfaction the thread was a good one and held. Unfortunately, I noticed out of the corner of my eye someone's head whip around and look in my direction.

I immediately dropped the thread and refocused on the field that was maintaining my invisibility. I hurriedly moved away from where I had been standing as two people wandered over into that space. I had luckily spotted them out of the corner of my eye through the blurry haze that the invisibility field was projecting around me. I couldn't see them properly but I could hear them talking as I crouched near the wall.

"What is it?" a male voice called over to the girl.

"I thought I saw something," she replied curiously.

"What?" The male voice grumbled, obviously disgruntled. "There's no-one there, come on, we're late enough as it is."

"There was someone there!" the girl insisted, but she grudgingly followed the man who was stomping angrily away.

"Well that was close," Renee's disembodied voice whispered in my ear. "I can't hear you by the way, just in case you're replying."

I nodded back even though I was pretty sure she wouldn't be able to see such a subtle movement from her distance and tried again. There was only a knife's edge of a margin of error. Any loss of focus would result in an instant degradation of power in either the mana thread or the mana field.

This delicate balance of focus that was more taxing that I thought it would be. I felt that I was sweating profusely already. With a flick of my fingers I sent a mana thread outwards from my palm, latching it onto the corner of a roof between two buildings. The world around me narrowed into two objects. The field surrounding me, and the thread that I'd latched onto the roof above me.

It was one of those moments where you're in the middle of doing something difficult and that little voice at the back of your head whispers 'Don't choke'. It's all you can think about and your concentration starts to waver and unless you're very lucky you will end up choking.

I had a choice at this point. I could either drop the mana field surrounding me, which would make me visible to the people below, or I could release the thread and drop down into the alley. As I was hanging from the second story of a building I didn't much care for either of my options.

"Just breathe," Renee's voice whispered into my ear.

I took another deep breath and found it wasn't so bad now that I was calmer. The little voice inside my head had been silenced and I completed my ascent. With a sigh of relief I gripped the side of the building and turned to look at Renee's ghostly form standing across from me.

She made a slight saluting motion with her hand and with a delicate flip swung from the building roof over onto another building a block away.

"Well done," Renee's voice floated over. "Now let's see if you can keep up."

It was an impressive leap. She'd covered almost fifty metres with one leap and now appeared to be waiting for me. I'd have to figure out how she was projecting her voice like that. I could see that there was a slight mana element in the air. It was nebulous and hard to see through my invisibility field. I'd need to see it closer while I wasn't invisible to try to figure out how she was doing it.

"Are you coming or not?" her voice demanded, disgruntled.

I took off into a running lope across the rooftops.

Once I reached the end of the block, I threw out a thread and latched onto one of the skyscrapers several blocks away. It was fortunate that I'd already practiced this before when I was skating in the car park of my local shopping centre several weeks ago.

This would be a bad time to make a mistake. I could clearly see the street below me and realised that I was at least three or four storeys in the air. If I dropped to the ground now I'd create a large pizza-shaped splatter on the pavement. I couldn't help grinning maniacally. This was quite a rush. I wish I'd thought to bring my skates. Now that would have brought back the old thrill.

I saw Renee launch herself from the side of her building to land gracefully on top of one of the buildings below us. She rolled into a tight loop and came to her feet instantly, taking off across the rooftops. I had the height advantage but Renee was closer to the target. It was a race. If I didn't do something drastic I'd definitely lose. With callous disregard for my own safety I threw myself free from my thread and free fell onto the roof just directly in front of Renee.

I broke my fall at the last minute by throwing a thread directly at the ground beneath and using it to stop my descent. The impact was jarring and I was forced down onto one knee as I landed but I was surprised at how well this had worked.

"Nice," Renee commented as I turned to block her from passing me.

"You're changing the rules." Renee chuckled as she

attempted to circle around me. "You're not supposed to block the other person's path."

I moved around to intercept her. I had no doubt that she could easily get past me but she seemed to be playing along.

"You never said there were any rules." I grinned. "What are you going to do about it?"

Renee laughed as a thread lashed out from her hands. I was taken by surprise as Renee took out my feet from under me. I wasn't hurt at all, but I was thrown to the ground and had the wind knocked out of me.

"Cheat." Renee laughed as she vaulted over me.

I quickly rolled onto my side and desperately threw a mana thread at Renee. I grinned as I felt it connect. It wrapped around Renee's waist and pulled her back down onto the roof. Renee let out a shriek of outrage but was back on her feet instantly. She lashed out with a mana thread at my torso which I intercepted with a flick of my own thread. I was pretty sure she was only toying with me, but it was fun nonetheless.

Renee sent a much harder swipe at head height. If this one connected I'm sure it would have taken my head off. I threw everything I had at it to deflect it away from me.

The impact of our mana threads caused a super nova effect in the mana particles within our threads and caused a loud explosion of noise and light.

"Hey! Play nice," I gasped.

Renee just grinned.

"You started cheating," Renee chucked as she launched her next attack.

Duelling with mana threads is nothing like fighting with swords. For one, unlike a sword, reach is not an issue. The mana thread can extend or decrease in length as required. The second factor is that mana threads can bend and weave as per the wielder's direction. This made it difficult to predict where an attack was going to come from. Renee would launch a feint which would be easily blocked and then with the same swipe, curl the thread back to attack from another angle. It made for a nerve-racking duel as any movement made by your opponent could be an attack. Any motion, however slight, could be twisted to launch a thread in a new direction. It was lucky that Renee wasn't trying to actively kill me, as I'm sure that she'd had the opportunity on several occasions.

"You're not even thinking about the invisibility field anymore, are you?" Renee asked as we passed in a particularly explosive exchange.

"No," I replied. I was surprised that I hadn't realised it until it had been pointed out.

"Not bad, Twitch. Not bad," Renee complimented as she launched a vicious swipe at my head.

I had already picked up on her habit of talking to act as a decoy for an attack so I wasn't surprised when her strike came. I threw myself to one side to avoid her attack and sent my own attack at Renee's exposed side. Renee cursed and had to throw herself onto the ground. My thread sailed harmlessly over her head.

"Okay," she grunted as she launched an attack from the ground, "but let's see what you do now."

Renee swivelled forward aggressively and rose to her feet. A second thread lanced out from her left hand and I frantically stumbled back as she brought two threads to bear. There was no way I was going to be able to manage two threads and a field. I didn't even try. I was amazed that I was doing as well as I was with a single thread, but it was now obvious that I was over-matched.

Renee had launched a particularly fast strike with her left hand, which I was amazed that I had managed to block. My mana thread had seemed to move of its own accord. Unfortunately this strike was only the beginning of my problems. As Renee spun around, her right hand came back around and her other mana thread swung around in an underarm arch towards my stomach. I don't know how but it was again hastily and luckily blocked.

I actively retreated at high speed across the rooftop. The problem was Renee was slowly and inexorably pushing me towards the triangular skylight in the centre of the rooftop and there was very little I could do to stop her.

"Do you give up?" Renee hissed at me with a grin as she spun towards me on her next pass.

"Never, I'll take anything..."

But I never got a chance to finish my sentence as with a vicious swipe Renee swept my mana thread out of the way and her second thread caught me just under the ribs. Time seemed to slow down for me. I could see her thread coming at me at high speed but there was absolutely nothing I could do about it. I attempted to drop the invisibility field and erect a shield at the last second, but I must have been too late. The impact of the mana thread drove my body backwards and through the skylight behind me.

This obviously wasn't Renee's intention as I heard her curse when I fell through the glass and down into the room below. I must have immediately gone into shock because I didn't really feel the impact. I appeared to have dropped into a kitchen of some sort, but it was too dark to really see where I was. The only light in the room was from the broken window above me.

"Shit," Renee called down. "I'm sorry! Are you okay?"

"My shoulder hurts," I called with a slight chuckle. For some reason I found this reply very funny.

"Don't move," Renee ordered as she prepared to jump down into the room.

I reached around and felt my left shoulder, which was stinging slightly. Strangely enough my side where Renee had struck me had gone cold but there was no pain. The only pain I felt was from my shoulder. I brought my hand back and I could see a dull red stain on my fingers.

It was clearly visible in the moonlight.

"Renee, I'm bleeding," I called out.

Renee landed with a slight grunt. "There's a lot of blood," she commented darkly as she moved towards me.

"Does it look bad?"

"Don't move," she ordered as I tried to rise. Renee leaned over me. Her face became a mask of horror and guilt as she inspected the scene. "I need more light," she muttered as she walked around to my right.

Renee raised her hand and built a small ball of mana into a sphere. She then flexed her fingers and launched it several metres into the air. When it reached the apex of its journey it exploded like fireworks. It may have been the blood loss or the shock, but the overall effect was breathtakingly beautiful. The mana cast a faint blue halo over everything. It was even casting shadows throughout the room… It was producing light!

Each mana particle was reacting with the air around it. I could see little droplets of mana igniting in the air and falling to the ground. It was like it was snowing mana. There was a faint sizzling noise as the mana wafted to the ground. The reaction repeated itself as each mana particle faded and fell to the ground.

I heard Renee gasp as she again looked down. I turned on my side and saw I'd basically splattered onto the side of a table in the centre of the kitchen.

There was so much blood, too much blood.

"Don't move," Renee ordered again calmly, but I could tell there was a degree of hysteria in her voice.

"Renee, it's okay," I murmured.

Renee rolled me onto my side and a choke escaped her lips. I couldn't tell if it was a laugh or a cry.

"Well, it's a light cut," Renee commented clinically.

"Light cut? That's a lot of blood for a light cut."

Renee swiped her finger along the edge of the table and brought it to my lips.

Tomato sauce.

"You must have landed on a bottle of tomato sauce." Renee smiled, her eyes glittering with nervous amusement.

"I tried to raise a shield," I explained tentatively.

"Yeah, I think I saw it as you were disappearing through the window," Renee commented. "Your shield must have broken your fall and crushed the tomato sauce bottle".

"Can I get up now?"

"I guess." Renee shrugged. "Be careful though, there's a lot of broken glass on the table, there must have been some glasses on the table too."

I tentatively leaned forward to allow Renee to better see the table under me.

"Your back looks like something out of a horror movie." Renee chuckled. "Fortunately it appears to be mostly sauce."

"I think you owe me a new shirt." I grinned.

"Lean further forward," Renee ordered. "There are bits of glass in your shirt."

I leant forward and let Renee inspect my back.

"Neat trick with the light," I commented.

"Quiet," Renee ordered curtly. "There's quite a bit of glass in your back, doesn't seem too bad though, it must have happened when you lowered the shield."

"Small mercies eh?" I chuckled.

My back was beginning to sting a little.

"We should probably get out of here," I commented, glancing around. "Someone may have heard the noise when I came through the ceiling."

"Yeah, I think I've got most of the big pieces, but we should go," Renee agreed. "We'll head back to my place and I'll patch you up properly."

"Do we need to do anything about the light?"

Renee shook her head. "No, it'll last about half an hour then it'll go out by itself."

She helped me off the table. I cringed slightly as my back began to tingle. I sent a mana thread up through the now gaping hole in the roof and pulled myself back onto the roof. Looking back through the smashed skylight I noticed with some degree of chagrin that we'd made one hell of a mess down there. The broken glass from the skylight was scattered across the floor and some of the pieces on the table were covered in tomato sauce. The whole kitchen had the feel of a particularly grisly murder scene. I had a brief moment of guilt and sympathy for the poor person who was to be greeted by that sight when they came into work tomorrow morning.

"It looks pretty bad, doesn't it?" Renee observed as she joined me on the rooftop.

My fall through the window had really done a number on this place.

"Come on. Let's get you bandaged up," Renee called.

I agreed wholeheartedly. My shoulder was really starting to ache.

I reactivated the mana field around me and made several small jumps across buildings. Renee led the way guiding me from building to building. She skilfully directed us towards the best places to land and to launch from. I got the feeling this wasn't the first time she'd done this.

* * * *

Renee let us into her apartment from the balcony door and in a brisk manner went to the hallway cupboard and retrieved two towels and placed them over her coffee table.

"Okay, lose the shirt," she ordered as she began to pour some water into a bowl.

"What? No flowers or chocolate first?" I quipped as I removed my shirt. Renee didn't comment as she was busy directing a lamp to shine down on to the table. It was beginning to look like one of those scenes in the movies where someone is about to be interrogated. After I had removed my shirt I noticed with annoyance that the left side of the shirt was completely shredded.

"You definitely owe me a new shirt." I grinned as I presented the shirt to her.

"I'll lend you one," Renee commented. "Now, lie flat."

I lay flat on the table and let Renee get to work. It wasn't the most comfortable of surfaces.

She had to adjust the light source several times before she was satisfied.

"Yeah, this doesn't look too bad at all," she murmured, dabbing my shoulder with a damp cloth.

I realised she was trying to pick up the small slivers of glass that still might be in or around the wound.

"We might not have to take you to hospital after all," Renee determined.

"Hospital?"

"Yeah, glass wounds can be bad," Renee explained, "especially when they're shatter wounds like yours."

"How do you know how to do this?" I flinched as Renee gently dabbed my shoulder with a damp cloth.

"I've had some experience with first aid," Renee answered.

"I suppose this kind of thing happens a lot, huh?"

"No, not really, but accidents sometimes happen. All in all you're not that injured… considering," Renee reflected.

"Yeah, I'd like to know why I'm not more seriously hurt," I asked grimly. "Some of those glass shards from the roof were huge."

It didn't take a whole heap of guessing to figure out what would have happened if one of the glass shards had come down onto me.

"I'd guess your shield held out until your impact with the table, or maybe just afterwards if you bounced. In fact I'd say that's likely the case. These cuts would be far more serious if you hit them from that height."

"Bounced?"

"Possibly." Renee shrugged. "You fell quite a distance."

"You're telling me," I chuckled.

"Your body really can take a pounding though. You've got to be impressed by that." Renee smirked.

"Gee thanks, it's always nice to hear a girl say that to you," I snickered.

"I think I'm almost done."

"It is starting to hurt less," I commented.

"I've removed three largish pieces of glass and God knows how many small ones," Renee remarked.

The largest piece was no larger than a twenty-cent piece.

"Okay, I'm going to apply some antiseptic now, this may sting," Renee warned.

It did, it stung a lot. I tried not to yelp but I did wince.

"Okay, I think we're good," Renee stated as she began to clean up.

"You've lost a little bit of blood. Might be best if you stay down for a while," Renee ordered as she deposited a glass of orange juice in front of me.

"I do feel a little light-headed."

"That's to be expected," Renee replied. "Next time though, learn to block."

She grinned cheekily at me as she moved to clean up the bloody towels and scraps of glass.

"Good advice." I nodded. "Although maybe next time, don't hit me so hard."

"Could have been worse," Renee retorted. "I could have knocked you in the other direction – onto the street."

"That's not really helping your cause."

"No, not really," Renee replied ruefully. "For what it's worth, I'm sorry."

"Hey, don't sweat it." I shrugged, wincing as my shoulder complained at the effort. "As you said – accidents happen."

"No, it's not right. I could have seriously hurt you," Renee replied, moving to sit down in front of me. "If my grandfather were here, he'd be seriously angry with me."

"It's okay. I'm fine, besides it all worked out okay," I assured her, peering into her eyes, which were only inches away from mine. "Besides, I learned a valuable lesson."

"What? Not to fall through sky lights?" Renee scoffed.

"Something like that." I grinned. "That was a pretty neat trick with the light though."

"It's pretty simple." Renee shrugged. "Want to learn it?"

"Can you show me now?"

"Sure." Renee nodded as she leant back into a cross-legged position. She then held out her hands in a cupping motion and began to move mana from her hand into a small ball. Wisps of mana left her fingers and collated into the shimmer ball of mana held in her palm.

"This is similar to the technique used for awareness right?"

"It's mana detonation theory, yeah," Renee confirmed with a nod.

"Look at how small I'm making the ball though," Renee explained. "The trick is to keep the actual detonation small."

"Oh?"

"Yeah, too large and it'll burn out too quickly," Renee continued. "Notice also how I'm building the wisps."

The wisps were wafer thin and slightly curved. They wafted gently from her fingers until they were absorbed into the mana sphere.

"The important thing is to keep your focus on the ball. Don't let it detonate before you're ready."

"Then what?" I asked, leaning forward.

"Throw and release," Renee stated simply as she threw the mana sphere into the air.

The ball exploded with a flickering sizzle and little particles of mana were flung from the centre and gently hung there in the air. It took several seconds before they began to flare and slowly fall to the ground like snow. Each particle flickered and emitted a faint light as it fell. It bathed the room in a blue halo of light. Renee switched off the light, leaving us illuminated entirely by the mana sphere hanging over us.

"Pretty," I commented.

"Better than a lava lamp," Renee said sarcastically. "Okay, now you try."

"Can I get that shirt you promised?" I asked, very aware that I still wasn't wearing a top.

"Oh, sure," Renee replied and disappeared into one of the other rooms. "I think this might be large enough," she grunted as she returned several seconds later. She threw a white shirt at me.

It did. But just, it was quite tight around the chest

and was uncomfortably tight on my now very tender shoulder.

"There's only one problem."

"What's that?" Renee asked as she returned to the couch.

"Sportsgirl?" I grinned, gesturing towards the logo emblazoned across the chest.

"What? Did you expect me to have men's shirts?" Renee smiled with a raised eyebrow. "Perhaps one with the Playboy bunny logo on it?"

"Well, no, I guess not."

"At least it's not pink with rabbits on it," Renee continued, "that was the other option. I don't have much that would fit you so count yourself lucky that I have even that one."

"Fair enough." I chuckled as I pulled myself into a seated position on the table. "Although I really doubt you have a pink shirt. You don't seem the fluffy pink rabbit type of girl."

"Perhaps not," Renee smiled.

I grinned at her.

"Are you going to try the spell or what?" Renee snapped.

"Oh, right." I smiled as I moved myself into a more comfortable position and readied myself.

"It's delicate work," Renee explained, "but not that difficult. It's usually one of the first spells we learn."

I concentrated on the small ball, slowly adding slivers of mana onto it.

"Too much," Renee instructed. "Try again."

It took me several tries before Renee was satisfied that I had it. When she was finally happy, I had a very small sphere of mana floating gently several centimetres above my fingers.

"Now what?" I asked.

"Okay, you're focusing on maintaining the mana now," Renee began. "What you need to do is throw the mana away from yourself and then detonate it."

"How?"

"The same damned way you detonated the awareness spell," Renee snapped. "I swear you're the most irritating student I've ever had. You do the advanced stuff more easily than the basics!"

"Natural talent?" I quipped with a grin.

"No, that's not it," Renee snapped. "Although that's part of it. You are very good at what you do manage to learn."

It was hard not to be overwhelmed by her inadvertent praise.

"…for a beginner," she added with a grin.

"You've done things with a skill level that would have most learner mages throw their hands up in despair and yet the most basic theories you can't grasp. It just doesn't make any sense," Renee accused.

"Hey! I get there in the end!" I complained, hurt by the accusation. "It's not like I'm stupid or anything."

"That's not my point," Renee cut me off. "Now detonate the damned mana."

I tentatively threw the ball into the air and willed it to detonate. With a small flash of light and a sizzling noise the mana exploded into small particles. I got to my feet to inspect one. I felt a slight tingle as my hand passed through the particle and watched as the particle was absorbed into my skin.

"Feels funny doesn't it," Renee commented.

I nodded in agreement. I was fascinated how they just appeared to hang in mid-air.

"Strange how they just hang there," I mused.

"They hang until they're out of power," Renee replied, "then they fall."

"Pretty though."

Renee simply nodded and casually reached back to turn off the lamp behind her. The interplay of lights on the wall increased in intensity as the other illumination in the room was removed.

"If I was a stoner, this would be better than Pink Floyd." I joked, sliding over onto the couch next to her, casually resting my arm on the back of the couch.

"Smooth," Renee teased as she leaned over and rested her head against my shoulder.

"Hey, at least I didn't do a yawn and reach," I protested.

"Good point, I'd have had to hit you if you did that," Renee smirked.

"I'm glad I didn't push it then, after the last time you hit me," I commented. "I'm not sure I'd survive the experience."

"Yeah," Renee agreed. "How's your shoulder now?"

"Itches a bit, but that's probably just the tacky shirt." I laughed.

"Suck it up, princess," Renee chuckled as she nestled further into the crook of my arm.

I sighed gently and pulled my arm around her protectively.

"Devon?" Renee whispered tentatively.

"Yeah?"

"Are you sure this is what you want?"

I didn't answer her at first. Instead I leant forward and kissed the back of her head, pulling her in close to my chest. "I'm sure."

"I'll be no good for you," Renee whispered desperately. "I'll end up breaking your heart and tearing your life apart, I won't be able to help myself."

I wasn't sure if she was trying to talk me or herself out of this.

"Our kind just doesn't play happy families," Renee reflected sadly.

"There must be a first for everything – even this," I whispered back, holding her tighter as I moved my face down next to hers.

"Don't say I didn't warn you," Renee whispered as she turned her head and our lips connected. The feel of her lips desperately pressing against mine sent a shiver down my spine. In that one moment I could feel her need, her desire. She wanted me, but what's more she needed me and I her. I guess I filled some dark part of her that she kept secret and hidden from the world around her. I couldn't tell you how I knew this, but I knew it with a burning intensity that filled my core. I knew this with the knowledge too that she had the same intuition for me.

She knew me as no other had and no other would.

I pulled her against me as I lay back onto the couch. The mana light was failing and casting the room in a dim light, but I could see the mana in her eyes flicker with her need, a need mirrored in mine.

It was that one perfect moment that they talk of in the romantic movies. I was just me and she was simply herself. No jokes, no pretence – everything we had built around ourselves for protection was swept away.

Pain, sorrow, loss and regret were all accepted and cast down as we revelled in the bonding of our union. Our bodies entwined as the mana flowed freely across our bodies, reacting to each other as the particles began a slow dance across our flesh. We never said another word to each other that night – there was no need. We simply lay under the fading light of the mana glow and watched with a contented smile the slight fizzle as the last mana particle that hung above us winked out of existence.

I woke up with Renee curled up in my arms, asleep with her head resting against my chest. In her slumber the lines on her face had softened and the mask of indifference and mocking was gone, replaced by a look of contentment. If I thought she was beautiful before, I was wrong. She was breathtaking. I gazed down at her as if it was the first time I'd seen her and knew in my heart that things would never be the same. I was forever changed by the experience, at long last I was hers and she was mine.

I have looked back on this night many times since. When the pain of remembering the past becomes too much I cast my mind back and remember that night with a smile. It has always been a beacon of hope for me in these dark days. I am not too shallow to admit that in a strange way Renee was my salvation and redemption. It was perhaps this fact alone that allowed me to stand when those around me fell and were cast down.

CHAPTER TEN

"…and then what happened?" Tony asked with a goofy grin on his face.

"Well, then I went back to Dad's," I replied with an equally cheesy grin, "and it was around then that I realised I had seven missed calls from him."

"Wow, was he pissed?"

"Yeah," I reflected sadly, "he grounded me."

"Sucks to be you," Tony teased.

"Actually, all in all, not so much," I replied. "I think I'd do it all again the same way."

Tony nodded and patted me on the shoulder causing me to wince.

"That's the shoulder, eh?"

"Yeah," I grumbled back, "so I'd appreciate you not whacking it."

Tony and I were walking home from school. I couldn't wait to tell someone what had happened and by necessity I couldn't exactly tell anyone else. This was the first time I'd gotten Tony alone all day.

"Did you get her number this time?" he asked.

"Yep."

"The right one this time?"

I nodded again.

"Are you sure?" Tony pressed.

I shook my head. "I'm too scared to try it."

"I can understand that," Tony chuckled. "You should call her though."

"What? Now?"

"Yep," Tony replied. "Go on, I'll wait."

I tentatively pulled my phone from my jacket and dialled her number and waited for the several rings it took before a soft female voice answered.

"Hello?"

"Renee?" I asked tentatively.

"Yes, who am I speaking with?" she responded.

"It's Devon – you know… from the other night," I babbled, not really paying much attention to what I was saying.

"Yes, Devon," Renee replied dryly. "I didn't need the reminder."

"I panicked," I replied. "I didn't expect this to actually be your number. You've given me so many fake ones."

"Third number's the charm," Renee quipped. "Did you actually want something? Or are you just calling me to prove you're even more annoying over the phone than in person?"

My mind was racing desperately to come back with an answer. Any answer that wouldn't make me look like a complete idiot. I didn't come up with much.

"… and now there's a stunned silence at the other end," Renee cut in after a few seconds. "Well done,

Devon, your phone manner is perfect."

"Hey, cut me some slack," I blurted out. "I was just ringing to see if this was actually your number."

"Didn't plan ahead as to what you were going to actually say then, huh?" I could just picture Renee's twisted smile as I heard her words.

"No, guess not."

"Want a do-over?"

"Please."

"Think it will help?"

"Probably not." I conceded.

"Well, I've got to go, but for the record it was nice to hear from you," Renee replied. "Call me again when you've actually got anything interesting to say."

"I will," I promised hastily. "Bye!" I shot in just before I heard the click of Renee hanging up.

"Well that went well," Tony commented as I put the phone back in my pocket.

"Yeah."

"Maybe you're getting better talking to women." Tony suggested.

"Maybe," I nodded.

"Wonders never cease. Are you coming over to Sarah's tonight?"

"No, why?"

"Some study group thing, I just assumed you knew about it," Tony continued.

"Well, better not then," I replied, concerned. Maybe Sarah was still avoiding me.

I knew she was still a little sore with me over the whole fiasco with Tina, but I didn't think it was this personal. It usually took Sarah a couple of weeks to get over things and then she'd be fine. Maybe this was going to take a little longer.

"No," Tony smiled, obviously noticing my expression, "I'm sure it was just that you weren't around when the plans were made."

I nodded half-heartedly. I wasn't so certain that this was the case.

"I'd turn up anyway."

"I don't think so," I said.

"You're really reading more into this than there is."

"Maybe," I replied, "but if I am right I really don't want to make a scene."

"You won't!" Tony announced, throwing his arm over my shoulders. "Besides, what's the worst that can happen?"

"You live your life by that philosophy. Don't you?"

Tony nodded agreeably.

"Well, it's all academic anyway," I replied dryly.

"Oh? How so?"

"I'm grounded."

"I thought you were just grounded at your dad's?" Tony grinned.

"It doesn't really work that way."

"Yeah, it's annoying when parents talk," Tony replied as we rounded the corner into my street. "Well, you'll be missed." Tony chuckled, tousling my hair and pushing me in the direction of my house.

"Have fun," I called as he turned to walk towards Sarah's. I headed straight home.

Mum had left some dinner for me in fridge and I spent the night hitting the books. I doubted that it was productive but it was long overdue. We got our results from our exam on the following day and as I'd expected I didn't do that well, but it could have been worse. At least I'd passed, barely. I suppose it's all a matter of expectation. I wasn't too upset with my result.

The results were supposed to be private but Sarah had demanded that I share mine with her. Tina was with her and I didn't really want her to know. Still, I told them.

Sarah muttered, "Well, that's better than expected," But Tina was appalled. "You need to do better for your finals," she said.

"Not really, I don't really need to get good grades," I reminded her. "I'm not going to university."

"I thought you were thinking of deferring," Sarah said. "You still need the grades."

"That's not even the point," Tina scolded me.

"So? What? I'm studying for study's sake?" I scoffed.

"No, you're studying to prove that you're capable of learning new information," Tina lectured. "University aside, the ability to teach yourself new things is a fundamental skill that you're going to need no matter what you end up doing."

"You've been practicing that speech a bit haven't you?" I teased gently.

"A little," Tina admitted with a smile, "but I do wish you'd take this more seriously."

"I will. I promise." I wasn't overly sure how serious my promise was.

There was an awkward silence.

"Tony tells me you're now seeing someone. That was quick? What's her name? Renee?" Tina said suddenly.

Both Sarah and I to turned to gape at her.

"Tony really should learn to keep his mouth shut," Sarah grunted angrily.

"No, no it's okay," Tina responded. "I asked why Devon wasn't studying with us last night."

"I got grounded."

"Yeah, Tony said that too," Tina continued. "Is she nice? Does she make you happy?" Her voice sounded bitter.

"I think so. It's early days though," I replied, hoping she'd drop the subject.

"Tony said you were interested in her before we went out." she pressed.

"Well, kind of, yes," I mumbled, scratching my head. "I'm sorry," I mumbled again, hoping another apology might help.

I could literally see Sarah's eyes targeting me like a laser. It was like she was daring me to put one foot wrong. Sweat began to form on my brow and my hands began to get a little clammy.

"Oh," Tina continued, "I'm so sorry, Devon, I realise now in hindsight that I did kind of force the relationship onto you."

I could see Sarah's eyes narrowing and taking aim. I felt like those guys in the action movies where they know they've got the sniper's laser target on their forehead but are too scared to move.

"No," I gasped, desperately trying to avoid both Sarah and Tina's gaze. "Don't apologise, you did nothing wrong – nothing at all."

"Did you have fun with me though? When we were together?" Tina asked nervously, her hands crunched up before her.

I nodded back and tentatively pulled her into a hug.

"Just, stop," I whispered. "There's really no need for this, when I was with you I was definitely happy, it just wasn't meant to be, you know?"

Tina nodded and pulled back.

"Thank you, Devon," she whispered as she hurried off down the corridor.

"Smooth," Sarah commented as we both watched her leave.

"Leave me alone," I grumbled. "I'm not really in the mood to be mocked."

"Actually, that was sincere," Sarah replied. "You're a good person, Devon."

"I'm going to kill your boyfriend when I see him next," I announced as we began our walk to our next class.

"Not unless I see him first," Sarah vowed.

* * * *

I caught up with Tony at lunchtime.

"Ouch!" Tony exclaimed as I clipped him over the head. "What was that for?"

"You know damned well what for!"

"Sarah already hit me for that!"

"It's true! I did." Sarah grinned.

"Well, I'm sure Sarah's girly punches don't count," I retorted, throwing myself into the seat next to Tony and placing my tray on the table.

"Oh? You want some of this mister?" Sarah blustered, flexing her arms.

"Sarah, as much as I love you, you'll never really be in the running for muscle woman of the year."

"Ouch!" I exclaimed as Sarah's right hook caught me just below the shoulder.

I could see Tony cringe as the blow impacted. She'd hit my injured shoulder. It hurt like blazes.

"Take it like a man!" Sarah exclaimed triumphantly, noting the expression on my face. "Now who's being girly?"

"Uhh, Sarah," Tony began, "that was Devon's injured shoulder."

"Oh my God!" Sarah exclaimed. "Are you okay? I didn't mean to! What injured shoulder?" Sarah blurted out quickly.

"It's nothing, I'm fine," I assured her.

"What happened?" Sarah pressed.

How could I tell her anything without explaining the mana though? Anything else would make Renee come out in a bad light. I wanted my friends to like her, to accept her. "It's nothing. I just fell through some glass and cut myself."

Sarah sucked all the breath into her mouth in one gasp and went a little white.

"I'm so sorry."

"It's okay," I assured her, "it's really not that bad."

A stunned silence descended over the table as none of us were much in the mood to talk. I was desperately trying to think of something – anything that would lighten the mood. Unfortunately I was coming up blank.

"Gee, way to kill the conversation, Sarah!" Tony snickered.

"Ouch!" he exclaimed as Sarah's hand clipped him across the back of the head.

"I thought you might have learned your lesson about hitting people," Tony muttered, ruefully rubbing the back of his head.

"At the moment, I'm tempted to throw you through a window," Sarah grumbled.

"I don't recommend it, it hurts!" I chuckled. This elicited a giggle from Sarah as she leaned forward and kissed Tony on the cheek.

"There, all better!" she cooed in his ear. I couldn't tell if she was being sarcastic or not.

"Well, I'm feeling quite abused today," Tony announced. "That's the third time this hour someone's hit my head and the day's not even half over!"

"Eh, no harm." I snickered. "It's not like you're going to damage brain cells."

"Hey! My brain cells are an endangered species, man! Endangered!" he drawled, drawing out the last word.

"They're practically extinct!" I shot back.

"There was no need to agree with me," he mumbled forlornly.

"So? Study group Monday nights, eh?" I asked once we'd stopped laughing.

Sarah nodded.

"You don't think Mondays are bad enough as it is?"

"Well, Monday just makes more sense." Sarah nodded. "We're all nice and fresh for the new week."

"Sadist!"

"Do you want to join us?"

"I can't! I'm grounded," I grunted.

"You know your mum would let you come to a study session! I guess you are trying to make a good excuse," Sarah said. "How long are you grounded for anyway?"

"A week."

"What did you do to deserve that?"

"I stayed out all night… And didn't tell Dad. I forgot to call him. I got home on Saturday morning and he was plenty pissed."

"Really? That seems kind of stupid," Sarah commented. "Your parents are pretty cool, and your dad is very chilled. If you'd called him he would have been okay with it".

"Yeah, I should have."

"Gettin' it 'awn," Tony drawled in a mock American accent, "can make a dude a bit distracted."

Sarah snorted into her drink. "Oh!" She laughed.

"Lucky Renee. Devon's not bad, I've had better though."

Tony and I snapped our heads around and gazed at her in shock. To my memory I'd never even kissed Sarah on the cheek. I was desperately trying to think when even a kiss might have happened and was coming up blank. What was she saying? Tony's eyes had narrowed and he was looking at me in a funny fashion.

"You should see your faces!" Sarah snickered, breaking out into a laugh.

"That's not funny!" Tony grumbled.

"Not funny," I agreed. "Besides," I said, grinning, "I'm much better than just not bad."

"Yeah," Sarah agreed readily. "Tina thought you were actually a pretty good kisser. A little eager though. Too much tongue."

I can't believe girls talk about this stuff. "And we're back to the insults!" I commented. "Story of my life really."

"Cheer up, buttercup." Sarah grinned. "Maybe your cougar girlfriend will teach you a few tricks!"

"I was wondering when someone was going to play that card," I smirked. "I thought it was going to be Tony though."

"Hell no, man – I think it's hot." Tony chuckled before being cut off by Sarah's hand clipping him across the back of the head again.

"How old is she anyway? Thirty?" Sarah asked, rubbing her hand.

"That one hurt, eh?" I grinned at Sarah, gesturing towards her cradled hand.

"Yeah, I clipped a knuckle that time."

"We're all just dripping with sympathy for you here," Tony smirked, rubbing the back of his head.

"You avoided the question," Sarah reminded me. "How old is Renee?"

"I don't actually know – in her twenties I think," I guessed. "A gentleman doesn't ask."

"I bet she's forty!" Tony chuckled. "Maybe in her fifties even!"

He intuitively ducked as Sarah's hand sailed across his head missing him narrowly. He didn't, however, dodge my fist, which landed solidly against his arm with a very satisfying thump.

"No fair!" he exclaimed. "You're ganging up on me!"

"Then don't be a prat!" Sarah admonished as Tony began rubbing his arm ruefully.

"That hurt!" he complained.

"Well it's nothing compared to what Renee would do to you if she had heard you!" I commented.

"Good point, I didn't think of that." Tony gulped as his face dropped. "You won't tell her will you?"

Tony's face fell as he realised the implications. He'd just mocked a girl who could telekinetically pick him up and throw him cleanly through a brick wall. Whilst I was pretty sure she wouldn't actually ever do it, it was amusing to let him think he was in trouble.

Well, it was funny until he actually started to look a little sick.

"My God!" Sarah exclaimed. "He's gone white! How scary is this girl?"

"She's really not scary," I protested. "Anyway you've already met her remember? That time at that club."

"Well, that was only for a few minutes and I didn't really get a chance to talk to her." Sarah's voice trailed off.

"Would you like to meet her?" I asked tentatively. I wasn't overly sure that Renee would want to meet my friends, but that did seem to be what Sarah was angling towards.

"Sure," Sarah replied. "We've got to make certain that she's got your best interests at heart."

"And if she doesn't?" I asked, worried.

"I'm pretty sure I can take her," Sarah announced, jokingly cracking her knuckles as both Tony and I exchanged furtive glances.

"Then let's hope it doesn't come to that," I agreed.

I had a dull ache in the pit of my stomach at the thought. Perhaps it would be better for all concerned if my friends never met her. Although I knew I could trust Tony, I didn't know how Renee would react if he inadvertently let it slip that he knew about mana.

Thinking back on my first experiences with her and the fury in her eyes when she first struck me I wasn't sure I'd survive that betrayal. Yes, perhaps it was best for everyone if they never met.

* * * *

The school week couldn't go quick enough for me. I couldn't wait to get back into the city on the weekend and see Renee again. Although I was technically still grounded I was pretty sure I'd be able to sneak away. Dad didn't actually spend that much time at home and I could make myself freaking invisible. How could he stop me?

I called Renee on Thursday night to check that she hadn't made plans for the weekend and wanted to hang out.

"Hey babe!" I greeted as Renee answered the phone. "How's it…"

"Don't call me that," Renee immediately cut me off, her voice dry.

"Honey?"

"That either."

"Darling?"

"No."

"Sweetie?"

"What am I? A low fat sugar replacement?"

"Pookie?"

"Okay buddy, now you're asking for it."

"How about snookums?"

"I'm going to seriously hurt you next time I see you," Renee promised "Seriously. Hurt."

"Snookums it is!" I grinned emphatically down the phone line.

"You call me snookums even once and it'll be the last thing you ever do."

"Fine, I won't call you snookums," I agreed with good grace, "though I do need to come up with a cute pet name for you though."

"I really don't see why," Renee replied. "Did you have a point to this conversation or were you simply trying to be more annoying than your last call?"

"I wanted to see if you were doing anything this weekend?"

"I do have some plans," Renee said coolly. "Why? Did you want to do something?"

"Yep." I agreed. "And I figured that now that you're my girlfriend and all…"

"Oh, so, now I'm your girlfriend, huh?" Renee asked pointedly, "just like that eh?"

"Yup."

"Oh, I don't think so, buddy boy," Renee snapped.

"No?" I stammered, a little confused and more than a little hurt.

"No, but if you're real nice to me, I might let you call yourself my boyfriend," she teased.

"Okay, that was just mean."

"I thought you'd appreciate it." Renee snickered.

"Okay… Well, what do you want to do?"

"Surprise me," Renee replied evenly.

"Um… well, you always see those couples sitting in Flagstaff Gardens. We could go do that?"

"Sounds boring." Renee yawned into the phone, but I was pretty sure she was faking it.

"Do you have a better idea?" I pressed.

"Well, no," Renee admitted grudgingly.

"Then my idea it is. We could bring a blanket and maybe some food, make an afternoon of it."

"When?" she asked.

"Saturday? Say one o'clock?"

"See you then, Twitch." Renee hung up before I could say, "See you then, snookums."

If she had heard that I was pretty sure that I would have paid for it, but damn me if it wasn't worth the risk.

Saturday afternoon couldn't come around quick enough to suit me. Friday school seemed to last for an eternity and I spent Friday night with Dad. He had grudgingly agreed to let me go out during the day on Saturday despite my grounding as long as I promised to be back in the evening. I'm sure the fact that I told him I was going to meet a girl had nothing to do with it. Although he had backed down from the argument pretty quickly after he had learnt that. It was possible that he realised that if he didn't give me permission I'd probably have just gone anyway. I reached the park twenty minutes early and surprisingly for a Saturday it was very busy. I'd occasionally walked through the park as it wasn't far from Dad's place, but I'd never been here on a Saturday afternoon though.

Renee hadn't arrived yet, so I selected a spot near a grove of trees off the beaten path, it had a fairly good view of the city skyline. Yeah, it seemed like a good spot. Renee was about half an hour late, but I wasn't that fussed. To be honest the sun was making me a little bit dozy.

"Nice spot," Renee called, waking me up.

"Yeah," I replied, "thanks."

"Were you asleep?"

"No, just resting my eyes," I murmured.

"Well, this is looking like it's going to be a pretty sub-par date then. If you can't stay awake." Renee rolled her eyes.

"This is a date?"

"Well, what would you call it then?"

"I'd call it a picnic!" I smirked cheekily.

"You're an idiot." Renee smiled as she threw herself onto the blanket next to me.

"True," I replied, "but I've got a pretty cute butt."

"How do you always know exactly what to say to make yourself seem completely devoid of any intelligence?"

"It's a gift!" I grinned, wrapping an arm around behind her. "Come on snookums, let's not argue!"

Renee's eyes narrowed.

"I bet you're thinking that with all these witnesses here I won't kick your arse around the park."

"I might like that." I leered.

"You're incorrigible."

"You're pretty," I whispered, kissing her on her forehead.

"That was the least smooth, most corny move I've ever heard."

"But it worked?"

"Do you see me kicking your arse around the park?" Renee smirked with a twisted grin.

"It worked? Man, you're a pushover!" I snickered.

"Shut up!" Renee sighed. "Before I put you out of my misery."

"I've brought some food," I announced. "It's in the hamper over there."

"No," Renee replied, "I'm good, maybe later."

She snuggled her head against my shoulder and pressed her body against my side.

"Yeah, me too." I sighed as I wrapped an arm around her and pulled her in close.

"Well, that at least was smooth," Renee whispered.

"You have to get in the last word, don't you?"

"Yes," Renee replied, "so shut up and let me and this will go much easier for both of us."

I think we may have drifted off for a while, which I suppose in hindsight probably wasn't the safest thing to do, but when I awoke Renee was sleeping gently in the crook of my arm. I was in the process of adjusting my arm which had fallen asleep when Renee stirred. Moving my arm must have woken her up.

"Sorry, didn't mean to wake you."

"That's okay," Renee replied sleepily. "I didn't mean to fall asleep."

"Yeah." I agreed. "I wonder how long we were out."

"An hour, maybe." Renee said, checking her watch for confirmation.

There were still a few people in the park but it had thinned out noticeably. There were several groups of picnickers sitting around talking and laughing, but for the most part we were pretty much alone.

"Want some food?" I gestured towards the hamper.

Renee nodded. "Is there anything to drink?"

"Um, no," I mumbled as I realised that I'd forgotten drinks, "but there's a store not far from here. I'll run and go get something."

Renee replied with a smile as she was inspecting the hamper.

"Just soft drink or something – but not cola," she called.

"Is mineral water okay?" I called back.

"Sure," she agreed readily. "Maybe orange or passionfruit flavoured?"

"No problems."

I had to pass through a grove of trees and then past a bowling green on my way to the store on the main road. It really wasn't more than a five-minute walk at a decent pace. I walked down an avenue of paths lined by trees one side and the road on the other. I wasn't really paying attention to where I was going until a flicker of light caught my attention.

I managed to see a figure quickly dart behind a tree a little way behind me. A circle of mana was evident on its chest. I grinned to myself. I didn't really understand the game, but it was obvious that Renee was following me. I began to whistle nonchalantly, which I realise in hindsight probably announced the fact that I'd seen her and began on my journey again. When I got going again the figure predictably began to follow me from behind the tree line. They were obviously trying to keep pace with me.

I could see the flicker of the mana circle from between the tree trunks as they passed from tree to tree. It would be interesting to see what would happen when I reached the road. Renee would have to come out of hiding.

I just hoped she'd remembered to bring the hamper with her. This garden was renowned for the possums being a little aggressive in the way of picnic food and it would ruin the day if we returned to our spot to find the hamper trashed. When I reached the road I couldn't see Renee. She must have gone around the other side of the bowling green. I crossed the road and made my way over to the store.

"Strange woman." I grinned to myself.

I paid for the drink and returned to our spot. Renee was sitting on the blanket with her legs crossed before her, slowly eating a sandwich. She was acting like nothing had happened.

"You're really awful at covert surveillance." I grinned as I sat down and passed the bottle over to her.

"Huh?" Renee asked with a raised eyebrow.

"I saw you."

"Saw me what?"

"Following me," I explained, a little less sure of myself.

"I wasn't following you." Renee looked genuinely confused.

"Sure you were," I insisted, "you were ducking around behind trees and stuff, trying to keep out of sight."

"I've been sitting right here," Renee retorted, "eating a sandwich."

She dutifully shook the sandwich at me in emphasis.

"Well, I saw someone," I insisted.

"Probably just someone walking their dog." Renee shrugged.

"Someone with mana?" I cut her off. "I definitely saw mana light."

Renee's face immediately fell and she got to her knees and set off an awareness blast. The mana rocketed out from her hands and the radius of the blast went out across the clearing.

Once the mana sphere reached the tree line we could both easily make out a figure lurking against the trees on the far side of the clearing. It had obviously been keeping its distance from us and trying to keep out of sight. However once the mana blast overtook it. It lit up like a beacon as the mana in its body reacted with that of the blast.

I glanced around, there wasn't too many other people in the park right now which I suppose was good, as this looked like it could get messy. The figure behind the trees shrugged and began walking towards us.

Renee's gasped and tensed up as she recognised the figure.

"Shield, now!" Renee hissed at me as the figure came closer.

With a quick flick of my wrist I wrapped a shield around myself, noting as I did so that Renee had already done the same. I hadn't even noticed her activating it. What the hell was going on? Renee was obviously rattled by this person.

The figure that emerged was a tall man, in his mid-twenties or maybe early thirties. He was wearing clothes that had obviously seen better days. Although that may have just been a stylistic thing as the jeans were quite ripped in several places.

He wore a khaki shirt over a white singlet and wore a long dusty black trench coat. He had long blonde hair that had been undercut and was pulled back into a ponytail. He was smirking as he approached.

"Hello Renee," he called as he got closer.

Renee didn't answer. Her expression was a curious mixture of rage and fear.

"That's far enough," Renee called harshly as he got closer.

He was only about ten metres or so away and came to a stop, his hands held outwards before him.

"Come now," he said, his arms held wide in a pose of submission. "This is all very rude."

He hadn't put up a shield yet and was still smirking widely. He had the feel of a crouching tiger about him and I didn't for one second doubt that should an attack come he wouldn't be found vulnerable.

"Come now, Renee," he repeated. "Surely this is unnecessary."

He gestured towards the shields surrounding us.

"Surely there's nothing to fear from an old friend who only wants to see how powerful you've become?"

"You're an unbalanced psychopath," Renee hissed at him, "and no friend of mine."

"I prefer to think that we simply took different paths," he replied with a chuckle.

Renee snorted but didn't answer.

I went to say something but Renee put her hand on my wrist, obviously indicating to remain silent. I quietly moved myself slightly in front of Renee protectively.

"Your bodyguard seems a little young," he commented.

"He's not my bodyguard," Renee snapped instantly.

"Looks like we hit a nerve did we?" He scoffed out a snorting laugh. "It's funny though, because he's acting like a bodyguard isn't he?"

"Don't," Renee whispered desperately. I wasn't sure who she was talking to – me or him.

"Apprentice then?" he continued, as he walked in a wide circle his eyes never leaving us. "Or perhaps he's your lover?"

His eyes almost glowed with a baleful intensity as he spat out the word lover.

"Aren't you going to introduce us?" He shrugged as his voice went playful again. It was frightening how quickly the tone of his voice changed.

"I think he's got a pretty good idea of what you are," Renee spat back.

"So, hostile little sparrow?" he almost sang in a singsong mocking voice.

"Don't call me that!" Renee hissed angrily. The mana immediately rose down her arms as she readied herself to attack. I instinctively readied myself to join her. I wasn't quite sure what good I'd be, but at least I was ready.

"Careful," he snarled, his voice going harsh again. "There's too many people here for that."

"Since when do you care about people?" Renee replied.

"Since you bring it up, I don't. But you do, don't you?" he answered. "Besides, aren't you afraid your little friend will get hurt?" He placed extra emphasis on the word *friend*.

"I think we can take you," I replied evenly.

I knew the type. He was a bully. He'd back down if we stood up to him. He was just like Mark Constance from school. There was only one way to deal with people like that, let them know that there were boundaries that would not be crossed.

"Oh? It talks?" he mocked, his head turned to one side as if examining me like some pet in a cage.

"Devon, please," Renee whispered.

"Does it think it can take me? Does it care to try?"

"Too many people," I grudgingly stated. I didn't want to appear to be backing down.

"I don't care about the damned people!" he snarled, mana leaping down his arms as both Renee and I braced ourselves for an attack.

"But in deference to Renee," he continued, his voice taking on that nasal sing song tone again, "I'll give you five minutes."

"Five minutes for what?" Renee asked.

"To get to somewhere where there are no people," he finished simply, "so we can do this properly."

"Go," Renee whispered in my ear.

I turned to look at her and realised with amazement that she was serious.

"Leave the stuff, just go."

"I'm not going to leave you," I whispered.

"I'll be right behind you. I want to make certain that he's not going to try anything," Renee ordered quietly.

"You go, I'll stay," I whispered, hoping like hell that he couldn't hear us.

"Would it help if I turned my back?" he mocked as he slowly and deliberately turned his back on us. "Four minutes – fifty seconds." He stated as if counting off time on a clock.

I was torn. He was just standing there, virtually undefended. He'd never even see my attack and I could finish this right now. I didn't know who this guy was, but it was obvious that Renee was terrified of him.

I could strike him down!

No, no, I couldn't.

That would mean striking someone down when they were totally defenceless and that I just couldn't do. I pulled Renee away and we ran across the park.

"Where are we going?" I asked as we ran.

"It doesn't really matter." Renee cursed. "He's probably not going to follow us anyway, at least not at first."

"What? Why?"

"He just wanted to prove to me that he could make me back down, make me run," Renee snarled.

"We could have taken him," I began. Renee didn't reply but instead threw an invisibility field around herself and telekinetically launched herself into the air. She landed on top of a building on the other side of the road. The building appeared to be a hotel or something.

A few seconds later I joined her.

We were relatively well protected on the rooftop. This meant that we'd at least see him coming when he came for us, but it was still too exposed. There was the possibility that someone from the office blocks behind us might see something. Renee stood looking out over the park. The figure was nowhere to be seen.

"Who was he?" I asked when I got my breath back.

"His name is Lester Vincent – Vin," Renee replied, "and we used to be friends."

"What happened?"

"I can't really answer that right now, but I will – I promise," Renee replied. "Please don't push this, just trust me – it didn't end well."

"I understand." I nodded.

"Would he have attacked us in the park like that?"

"I don't know," Renee sighed. "Maybe… He definitely would have gone for the kill if we'd attacked him first."

"Kill?" I repeated incredulous.

"Kill," Renee confirmed. "Well, maybe. I don't know."

Suddenly it all made sense.

Why Renee lived alone in a city without any friends or family. Why her grandfather only visited her occasionally. Why she had so aggressively attacked me when we first met. She was a fugitive in hiding.

"I might be able to talk some sense into him," Renee concluded.

"I don't like the idea of you seeing him alone," I stated.

366

"To be honest I don't much like it myself," Renee agreed, "but if I can get him to see reason I think I can get him to leave us alone."

"He's the one you're hiding from then?" I commented, taking a swing on my hypothesis.

"Yeah," Renee confirmed quietly, "figured it out did you?"

"Well, it seemed obvious after this," I continued. "Are you sure you can talk reason into him?"

"Yeah, well, as I said, Vin and I used to be friends."

"He didn't much seem like the reasonable type."

"No," Renee agreed, "but I have to try."

"I don't like it," I repeated.

"You'd better go," Renee replied, ignoring me. "Jump down into the alley and go straight home. He won't come after you."

"No, I'll stay, you might need help."

"Yes!" Renee retorted immediately. "Go. You can't do any good here. I'll just worry about having to protect you."

"Not yet," I argue. "Let's wait a half hour or so and make sure he's not coming after us."

"He'll be waiting for you to go," Renee commented bitterly. "He'll find me when you're gone."

"That doesn't comfort me very much."

"I wasn't trying to be comforting."

"We could take him?" I suggested tentatively.

"Are you sure?" Renee replied gently. "Really sure?"

"No," I replied softly.

"Then go."

I didn't like the idea of leaving her to face that obviously unhinged maniac alone. I didn't like the idea of being sent away whilst the adults talked. In fact I didn't like any damned part of this entire situation, but I didn't particularly have a choice here.

"Okay," I grudgingly agreed. "I'll go, but call me when you're done and if you don't call by nightfall I'll come looking for you."

"Sure," Renee shrugged. "Just go. I'll be okay."

I nodded and made my way to the edge of the building preparing to drop back to the ground below.

"Devon?" Renee called.

"Yeah?"

"I'm sorry I got you messed up in this."

"Don't mention it." I smiled back and gave her a mock salute as I raised an invisibility shield around myself, latched a mana thread onto the side of the roof and dropped off the side of the building to the ground. I felt like scum, the whole way down. Renee called me later that night and told me she'd sorted the problem out.

The only problem was – I didn't believe her.

I trusted Renee and didn't think that she'd lie to me or that anything was going on romantically with Vincent. She had made her feelings about him quite clear in that regard. There was something about the way Vincent was acting that led me to believe that he wasn't going to just simply walk away that easily. Renee had claimed that his primary interest was in humbling her and appearing to be the more powerful of the two of them. When Renee and I had run from him he'd gotten what he wanted. She claimed that she'd convinced him to return home but I wasn't convinced. I had one of those gut-feeling premonitions that he wasn't going anywhere. The problem was – I was right.

CHAPTER ELEVEN

"And so as we move into the final phase of your high schooling," Mr Saunders' monotonous voice boomed across the assembly. "It's important to take the time to consider everything you've experienced in high school and what lessons you have learned that may serve you in the time to come."

Mr Saunders speech had been droning on for about a half hour and showed no signs of slowing down. I didn't mind this at all. I'd had a lot on my mind since Saturday that would keep me more than distracted.

Renee had been awfully close mouthed about her meeting with Vin and I couldn't help but wonder if she may not have been telling me all the truth. I could tell from the expression on Renee's face that she hadn't been happy that I'd guessed she had been hiding in Melbourne from Vin.

Everyone is entitled to their secrets, I suppose. The more I thought about this the more it sounded like the type of stupid teenage drama that you're supposed to grow out of when you reach Renee's age. It sounded like something you'd go through when you're my age. The one factor that made me rethink this assessment was that she'd been genuinely scared when she recognised Vin in the park. She had been the kind of scared that you just can't fake. There was something about Vin or something that he'd done that terrified Renee and given that she could quite easily finish me off with little effort gave me cause for thought. Something wasn't right.

Mr Saunders eventually trailed off and we sluggishly got to our feet and ambled from the hall.

"What are you thinking about?" Sarah asked on our way out the door.

"What? Oh nothing much," I replied, as we entered the corridor. "Just stuff."

"Just stuff, eh?" Sarah pursued. "It kind of looked like you were arguing with yourself during the assembly."

"No, it's nothing, just thinking about Renee," I explained.

It was kind of difficult to talk amongst the throng of people in the crowded corridor so our conversation stopped and started as we weaved through the crowd. Eventually we cleared the corridor into the less crowded locker room.

"Oh, can't have been good then," Sarah mused as she opened her locker. "You had an awfully determined expression on your face."

"It's nothing."

"What? She cheat on you already?" Sarah laughed in a playful fashion.

I didn't answer her back. It wasn't that I thought Sarah was right. I just couldn't shake the feeling that I wasn't being told everything.

"My God," Sarah gasped, "she didn't, did she?"

"No, of course not," I retorted. "We just met someone the other day…"

"Like an old boyfriend? That can be awkward," Sarah guessed.

"No, maybe, I don't know."

"She got overly chummy with him eh?" Sarah teased again. "That can be uncomfortable for the new guy."

"No, it wasn't like that at all," I snapped. "She was physically scared of him."

"We've all had relationships that have gone bad before, sometimes these things get exaggerated," Sarah replied.

"I don't think so," I reflected sadly. "I really don't." "Are you saying that Renee isn't making you happy?" Sarah asked tentatively.

"No, I'm not saying that at all. What the hell?"

"Just asking is all," Sarah replied simply.

"But, why?"

"Because, if you're not happy, you should end it. Wasn't that the advice that Renee gave you before?"

"Is this some kind of sick joke to you?" I was little hurt that Sarah would say these things.

"No, Devon, of course not," Sarah replied, touching my shoulder. "But you've got to admit, that sometimes you get what you want, and other times you get what you go for."

"What does that mean?

"It means be happy with what you have," Sarah

reflected sadly, kissing me gently on the cheek. "Because sometimes, the grass on the other side of the fence is just grass."

Sarah left it at that. I called Renee that night and asked her directly what was going on. I asked her whom she was hiding from and what had happened between her and Vin. Renee informed me that she didn't want to tell me over the phone but promised to tell me everything this weekend. She'd come to the conclusion that she probably should tell me everything before I had called, as I deserved to know. She said she'd tell me anything I needed to hear – she said we needed to talk.

'We need to talk', the code for lovers in trouble.

I was nervous about my upcoming meeting with Renee and I was obviously taking it out on my friends. I must have become intolerable as even Tony took to avoiding me. I'd arranged to meet Renee at her place on Friday night for our talk and I was quite unsure of how that conversation was going to go.

I feared the worst. To make matters worse Dad had called mid-week to say he'd be out of town for the weekend. This meant that I had no other reason to go into the city. Hopefully I could patch things up with Renee and spend the night there. If not, then I guess I could simply take the train back home. I wasn't going to miss meeting Renee for anything. By the time I got to Renee's she was already back from university and was waiting for me. I rang the buzzer and she let me into the building.

I climbed the stairs with a lump in my throat and knocked on the door. Renee opened the door and ushered me inside. I couldn't make eye contact with her and noticed that she wasn't making eye contact with me either. I wasn't sure how this was going to go.

"Devon," she whispered, touching my cheek. I think that was the first time she'd used my first name.

"Yes?"

"We need to break up."

"Why?"

"You know why."

"It's not fair," I replied.

"No-one claimed life was fair, kiddo."

"No, don't call me kiddo," I snapped. "I am not a child".

"You're not an adult either," Renee replied sadly.

"Then, neither are you!" I shouted, angry at both Renee and at myself at the same time for getting angry.

"No, probably not," Renee replied sadly.

"I don't want to break up."

"Neither do I," Renee replied.

"Then why?"

"Because it's the right thing to do," Renee said.

"Why?"

"Because you'll get hurt if we don't," Renee replied. "And I don't think I could live with that."

"I don't care," I murmured brokenly. "You've told me that before and I said that I don't care."

"Well, I do care," Renee replied, "and things are different now."

"Is this because of that guy?" I replied, close to tears now.

"Yes," Renee answered simply.

"You said you sorted that out," I accused. "You said you'd gotten him to go away."

"I lied," Renee replied. "You know I lied. You couldn't have helped but know."

"It's not fair!"

"I know," Renee repeated again. "I think you need to go now."

"No," I gasped brokenly, tears running freely down my face. "Don't send me away," I pleaded, throwing my pride and all decorum to the wind. "I can help you! I need you!" I murmured tearfully into her shoulder.

Renee was slipping away from me, I could feel it. Renee smiled sadly at me and wrapped her arms around me, pulling me against her as I wept uncontrollably against her shoulder. Her hand trailed up and wrapped itself around the back of my head stroking my hair.

"Goodbye Devon," she whispered. I could feel her tears on my cheek.

"You don't want this," I murmured brokenly.

"No," she replied. "But what I want doesn't count."

"I don't want it either."

"What you want doesn't count either."

"It's not fair," I demanded. "We're not like everyone else, we're special! What we want should count!"

Renee's face lost its sadness and her eyes grew cold and dark. She suddenly looked far older.

"Devon, please understand. No matter how powerful you become or how special, sometimes things just happen. You can't just force your life to adhere to your will."

"Some people can!"

"No," Renee reflected sadly, "they're just better at convincing everyone else that they can."

"It's not fair," I said again.

"No," Renee replied, "but that's the way it is".

"It's not fair!" I repeated, with more emphasis.

"Stop saying that!" Renee snapped angrily. "You think I don't know that?"

I kissed her on the forehead. I said nothing and a stunned silence descended between us. The door remained open but I refused to leave her, I stood with my arms wrapped around her and my face resting against her shoulder.

"You want to fight this then?" Renee snarled. "You want to take on the world?"

"No," I replied, my tears having dried. "I simply want you."

"Oh, Twitch," she sighed as she nuzzled her face into my neck, "you don't know what you're saying."

"Then tell me!" I whispered.

"I can't."

"Why not?"

"Because, if we do this, then we'll become something we can't be."

"At least we'll be together," I murmured brokenly.

"Okay," Renee replied, giggling suddenly. "Have you

got a book of bad romantic lines stuffed up your shirt? That was corny – even for you."

"Is it working?" I said, wiping away a tear from the corner of my eye.

"No." Renee sniffed, wiping her hands across her face. "You don't understand. It's just not a good idea."

"Then tell me everything. Explain why not," I urged. "Let me in! You can't keep pushing people away forever."

"Well, I could until you showed up," Renee retorted with a twinkle in her eyes.

I breathed out slowly. I could see from her expression that'd she'd come to a decision. I'd convinced her.

"Tell me," I repeated.

"Okay," Renee whispered, her voice going soft and almost silent.

And so we talked.

Renee told me about how her mother had been murdered when Renee was only a little girl. She continued with how her father had been suspected of the crime and had fled. She finished with how her grandfather had taken her in and raised her as his own.

How when she was six she discovered that she had the talent.

She described in detail how her grandfather began to train her in the arts and it turned out that she was gifted with mana. She grasped concepts and theories like they were second nature to her and she told me how she adored the magic and the power that it gave her.

She then told me how she met Vin and about how he

had been sent to her grandfather for training. Renee's grandfather was considered a great teacher amongst our kind and that promising students were often sent to him for training.

She told me how Vin was at first. How he was shy, thoughtful and introspective. Renee continued with how they had studied together and grown up together and how Renee had thought herself in love with him with all the heart and earnestness of a sixteen-year-old girl. Renee spoke in simple truths and it was hard not to be hurt by her frank retelling. She continued on with her story explaining that as Vin became stronger in the arts and learned more, he began to change. It manifested in small ways at first and Renee hadn't noticed it. Then Renee found that he had begun testing the local kids in the local school. A school that both Renee and Vin attended at the time. He would play games with them, seeking out their weaknesses to prove that they would never be as strong or as smart as him. He became cruel and reckless as he flaunted his powers without ever revealing his powers directly to them.

Renee's grandfather had placed stern restrictions on them both against revealing the magic to outsiders. Each month that passed Vin was skirting closer and closer to breaking the rules. He would scare the students and torment them more and more and as time passed he became more reckless.

He became arrogant and proud of his abilities. He spurned his master's teachings and began to actively seek out ways to test himself and to improve his abilities. He sought to prove that he was stronger than those around him. In the end, he tired of tormenting the 'normals' as he dubbed them. This only left one option, there was only one on whom he could really test himself – Renee.

It came to a head when they had finished high school. Renee chose to attend university and Vin did not. Vin saw no value in formal education and scoffed at Renee's choice. He obviously saw this as a sign of weakness and began to exploit it.

This competition began in little ways. Vin would create stupid challenges to see who could project the strongest mana thread or who could detonate the most mana. When he inevitably lost he would become cold and distant.

He had no patience with being bested by a woman and it soon began to show. Renee described how the two began to argue, often loudly and how one night after a particularly stupid argument she had slapped him and demanded that he go away and leave her alone.

He had taken it badly.

The argument had made Renee's grandfather concerned and he chose to send Vin away. Vin had refused to go and instead moved into the local town to stay close to her. He became fixated on her and began to follow her, often turning up unexpectedly at her university campus.

At the conclusion of her first year at university, Renee's grandfather arranged for a trip for Renee and several of her friends. It was an amazing holiday opportunity. Renee found out later that it was merely an excuse to get Renee out of the way so that her grandfather could deal with Vin.

Renee spent the next several weeks travelling around Europe with her friends in what she described was the best time of her life. It wasn't until Renee returned from her trip that things turned horrible. In her absence Vin's fixation had increased. Renee's grandfather's plan had obviously had the opposite effect to what he had intended.

Renee and her friends were returning home from the airport via a bus when Vin caused the bus she was travelling in to have an 'accident'. He telekinetically sent the bus tumbling over the side of a cliff on the road leading back into the town.

The accident made the papers, as dozens of people were injured and several people were killed, including the driver. There were rumours that the bus had swerved to avoid someone standing on the road, but Renee knew better. She had seen the mana threads wrap around the bus that had sent it hurtling over the edge. She'd seen the driver on the brakes and grasp at the wheel in panic. This was useless as he had no control over the vehicle any longer. In vain she had tried to steady the bus using her own powers, but it all happened so fast. It was all she could do to brace herself and those around her as the bus fell to its inevitable and fiery end.

She awoke amongst the ruins of the bus. Her arms

were battered and bruised and she had a cut to her forehead. A red mist covered her eyes as she spotted Vin on the roadside looking down upon what he had wrought.

In fury she stormed from the bus, leaving dozens of confused and hurt passengers in the wreckage behind her as she leapt to the top of the ravine where Vincent was waiting for her. He gloated, saying that she wasn't powerful enough after all. That at the end, when it had really mattered he had beaten her.

She didn't even listen to him in her anger and she struck him, again and again and again. The accident weakened her and put her off balance and her magic wouldn't respond to her the way it used to. She was unable to penetrate the shield around him.

He'd laughed at her and called her pathetic. He shrugged off her attacks with his mocking laugh as if they were nothing. Renee stuck him again and again, her rage lending her more strength and power but it simply wasn't enough.

Then, when he had decided it was time, he struck back.

With a contemptuous flick of his wrist he sent a powerful thread against Renee. Due to the accident she had just survived and her own expenditure of energy Renee wasn't able to stand against it. Renee was just barely able to shield his attack in time, but the blow sent her tumbling back over the side of the cliff. Renee wasn't sure what happened next, but had supposed that the impact with the ground had caused her to black out.

Renee's grandfather found her several hours later unconscious at the bottom of the ravine. The trees around her had been crushed as if something far larger had come tearing through the woods.

Renee didn't see Vincent after that. The bus accident had been investigated and it was blamed on a driver fault that had caused the bus to swerve over the side. An investigation into the fault was launched as to how it could have happened, but had come back inconclusive.

Renee suspected that her grandfather had involved himself in the investigation to hush matters up. She was never able to prove that this was the case though. A small service was held in the town for the victims of the accident. Amongst the victims were two of Renee's close friends from university.

Renee had fallen into a deep depression after the accident as she blamed herself for the death of her friends. After all, if it hadn't been for her friendship with Vin the accident would never have happened. Renee's grandfather had decided that Renee had to be sent away until Vincent could be found and stopped. She could not be adequately protected where they were. She needed to be sent far away while he dealt with matters locally.

Renee's grandfather arranged, through his contacts, the apartment in Melbourne. It was as far away as he could arrange in a city that had a good university for her to continue her studies. She didn't want to leave but grudgingly agreed.

She moved and took up film studies (something she'd always wanted to do) and a part time job in the bookstore, finding as she did so that she didn't need to draw upon the magic like once she did. In fact, she found very little need for it at all. She still used it of course, but she didn't get the same joy from the experience as she once did. She'd actually done a pretty good job of leaving her past life behind until she met me.

When she met me, her love of the magic returned with renewed vibrancy and temptation. She realised that it was a part of her life that she simply couldn't do without. No, that wasn't true – she didn't want to live without it.

When Renee had first met me at the club she had thought that I was a threat. She thought I was someone sent by Vin to find her and bring her back to him. She knew he would still be hunting her and that he'd never give up. When Renee saw the state that I was in as my body was coming to terms with the mana, she knew she had to help me. She knew from her studies that this is a dangerous time in our development and that it can easily lead to death if it goes badly. In the end, against her better judgement, she decided to teach me.

It might have been easier for her if she'd turned her back on me and let me go my own way. Renee had found that she enjoyed helping me, teaching me and sharing her knowledge with me. Although it hurt when she said it, she said it reminded her of the good times with Vin.

And that was the problem.

She began to look for signs in me, a smirk or gloating comment that would make her believe that she was creating the very same monster that she was trying to hide from. And so she said she had watched me and kept her distance from me. Then Renee told me that she loved me. We didn't break up that night. I had asked her if she truly thought Vincent would leave me alone just because we weren't together any longer and Renee had remained silent. She couldn't answer me, but her silence had answered the question nonetheless.

Vin would eventually come after me anyway. It was obvious that he'd feel that I represented a threat to him. It would be a threat that he'd inevitably feel the need to test himself against. I wasn't sure that I'd survive the test, let alone pass.

I often look back on this night with the wisdom that comes with hindsight and ponder what would have happened had I just decided to turn and run. I doubt had I chosen that path that I would have retained my self-respect, but the path I chose cost me that anyway. Turning tail and running probably wouldn't have hurt anywhere near as much.

* * * *

The ticket machine clicked with a dull thud as my ticket was returned to me. I moved through the security check and onto the train station platform. It was dark by the time I left Renee's and although I had vague plans of staying the night there, Renee didn't think it was good idea given the circumstances.

She'd seen Vin stalking her during the day and guessed that he probably knew where she lived. She didn't think it was a good idea to antagonise him by staying the night. I think I was a little obvious in my disappointment, but Renee was firm with me. My phone buzzed in my pocket and I fumbled for it and brought it to my ear. I was a little out of breath as I answered it as I'd had to run as I thought my train was about to leave the station.

"Hello, Renee?"

"Where are you?" she demanded down the line, in way of greeting.

"I'm at the train station."

"Have you seen Vin?"

"No, why?" I replied. I glanced nervously about the abandoned station. It was pretty dark and there were several other people on the train and platform, but I'd have never missed the tell-tale evidence of a mana circle. Vin wasn't here.

"Can you see any small particles of mana in the air?" Renee demanded, ignoring my question.

I glanced around frantically. I couldn't see anything unusual about the place.

"It'll be very hard to see," Renee continued urgently. "Look for reflections of light out of the corner of your eye where there shouldn't be any. It's kind of like when a light reflects off a mirror."

"Maybe," I reflected as a flash of light caught my vision.

"Okay," Renee said. She sounded calm but it was obvious from her tone that she was more than a little concerned.

"Yeah, I'm definitely seeing something funny going on," I continued. The flickering became more and more obvious to me now that I had noticed it.

"Right, set off an awareness blast now!" Renee hissed down the line.

"I can't, there are people here," I disagreed.

"Then do it quietly! It won't need to be that big, just do it now!" Renee retorted.

"What will this prove?"

"I think you're being watched," Renee replied darkly.

"Does it matter?"

"Of course it fucking matters," Renee snapped, finally losing her patience. "Don't be stupid!"

I didn't argue the point any further. I simply moved to a seat where my hand motions couldn't be seen and set off a small blast. To my amazement the small amount of mana I used covered the entire carriage, most of the two on either side and a good portion of the station platform.

"Did you do it?" Renee nervously asked.

"Yeah," I replied as I looked around.

I could see an arc of mana curving onto the station platform where I had been catching the twinkling lights. It was like no mana thread that I'd ever seen before. The mana particles were wound loosely around a central core but weren't really attached to it. I had no idea how it was maintaining its stability.

This was something far beyond my abilities.

"What do you see?" Renee interrupted my observation.

"It looks like a mana thread on the station. It's kind of, I dunno, more loosely built," I replied.

Renee cursed down the line.

"What is it?"

"Scrying," Renee replied. "Where does the thread appear to be going?"

"I don't know," I replied nervously. "Up out of the station."

"What direction?" Renee almost snarled down the line.

"I don't know."

"Guess."

"North Melbourne?" I guessed, trying to estimate where the thread headed.

"Right," Renee replied determinedly. "Stay put – call me if you see anything."

Renee hung up. I stood and watched the mana thread for a good five minutes before eventually an announcement came on indicating that the train was about to finally leave the station.

I watched owlishly as the door to the train closed with a small hiss and the train gently rocked itself into motion. I quickly looked around the carriage, taking note of each occupant. There was a little old lady with a young man who I could only assume was her son.

There were also a few guys in the corner who were obviously a little worse for drink. The last occupant of the carriage was a weary man in a rumpled suit who was staring forcefully out the window ignoring everything else around him. I breathed a sigh of relief as the train left the confines of my awareness spell and left the station.

Renee rang as I passed the first station to check in. She hadn't been able to locate Vin, but noticed that the thread of mana had stopped. I promised Renee I'd call if anything unusual happened and quietly slipped my phone back into my pocket and positioned myself near the aisle just in case I needed to make a quick getaway.

The train dipped into the subway and it wasn't long before the motion of the train sent me into a light doze. It couldn't be called sleep, but I certainly wasn't alert either. I had meant to stay alert, but given the time it was difficult. Besides, I doubted that anything would happen anyway.

We passed several more stations, taking us out of the underground loop. No-one had gotten into my carriage from any of the city stations. This wasn't that surprising given the hour and pretty soon the train was making its way out of the city and into the suburbs.

I was on the home stretch now.

A whooshing noise followed by a door slamming brought my attention back into the carriage. I wasn't overly concerned by the noise but it had startled me. It was just someone moving between carriages. It was unusual, but hardly noteworthy. It was only when I noticed exactly who had entered the carriage that I sat bolt upright in my chair.

Vin was sauntering down the aisle of the carriage on his way to me. Fortunately he'd entered from the opposite side of the carriage and was thus immediately visible. I wouldn't have liked to have thought of my reaction should he suddenly have appeared from behind me. It certainly wouldn't have been conducive to the healthy state of my underwear.

I vaguely contemplated ringing Renee but quickly discarded that idea. It would be obvious that I was calling for help and I wasn't ready to admit yet that I needed it. The second reason was that Vin was too close. He'd hear everything said and I didn't like the idea of that either. I decided to play it cool and wait and see what happened. Probably not the best plan in hindsight.

Vin had a smug grin on his face as he reached the row of chairs I was occupying and he threw himself into the chair opposite me. He lazily stretched his legs forward to rest them on the chair opposite. This forced me to scoot down the row of chairs further towards the window.

He'd blocked me in.

"I don't think we've met," Vin grunted after several seconds of silence.

"Just briefly," I replied, not making eye contact.

"Hardly formally introduced though. Renee was quite rude in that department especially considering that we're such old friends." He smirked as if making a joke.

I didn't comment. I could tell I was being baited.

A stilted silence ensued and I could feel Vin's eyes dragging across me attempting to find any weakness. It was like he was tearing me apart and inspecting the pieces, looking for defects.

I had no intention of giving him any further opportunities.

I was seconds away from throwing a shield around myself and making a run for it. The rational part of my mind insisted that this would do no good however an irrational part of my mind was screaming at me to get the hell out of there.

"Quiet type, aren't you?" Vin continued in his mocking drawl.

"Yeah, I guess," I replied. "Don't really have much to say."

"I guess it seems that Renee's rudeness rubs off on her students."

I winced slightly at the way that Vin cut off the word '*students*', but didn't reply.

"Is Renee a good teacher, do you think?" he continued conversationally.

"Good enough," I grunted.

"How good would you say?" he pressed.

"She's the only mana teacher I've known, so I'm not really in a position to judge now, am I?" I replied, letting my voice get a little cutting.

"Really? That's interesting." Vin smiled. His tone gave me the indication that I'd just said something that I shouldn't have.

His eyes were almost glowing in the reflected light from the window, giving his face an almost skeletal mask across his features.

"You're certainly committed to the story, I'll give you that," Vin continued.

Again, I didn't reply.

"Your attitude is starting to verge on the insulting," Vin stated, his voice becoming cold and hostile.

"Look, what do you want from me?" I snapped.

His eyebrow rose slightly at my response but I had no idea what he was thinking. His expression certainly didn't change.

"I'm not sure what I want from you. I probably want nothing," Vin continued, smirking at my response. "I'm trying to figure out if you're in my way or not."

"Let's just assume that I'm not, and you can go back to where ever you came from," I replied dryly.

Vin snorted with amusement

"You've got balls, kid – I'll give you that."

I ignored the backhanded compliment and kept a watchful eye on Vin as he stared back at me. His mouth was still curled into that mocking sneer of his. Nothing was said for what appeared to be several stations. I looked at him – he looked back.

I couldn't take it any longer.

"Look, we both know you're not going to do anything here with all these witnesses about," I snapped, gesturing towards the other people in the carriage behind us, "so just fuck off."

His face dropped at the shock, but quickly resumed its usual smirk as he leaned forward and got to his feet. At first I thought he was going to attack me. If he had chosen to do so I would not have had time to defend myself. It was fortunate though that he walked several rows up the carriage to address the rest of the carriage.

"My friend and I need this carriage – please leave!" He ordered in a clear authoritative voice.

There was a stunned silence in the carriage as his words sunk in. The little old lady and her son swiftly got to their feet and were assisted into the next carriage by the business man. All three of them must have assumed that it wasn't worth the effort of arguing. I couldn't see Vin's face but from the way that all three kept looking fearfully at him I could see he'd definitely made an impression.

"Who're you to make us?" one of the drunks called from the other end of the carriage as he rose to his feet unsteadily.

"I've asked nicely," Vin replied in his sing song tone and holding his arms out each side of him.

"So what? It's a free country!" the drunk called back, egged on by his friends. I could see that Vin was readying himself for something. This wasn't going to be pleasant.

I vaguely thought about attacking Vin at this point whilst his attention was diverted, but I again decided against it.

"You've really got to hand it to Australians..." Vin called out to the drunks.

Vin didn't bother to finish his sentence and we never got to find out what exactly he was handing to Australians. Without missing a beat, a mana thread erupted from his already outstretched hand and smashed into the security camera on the roof. I could see the mana thread but all the drunks would have seen was the camera suddenly implode in on itself without any obvious cause.

Each drunk reacted in a different way. The leader appeared to find this funny and notably snickered as if this were the funniest thing in the world. Both of his offsiders however went noticeably white.

One of them looked like he was on the verge of running. He was obviously the smartest of the lot or he was simply the most sober. With another wave of Vin's hand, the second and last camera in the carriage shattered and a third swipe smashed the window directly behind the drunks, showering them with glass. I quickly activated a shield around myself anticipating an attack, but one never came. Vin glanced back to see what I'd done but kept his attention firmly focused on the drunks.

I scooted over the back of the seat into the entry way of the carriage near one of the doors.

"I asked nicely," Vin repeated. "So, you leave – that's the way it works… isn't it?"

Two of the drunks made a quick dash for the doorway behind them, pulling their spokesperson along with them. The leader appeared to finally get the idea, as his eyes were as wide as saucers as he was dragged away.

To his credit, he didn't appear to be struggling that much.

"Well, we appear to be alone now," Vin observed as he swung around gracefully to face me. The mana threads were still looped around his hands.

"You've made your point," I murmured sullenly.

"No, I don't think I have," he contradicted.

"I don't believe that you're a student," he continued. "In fact, I think if I provoke you enough the truth will come out."

"I don't know what you're talking about," I snapped, playing for time waiting for the next train station to come up. I had decided to make a run for it at the next station. Worst comes to worst, I could throw myself out the doors and into the relative safety of the station. Hopefully the station would be busy or something as surely Vin wouldn't continue his attack on a crowded train station platform. Well, probably not anyway.

I anticipated the attack when it came. I had noticed before that he had struck at the drunks before he'd finished speaking. So it came as no great surprise when the thread uncurled itself from around his fists and lashed in my direction.

I let the shield take the impact and winced as it noticeably buckled. It wouldn't be a wise idea to do that again.

"After all," Vin snarled, "out of Renee and myself – I was always the stronger."

I wasn't going to give him a chance to strike again, and with a sharp intake of breath I struck with everything I had. It was a good solid mana thread and it lashed out from my hand with pin-point accuracy at its target.

Had it been allowed to impact I'm sure it would have taken Vin out. He had after all not bothered to raise a shield. Unfortunately, with a contemptuous flick of his wrist Vin intercepted it with his own thread and deflected my attack away from him.

The arrogant bastard hadn't even raised his shield in defence.

His counter attack when it came was predictable and I was able to pull my thread back to intercept it, which caused a loud crash as the two particle threads collided.

"Pathetic," Vin called as he stalked back down the carriage towards me.

He launched several over arm attacks at me. I parried those too, but it was getting close and it was obvious that I was over matched. He wasn't giving me any opportunities to launch an attack of my own in retaliation. Eventually he'd break through my defences.

"You know, I'd almost be prepared to believe that you actually are a student," he laughed as he launched another attack. I grudgingly gave ground before him.

It was fortunate that I had chosen to sit near the middle of the carriage when I'd sat down. This means that I now had approximately half the carriage to retreat into. It looked like I was going to need all the space I could get.

Vin launched into a lazy over hand strike at me, which I easily parried. As he struck he gave me the impression that he was playing with me and could finish me at any time. I hated him for it, but there was nothing I could do. A second sweeping attack came from the opposite side, crashed against my shield, and sent me tumbling down into a row of chairs. I hadn't even seen it coming.

He was just too damned fast. He waited until I regained my feet before launching a spearing attack at my torso. I had no doubt that should this strike have hit it would have impaled me directly through my chest and have ended my life immediately. It was only by throwing myself to one side and putting everything I had into a thread against it that I was able to push his attack firmly to one side. As a consequence his mana thread speared through one of the train windows.

"Ooh, nice," Vin snickered smugly. "I hadn't expected you to block that one."

Why hasn't this train stopped yet?

Surely someone must know that something strange was going on. The smashing noises alone must have gotten someone's attention. The sound of the wind howling through the broken windows was almost deafening.

Someone must have surely raised the alarm by now.

I noticed with some degree of frustration that there were three faces pressed up against the window of the opposite carriage. It was the drunks from before. Surely one of them would have thought to press the damned emergency button, but no such luck. I couldn't see the old lady or the businessman either – what the hell were they doing? Couldn't they see that I was in trouble here?

A snapping attack launched at my head ricocheted off my shield causing my head to snap to one side. A whiplash of pain tore through the left side of my neck and down my back.

Great, I was sure I'd be feeling that one come winter.

"Focus, focus," Vin chanted in his annoying sing-song voice. "You mustn't let yourself be distracted."

My head throbbed a little but I was otherwise okay. I replied in the form of another attack that led into a small but savage exchange of blows. It was infuriating. Try as I might I just couldn't get through his guard and I was still slowly but surely losing ground. I was gasping for air but it couldn't have been more than two minutes since the first strike.

"Well, I'll give you one thing boy," Vin grunted as our heated exchange slowed. "You've certainly got stamina."

He didn't appear to be as out of breath as I was, but I could see a notable layer of sweat on his brow. I didn't respond. There didn't seem to be much point. I used the time to catch my breath.

It was almost by an unspoken agreement that the two of us launched our attacks again. I could see the gleam in his eyes as he launched his attack. The bastard knew as I did that eventually I wouldn't be able to return fire. He was revelling in it and there was nothing I could do about it. The simple fact was that he was more skilled, stronger and faster than me.

If I didn't do something to even the odds I was going to lose, it was only a matter of time. The problem was, I didn't know what I could do. There really wasn't much room to manoeuvre in the cramped walkways of the train carriage so if I couldn't block out of the way, I had to rely on my shield and pray that it held.

He'd only caught me with glancing blows so far but I was certain that a direct strike would shatter my shield and end me in one fell swoop. With a quick series of strikes, Vin pushed me back further, forcing me to leave the protective cover of the rows of seats. This was a mixed blessing as whilst I was sacrificing the cover afforded by the seats, I now had a greater freedom of movement and could attempt to use this to my advantage.

"Looks like you're out of space, boy," Vin grunted.

I frantically looked around looking for an escape, but he was right. There was no way I'd be able to escape into another carriage as he'd finish me before I could get the door between carriages open.

A quick glance out the window informed me that it was at least two or three minutes away from the next station. Vin would easily finish me off in that time now that he had me trapped. I needed to do something, anything to turn the odds.

I needed to get out. I didn't have any other option. It was something that I never would have considered doing if I had any other choice. I sent a thread arching towards Vin's head and was satisfied when he easily deflected it into the direction I'd suspected that he would block that one to. I used this to my advantage and placed all my strength behind the redirected thread and watched with devilish delight as it slammed into the carriage door to my right.

The mana hit the carriage door with full force and easily smashed the door open. There was a satisfying crunching noise and the sound of twisting metal being torn from its frame as the door came loose. The wind rushed into the carriage through the wrecked doorway, pulling at my clothes and hair.

One of the carriage doors hung on its railing from the side of the doorframe but the other had been torn completely away leaving a gaping hole in the side of the carriage. I had my escape. I just couldn't let Vin know it yet or he'd move to stop me.

"Now look what you've done," Vin smirked.

"I know," I replied as I took a deep breath.

Although I'd planned this, I was now having doubts as I looked at the power poles flashing past the doorframe. It looked like the train was going awfully fast and it would really hurt if I hit one of those poles on the way through. I didn't have a lot of time to let my fears linger as Vin looked like he was gearing up for another attack. It was now or never.

I timed it so that as Vin was just about to attack I threw myself on to my side under his attack. I leapt back to my feet and began running towards the gaping hole in the carriage. Before Vin could do anything about it, I'd thrown myself from the moving train carriage. I'd just jumped off a speeding train.

I hit the ground hard. Fortunately, due to a combination of the trajectory at which I landed, and the relative softness of the ground below I wasn't too hurt. The fact that I still had had a shield around me when I actually hit the ground was probably the only reason I was unhurt by the fall.

When I turned to look back at the train I saw Vin hanging onto the side of the carriage door as the train swept away. I could just make out his mocking grin as he disappeared back into the carriage.

It was a long walk back home as I was still about three or four stops from my station when I had 'disembarked' from the train. I made a pretty quick pace as I wasn't sure if I had been spotted jumping from the train or not. Furthermore I wasn't sure if Vin was going to pursue me further.

After the first hour I came to the conclusion that I needn't had worried anyway. Vin had obviously gotten his victory in that he'd forced me to run away. If Renee was right then that was all he was after anyway. He wanted an acknowledgement that he was better than me. I gritted my teeth with anger at the admission, however there was little I could do to ignore the simple truth of the statement. He was better than me.

There was no denying the fact that everything I tried, every tactic I had employed or the strength I applied he simply matched and then exceeded. I opted not to inform Renee of the incident as no harm had come from it and she would just needlessly worry. With any luck the police would pick Vin up at the next station and he'd do something stupid and then the problem would be solved for us.

* * * *

I'd managed to get home not long after midnight and my feet were sore from the long walk home.

I hate walking.

I'm quite active in other ways, such as roller blading or bike riding but I can't walk to save my life. If I'd had any other option last night, I would have taken it. It took me almost two hours to walk home. I suppose in hindsight I could have simply walked to the next station and taken the train, but to be honest I was a little jittery about running into Vin again.

I spent my first waking moments on my laptop looking through the major news websites for a report on mysterious train attacks or damage. There was nothing there, absolutely nothing. How can this be? We broke at least three or four windows on the carriage and the doors were completely ripped off their hinges, how could this not be news? Not to mention that this happened under the noses of at least three witnesses.

Although last night I'd determined that I wasn't going to tell Renee, in the cold light of day it was obvious that I had to. I reached back and flicked my alarm clock around to check the time. It was a quarter past nine.

I'd let Renee sleep in for a bit before I called her. I wouldn't want to be woken up first thing on a Saturday morning with this news. I didn't even like thinking about it. The reality of the situation pained me like a sore tooth. Someone had just tried to kill me.

It's a very simple statement to make but the implications of this are life changing. Your whole world narrows down into a single statement of fact. Vin had tried to kill me and would probably try again.

I had begun to shake as I reached for the phone and dialled Renee's number. It took me several tries to get the number right.

"Devon?"

"Yeah," I replied, a slight tremor creeping into my voice.

I breathed a deep breath to attempt to steady myself. I hadn't planned on breaking down like this but I couldn't seem to get the words out properly. I'd simply planned on repeating a rehearsed statement of fact. Unfortunately that didn't look like it was going to be likely now.

"Are you okay?"

"Yeah, I'm fine," I lied.

I wasn't overly sure why I lied. It was just one of those things. When someone asks you if you're fine, you say yes. I mentally kicked myself.

"You don't sound fine," Renee retorted.

"No, you're right, I'm not." I sighed. "Vin came after me last night."

"Why didn't you call me?" Renee thundered down the line. "I told you to call me!"

"There wasn't time," I protested. "It all just happened so fast."

"You could have called me afterwards," Renee continued icily.

"It was late. I told myself I'd call you in the morning."

"Are you okay?" Renee's voice softened a little.

"Yeah, I got away okay, I'm not hurt."

I could hear Renee's sigh of relief clearly down the phone line. I braced myself as I approached the subject I didn't want to reveal.

"There were witnesses," I murmured tentatively. This was the part of the conversation I wasn't looking forward to. Renee had made her opinions about media exposure very clear.

"How many?" Renee replied dryly.

"Three or four, at least," I whispered.

"That's not too bad, what happened?"

I gave Renee the details of last night's encounter and to her credit Renee remained silent throughout the whole story until the end.

"Well, it sounds like he didn't give you much of a choice," Renee concluded.

"No, not really," I agreed dryly.

"For what it's worth, it sounds like you handled yourself well," Renee commented.

I shook my head.

"He was playing with me, he could have ended it at any point."

"I know," Renee agreed. "But I've seen him play – he

plays rough, the fact you're unhurt is actually kind of impressive."

I wasn't sure if Renee was trying to reassure me or she genuinely felt that way. In either event I was touched at the approval in her voice.

"We need to do something about him," I grunted.

"What do you suggest?"

"We need to track him down and confront him. Together," I urged. "We can take him, I know it."

"You're probably right," Renee conceded. "But it will get ugly, he's not going to walk away from this."

"What's the alternative? Let him find us alone and vulnerable again?"

"I don't know," Renee whispered. "Maybe I should call my grandfather."

I hadn't considered that idea, but I didn't like the idea of running for help and in any event her grandfather was overseas – it'd be at least a few days before he could get here.

"All we need to do is scare him a little. To make him realise that if he keeps this up we're going to hurt him," I continued.

"I wish I had your confidence that it would go down that way," Renee whispered.

"We don't have any choice. Eventually he's going to come for us again. Better that it happen on our terms."

"Okay," Renee sighed.

I knew I hadn't convinced her but she, like me, could not see any other option.

"Just promise me one thing," Renee murmured.

"What?"

"If I say, run, we run."

"Okay," I conceded. "So how do we do this?"

"Come back to my place tonight. We'll go somewhere quiet and make a lot of noise. That's bound to attract his attention, and when he comes for us – we'll take him."

"Sounds good."

"Right," Renee replied forcefully. "I'll see you tonight."

"Okay, I'll see you tonight then."

Mum was waiting for me in the kitchen. She'd already made herself a bowl of cereal and had left the box and the milk on the counter for me.

"Were you on the phone to your girlfriend before?" Mum pressed.

"Yeah, were you listening in on my calls again? You promised you'd stop doing that!" I grumbled.

I'd already come to the conclusion that she hadn't heard what we were saying – if she had heard the conversation, I doubted that would be the question that she'd open with.

"I wasn't listening, just heard you as I walked past," Mum protested. "Although I must say I like Tina, she seems good for you – a stable influence. I heard that she's going to do Medicine at Melbourne University."

"Um, actually it's not Tina. We broke up," I grunted as I sat at the table.

"Oh? I'm sorry to hear that," Mum commented.

"It's okay," I replied, "just wasn't meant to be."

"So who's the new girl then?"

"Her name is Renee," I replied.

"…And?"

"I like her," I replied, not in the mood for an interrogation.

"Do I get to meet her?"

"It's a little soon for that." I shrugged.

"Does she go to your school?"

"No, she lives in the city," I replied.

"Oh," Mum replied simply.

"I'm going to go see her tonight."

"Really?"

"Is that a problem?".

"Well, no, but your father is away this weekend, isn't he?"

"Yeah."

"Well, it's an awfully long way to come back here afterwards."

"I was planning on sleeping there."

"Oh," Mum mumbled, obviously flustered. There was several seconds of silence before Mum followed up with, "I'm not sure that's a good idea."

"Either that or I'll come back here on the late train," I replied to mollify her.

I had no intention of coming back here if I could help it.

"If you need to, you can always call me and I'll come get you."

"No." I yawned as I stretched, pushing myself away from the table. "I don't want to put you to any trouble."

"It's no trouble," she assured me.

I moved to the bench and began to give my bowl a cursory scrub before putting it in the dishwasher. There's nothing like the apparent task of manual labour for delaying the answering of a question.

"We'll see," I eventually replied.

"I'd really be more comfortable that way," Mum insisted.

"I am eighteen, you know," I snapped.

"Yes, and I'm still your mother, so you'll do as I say," Mum replied calmly.

"Sure, fine – whatever you say," I answered.

I slammed the bowl into the dishwasher and not-so-graciously stormed off into my room. I can't say that at this point I wasn't excited, the thrill of hunting down and vanquishing someone who had wronged me pumped through my veins. I finally understood the desire that burned within the comic book heroes. However, this passed with time, and excitement gave way to doubt, doubt gave way to fear and fear gave way to despair.

It wasn't until I was on the train that evening that I fully realised the extent of what we were planning. If Vin proved intractable or too strong, someone could get hurt, maybe even killed. The thought gave me visible shakes and made me sick to my stomach. Could I kill someone if I had to? Could I take someone's life? Could I end someone? Intentionally?

As blasé as I was about the topic on the phone this morning, now that it was actually happening I was having doubts. If it came down to his life or mine – I still wasn't sure I could go through with it. Would you kill to save your life or the lives of those you loved?

No.

The simple fact was that I didn't believe that I could. I could sacrifice myself to save those I loved, but that was a coward's way out. In the cold light of day I just don't think I could consciously and with full understanding of the consequence of my actions take a life. I just wasn't built that way and I didn't believe in the story archetypes of the hero and villain facing down at dawn – with only one man walking away.

I just don't think life is like that. Life is not a storybook and not subject to the conventions of narrative device. The truth of the matter was that under examination I wasn't sure I could cause death and this led to an unfortunate realisation. Vin obviously could, he'd already done it. This meant that I was at a very real disadvantage and there was nothing I could do about it.

I was so lost in my thoughts that I completely missed my station. It wasn't a big deal though as I simply took a connecting tram from a little further down the line. I arrived at Renee's a little late, but that was okay because I'd called ahead to let her know.

Renee looked dishevelled when she answered the door.

"What's wrong?"

"Do you have a passport?" Renee cryptically asked, ignoring my question.

"Um, yeah… why?" I replied, a little confused.

"I called my grandfather. He wants me on the next plane out of here."

"Maybe you should go?" I suggested. The words tore me up on the way out of me. I didn't want her to go because I instinctively knew that should she go I'd never see her again.

She would never return to Melbourne and I'd lose her.

"I can follow later, once school is finished."

"I'm not leaving, not without you," Renee replied.

I breathed a sigh of relief.

"If I leave you here, Vin will most certainly try to find out where I've gone through you."

Well, that wasn't the grand romantic statement I'd been hoping for, but at least it showed she cared right?

"Besides, I'm pretty sure I'd miss you," Renee continued with a smirk. "Well at least a little bit. Don't think I didn't notice your expression before – that's one hell of a puppy dog eyes look you've got going there."

I chuckled as I pulled Renee into an embrace.

"So what are we going to do?"

"Well, my grandfather wasn't happy about my decision, but he eventually agreed."

"Okay," I prompted, unsure of where this was going.

"We're going to go on a trip."

"How long for?"

"We probably won't return," Renee replied simply.

"I can't do that!" I exclaimed, "I've got friends and family here – I can't just disappear!"

"You can if you don't want them mixed up in this," Renee replied. "I know from experience that Vin isn't above using your loved ones to get to you."

"When?" I replied bleakly.

"As soon as possible, once you've finished your last exams," Renee continued.

"After my exams? Why not just go now?" I asked. I didn't care one way or the other about exams.

"I've fucked up your life enough without ruining your education as well," Renee snapped harshly. "Besides, it will take Vin some time to track down where we've gone. We should have more than enough time."

I nodded. I wasn't sure how she was planning to elude Vin for that long, but she seemed confident. There would be no argument with her. I was kind of glad actually, this gave me enough time to try to figure out how to say goodbye to my friends and family.

"How long until your exams? Four weeks, yeah?" Renee asked.

"Yeah, about that."

"Okay, that's not too bad. First, we're going to stop coming into the city. In fact we're going to avoid going out in public as much as we can. I'm going to get a hotel out near you so I can keep an eye on you. Secondly we're not going to use any mana until we leave."

"He's tracking us because we're using mana?" I asked.

"Probably," Renee replied dryly. "It's what I would do."

"Okay, that's not too difficult." I nodded, not thinking of the implications of this.

"Speak for yourself," Renee disagreed curtly. "I get the shakes and a headache that makes the flu look mild by comparison."

I'd forgotten about that, withdrawals from mana use weren't pretty. I'd already gone through that once and wasn't looking forward to going through it again.

"With any luck, by the time he's tracked us down, we'll be long gone. He won't use an Awareness blast for fear of tipping us off."

"I'm not sure about this," I murmured.

"I warned you when you pursued a relationship with me that there would be costs," Renee replied, her voice going cold.

"I know, but I wasn't prepared for anything like this," I replied.

"Are you saying that you don't want this?"

"You're asking me to give up everything here, my whole life," I retorted.

"Are you saying that you don't want this?" Renee repeated, her voice almost going to a whisper.

"No, I definitely want this," I replied, moving to pull her into my arms.

"What about you?" I murmured, stroking her hair. "Won't you miss your life here?"

Renee sighed and whispered, "No, not really, there never really was anything for me here... well, except for you."

"I'm coming with you."

"I know, that's why there's nothing here I'll miss," Renee continued.

With those simple words, my mind was made up –
I'd give up everything: my friends, my family, my whole
life. I'd throw it all away and follow Renee. I had no idea
where we were even going – but that didn't matter. I
would be with her and she would be mine.

I often wonder in hindsight how our lives would
have worked out had our plan come to pass. But alas,
plans made in haste are often cast astray by the hand of
the fate. And to be honest, I think the fates hate me.

CHAPTER TWELVE

Giving Renee my passport had proved to be more complicated than I'd originally expected. When I had handed my passport over to her she passed it immediately back. It was due to expire very early next year. I hadn't noticed this small fact.

I would need to get it renewed.

It was fortunate that I was now eighteen and didn't need parental approval for renewal. This meant that it was simply a matter of getting the other required forms of identification. I'd always known where my birth certificate was kept so that wasn't too difficult to obtain. I already had the other required forms of ID.

Things were falling into place. One thing I hadn't counted on, however, was that because I needed the passport relatively quickly I'd have to go into the city to the Passport Office. This meant that I would need to skip school on the following Monday to go into the city to sort out the paperwork. I could then have the passport mailed to me.

Renee had provided me with a post office box number to have the passport sent to. I couldn't risk my parents wondering why I was having a passport sent to my home address. The process turned out to be a lot easier than expected and it was shortly before lunch time on Monday that I walked out of the application office with the forms filled out and my new passport on its way.

I called Renee to let her know that things were progressing well as I made my way back to school. I wandered into the school yard about half way through lunchtime. I'd already told Tony and Garry that I was ducking out of school, though I had neglected to give them a reason.

"All sorted?" Tony called as I ambled up to our usual lunch spot.

"Sorted?" I asked as I threw myself down onto one of the park benches.

"Yeah, whatever it was you needed to sort out this morning," Tony replied.

"Yeah." I nodded nonchalantly.

"What were you doing?" Sarah asked.

"Sorting out a passport," I replied.

"Are you travelling somewhere?" Garry asked.

"Well, obviously… dumbass," Sarah cut him off. "Where are you going?"

"I'm visiting Renee's folks."

Well, so far I hadn't lied to them. I just hadn't mentioned that I wouldn't be coming back. I felt terrible for even this small deception. I had no idea how I was going to tell my mother.

Renee had counselled just upping and leaving, but I was beginning to suspect that Renee didn't really like the soft touch when it came to dealing with family. This wasn't really surprising considering – but her advice wasn't that helpful.

"That'll be nice." Sarah murmured, her eyes narrowing with suspicion. She knew me too well and knew without a doubt that there was something that I wasn't telling her. I could tell from Tony's silence and the expression on his face that he knew something was up too.

"Yeah," I replied weakly. Fortunately for me neither Sarah nor Tony chose to pursue the matter with the others around.

Tina was looking at me a little strangely, though I suppose hearing that your old boyfriend was going on a holiday to meet the parents of his new girlfriend so quickly would put anyone out of sorts. It wasn't until the school bell went and everyone made their way back to the locker bay that Sarah and Tony cornered me.

"Okay, buddy," Sarah hissed, poking me in the chest, "what's really going on? The truth this time."

My eyes narrowed in suspicion. I'd expected her to try to talk to me about it, but I didn't expect an outright demand. What else did Sarah know? How much did she know? Had Tony finally ratted me out after all? I turned to look at Tony's face, trying to see any hint of betrayal in his features. The look on my face must have given me away because Sarah immediately turned to look apprehensively at Tony.

"I didn't tell her," Tony replied simply and I believed him.

"Tell me what?" Sarah exclaimed.

"But you should," Tony continued.

"One of you had better tell me what's going on soon." Sarah turned to face Tony.

It wasn't immediately obvious whom she was angrier at, if it was me or her boyfriend who had been keeping secrets from her. I wasn't sure if it was a good idea to tell Sarah or not. Renee had made it quite clear that she didn't want anyone knowing and telling Sarah could expose her to danger from Vin. He had proved that he wasn't above threatening friends to achieve his goals. All these were good reasons not to tell her. In the end though it came down to one simple truth, she was my friend and she deserved to know. The final reason which was perhaps the most compelling was that I didn't want her to come looking for me after I disappeared with Renee.

"Okay, I'll tell her," I declared, "but not now, not here."

"You're sure?" Tony replied with a quizzical expression.

"Yeah, if I can't trust Sarah, then I can't trust anyone."

"Thanks, man," Tony replied. I hadn't realised it up until now, but keeping this from Sarah must have been placing a lot of strain on them.

"After school, meet me by the oval. Then I'll tell you everything."

"Okay," Sarah replied, a look of confusion on her face. This clearly this hadn't gone the way she'd expected. I wasn't sure exactly how much I was going to tell her, but it was worth it just to see the look on her face now.

Halfway through the next period we had a call come over the speakers calling for a special assembly for senior level students. I assumed that it had something to do with the upcoming exams. This assumption was wrong – very wrong.

When we arrived at the senior common rooms, there were several police officers standing with the teachers. Our head of level introduced the policemen to us and indicated that they were there to give a lecture on how we should conduct our Muck Up Day.

Muck Up Day is a silly tradition where the final year students are given free range of the school grounds before they go into exams. The tradition usually led to running water fights, occasional egg throwing and general mayhem. The school usually looked upon this with controlled tolerance until last year when a whole bay of lockers were removed from the locker bay and formed into a recreation of Stonehenge. The resulting mess had been unoriginally dubbed 'Locker Henge' by the school society.

It had actually caused quite a lot of disruption, as it wasn't immediately easy to tell whose locker was whose. I remembered being highly amused at the whole affair. Although my locker had been one of the one's used it hadn't really affected me that much as I didn't really use my locker anyway. I assumed that this assembly was simply a show of force by the school in an attempt to curtail any more unorthodox pranks. Again, my assumption was dead wrong. I hadn't noticed during the assembly but the second police man was taking notes and looking at faces. They were looking for someone.

By the time the policeman's speech ended, I'd already planned on several places I could lodge lockers where they'd have no idea how we'd got them there. It's possible that I may have missed the point of his speech somewhat. The students began to file out from the assembly room after being dismissed. Tony and I made our way to the door.

"Mr Wills, if we may have a moment of your time," Mr Saunders voice boomed across the hall.

Both Tony and I stopped and turned to see Mr Saunders standing off to one side with the two police officers.

"I'll wait here," Tony declared.

"No, you go on." I nodded to Tony. "I'll catch up."

"Perhaps, Mr Ward, you should go to class. As tragic as it is to break up the greatest comedy duo since Huey and Lewis, I think we can manage without you," Mr Saunders instructed dryly.

"Sir, that's one dude! He sang a bunch of songs in the '80s," Tony declared.

"Well done, Mr Ward, but everyone knows that – that's old news," Mr Saunders replied dryly.

"That was very nearly a joke, sir!" Tony drawled.

"Tony!"

"Yes, sir."

"Go away."

"Tony likes his '80s rock," I said as Mr Saunders led me into one of the study rooms.

The two policemen remained behind, obviously conversing with each other.

"Clearly," Mr Saunders replied. The policemen hadn't entered the room yet.

"Devon, I'm not sure what the police want with you and quite frankly I'm a little surprised. I never picked you for the troublesome type."

"The police want to talk to me?"

Saunders just nodded. "Just answer their questions honestly and everything will be okay," he advised. "I'll just go see if they're ready for you."

"Okay, sir," I was actually kind of glad he was there, which was a first for me.

Something wasn't right here.

When the policemen arrived into the room they were all business. The more senior of the two placed a picture on the table and looked at me. Mr Saunders placed himself behind me leaning against the wall. I had no idea what he was still doing here.

The photo on the table was a picture of Vin.

"Do you know who this man is?" the policeman opened.

I shook my head, but it must have been obvious that I was lying as I saw the policeman's eyes narrow with suspicion. He looked at his partner who shrugged.

"Fine," he continued with poor grace as he stomped over to the chair and sat down, putting a manila folder on the table between us.

"Mr Wills is it?" he confirmed, double checking on the page in front of him.

"Yes," I replied. My mind was racing. I had no idea what I was going to tell them. I obviously couldn't tell them the whole truth.

"Where were you last Friday?"

"School, sir," I replied straight faced as my stomach tied itself in knots.

"Friday evening?" he amended sternly.

"With friends," I replied simply.

"Did visiting these friends involve using the train at all?"

"They're in the city, yeah," I replied.

I wasn't prepared to overtly lie to the police yet, but I obviously couldn't tell them everything. I just wasn't sure what I could tell them and what I couldn't. I resolved to tell them as much of the truth as I was able. This was exactly the situation that Renee had warned me about.

"What time did you take the train?" the officer asked.

"Late afternoon, straight after school," I replied easily.

"And did you return that evening?"

"Yes."

"At what time was this?"

"I don't know, it was rather late."

"I get the feeling that you're not being as cooperative as you could be," the policeman warned as his voice went a little frosty.

Before I could answer his partner pulled a second photo from the manila folder and swung it around

422

to face me. It was another photo of Vin; however, in this photo you could just make out my profile in the background. It wasn't the best photo, but it didn't take too much imagination to figure out the other figure in the photo was me.

"Is this you?" he snapped, pointing at my face in the photo.

"I think so, I'm not sure," I stammered, hoping that there were no better photos of the event. I had no idea how I was going to get out of this one.

"It's from the security footage of one of the Glen Waverley night trains," the officer informed me.

"Are you planning on arresting Devon?" Mr Saunders cut in immediately, preventing me from saying anything.

"Well, no," the officer stated, "we're actually more interested in the other person in the other photo." It was at this point that his partner leaned forward and spun Vin's photo around to face me.

"You know who he is," he declared. "I can see it from your face."

"Look, I'm sorry. I really don't know who he is," I lied. "He was on my train, and just went nuts and started breaking things."

"I got off at the next station, after he started going berserk," I finished lamely. This was kind of true.

"There was extensive damage to the carriage," the officer prompted.

"Once he started smashing windows I decided to leave," I replied.

"Did he have a weapon or something that he was smashing the windows with?" the partner asked. I was beginning to hate that partner.

"I didn't see one. To be honest I didn't really want to get that close," I replied.

"Fair enough," the first officer commented. "Understandable." The second interjected.

"And he just let you go?" the second officer pressed. "Only it looks like he's talking to you in this photo."

"He was talking to me," I replied. "I wasn't really listening though, I thought he was drunk and I was trying to ignore him."

The policeman nodded and took some notes in his book.

"Then he just went berserk and started smashing things. I decided to leave the train shortly after that."

Again the policeman took notes in his infernal notebook. In the action movies they never seem to show you how difficult it is to lie to the police. The plucky action hero always has the right lines and dialogue. It was much harder in real life.

"He was involved in an altercation with one of the train line security patrols at Mount Waverley Station, but you wouldn't know anything about that, would you?"

"No, I got off before there," I replied.

"They were quite badly hurt," the officer continued. "Hospitalised. One may never walk again."

He continued as if reading the phrase from his notebook. I sat in silence as the ramifications of this hit me. This was my fault. I had stirred him up. I was the one he was after. He had only taken his ire out on those guards when I fled. I had even hoped that the security guards had picked him up. I'd just never imagined that this would happen. I chose to say nothing. After all there was nothing I could say.

"You have no comments to make regarding that?" the second officer pressed.

"I wasn't there!" I protested loudly. "I never saw any security guards!"

"Yes, but you know who this man is!" the officer demanded, curtly jabbing his finger at the photo of Vin.

"No," I repeated. "He was just some maniac on the train – I'd never met him before."

"I don't think we're getting anywhere here," the first officer cut back in. "Look, Devon, we're just trying to find this man. He has seriously hurt some people and this is really the only clear shot we have of him."

"I understand that," I began, "but to be honest, I've been trying to forget that night."

"Understandable," the first officer replied. "However, anything you remember may help us track him down before he hurts someone else."

"Okay," I replied in a soft voice.

"So, if you remember anything else, anything at all, you'll call us? I'll give you my card."

"Yes, sir," I promised as the officer passed his card across the table.

"Then I think we're done for now," the first officer

concluded. "Thank you for your time, Devon."

I nodded back to them as both Mr Saunders and I got to our feet. The first officer collected the photos from the table and slipped them back into the manila folder.

"Devon, wait here. I'll see our guests out," Mr Saunders ordered as he moved to direct the policemen to the door.

After several minutes Mr Saunders arrived back into the room and closed the door.

"Thank you, Devon, I realise that this couldn't have been easy."

"No problem, sir," I replied, mocking a tip of the hat motion to him.

"Stop making light of this, Devon. You were assaulted by what was obviously a drug-addled maniac. This isn't something you can just shrug off with a laugh."

"I'm okay," I protested. "I really am."

"Well, you seem to be," Mr Saunders replied. "But if you find you have trouble sleeping or anything, the school can recommend a good counsellor."

"I think that's a little extreme, sir," I replied.

"I think we can drop the sir now, don't you, Devon?" Mr Saunders commented dryly.

"Sure, okay," I replied.

"Look, Devon, what you went through can't have been easy. But it's important that if you remember anything about this man you inform the police. You'll do that, won't you?"

"Yes, sir, of course," I replied.

A look of wry humour crossed his face at the use of the word *sir* again.

"Sir," I began tentatively. This was new ground for me.

"Yes?"

"Thank you for being here with me, I really appreciate it."

"Don't mention it," Mr Saunders replied simply. "Now, you'd better get to class."

Tony was waiting for me when I got out of the assembly room. I noted the look of resigned displeasure on Mr Saunders face as he spotted Tony waiting for us. He didn't comment but just waved his hand in the direction of the door.

"What was that about?"

"An overdue library book," I replied flippantly.

"Seems extreme." He chuckled with a grin.

"The school is taking a hard line on overdue fees." I chuckled.

"What was it really about?"

"I'll tell you later. This really isn't the place to get into it."

"Sure." Tony shrugged. "I wanted to talk to you anyway. Are you sure about telling Sarah everything?"

"Yeah," I replied. "I don't really have much choice now, but it's something I probably should have done earlier."

"Thanks, man, it's been difficult keeping this from her."

"Yeah, I can imagine," I replied.

"What was going on with Saunders? He doesn't usually joke around like that."

"I'm not sure," I replied, "but he was being awfully nice, uncharacteristically nice."

"Yeah, freaks me out," Tony replied.

"Anyways, I'm in here." I finished, gesturing towards a class that had already started. Tony gave a mock salute to me as I joined the class.

The remainder of the school day went relatively quickly and it didn't feel that long until I was waiting apprehensively at the oval.

I didn't have to wait too long before Tony and Sarah made their way over to the where I waited at the edge of the oval and the basketball courts. Tony had a basketball casually held under one arm.

"What's the basketball for?" I asked as they got close enough.

"For a small demonstration." Tony replied.

"He wouldn't tell me either," Sarah replied glumly.

"Devon is going to show you something now. I don't think you'd believe what we've got to say without some form of proof."

Tony casually threw the basketball at me.

"Okay," Sarah replied, a little lost, "whatever this thing you two have been scheming has to do with sports?"

"Not even a little bit." I grinned.

I had an idea of what Tony had in mind and to be honest it was kind of clever. I doubted Sarah would believe us unless some display of the power occurred and this seemed as good a way as any.

We certainly wouldn't appear out of place on a

basketball court throwing basketballs at the hoop. Provided that no-one paid undue attention to what we were actually doing, we should pass unnoticed. We made our way onto the court and moved towards one of the basketball rings.

"Right, Devon here is going to throw that ball through that hoop," Tony explained, gesturing towards the hoop as if he were some stupid stage magician.

"That's really not that impressive," Sarah replied. "People do that all the time."

"He's going to do it from the other end of the court," Tony finished.

"Shit man! I can hardly see the hoop from the other side of the court!" I protested.

"Just shut up and do it," Tony replied with chuckle.

I ran down to the other end of the court. It was located just behind the ring on the far side. I'd never really realised how long a basketball court actually is. With a flick of my wrist I looped a thread of mana around the ball and very gently lobbed the ball in the direction of the hoop at the other end. I didn't even really have to aim and it only took some minor correction to cause it drop with ease through the ring on the other side into Tony's waiting hands. I wandered back up the court to where Tony and Sarah were talking.

"Well, that's all very impressive," Sarah replied. "But I don't see what this has to do with anything, unless you're telling me you're trying out for the school basketball team."

"What are the odds that he could do it again?" Tony pressed.

"I dunno, not good I'd say. That looked pretty difficult," Sarah reflected.

"What if I were to tell you that the odds are one hundred per cent?" Tony asked. "And that he'll do it every time?"

"That's what one hundred per cent means, dumbass," Sarah replied briskly, "but I'd have to say that then there's obviously a trick to it then. He's cheating somehow."

"But I can't see how he'd be cheating," Sarah continued thoughtfully.

"Do it again," Tony ordered.

"Christ, man, can't I just do it from here?" I complained.

"Same shot," Tony replied forcefully, taking a quick glance around the court. It was fortunate that no-one was really paying us much attention.

I returned to the other side of the court and repeated the shot. Sarah's face took on an expression of incredulity as I sauntered back up the court.

"How did you do that?" Sarah asked as I got close enough.

Tony cut me off before I could answer the question. "Okay, now he's going to balance the ball on the edge of the ring," he called, throwing the ball at me.

"From here? Or do I need to walk up and down the court again?" I grumbled with poor grace.

"From here is fine," Tony nodded.

Without even really setting myself I lobbed the ball up into the air and caused it to take a ninety degree change in direction to rest gently against the rim of the hoop. Sarah gave a startled yelp at the sudden change in direction of the ball and her eyes narrowed with suspicion at the ball. It was just sitting there appearing to be perfectly balanced on the edge of the ring. In reality, however, my mana thread was holding it in place, but of course Sarah couldn't see that.

"That's... unbelievable," she whispered. "How are you doing that? Is there a magnet in the ball or something?"

"Pick a direction," I ordered.

"What?"

"Clockwise? Counter clockwise?" I prompted.

"Um, clockwise I guess," Sarah replied, confused.

I gently made a sweeping motion with my fingers and caused the ball to begin to slide around the rim of the basketball ring.

"Err, that's counter clockwise," Sarah commented dryly, "but I get your point."

"Oh, sorry." I grinned, reversing the direction.

"Okay, so you've got a remote control ball or something," Sarah replied.

"Nope," I replied simply as I let the ball fall back through the hoop.

I brought it into my outstretched hands again by changing its direction from straight down into a ninety degree loop to lump into my hand with a satisfying thumping noise. Sarah had watched as the ball zipped past her face with an expression on her face that bordered on hysteria.

"How…?" was all Sarah managed to get out before she trailed off.

I simply turned my hand over so that the ball was resting in the palm of my hand and with a slight flex of my hand caused the ball to lift slowly from my palm. Sarah's expression narrowed and she ran her fingers through the air around the ball. It tingled a little bit as she ran her fingers through the mana thread. I noticed that there was some disruption to the mana thread as it happened, but it soon stabilised.

"This must be a trick ball," Sarah commented, her face taking on an analytical pose as she examined the ball.

"Okay," I replied, feeling a little like a sideshow magician revealing a trick. To be honest I was enjoying this more than a little bit.

"You pick the object then."

"Something small preferably," Tony cut in, still glancing around the school yard. Fortunately, most people were focused on going home and weren't really paying us much attention.

Sarah removed a small notebook from her bag and I latched a mana thread onto it before she could offer it to me and gently caused it to rise from her hands. Sarah gave a small yelp and pulled her hands away in fright as the notebook began to float of its own accord.

"How are you doing this?" she asked, her eyes wide and her voice still a little high.

"It started about mid-year," I began. "Remember that day when you said you saw my eyes go strange?"

"Yeah," Sarah said, "but I thought I dreamt it."

"Look at my eyes now,"

Sarah gave a strangled gasp as she looked me in the eyes, "That's just not natural."

"I don't think I need to tell you how serious this is," I declared. "You can't tell anyone about this – ever."

"How did this happen? You didn't make a Faustian deal or anything did you?" Sarah asked in a high pitched voice.

"Faustian?"

"Oh! I know that one!" Tony quipped, "Faust was some dude who made a deal with the devil. Some eighteenth century poem or something. Sarah went nuts over it for a while."

Sarah rolled her eyes at her boyfriend's explanation.

"No." I chuckled. "It was nothing like that. One day I just woke up and I could see these little blue lines everywhere. I thought I was going crazy at first, but then I met Renee."

"Renee? What does she have to do with this?" Sarah's eyes narrowed. It was becoming more and more obvious that she didn't much care for Renee.

"She's been teaching me," I replied.

"So, she's like you?" Sarah interjected.

"Yeah… only she's more powerful."

"Is it possible to teach someone, anyone … this?" Sarah asked with a slight catch in her voice.

"I don't think so, if you can't see the mana, then no, probably not."

"Mana?" Tony interrupted. "What the hell is that?"

"The magic," I replied simply.

"What does it look like?" Sarah was obviously intrigued.

"Umm, it's kind of blue and sparkly, I guess," I explained. "I can see it pulse up and down my arms."

"You're blue and sparkly?" Tony quipped in. "So you're covered in blue sparkly things? What you're saying is that you look like a flamboyant Smurf?"

"Thanks dude." I nodded. "You always know just what to say to make me feel better."

"Yeah, it's a public service really," Tony chuckled.

"I appreciate it. I really do." I snickered.

Sarah had a wild look in her eyes as she looked at me. She refused to look me directly in the eyes. Her eyes darted wildly between the ground and Tony as if seeking reassurance that this was actually happening.

"Why didn't you tell me any of this earlier?" she demanded.

"I didn't really know what was going on at first," I explained. "I only told Tony a few months ago as Renee asked me to keep it a secret."

"Why does Renee want this kept so quiet?" Sarah interjected.

"Would you announce something like this on public television?" I retorted.

"Yeah, okay… fair point," Sarah conceded.

"But, she did have another reason …" I trailed off.

"Which is?"

"She's a fugitive."

"Who from?" Sarah immediately demanded.

"Well, I'm not one hundred per cent sure of the relationship, but I suppose you could say that he's an old boyfriend of hers," I said.

"So? We've all got baggage," Sarah replied critically.

"This baggage is dangerous. I've met him and he's completely deranged," I answered.

Sarah raised a quizzical eyebrow.

"I ran into him on the train on Friday night," I explained. "That's incidentally what the police wanted with me today during the assembly, apparently he hurt some security guards after I escaped from him."

"You escaped him? Whoa, dude, back up, what happened?" Tony stopped me. "You never told me any of this."

"He confronted me on the train back home. We were between stations. I couldn't get away."

"What did you do?" Sarah asked.

"Smashed the door and jumped out."

"While the train was moving?" Tony prompted.

"Yeah."

"That's really cool, dude," Tony replied, grinning and patting me on the shoulder.

"You smashed a train door open?" Sarah asked incredulously.

"Ripped it right off its hinges actually," I replied smugly.

I was strangely proud of the achievement. I hadn't considered how this must have sounded to Sarah.

"Wait a minute," Sarah demanded. "Throwing balls into the air and lifting notebooks is one thing. But ripping train doors off their hinges isn't even in the same league! Just how powerful are you? Just what could you do if you had to?"

"I don't know actually. I've never really tried to test myself," I replied, a little taken aback at her attitude.

"I could probably tear these basketball poles from the ground and hurl them across the court or maybe even throw a car," I added, a little intrigued by the possibility.

I'd never really tested the limits of my lifting power – certainly everything I'd tried to lift I'd been able to lift without great difficulty.

"And you think this is a good thing?" Sarah asked defiantly.

"Of course it's a good thing!" I replied, irked by her attitude. She was my friend, she should be happy for me. "How can this be anything but good for me?"

"What you're talking about is absolute power with no restraint," Sarah continued. "Power corrupts and absolute power corrupts absolutely."

"Don't quote your rhetoric at me," I snapped angrily.

"You're not stupid, Devon! You must see what's happening to you!" Sarah urged. "This must be having an effect on you. I knew you weren't acting like yourself recently!"

"Hey! I didn't get a say here!" I argued. "I didn't ask

for this to happen to me. And I certainly don't need you criticising me for a decision I didn't make!" I finished angrily.

"You might not be making the decisions, but you're certainly not thinking about the repercussions either!" Sarah snapped. She hugged me.

"Damn it, Devon, I'm scared for you!" She pushed me back. "You come here and blatantly tell us that you're in possession of superhuman power and that some deranged maniac is trying to kill you and you don't see that this could be a problem?"

"Well, this is something I've been dealing with by myself for a long while now," I protested.

"Well, it's fucking scary," Sarah continued. "You're sounding more and more like a deranged maniac yourself."

"Believe me, I know. This is crazy, but I just don't know what to do," I sighed. "I mean, who do I talk to about this kind of stuff? Renee treats it like it's second nature and like it's nothing special. You've got to admit that this isn't the sort of thing I could talk to Tony about."

"I had no idea it was this bad, dude," Tony interjected. "I would have listened."

"You could have talked to me," Sarah demanded.

"What? And have you look at me exactly the way you're looking at me now?"

"And how am I looking at you?"

"Like I'm a freak and that you're scared of me."

"I am scared," Sarah replied. "But I'm scared for you, not *of* you."

Sarah pulled me into a second hug and whispered in my ear. "I'm your friend, always your friend, never forget that."

"I didn't want to burden you with all this," I whispered back.

"You're never a burden," she replied. "Never."

"Thank you," I said brokenly as we broke the hug.

"So what are you going to do about this deranged guy then?" Tony asked.

"Well, that's the last thing," I sighed.

This was harder to broach with my best friends but they had a right to know. Unfortunately, I had no idea even where to start to tell them. How do I tell my best friends in the whole world that I was running away and leaving them?

"You're running away with Renee," Sarah interjected. "You're going somewhere where he can't find you."

"How did you know that?"

"You told us about the passport this afternoon and I knew it sounded strange," Sarah continued.

"How long will you be gone for?" Tony asked.

"I don't know," I replied.

"Maybe forever?" Tony prompted.

"Maybe." I nodded in agreement.

Tony remained silent for a few seconds. "Is this all set in stone?"

"Kind of."

"Can't Renee just go?"

"It's not that simple, buddy," I sighed wistfully. "If I

remained behind he'd simply try to figure out where she went through me. I doubt I'd survive that experience."

"I understand." Tony replied. "Though I think it sucks."

"I do too." I agreed. "I do too buddy."

"Couldn't you just convince him to leave you alone?" Sarah interjected. "He can't be totally without reason."

"Renee doesn't believe that's possible. She thinks he'd force a fight. I believe her."

"You couldn't take him together?" Tony asked.

"Tony! That's not an option!" Sarah snapped irritably. "Fighting with this guy can't end well."

"Well, to be honest, I wanted to," I replied to Tony. "I was all ready to throw down, but Renee decided it wasn't a good idea. She wasn't sure we'd win. So she convinced me not to."

"Or she was concerned that you'd get hurt?" Sarah suggested.

"Or that, yeah.".

"That's the first intelligent thing I've heard you say about that woman," Sarah muttered darkly.

"Hey, cut her some slack," I retorted. "She's as much a victim in all this as I am."

"If it weren't for her, you wouldn't be in any of this."

"If it weren't for her, I probably wouldn't be here at all," I snapped angrily.

"What?" both Tony and Sarah exclaimed almost in unison.

"There was a point where I was coming to terms with all this that I was in danger – serious danger."

"Danger? From who?"

"Well, no-one really. There's a coping mechanism that the body goes through when this all happens. It's something about the way that the body adjusts to the mana."

"Right… and?" Tony prompted.

"Well, it's apparently a very dangerous time for our kind."

"Our kind?" Sarah interjected. "Christ, you make it sound like you're no longer human anymore."

"Anyway," I replied, ignoring Sarah's comment, "it can be fatal. The body burns itself out or something, and Renee helped me through it."

"Oh?"

"Yeah, apparently I wasn't doing so well. It's entirely possible that without Renee's intervention I would have died."

"Really? When was this?" Sarah asked tentatively.

"Earlier this year," I replied frankly.

"What? When you were getting all those headaches? And couldn't sleep and such?" Sarah asked.

"Yeah, all I know is it wasn't pleasant and I'd never want to go through it again."

"Yeah, you looked pretty wrecked for a while there dude," Tony muttered.

"Is it likely to come back?" Sarah asked.

"No, I don't think so, at least from what Renee told me it won't."

"Kind of like puberty for wizards then, eh?" Tony snickered. "Told you you'd hit puberty eventually."

440

"I guess." I nodded, not really wanting to entertain Tony's jibe. "The important thing is that now you know, I need you to keep this a secret."

"You don't even have to ask," Sarah replied immediately.

"Thank you," I replied.

It felt so much better to get all that off my chest. I hadn't realised how long I'd been holding on to all of that. It was hard keeping it all to myself without talking to anyone about it. I had a tendency to brood if left alone and didn't really deal with my problems that well.

"Now let's go home," Tony declared as he threw an arm around my shoulder and pushed me towards the school gates.

"Don't you have to return the basketball?"

"Eh, I'll do it tomorrow." Tony chuckled.

It wasn't until halfway home that I remembered Renee's instructions. Do not use the mana for any reason. A chill went down my spine. I may have just given everything away. In my callousness and my foolishness I could very well have given Vin the clue he needed to track us down.

Even today I'm still not sure if it was my actions on the basketball court that led to Vin finding us. Despite all evidence to the contrary, I still blame myself for what came next. I'd been warned and it had been very clearly explained to me the consequences of my actions. However, when the chips were down, I took the opportunity to show off for my friends and ignore my responsibility.

* * * *

Renee called to check on me later that day. I neglected to tell her that I'd used throughout the day. She had actually called to tell me that she'd booked a motel room for a few weeks. The motel wasn't far from the school and she'd quit her job. All we were waiting on was for my exams and then we'd be out of here.

I wasn't sure how I was going to break the news to Dad. I'd called him the night before to ask him if it would be okay if I didn't come into the city for the next few weekends as I wanted to cram for the exams. He said he understood, but I could tell he was a little hurt by the request.

I hadn't said anything to Mum. I had no idea how I was going to cross that particular issue. Again Renee was no help as she herself admitted she didn't exactly play happy families. She and her grandfather pretty much went their own ways and tried to stay out of each other's way. In the end, I determined to deal with it the same way I deal with all issues that I didn't want to deal with. I ignored it.

Renee had agreed to come to the Final Year Formal Dance. It was a school tradition that on the weekend before the exams the Year 12s would attend a formal dance to celebrate the end of the school year.

I'd done some checking, and whilst it was unusual it wasn't against the rules for students to bring dates from outside the school. I couldn't think of anyone I wanted to take more. A week had passed and we'd fallen into a routine. We hadn't seen anything of Vin throughout the time and so it was looking good that we'd eluded him – at least for now.

Neither Renee nor I had used mana since my small slip up on the basketball courts and it was beginning to show. I was starting to get those headaches again and becoming short tempered. Fortunately Sarah and Tony now knew what I was going through and cut me some slack. Renee seemed to handle the withdrawal better than me, but you could tell there was a tension behind her eyes. It showed especially when she looked at me, but she certainly didn't appear to be developing headaches or snapping at me anymore than usual.

The school formal was the weekend after next, followed immediately by exams. It was frightening how quickly time was running out. I still had no idea how I was going to say goodbye to my friends and family. Although Tony and Sarah knew I was going, we all were treating it like it was only for a few weeks. The reality of the situation hadn't hit home. Renee and I had talked about where we might go, but Renee had claimed that her grandfather was preparing a place for us. She just wouldn't tell me where it was. I could tell she was a little nervous about introducing me to him and to be perfectly honest, I was terrified of the prospect.

I'd come to the conclusion that I was the one who was responsible for Vin finding Renee. After she had inadvertently let slip that Vin was tracking us via our mana use I thought back about everything we'd done and remembered with startling clarity the mana burst I'd sent out across the Melbourne skyline.

That display must have been a beacon from many miles away – there was no way any of our kind could have missed that. The fact that Vin had shown up only a few weeks after that seemed to support my theory.

I wasn't looking forward to standing before Renee's grandfather being the responsible party for Vin finally locating her. Renee had told me he didn't cope with fools well, and at the moment I felt very foolish.

* * * *

It was the week before the school formal. Next week would be exams. I wasn't really freaking out about the exams, however, as all my terror was reserved for the decision I'd already made. I was leaving.

It wasn't that I had begun to second guess myself. It was more a case that I wasn't sure that I could pay the price of my decision. Everything I knew, everyone I knew was here – I'd be giving it all up.

"Wow, you're really out of it." Garry grinned, punching me on the shoulder. We were sitting in the food court of the shopping centre after school. We used to come here quite regularly after school until they'd instituted a no school uniform policy. Considering it was this close to the end of the school year we figured that they didn't care anymore. We never really worried about the rule anyway, but it would be nice not to have to worry about keeping an eye open for a teacher doing a random check.

"Yeah, sorry mate," I grumbled.

"Actually, you've been out of it for a while now," Garry continued. "You nervous about exams?"

I could see Tony and Sarah exchange glances. I could see them wondering how best to derail Garry's line of conversation. They'd obviously realised what I was brooding about and that I couldn't just come out and discuss it openly now.

"Yeah," I said, "and starting to wonder if I've made the right decision."

"What? About not going to university?" Tina piped up.

She and I had had vastly different views on that topic, so it wasn't surprising that she'd go there. This turn of topic would do nicely.

"Yeah," I said, playing along.

"I didn't think you had a choice," Sarah replied.

"No, I don't really," I replied dully.

"Of course you do!" Tina jumped in, flashing an angry glance at Sarah. "There's always a choice, you've just got to fight for the things you want."

"Fight?" I asked.

"Yes, if something is important, it's worth fighting for," Tina protested.

"What if there's no chance you'll win?" I asked.

"There's always a chance," Tina said with a strange look on her face. "Are we actually talking about university here?"

"Of course," Sarah replied quickly – too quickly.

"Only it seems, from the way you and Tony keep glancing at each other, that there's something else going on here," Tina commented shrewdly.

Sarah and Tony shared another covert glance.

"Glances like that?" I chuckled.

"Yeah." Tina grunted darkly..

"I have no idea."

"Thanks, Dev, that's very helpful." Sarah said, not so subtly flashing me a look of annoyance.

Her look was very clear. It said without a doubt '*we're trying to help you. You could at least help us in return*. She was right. I shrugged slightly in an apologetic fashion. Fortunately Tina was distracted with talk of formal dresses, which I suspect had been Sarah's intention. Talk soon turned to the formal, which the girls were very much looking forward to.

"You're bringing Renee, right?" Tony asked before catching a warning glance from Sarah and trailing off.

Sarah and I were looking at Tina, waiting for her reaction.

"What?" Tina asked, glancing at us. "I'd like to meet her actually."

"Oh? Why so?" Garry grinned. "Going to take out the competition, eh?"

Both Sarah and I punched him from opposite sides.

"No fair! No ganging up on me!" Garry grumbled, rubbing both his arms.

"Yeah," Tony mumbled sympathetically, "they do that to me too."

"Only when you're being an idiot," Sarah shot back, "and you deserved it Garry!"

"Well, I want to see what kind of woman she is," Tina continued, answering Garry's question even though it really wasn't required.

The conversation eventually returned to talk of the formal and I was kind of glad that I wasn't paying attention.

"Good God, Devon!" Tina hissed. "Are you okay?"

"He's gone white!" Sarah commented, glancing around.

Standing on the opposite side of the food court leaning casually against a railing and looking back at me was Vin. He had a smirk on his face and a knowing look in his eye.

"Give me a minute," I grunted as I pushed my food tray away and got to my feet. Tony moved to stand up but I waved him down.

"I'll be okay," I assured him, hoping like hell that this was in fact the case.

Vin watched me make my way across the food court, which wasn't an easy task as the court was quite busy. This was a mixed blessing as there were surely far too many witnesses for Vin to try anything funny. Which raised a further question, what the hell was he doing here? And why reveal himself to me now? I vaguely thought about ringing Renee but I doubted she'd be able to do much more than I could here – it was too open. Besides, there were plenty of people here, and I was safe for the moment. I'd call Renee as soon as I could. Her motel was only five minutes' walk from this food court and I didn't want Vin knowing she was so close. Vin didn't say anything as I approached.

"What are you doing here?" I accused when we got close enough to talk privately.

"At the moment, nothing," Vin replied, "at the moment…"

"Is that a threat?" I snapped coldly.

"Listen boy, I don't make threats," Vin retorted, his face twisting in a savage distortion of his features as he sneered down at me. "You know damn well why I'm here."

I didn't respond.

"Where is she?" he asked. "I'm not interested in you. Tell me where she is and I'll leave you alone."

"Like I believe that," I scoffed.

"Believe what you want." He nodded. "I've really got no reason to bother myself with the likes of you."

I contemplated his offer but I wasn't tempted for a second.

"She's not at her apartment and it looks like she isn't planning on coming back," Vin continued. "So where is she?"

"I don't know," I lied. "She called me several days ago and said she was going away. She told me to watch out for you."

Vin grinned darkly but his eyes did not reflect the mirth.

"You're lying," he accused.

I didn't respond.

"I'll find her, one way or the other," he promised.

"You go do that," I replied, turning to go.

I doubted he'd just let me go, but he made no move to follow me.

"Are those your friends?" Vin called as I got several steps away. "Nice school uniform, by the way."

I didn't reply. I just kept walking and by the time I returned to the table, he'd gone.

"Everything okay?" Sarah asked delicately as I resumed my seat.

"Yeah." I nodded as I started fishing through my backpack for my phone.

I took a quick look around the area for Vin, but I was pretty sure he'd gone – it wasn't like he could be hiding amongst the crowd. The mana would give him away far too easily. I rang Renee's phone, but it rang out. This was odd as she was normally pretty good at picking up calls. I shrugged a little and figured she'd ring me back.

"Who was that guy?" Tina asked once I hung up the phone.

"An old friend," I grunted, "and someone I didn't particularly want to see."

"He didn't look very friendly," Tina continued.

"He's not."

"Are you in some kind of trouble?"

"No, I'm fine." I grinned disarmingly. I wished that this was actually the case.

I had a dark sense of foreboding at this whole situation and couldn't shake the feeling that something was very, very wrong.

CHAPTER THIRTEEN

Renee hadn't answered my call again. I put down the phone in frustration. She hadn't returned the subsequent two calls that I'd made the following day either. Paranoid theories ran through my head. Maybe she'd gone to confront Vin by herself or maybe she had come to the conclusion that I'd be better off out of all this and had left without me. Despite my paranoid musings I wasn't overly worried about her. The last time we had spoken she had indicated that she might be unavailable for some time. She hadn't given me any more details, and I hadn't pressed her. She hadn't exactly been easy to deal with while she was undergoing mana withdrawals.

I stopped by her motel room in the morning before school, but there was no answer. I tried peeking through the windows and could see her suitcase and stuff still on the floor by her bed. I took that as a good sign. It meant that she was planning on returning here at some point. Unless it meant that she hadn't planned on going and had had to leave in a hurry. The nervous unease in the pit of my stomach was quickly turning into a rising terror.

I didn't know what to do now. Should I start looking

for her? Setting off an awareness blast would only call Vin back and give away my location and I definitely didn't want to do that. Maybe that wasn't such a concern. After all he'd found me yesterday. I was still running wild theories through my head as I wandered through the school gates. No matter which way I played this – I really had no idea what to do now. I had vague plans of confronting Vin and demanding to know what he had done with her, but I wasn't sure that that would be a good idea. After my last confrontation with him, it was clear that I was outmatched.

Fortunately school wasn't that stressful any longer. I'd already completed the assignments I'd needed to complete and as long as no-one asked too much about the quality of those assignments I'd be okay. I tried ringing Renee again during lunch but again it rang out.

During the afternoon classes I began pondering exactly what Vin meant by '*Nice school uniform*' and '*Are those your friends*?'

Aside from the obvious threat, it was clear that he was going to attempt to strike at me through my friends, unless of course he was simply playing mind games with me which I grudgingly conceded was possible.

"Walk home together?" Sarah interjected from my reverie. "Tony's got himself into detention again."

"Um, I'm not sure that's a particularly good idea," I replied darkly.

"That guy yesterday, at the food court – he was the guy, right?" Sarah guessed.

"Yeah."

"Well, that's not good," Sarah reflected. "And you're afraid he's going to come after you?"

I nodded grimly.

"What are you going to do?"

"I don't know."

"You could go to the police."

"That's a possibility," I replied, my hand caressing the policeman's business card in my pocket. I'd already had the same thought.

"I don't know if that's the right thing to do. I get the feeling that that would just lead to a massacre."

"As much as I hate to ask, what does Renee think?" Sarah asked darkly.

"I can't get hold of her," I replied.

"What – you think she's done a runner?" Sarah exclaimed, stating my darkest fears.

"No, her stuff is still at the motel, but she's not answering her phone."

"What are you going to do?"

"I don't know," I replied. "I simply don't know."

"Well, I think you should walk me home anyway," Sarah replied promptly.

"Okay," I replied cautiously, getting a strange sense of déjà vu. "But, if I say run, you run, okay?"

"Okay," Sarah agreed readily.

"Thanks, Sarah."

"I wasn't going to leave you on your own in this mood," Sarah added.

Vin didn't come after us on our way home, but it was a strangely quiet walk home. I kept jumping at shadows and to be honest I think Sarah was as relieved as I was when we reached her house. She didn't invite me in, and frankly I didn't blame her. She didn't need to be involved in any of this and the less time she spent with me, the better. The next day was the day of the formal. The school had graciously given a half day to the final year students but it was expected that we attend in the morning. I hadn't slept at all that night. I'd sat perched in my window frame, watching the street outside, waiting, watching, and slowly going insane through lack of sleep and dread. I was almost at the point where I actually wanted something to happen, anything to happen just to stop this infernal waiting game.

I could almost feel Vin out there watching me, judging me. It felt like he was waiting for a moment of weakness to strike. The only upside was that fear for one's life just happens to be one of those factors that makes the school day appear to go much quicker. Before I realised it the half day was over.

I tried ringing Renee again, hoping against hope that she had just been busy the previous times I'd called. As usual the phone rang out. I walked over to Renee's motel room, no change there. On a hunch I tried the phone again. Listening carefully I could clearly make out the sound of Renee's phone ringing inside. Her mobile phone was in her room! Shit! She might be hurt!

Why hadn't I thought that sooner?

The mana came to my hand far quicker than expected and with a directed flick caused the lock on the door to almost implode into fragments. I stalked into the room, half fearing to find Renee unconscious on the ground. The apartment looked untidy. Her phone was lying on the floor by the bed, next to a glass of water which was half-finished on the stand. Her suitcases were still fully packed and from a cursory inspection I couldn't see anything that was obviously missing. Why was her phone on the floor?

Had she fled the apartment in a rush? No – her keys were on the mantle by the doorway. She'd left without her keys and phone? What the hell was going on here?

With a deepening sense of fear, I noticed that Renee's hand bag was thrown haphazardly over one of the arm chairs. A quick inspection revealed that her purse was still in the handbag. She'd left the apartment without any of her personal effects. There was only one conclusion to be drawn from this – she'd left against her will.

No, that wasn't right. There didn't appear to be any sign of a fight or disturbance. if a fight had happened here then there'd be something. The more I thought about it the more I came to the conclusion that something unexpected had happened. If a Mage fight had happened here the whole motel would be in ruins. I had just about calmed myself back down when there was knock on the door, and a voice calling out. I quietly cursed and threw an invisibility field around myself. Someone from the motel wandered into the room from outside. She entered the room tentatively. I could see from her expression that she was obviously worried about the damage to the door and of the possibility of a robbery. It was one of the maid staff. As she glanced around the room she obviously came to the conclusion that the room was empty. She checked the bathroom and kitchen areas looking for intruders. Once she entered the bathroom I took the opportunity to slip out the front door. I had what I wanted anyway. Renee wasn't here. The first trick would be to find Renee, I wasn't sure even where to begin with the second, but I was sure once I had found Renee, together we could deal with the problem. Making my way back home I had to force myself to prepare my clothes for tonight. I thought about skipping the formal tonight, but thought against it. Renee had promised to go – it was possible that she still might turn up. My optimism aside, I was also considering where I could set off an awareness blast that would give me the most ground, probably from the top of one of the larger buildings. Glen Waverley wasn't exactly an inner suburb, but it did have several large buildings that would suit the need. If I waited until it was dark, I'd be able to spot Renee's mana signature from a far greater distance.

I made plan after plan after plan, until I had pretty much discounted all of my available options and then I started again from scratch.

"You're pacing," a quiet voice interjected into my brooding plotting.

I don't know if Mum realised that I was quietly simmering away into a pit of anger and fear or simply assumed that I was nervous about the formal tonight, either way I needed a break. I threw myself onto the couch and attempted to calm myself down. Watching the mana particles pulse up and down my forearm gave me a strange sense of peace and assurance. it would all work out, Renee was okay, she'd meet me later tonight. It would all be all right.

"Does Renee need to be picked up?" Mum asked. She'd offered to drive me to the formal. I had refused as Tina would be picking us all up in her car and we'd all go in together.

"No, we're meeting there," I lied.

"Oh, that's unusual, it's more traditional for the gentleman to pick up the lady," Mum commented.

"I don't have my full driver's licence," I scoffed. "That'd look really traditional – with the gentleman's mother in the passenger seat correcting his drifting."

"Well, you do tend to drift," Mum reminded me.

"And besides, it's your fault you don't have your licence – I offered to pay for the test."

"I didn't have time," I replied.

To be honest I'd avoided the test because I wasn't sure that I'd pass and wasn't sure that I could handle the mocking I'd get from Tony.

"If you say so." Mum smiled.

She knew as well as I did that I really was quite full of it at times, but she let it pass.

"Mum, I'm not quite sure what's going to happen tonight," I began, "but, thanks – for everything."

She turned to look at me, a quizzical expression on her face.

"What's all this about?"

"Well, nothing really," I coughed, trying to avoid making eye contact. "Just wanted to thank you is all – you know … for school and stuff." I was a horrible liar.

"Well, you're welcome," Mum said, still giving me that strange look.

I chose not to push the subject any further; however, by way of punishment Mum made me pose for photos in what I considered to be an overly decorative monkey suit, rather than a formal dress suit. However, I think I owed it to her and the photos seemed to make her happy. Some of the photos hadn't turned out that bad either, considering I'm not an easy person to take a good photo of. A few hours later Tina's car pulled up in my drive. Mum called out and I answered the door and went outside to meet them. Tina had already picked up Sarah and Tony.

"You guys look amazing," I gushed as I got into the seat.

The advanced cosmetics practical that had been going on at Sarah's house this afternoon had paid off. Tina and Sarah had chosen to spend the remainder of the day getting ready at Sarah's house.

"Why thank you, kind sir, I do believe we look appropriate for the event," Sarah snickered, doing her best impersonation of an eighteenth century southern woman and mocking a curtsey. This was actually kind of impressive considering that she was currently seated in the front seat of a car.

"Tony, you look as trashy as ever," I grinned, nodding to him. just being around my friends brought an immediately sense of relief and comfort as I fell back into our old routines. The world could be crumbling around us, and we would still be ragging on each other about mindless crap.

"And you too, sir." Tony smirked. "You look like a hobo that's really decided to let himself go and start dressing in casual."

I couldn't help but chuckle at that.

"Well, I think you guys look good too. It's nice to see you dressed up for once!" Tina piped in from the front.

Tony and I grinned to each other.

"Don't encourage them," Sarah scoffed. "They know they're all dressed up and looking good, they're just being idiots."

"Why, ma'am, I do believe that was a compliment, most untoward from a lady of unmarried virtue," I replied.

I was talking utter garbage and doing my best Colonel Sanders impression, in actual fact it was more Foghorn Leghorn but I think the gist came across.

"Devon?" Sarah called from the front.

"Yeah?"

"Shut up."

"Yes, ma'am." I grinned.

We weren't far from the school now and were just pulling into the road between the school and the shopping centre. Surprisingly for this time there was a lot of traffic on the road. I suppose a lot of people had chosen to drive to the formal.

"We're going to be late," Tina fumed. "I think it's already started."

"Relax, Tina, it's fine," Tony called. "It's not due to start for another ten minutes at least. Not everyone needs to be half an hour early for everything, all the time."

Tina's response to this was cut off by a sudden twisted complaint of metal and noise as the engine immediately revved up. The car was jerked suddenly to the side, throwing us hard against our seat belts.

"What's going on?" Tony gasped as the car lurched again.

"I don't know! I can't seem to control it!" Tina called hysterically. Her head was whipping around frantically from side to side as the car buckled again. The noise was incredible from inside the cabin. Each metallic shriek was amplified within the cabin of the car. I could barely hear it though, not over the shouts and cries of my friends. This was my fault.

I breathed out a sigh of futility. I knew what was going on. I could see it. Mana threads had looped themselves around the car and were pushing against it. They were slowly but surely pushing it onto the other side of the road. I couldn't' see where they were coming from, especially with the car bucking around so much, but it was obvious that this was Vin's work.

Tony looked frantically at me as the car immediately jumped several metres in the air.

"Are you doing this?" he shouted, his eyes wide with horror.

I shook my head.

"Him?"

"yes."

There was a resounding thump and the rear end of the car swung ponderously around. We'd just collided with a car on the other side of the road. Tina and Sarah were both screaming in the front and Tony had gone white.

I needed to do something, and quickly.

Time appeared to slow down for me. I could see with stark clarity the mana threads encircling the car and slowly dragging us onto the other side of the road. I unlatched my seat belt and threw myself onto the opposite side of the car and latched my own mana thread against the ones wrapped around the car in an attempt to slow our motion.

The only reason we weren't dead from the impact before was that the car hadn't been moving that fast. This wasn't about killing us – this was about humbling me. This was about forcing me to accept him as my better – this was another of Vin's damned games.

My efforts had at least slowed our movement and I could feel the motion of the car get jerkier and more frantic. At least our sideways motion had stopped though. Due to the effort of our contest the car now appeared to be floating several metres above the road. I could feel the tension in the car frame between us as I began a deadly game of tug of war with Vin.

"Devon! What are you doing? Get back in your seat!" Tina screamed frantically, her hands gripping the steering wheel.

I could feel the motion of the car as it slowed and it appeared that I was winning. I was actually pulling the mana thread from around the car. Vin obviously felt so too because in swift motion he released the car and let it plummet back to the ground with an audible crash.

The impact knocked the wind out of me. We were only several metres above the ground, but the shock of the car hitting the surface drove the air straight out of my lungs. I breathed a sigh of relief, which turned out to be premature as Vin wasn't finished. Not by a long shot.

The sound of a car horn blaring out was the only warning we had before an oncoming car was telekinetically hurled into the front driver's side of our car. I called out and attempted to throw a shield around the car. Forming a field that large was difficult and I had the shock impact of feeling the field unravel before everything went black.

There was a long monotonous buzzing sound that brought me round.

My head was resting against Tony's leg and I could feel blood dribbling down the side of my face. There was a smash mark in the window behind Tony. I wasn't sure if it had been caused by my head or Tony's. I checked my head and my hand came away red with my blood. It didn't feel too bad. I only found a small cut on my forehead. It was a small cut but it was certainly determined to bleed. Other than that I was a little shaken but appeared to be okay.

Tony was unconscious in his seat, but didn't appear to be too badly injured. The seat belt had obviously kept him in his seat. He was the furthest from the impact point. A groggy inspection informed me that the front of the car was a complete mess. I don't know how hard the other car had hit us, but it must have been hard.

I could see Sarah and Tina, but they weren't moving. I couldn't tell how injured they were. I must have nudged Tony as I was moving around as he groaned and opened his eyes.

"What happened?"

"He threw a damned car at us," I cursed.

"Is Sarah okay?"

"I don't know," I replied grimly. "I hope so."

I pulled on the door lever to Tony's door as the one on my side was a complete mess. The fact that I hadn't been in my seat at the moment of impact had probably saved my life. I hurriedly pulled on the door handle to Tony's door, but I wasn't overly surprised that this door had jammed too. The whole carcass of the car was a rumpled mess.

I'd heard somewhere that cars are designed to

crumple in on themselves to absorb the impact and protect the occupants. Looking at this mess from the inside, I believed it. I took my jacket off and threw it over Tony's left side to cover him from what I was about to do. The window on his side hadn't shattered and I didn't want to shower him with glass.

"Brace yourself," I ordered Tony as I sent a mana thread smacking against the door frame. The impact of the thread sent the door screaming with a metallic complaint across the road.

The car wreck was sitting on the sidewalk near the shopping centre entrance. The two cars formed a v shaped wreck with the car that had hit us wedged into the driver's side. I could make out the driver of the other car through a smashed windscreen but he was slumped over the wheel and was unnaturally still.

Several people were approaching the car cautiously. They were looking at me with a strange mixture of fear and concern. They had just seen a car door fly from its hinges and me emerge from the wreckage. The noise must have brought Sarah around as I could hear her groan from the passenger's front seat. Tina, however, hadn't moved since the accident. I could see her body, but there were so many rumpled up pieces of wreckage around her that I couldn't get to her.

"Look after her, I'm sure an ambulance will be on its way," I ordered as I turned back to Tony.

"Where are you going?" Tony called.

I didn't answer. I couldn't answer, I don't suppose

I even knew myself, all I knew was that I had one overwhelming desire.

I'd make Vin pay for this.

I'm not sure I heard people calling out into the car. I vaguely recall someone asking me if anyone was hurt. I know for certain that several other cars had pulled over and I even vaguely recall hearing the sound of an approaching ambulance. But I can't clearly recall any of the details of the accident. It was all red mist.

I set off an awareness blast which rocketed out from the car and covered the surrounding area. This informed me that Vin had obviously fled into the shopping centre. I burst from the accident site at a fast run using mana threads to enhance my speed. I leapt up the stairs taking several steps at a time and made my way into the centre. I heard from behind me the gasp from people behind me as they witnessed my ascent.

My legs were grudgingly complying at the rough treatment although there was indication that there would be a price to pay later. My head had begun to clear as I ran up the stairs into the shopping centre and the annoying ringing in my ears had begun to subside.

I wasn't surprised to find that the doors to the centre already had been smashed open. There was a lot of glass on the ground and the metal frame bent almost to a 90 degree angle. The centre had been closed for hours now, although the supermarket was still open at the other end of the centre. This end of the shopping centre was closed and was locked down – entry was prohibited. However, it's difficult to keep our kind out of somewhere we want to go.

The deserted shopping centre was a good sign. It meant that there'd be no-one to get in my way. The stores had an empty quality that was almost haunting. The main lighting remained on in the centre but the interior lights in all the shops were switched off. This gave the impression of shrouds of darkness where there used to be light.

Small sounds echo loudly throughout the centre, which you don't notice during the day because of all the background noise. Without these sounds my footsteps were discordant and distracting. I wasn't concerned about Vin knowing I was coming. I'd already announced my intentions with my awareness spell. I hadn't used that much power with the blast and as a result the effect was fading quickly. It was still sufficient for me to find him.

I knew where he was and therefore he obviously knew where I was too. I could still see Vin clearly from the awareness blast I'd used earlier. He appeared to be a floor up from me in the main corridor of shops.

I vaulted onto the side-rail of the escalator, which had been blocked off by a portable barrier, and ran up it. I picked up speed as I ran and latched a mana thread to the top of the roof above me, which allowed me to pull myself into a rough form of leaping flight.

I barrelled from the escalator pit at great speed and leapt high into the main corridor. I could see Vin standing at the other side of the corridor. I didn't even give him a chance to say anything. I raised a shield around myself and launched a mana thread straight at him from the high angle of my attack. This gave me the perfect angle from which to strike and I bore down on him like an avenging angel striking from the heavens.

Vin countered my thread without too much difficulty which caused me to smash a potted plant display to the left of him into shards. I landed without much magical assistance, relying on my shield to absorb the majority of the impact.

The breath was forced from my body and I felt my legs jerk as I rolled into a tight ball. I curled myself into a somersault forward and launched myself at him again. I'd expected him to block my first strike. My whole plan was him not being prepared for the second. I immediately came back to my feet and launched a second thread, bringing my arms around in a wide round arc. An arc he wouldn't be able to avoid.

Vin's face turned from smug condescension into panic as he raised a shield – it had worked! He obviously hadn't expected me to be able to return the attack so quickly. I watched with a small degree of satisfaction as my mana thread impacted solidly against his shield. This caused him to wince and take several staggered steps back. My victory was short lived however as he immediately countered with a savage strike that I narrowly managed to parry by throwing myself to one side. With a jarring impact our two threads struck each other. I quickly countered again, by sliding my thread around and aiming for his face. However this time he was prepared and easily defended my attack. I noted with some degree of smug triumph that he had retained his shield.

His response was aggressive and fast. His mana thread pounded against mine again and again and I was amazed that my thread was holding against it let alone that I was even still able to block. I'd obviously improved since our last encounter and I had no idea how, or why.

However, as good as I was it still wasn't good enough.

I was now as fast as him and able to counter his strikes but I couldn't match him for raw power and what little ground I had gained I was quickly losing. He had already forced to me to retreat back past the escalator pit and to the shops behind me. Although both of us had scored several successful strikes, due to the strength of our shields and the fact that we'd only scored passing shots the shopping centre was actually taking the worst of our fight. Invariably our missed or deflected strikes would hit both shop window frontages or centre decorations. We were quickly leaving a path of broken glass on the floor behind us and a swathe of destruction through the centre.

The strain of the battle was finally starting to get to me. I'd never used a concentrated thread of mana for this length of time before. The reality of the situation was that although the battle had only lasted a few minutes it felt like several hours had passed. My arms ached from the effort of controlling and directing my attack and my breath was coming out in gasps.

I was physically panting when I made my first mistake.

It was a small mistake, the angle of my thread was wrong and Vin easily slipped his attack underneath it and connected solidly with my side. The shield took the majority of the impact but the dull thump still swept me from my feet and slid me across the ground. Fortunately Vin was obviously too tired to finish the attack and his delay allowed me time to regain my footing. The delay had cost him, but the battle was still far from over.

I pulled myself wearily back to my feet and launched a half-hearted overhead attack at his head. His counter was with his usual speed, causing my thread to obliterate the railings covering the walkway over the gap between this level and the one below.

"I've just about finished toying with you, kid!" he snarled.

He appeared confident and proud but I could tell that he was struggling to catch his breath and that this was at best an attempt at intimidation. I didn't respond, but instead I pressed forward my attack. The reality of the situation was that I was still losing. Like in our encounter in the train carriage I was being forced to concede ground. There were only three shop lengths before I ran out of mall and unless I did something clever I would lose.

He was just too good at being able to spot and predict my attack angle. His threads now didn't appear to be any stronger than mine and he didn't appear to be hitting any harder than me, our fatigue had made us equals in that department. It was just that he appeared to be able to predict and anticipate where I'd attack from with almost preternatural accuracy. Until I neutralised that advantage, I was doomed to defeat. In desperation my mind scrambled to come up with some solution that would allow me to overcome this single element of his attack. In a burst of inspiration I realised what I needed to do. It wasn't that he was better than me – it was that he had more experience in analysing what I was doing.

I needed to make it harder for him to see what I was doing and I knew just how to do that.

And then, well. Then I'd have to run. There was no way I was going to win this.

The cold reality of the situation had cooled the rage that had fuelled my attack. I had no desire to continue this battle any longer than I had to. It was a desperate gamble – if I were able to distract him, I'd be able to get away. To look at him now, I was sure he wouldn't pursue this. I'd made my point. He'd have to leave me alone. He'd have to. He had to.

I didn't even bother blocking his next attack. I simply slid to my knees and rolled forward under his thread, coming up much closer than we'd normally been getting. At almost point blank range. I was almost right under his nose. I rose with fury from beneath him, the mana building in my hands into a ball of swirling energy and with a flick of my wrist I released. A bright light burst out from my fingers causing me to avert my eyes as the glow spell detonated the mana straight into Vin's face.

Vin yelled out as the mana detonated right before his eyes and his mana thread disintegrated immediately. He quickly reformed it but the lapse had definitely cost him. The mana was bursting into little flecks of light around us, burning up and falling to the ground creating a virtual symphony of magical noise.

Vin struck out wildly and it was obvious that he was having trouble seeing. Unfortunately for him he'd struck where I'd launched my glow spell from and not where I'd ended up. I was easily able to deflect his strike, sending his mana thread arching about and breaking the ceiling, causing glass to shower down upon us. He made several more wide strikes, almost at random. He was flailing and trying desperately to keep me at bay.

It was easy to avoid this new tactic and I sidestepped to one side and launched my attack. Whipping my mana thread around savagely into a full chest strike I launched my attack with everything I had and watched with satisfaction as the thread tore into Vin's shield and sent him spiralling back into the shopfront behind him. This showered him with more shards of glass as they fell from the store shopfront.

I didn't even stop to look, the moment he'd hit the glass I was already running. I was desperately trying to make it to the closest exit. I couldn't go back the way I'd come as by now there were sure to be ambulances and perhaps even police at the car accident zone. There was another exit that led into the high rise car park on the far side of the shopping centre, from there I could make good my escape. All I needed to do was drop down a flight of stairs and run down a small plaza that would lead me to my destination. Once I made it into the car park, I'd be okay.

And you know what? I almost made it, I really did. I was so close. I could see the doors in sight just before me and was getting ready to hit them with a mana thread to smash them open and disappear through them. I never got the chance. This isn't to say that I didn't end up breaking through the doors. I did – just not the way I'd expected to.

If I hadn't still had my shield around me, I think the strike that hit me probably would have killed me. It struck me on my lower right side and lifted me into the air, propelling me through the glass doors. I felt the impact of the doors and I felt them give way. The impact shattered my shield and the impact with the ground left me dazed and hurt. I felt my legs jar as I hit the cold concrete surface of the car park floor outside and felt a click in my ankle as I landed.

In shock I turned to look at the remains of a doorway that I'd just flown through. It was a mess: both doors were twisted wrecks hanging off their railings and Vin was walking calmly down the stairs behind them. He walked across the floor with a self-satisfied grin on his face.

I tried to get to my feet and gasped as it felt like a brand of fire had been shoved into my ankle. With a strangled cry my legs gave way and I tumbled back to the ground. Vin gently pushed the wrecked doors to one side as he moved through them. His face was twisted into a savage smirk and his eyes glittered with barely concealed hate.

"So it comes to this," he snarled. "You should have just told me where she'd gone."

I pulled myself onto my side and gazed at him. There was no hint of anything remotely recognisable in his eyes as he gazed down on me. There were no traces of humanity or morality. There was only that damned evil smirk. Vin shrugged and pulled off his trench coat, which was mostly in shreds now anyway. I noticed he had several cuts along the left side of his face that bled freely.

"I've given a lot of thought as to how I'm going to kill you," he explained, taking his time to enunciate each syllable.

I sighed wistfully. There was very little I could do to prevent him with my ankle like this. I couldn't very well run and he would most certainly be able to defend himself from any attack I launched now. Perhaps it would be easier to just lie back and await the inevitable. I was tired of fighting anyway, tired of the constant struggle. Perhaps it would be better to just bow down and await the end.

"I'm going to make you suffer," Vin hissed as he stepped away from his fallen trench coat.

"Just do it already!" I snapped angrily. I figured if I made him angry enough he'd finish it quickly. He was probably the type that this would work on if the action movies were to be believed.

Vin smiled again and his face took on a twisted smirk as he tilted his head back. He brought his hands up in front of him and I watched as the mana ran down his arms and into the palms of his hands. Two jets of flame burst from each palm and engulfed his hand. The flame was running like quicksilver up over his wrists and across his forearms. Vin's face took on an ecstatic tilt as the magical euphoria overtook him.

His dark eyes glittered as they reflected the hell fire now contained within his grasp.

With a small gesture he sent a jet of flame jetting in my direction. It caught my right foot before I could pull it away. I gasped with pain as I felt my foot blister and burn within my shoe. I watched as the leather on my shoe blackened and burned and the pain was unbearable. I pulled my foot from the jet and clambered onto my side and painfully began to pull myself away. Crawling away wasn't really going to do that much, but I couldn't endure a death like this. I had to get away.

"Yes! Run away!" Vin shouted, his voice breaking off into a fit of maniacal laughter.

"Not like this," I whispered quietly to myself as I looked for something, anything that could prevent what appeared to be the inevitable.

There were no cars I could hide behind. This would have only granted me a temporary reprieve in any event. There was no-one to interfere or stop him. Not that

Vin wouldn't have been able to deal with anyone who attempted to try. No. I was completely on my own.

Vin sent several more jets of flame bursting into my direction. I had raised my shield by now, but I could still feel the heat scalding my back and causing me to gasp and roll over. This was pointless. He'd won. I turned onto my side and faced him.

If I was going to die, then I was going to die facing him and accepting my fate. He wouldn't find me snivelling and begging him. I'd face him down and when he finished it, god damn it, at least he'd respect me for it.

"You're nothing," Vin hissed as he stepped forward again. The flame was now billowing across his arms and upper torso almost as if it were a liquid. Under any other circumstances it would have been beautiful, however under my current position I was less than objective about its beauty. The look on Vin's face hardened and I realised that he was through playing.

This was it.

I needed something to protect myself, anything. I began to frantically look around for something, anything to protect myself when I noticed that near the entrance to the shopping centre were two industrial sized garbage skips that were used by the shopping centre for waste disposal. I couldn't envisage a way in which they could be used as a weapon, but I might be able to use them as a shield.

I gasped as I pulled myself forward onto my knees, gritting my teeth and ignoring the searing pain from my injured foot. I wrapped a mana thread around the skip.

Vin, obviously assuming that this was an attack of some sort, sent a volley of flame my way. Through either fate or perhaps incredibly motivated self-interest I managed to bring the dumpster directly into the path of the volley of flame.

I could hear Vin's laughter over the sound of the flame hitting the side of the skip. The strong stench of burning paper and plastic assaulted my senses as I held the skip before me. I dropped my shield as it wouldn't have helped me that much anyway and rallied my strength into holding this simple object in front of me.

"Oh well done!" Vin called as he burst into laughter once more. "You're quite inventive!"

I didn't respond. I could see that Vin had increased the ferocity of his attack. The plastic lids to the skip were warping and melting and beginning to slowly slide down the side of the skip. He obviously intended to burn his way through the skip.

"Do you really think this will save your life?"

I gazed at the disintegrating structure of the garbage skip before me and saw the metal turn bright with the heat poured against it. I saw the skip sag as the integrity of the construction finally gave way and I was now holding no more than several chunks of intensely hot burning metal.

"You're just delaying the inevitable!" Vin called as segments of the metal structure burst into flame. Each piece was glowing red hot with the force that Vin was applying.

"I'm strong enough to burn straight through this," he called mockingly.

I'm not exactly sure when I became the villain of my story, but I am sure when I became a murderer. When I looked into the darkest depths of my soul and knew without a doubt that this was something I could do – that this was something I had within me to do.

I could use terms like self-defence and justifiable cause, but I know those for what they are. They are validations that people use to get them through the horror that they inflict upon themselves in their most honest moments.

I glimpsed at the heart of darkness beating within my own breast and I whispered, "No more."

Vin didn't hear me of course. He couldn't have heard me. All sound was obliterated by the noise generated by the burning of the garbage skip and the rushing howl of intense flame. I could see him now, through the tattered remains of the dumpster. I looked into the madness that was his eyes and I softly sighed. His face took on a quizzical look as I let the magic do its grim work.

With a flick of my hands I sent the twisted wreck of semi-molten metal that was the remains of the garbage skip flying towards my foe. He could see me and I could see him. I looked into his eyes as the metal hit him. I saw the mirth on his face turn to concern and then to fear as he saw his death approach.

At the last moment he had raised a shield and he began laughing again, his laughter cackling as his shield repelled the burning oblivion that was bearing down on him. His face then twisted and took on a strange expression and the laughs turned to a strangled yelp.

With bands of mana stronger than steel, I wrapped my magic around him and tightened my grip. With an audible crash akin to thunder I squeezed the metal around him and his shield collapsed under the pressure.

I looked into his eyes as I wrapped the molten metal around him, using bands of mana to twist his death against him like a python's embrace. His screams became cries, and his cries became shattered unintelligible moans.

I held him in the air before me with the power of my magic. I kept him there, held tight and firm. The metallic complaint of smouldering steel and the smell of his own burnt flesh were his only companions and mute witnesses to his end.

It was long after he stopped screaming that I came to my senses and released the shattered wreck. A misshapen and horrid mixture of human remains and twisted metal fell to the ground with a resounding thump. As the magic fled me I turned to limp away. I didn't look back. I didn't even feel the urge to look back. I cannot say with any truth that I held any remorse nor regret for Vin. He was a monster and perhaps some might say that he deserved the end to which he had wrought.

I'm not sure if it was fate or perhaps it was chance that I was the one who walked away from our encounter and not he. I'm still not even certain, in the darker moments of my recollection, if I even give thanks to be the one that did walk away.

In a strange way I owe Vincent my life; had he not taught me the harsh lessons I learned that day then I never would have survived my own trial through fire. Though I passed mine, I was scarred and forever changed by it. The dark lessons that Vincent had taught me about power and its corruption kept me pure when those around me fell.

When the temptation beckoned and the whispering seduction of power and prestige became too much, I only had to look back at this day and look at the lessons I learned from Vincent and whisper quietly to myself.

"Yes, I'm a villain … but I'm not a monster."

To be continued.

ABOUT THE AUTHOR

As an avid science fiction and fantasy reader Christopher George has been immersing himself in books from a young age. In 2004 Christopher completed his Bachelor of Multimedia at Monash University and has been working as an IT professional ever since. He currently lives in Melbourne with his partner, her daughter and three cats.

Mage Catalyst is his first completed novel and was written in a variety of hotel rooms and airports across Australia. Catalyst is his first non-technical piece and he finds it much easier to write fiction than software documentation.

It's also very recently come to light that he is simply awful at talking about himself in the third person.

For more information about the book and the series go to

www.christophergeorgenovels.com

or like us on Facebook